The Rocks

ALSO BY PETER NICHOLS

RIVERHEAD BOOKS

a member of Penguin Group (USA)

NEW YORK

2015

The Rocks

PETER NICHOLS

RIVERHEAD BOOKS
Published by the Penguin Group
Penguin Group (USA) LLC
375 Hudson Street
New York, New York 10014

USA · Canada · UK · Ireland · Australia
New Zealand · India · South Africa · China

penguin.com
A Penguin Random House Company

The author gratefully acknowledges permission to quote from "Ithaka" by C. P. Cavafy,
from C. P. Cavafy: Collected Poems, edited by George Savidis, translated by
Edmund Keeley and Philip Sherrard. © 1975 Princeton University Press.
Reprinted by permission of Princeton University Press.

Library of Congress Cataloging-in-Publication Data

Nichols, Peter, date.
The rocks / Peter Nichols.
p.   cm.
ISBN 978-1-59463-331-7
1. Secrets—Fiction.   2. Majorca (Spain)—Fiction.   I. Title.
PS3564.I19844R63   2015   2014022801
813'.54—dc23

Printed in the United States of America
1   3   5   7   9   10   8   6   4   2

Book design by Susan Walsh

For my son, Gus

And for David, Lizzie, Cynthia, Matt, Annie, and Roberta

As you set out for Ithaka
hope the voyage is a long one,
full of adventure, full of discovery.
Laistrygonians and Cyclops,
angry Poseidon—don't be afraid of them . . .

Keep Ithaka always in your mind.
Arriving there is what you are destined for.
But do not hurry the journey at all.
Better if it lasts for years,
so you are old by the time you reach the island,
wealthy with all you have gained on the way,
not expecting Ithaka to make you rich.

Ithaka gave you the marvelous journey.
Without her you would not have set out . . .

—C. P. Cavafy, "Ithaka" (1911)

The Rocks

2005

Together Again

One

H*er guests had always* marveled at how young she looked.

"Lulu, don't be ridiculous, darling—you can't be *eighty?*"

In her ninth decade, Lulu Davenport still had the slim, supple body of a much younger woman. Her thick, straight hair, which she still kept long, usually braided or coiled into a loose bun with fetching whorls escaping at the nape of her neck, had gone completely white in her thirties and had always seemed part of her abundant natural gifts. Lulu had never been concerned with health or beauty. These were accidents of nature and one had simply been lucky. She walked everywhere, she gardened, and she ran Villa Los Roques—"the Rocks," as everyone called her little seaside hotel at the eastern end of the island of Mallorca—and charmed her guests as she had for more than fifty years. That had kept her vigorous and happy, until one December afternoon when she was found sprawled in the Mediterranean sun among her yellow rosebushes by Vicente the handyman.

She looked no different after her stroke. She soon recovered her marvelous strength. In almost all respects, she appeared unchanged. But with the sudden tiny dam-burst of blood a tumbler had turned in Lulu's brain, and she began to swear. Her new vocabulary was Lawrentian: *fuck, cunt, shit, piss.* She talked of the same things as always, with appropriate logic and context, but with her arresting new expressions filling and punctuating her speech. At first, her friends were hugely amused to sit and chat with someone they knew so well who spoke in a new, rather cinematic language. Yet after a while it was strangely alienating—it was, after all, a neurological disorder. Was this still really Lulu?

The other change was to her schedule. Its former rigidity eased—nothing extreme, no getting up in the middle of the night to trim the roses or take a walk—but after her stroke it was erratic. She set off to the market with her straw bag over her shoulder as ever, but at random hours. In this way she encountered her first husband, Gerald Rutledge, one afternoon late in March. They had both remained in the small town of Cala Marsopa after their divorce in 1949, yet by evolving antipodal routines they had managed to avoid each other almost entirely for half a century.

Though they were the same age, Gerald had not been as blessed by nature. He'd been a smoker all his life and now had emphysema. He'd suffered from arthritis for years. His hips needed replacing but he had a horror of hospitals and had resisted such a dramatic procedure. He walked slowly with a stick.

He was stooped, puffing a Ducados, gripping a small four-pack of yogurt in a tremulous hand when they ran into each other at the local *comestibles*. His brown legs and arms were wrinkled and emaciated in his baggy khaki shorts and short-sleeved pale blue shirt, cheap polyester garments bought at the HiperSol in Manacor. There were scabs of sun cancer on his scalp beneath the thin, lank gray hair.

"God, Gerald, you look fucking grim," said Lulu. "Why are you here anyway, you cunt?"

Gerald's mouth opened to form an answer, but his mind skittered off into confusion. Its tracking mechanism, unsteady these days anyway, was thrown further off balance by the coarseness of Lulu's greeting. His memories of her—almost all of them stemming from the few happy weeks of their marriage almost sixty years before—could not reconcile such stark filth and venom. As his jaw moved, trying to form words, his eyes sought and found the small white scar, still visible, on her chin.

Lulu's eye was caught by a heap of splendid blue-black aubergines.

She began to move away and Gerald's hand shot out and grasped her upper arm.

She turned toward him again. "Piss off, you wretched shit." Lulu pulled her arm free. She walked away, toward the aubergines, pleased at the opportunity to cut Gerald, and at how decrepit he looked. She'd been mortified by her stroke; it wasn't like her. And while adjusting to the unsettling intimations of mortality, it had occurred to her that Gerald might outlast her. She wanted him to die first, with urgency now.

She picked up an aubergine, rubbing her thumb across its firm squeaky skin. She finished her shopping with brisk efficiency and was soon outside.

Gerald stared after her. Some moments later, he became aware of a sensation in his hand. He looked down and saw that he had squeezed the yogurt containers too hard. Creamy curds of *frutas del bosque* were dripping from his trembling fingers.

A*fter a day* of cloudbursts, the clouds departed, as if they'd been waiting for an improvement in the weather themselves, moving away eastward across the sea like pink and purple galleons. Lulu walked home along the sandy, unpaved, still-puddled road between the white villas and their gardens of fruit trees and bougainvillea and the limestone shore stretching beyond the harbor. The road carried mostly foot traffic and mopeds, a popular, out-of-the-way walk in the summer but deserted the rest of the year. In places, the rough spongiform beige rocks between the road and the sea offered flat spots near their edges where for years Lulu and the Rocks' guests who didn't want to walk as far as the beach had spread their towels to lie in the sun, launched themselves into the cool water, and climbed back up again.

Lulu walked happily and slowly, enjoying the warmth of the sun—it had been an unusually cool and rainy winter in Mallorca. She was comforted by the familiar nubs and contours of the rocks and the gentle sound of the sea that rose and sucked at them.

She didn't notice Gerald following her. He was walking at a speed that had become unusually fast for him, though no more than a normal walking pace. His legs weren't working properly. Everything in them was worn, and the regular mechanisms had grown so sloppy that they were threatening to fold the wrong way and collapse. His hips were killing him. Sweat beaded his forehead, his neck and upper lip. His face had grown pale as the depleted oxygen in his blood chugged toward his heart and lungs, leaving him panting, wheezing heavily. He was dying to stop and light a cigarette but then he would lose her. He pushed furiously on, like a man walking underwater.

He caught up with Lulu just outside the Rocks. He grabbed her arm again with strength fueled by rage, and spun her round.

"You never—" he started, with a smoker's bubbling growl, but his chest was empty of air, heaving spasmodically.

Again, Lulu shook off his grip. But she was surprised and immensely pleased to see the effort Gerald had made, how overwrought, breathless, and unwell he was. It occurred to her that with just a nudge he might easily die of a heart attack right in front of her. "You're *pathetic*, Gerald. An empty, hobbling husk of a man." A flame of old anger rose in her. "You're a bolter! A miserable, wretched shit of a fucking—"

"*You never developed the film! Did you!*" The furious, strangled words erupted wetly out of Gerald's chest, his body pitching forward. "*I lured them away! Do you understand? I got them away! I—*" His blue-and-gray glistening face thrust into hers, but he had no more breath.

Lulu involuntarily snapped backward from the waist, repelled. But she recovered—or was recovering, as her shoulder bag, laden with aubergines, lemons, cheese, and wine, still swinging backward, tugged at her, and she began to lose her balance.

Gerald grabbed her arm again, this time—his instinct sure—to steady her, and Lulu clutched at his shirt, but they both leaned well past recovery and began to fall. As they fell, the sight of Gerald's face so close to hers, spittle gathered in the corners of his thin rubbery lips, was so repugnant to Lulu that she whipped her head sharply aside with disgust. When they landed, her right temple hit a jagged spur of rock.

Gerald's knees smashed into sharp, serrated limestone. He screamed—a brief empty wheeze—and writhed, pushing with his torso, his excruciating hips.

They rolled together, not toward one of the flat spots where guests spread towels. They tumbled off a ledge into the sea.

Two

A according to the report of the coroner, the deaths are from drowning," said the police inspector, flicking through pages on his desk. He was a slim young man, with the confident demeanor and close-cropped spiky-gelled black hair of a detective in a *telenovela*. "There was water in the lungs of both persons. But there are the external injuries, primarily in the head of Señora Davenport and the knees of Señor Rutledge . . . and there are other abrasions. . . ." He looked up at the middle-aged man and woman across his desk. "However, nothing is missing. We found Señora Davenport's purse in her bag, and money in Señor Rutledge's pocket. Nothing was taken from them, so we don't believe it was an attack—a robbery. More probably, these lacerations occurred during the fall into the water."

He spoke in Spanish. Luc Franklin, the son of the Davenport woman, and Aegina Rutledge, the daughter of the Rutledge man—both of them *ingleses*, as were the deceased—had addressed him in fluent Spanish during their introduction. The Rutledge woman appeared completely Spanish to the inspector. Dark hair, dark eyes, olive complexion, old enough to be his mother, but still, as a woman, very attractive—perhaps a certain polish from the English side. The man, Franklin—he spoke Spanish well, though his accent was not as good as the woman's—looked like simply another graying middle-aged *inglés*. They showed no emotion as he talked of the death of their parents and detailed the *contusiones* found on the bodies. But that did not fool the inspector. He noticed they had barely glanced at each other. They avoided expressions of warmth and comfort that would have led to tears, at least embraces or hand-holding between old friends, and proper expressions of grief, for which the inspector had well-tested soothing words to offer.

These two didn't like each other.

The inspector continued. "There is only the question of why they fell."

"My mother had a stroke in December," said Luc Franklin. "Maybe she had another one and Gerald—Señor Rutledge—was trying to help her."

"They were very old friends," said the Rutledge woman, supporting this scenario. "If she'd been in trouble, I'm sure my father would have tried to help her, even though he wasn't well himself."

"*Claro*," said the inspector. "This seems most likely what happened. Señora Davenport had a head injury, here"—he touched his temple—"probably because of a fall on the rocks, perhaps as you say, because of another stroke, or"—he looked at the Franklin man, suggesting gently—"perhaps she just fell—she was quite old. She was carrying a heavy bag. It happens."

"Possibly," said the Franklin man. He appeared strangely uninterested. The inspector had seen this before: grief expressed as detachment. The dead were now dead, how they got that way no longer mattered.

The inspector pressed on, limning a scene that spoke for itself. "Yes. And Señor Rutledge was there"—he looked over at the daughter, his face showing the unselfish kindness he presumed of her father—"he attempted to help her. They fell, perhaps together, first onto the rocks beside the road, and then—it is not wide, the rocks there, I went to see—into the water. The injuries are consistent with such an accident. Unless you have reason to suspect somebody attacked them—"

"No, no, not at all," said the Franklin man, now impatient.

"I'm sure it was an accident," said the Rutledge woman.

The inspector nodded gravely. "A tragic accident for such old friends." He rose. "My deepest condolences."

Together *they rode* the elevator down to the underground police parking garage. They were silent until Aegina said, "Luc, I'm sorry about your mother."

"And your father," said Luc, glancing at her reflection in the brushed aluminum door just as it opened and erased her.

They walked toward the parked cars.

"Luc." Aegina stopped. "You don't think—honestly—they actually had a fight?"

"Aegina . . ." He shrugged. "I don't know."

"But what were they doing together? They haven't seen each other for . . . since Algeciras?"

At the mention of Algeciras, Luc looked away to some bleak corner of the garage. "I wouldn't know."

"I can't imagine why he was there, outside the Rocks," said Aegina. But she remembered episodes as she spoke. She looked at Luc. "How are you feeling?"

"Numb," he said. "The way I always felt about her."

"I'm sure that's not true."

"Well, never mind." He glanced at her again. "I'm sorry about your father. I liked him." He turned and walked toward a white Land Rover, Lulu's car. It beeped and blinked its lights as he pressed the remote locking device.

"Are you going to be here long?" she called.

"I don't know," Luc said, opening the door. He climbed in and shut the door and started the engine. She stood aside as the Land Rover backed out. She watched it speed off toward the exit.

Aegina looked around the unpainted concrete cavern, trying to remember what car she had rented that morning. She had driven straight from Palma airport to Pompas Fúnebres González to see the body, and then to the police station.

Driving up the long, still-unpaved track to C'an Cabrer, her father's farmhouse, Aegina couldn't believe he wouldn't be there. The drive from Palma, through the villages, or now more often than not on the new roads built around them, past the endless new developments of blocky little villas, finally the shimmering sea opening up ahead, and up the hill through the olive trees to the house—the whole headlong journey from London or anywhere else had always been filled with the anticipation and certainty of seeing him at the end of it. He had come up to London only twice in her life. Otherwise, whenever she had seen him, it had been here, in this one place. There had never been a time when she had been in the house and her father had not been there, or out and shortly expected back, as constant and fixed as the stones of its structure and the land around it.

High on the hill, the drive turned sharply and ran level through a stand of lemon trees toward the old pigsty—her father's workshop—at the side of the house. Aegina stopped the car and got out. It was hot now; the air buzzed with cicadas.

She climbed the steps at the side of the house and entered the large kitchen. Aegina stood still. A teapot, its strainer and top, a chipped mug, a china plate, a large bone-handled dinner knife, lay clean and dry in the wooden dish drainer above the large, square, ceramic sink. He had cleaned these things and then gone out and died. Now she knew she would not find him, either here making tea, or in his study, or reading in the living room, or wandering through the gardens or the olive and lemon groves—what was left of them—on the hill surrounding the house.

She walked through the book-filled rooms into her father's bedroom. He had made the bed neatly too—shipshape as always—before going out to the market that last morning.

She had been conceived here.

Beside the bed stood the small, rough, old bookcase made of local pine that contained the original core of her father's library, the books he had brought ashore from his boat—or saved when it sank, she was never sure which—in 1948: J. B. Bury's *A History of Ancient Greece*; Seymour's *Life in the Homeric Age*; various editions of *The Odyssey*; a book of photographs of the Aegean, the sea her father had named her for.

She sat down on the bed and pulled out a faded blue Oxford University Press hardback. Its pages long ago rippled from damp, *The Odyssey of Homer* embossed on the spine. On the front cover, in faded gold on top of the blue cloth, was a circular indented depiction of a small fourteen-oar galley. The figure of a bearded man, Odysseus, was bound by ropes to the mast. In the water below the ship, looking up at him, singing, were the Sirens who bewitched anybody hapless enough to draw within hearing of their liquid song—wingèd harpies clutching bones in their talons, who captured and imprisoned sailors and turned them to skeletons as the skin withered upon their bones.

Aegina opened the cover. The inscription, written in faded black ink on the first blank, yellowed, damp-spotted page:

For Lulu. An odyssey.

Love always, Gerald

20 July 1948.

1995

Golden Oldies

One

Why *shouldn't I go? It's* her seventieth birthday," said Charlie. He was slouched in a chair at the large oak table in the center of the kitchen, picking from a small pile of raw almonds in front of him, one nut at a time. "Just because you and Grandpa loathe her guts—"

"That's not true, Charlie," said Aegina. She was making dinner, chopping onions and garlic and pine nuts at the other end of the table. "I don't loathe her. I don't even think about her."

"Yes you do," said the boy.

"I don't have the energy to loathe anybody. And I agree with you. Of course you should go if you want to. Have you been invited?"

"Mum," he said with pitying exasperation, "you don't have to be invited to go to the Rocks. People just go. I've been going there all my life."

"I know, but isn't it going to be a big to-do?"

"Yeah, that's the point: everyone's going. But as a matter of fact, Lulu invited me."

"She *what?*" came the voice from the living room.

A moment later Gerald appeared in the doorway. "Why did she invite you? How does she know you?" He looked over his reading glasses at his grandson, who was tall and lithe, with his mother's dark Spanish coloring. The boy had leapt across some boundary from childhood into strapping youth since the previous summer when Gerald had last seen him. He was a foot taller, already shaving. He looked like a louche young matador, Gerald thought. God help him.

"Grandpa, I've been going there for years," said Charlie. "Of course she knows me. She's asked me to be the DJ for her party. It's a job. She's paying me five thousand pesetas."

"That's nice," said Aegina evenly. "Why you, sweetheart?"

"She likes the music I like. And I like what she likes."

"Like what?" asked Aegina.

"Oh, old stuff, newer stuff. She's got a turntable and all these classic old vinyl LPs. You really should come down and see sometime—if you don't hate her guts."

"Now stop it, Charlie. I've just got plenty to do, and I like to spend my evenings here."

"I'm sure she likes your concentration camp music," said Gerald.

Charlie's latest enthusiasms, played more than Gerald would have liked on the gramophone in the living room, were Henryk Górecki's Third Symphony, *Symphony of Sorrowful Songs*, with Dawn Upshaw's ululant soprano filling the house with waves of mournful music—lyrics, Charlie informed his grandfather, that had been scrawled on the wall of a Gestapo cell—and Olivier Messiaen's *Quartet for the End of Time*, composed in a German prisoner-of-war camp. Charlie's music teacher at school was currently keen on Holocaust music.

"She doesn't have any of that."

"Lucky her," said Gerald. He stood irresolutely in the doorway for a moment, and then said: "Does she know who you are? I mean, that you're connected to . . . us?"

"Of course she does, Grandpa. Lulu knows everyone."

Gerald glanced at his daughter. Aegina met his eyes before looking down at her chopping board.

"Sounds like you two are terrific chums," he said.

"Well, Bianca and I go there a lot. She invited both of us to her birthday party."

"Ah," said Gerald. Bianca, the daughter of Aegina's best friends in Cala Marsopa, was Charlie's age, fifteen. She had grown up noticeably the past year. She now looked at least twenty-five, he thought.

"And people your age go to the Rocks?"

"Sometimes," said Charlie, nonchalantly munching almonds. "After dinner."

"They don't serve you drinks, do they?"

"No, Coke. Or TriNaranjus."

Coming from Charlie, this lolling, smoldering youth, it sounded like a joke. Gerald was unsure if his leg was being pulled. Perhaps they drank like fishes now at fifteen and he was the last to know. "Really?" He looked over at Aegina.

"They drink Coke, Papa."

Gerald said, "Hmm," in a way that he himself detested as soon as he heard it because it made him sound like a hopelessly reactionary dotard.

"Will Tom and Milly be there?" he asked.

Aegina looked up at him. "Papa, they've been dead for years."

"Oh, right."

He returned to the living room, sat on the old sagging leather couch, and picked up what he had put down before going into the kitchen: his book, *The Way to Ithaca*. Out of print for more than forty years, a new edition was being brought out by Doughty Books, Ltd, in London. Doughty had published a line of short works about ancient history, small, attractively designed hardback books written in lively, readable prose by experts who managed to avoid the pedantry of scholarship. They had proved popular and sold well. Founded only seven years earlier, Doughty had twice won *The Sunday Times'* Small Publisher of the Year Award.

Ten months ago, out of the blue, Gerald had found a letter from Kate Smythe, Doughty's editor in chief, in his dusty letter box under the carob trees at the bottom of the drive. One of her authors had "discovered" *The Way to Ithaca*, the original John Murray edition, in a library sale and sent it to her. She thought the book "absolutely brilliant in its accessible and charming approach to the modern, nonnautical, reader, and still as relevant to the world of today as on the day it was first published." Everybody at Doughty believed that with a "very little light editing," it would stand neatly alongside their recent books on the Parthenon, the Greco-Persian Wars, the Elgin Marbles. They agreed that Gerald's original black-and-white photographs were "essential to the book, classic in composition, and conveying a timeless sense of the Mediterranean that appeared to give the modern reader contemporary snapshots of the Homeric world." (In other words, Gerald had remarked to Aegina, they think I'm three thousand years old.) Did Gerald have a literary agent to whom they could present their offer? If not, Kate Smythe would be happy to refer him to an agent with whom Doughty did frequent business and whose impartiality and commitment to Gerald's best interests were guaranteed. And did he have a phone number?

Skeptical, suspecting this offer would evaporate before anything came of it, Gerald had written back that he did not at present have a literary agent (he'd never had one) but that he would be pleased to consider their offer. Within days of dropping his return letter in the yellow Correos box in Cala Marsopa, he received a gushing phone call from Kate Smythe in London. She sounded sincerely enthusiastic. She told him again how much she loved his book, how excited Doughty would be to bring out a new edition, how well they thought it would do.

"How very nice," Gerald told her, still not convinced, looking abstractedly at bottles of his own honey-colored olive oil that sat on the shelf beside the phone. (When he'd finally allowed the installation of a phone in 1987, he'd wanted it out of the way and put it in the larder.)

Less than an hour later, he was back in the larder, answering the phone again. The caller identified herself as Deborah Greene. She was a literary agent, authorized by Doughty Books to convey to Gerald their offer of an advance on royalties of fifteen thousand pounds.

Gerald had left England many decades before decimalization had shrunk the pound to one hundred recessive pence from the glories of its twenty shillings and two hundred forty useful pennies that had formed notions of plenitude in his childhood; when a thrupenny bit had purchased sixteen lemon drops at a farthing apiece. Gerald still thought of wealth in terms more suited to living on a boat: a sufficiency of food, properly stored against weather and misadventure, to last a fixed period into the uncertain future. Fifteen thousand pounds was a sum he could associate only with train robberies or the wages of film stars.

As the literary agent spoke, Gerald stood in the larder, staring again at his olive oil. For a long time afterward, whenever he thought of his new publisher and his fifteen-thousand-pound advance—and whenever he came into the larder for any reason—he envisioned a rich oil-like sap sliding over him to encase him like a golden amber.

Deborah Greene was saying something about foreign rights, Doughty already having a strong response from an American publisher, the book going into profit quite quickly, Gerald might see additional royalties in the years following publication—he didn't understand most of it.

Gerald either did or didn't say aloud, "Whatever you think best."

She asked if he had another book idea that might serve as a follow-up, for which she believed she could secure an additional healthy advance. He didn't, offhand, but he would have a think, he told her.

He had staggered out of the larder and finally made a pot of tea.

A few weeks later, a check for £6,375 (half of his advance, after his new agent's commission, the remaining half to follow on publication) arrived in his letter box beneath the carob trees. He deposited it in his account at the Banco Santander in Cala Marsopa and wondered what to do with it. Months later, he decided to have some roof tiles replaced. He sent a check for a thousand pounds to Aegina for her birthday—"Of course, it will all be yours someday," he wrote grandly—and a hundred pounds to Charlie for his birthday.

Now, almost a year after that first letter from Kate Smythe, his new book, this late-life miracle coming when he was seventy years old, lay open, pages down on the leather cushion, in front of Gerald. The publishers had added a subtitle: *A Sailor's Discovery of the Route of Homer's Odyssey.* The dust jacket showed a detail of an old wall mosaic of Odysseus surrounded by the six heads of Scylla, a vivid scene full of action, rather than the stilted two-dimensional Grecian-vase rendering one might expect. Here, inside this book—as Kate Smythe had put it to

Gerald over the phone—the cover promised a big, action-packed story. He thought it very handsome, the mosaic surrounded by a Mediterranean blue that was somehow aged and watermarked—very clever.

But the elation, and the pleasant if vertiginous sensation of having so much money in the bank, had given way to panic. The publishers had invited him—pressed and flattered him, with phone calls from Kate and her editors and production team, and even Aegina had joined them in urging him—to come to London for the book's launch party. This was to take place in three days' time, in the Duveen Gallery of the British Museum, which housed the Elgin-looted Parthenon Marbles, and Kate had, by some sleight of evolving phone calls, got Gerald to agree to read an extract from his book at the party. He'd spent the last few weeks in the grip of a virulent and mounting stage fright. He woke now in the predawn hours in a sweating panic, picturing himself surrounded by a Scylla-like throng of smiling, teeth-gnashing heads belonging to clever, literary academics, all of them vastly more knowledgeable about his subject than himself—a Cambridge don whose specialty was the Parthenon was among Doughty's recent authors. He was sure he would stammer, splutter, find himself robbed of the power of speech, possibly even have an accident in his trousers, or be so inclined to do so that he would be unable to leave the museum's toilet. Meanwhile, he had to prepare for this "impromptu" address. He had to find something in his book to read; something "fun," Kate had suggested.

As he picked up the book again, Gerald's synapses snapped him back to what had made him put it down minutes before and go into the kitchen: hearing his grandson talk of that woman. He looked down at the beautiful cover and realized that, in any edition, the book itself would always carry an ineradicable taint.

Charlie passed through the room. "See you later, Grandpa."

"Aren't you staying for supper?"

"No, thanks. I'm going to eat with friends in town."

Soon Gerald heard the strong torrent of Charlie's urine stream crashing heedlessly into the toilet bowl in the adjoining bathroom. Such an enviably strong, vigorous contrast to his own sadly diminished and fitful effort.

"You don't mind him going to that party, then?" Gerald asked as he and Aegina were eating in the dining room.

"No. They all go there. I don't want to spoil it for him."

"And you feel all right about leaving him here? I've told you, I'm quite capable of getting myself to London and back."

"I'm not sure about that. He'll be fine, Papa. Penny and François are very happy to have him—"

"I'm sure Bianca will be too."

"Yes, she will. They're wonderful friends."

"But are they . . ."

"Are they having sex? I don't think so. I expect they're kissing. Maybe a bit more. But they're close friends. I think it's all right. Anyway, you're mad if you think I'm not coming to your fabulous book bash. I mean, come on—the British Museum. And the relaunch of your book, which had basically disappeared before I was old enough to read it. I want to see you in your hour of glory."

"Humiliation, more like."

"You'll be great. They're so impressed by your book. You don't have to make a speech or anything. You just say, Thanks so much, read a few words, and they'll do the rest. It'll be fun."

"Hmmm," Gerald said again. They ate silently for a minute. Aegina had made the tumbet she had learned from her mother: a Mallorcan dish full of aubergines, tomatoes, onion, garlic, goat cheese, and olives from Gerald's trees. His eyes ranged over Aegina's paintings that hung on the walls: landscapes around his property and eastern Mallorca in a range of burnt and raw umbers, lines and shadows as familiar to him now as the veins and splotches on the backs of his own brown, weathered hands. They'd hung there for many years.

"Are you painting much these days?" he asked her.

"No. Not at all, actually. I'd like to get back to it at some point, and I will. I don't seem to have had the time—well, I guess that really means I haven't had the interest."

"I hope you will. I love your paintings, you know that. You're a very fine artist."

"Sweet of you, Papa."

"Does Charlie paint, or draw?"

"No, just the music. Well, you've heard him play his keyboard in his room."

"I know, he's amazing. But you were musical too. Always playing songs on your little record player that you took everywhere with you. I remember that one you liked about flying to the moon."

"'Everyone's Gone to the Moon.'"

"That's it. Rather a lonely song, I thought."

Two *days later* they stood in a long line of sun-blistered British tourists—most of them dressed as if they'd just come off the beach—and their piles of luggage snaking toward the Iberia check-in counter at Palma airport.

"These people can't all be on our flight, surely?" said Gerald. He was neatly dressed in faded blue canvas trousers, tennis shoes, a white shirt so laundered that it had become almost transparent, and a threadbare but clean cream-colored linen jacket of a type popular with British school-masters in the 1930s.

"They are," said Aegina. "And more coming."

"How can they possibly fit them all onto a single aeroplane?" asked Gerald, for whom there would always be only one spelling and pronunci-ation of the word—that machine forever being the size and kind that he had come to know during the war. In 1942, after he'd lied about his age and enlisted in the Royal Navy, Gerald sailed aboard the battle cruiser turned aircraft carrier HMS *Furious*, as she ferried RAF Supermarine Spitfires and Hawker Hurricanes between Portsmouth and Malta.

Dainty aircraft, pretty as small sailboats and operating in much the same way: featherlight airfoil sections controlled by wire the size of fishing line. They had the tenuous rigidity of large box kites and wobbled like shrubbery as they were pushed about on the flight deck. Gerald thought them marvelous until he began to see them crash. Pretty aeroplanes hurtling from the sky in fiery descents, in every case to explode spectacularly into the sea or on rocky coastlines. Even without antiaircraft bombardment, they suddenly seemed too improbable, the conceit of mad inventors. During the war and after, Gerald sailed all over the Mediterranean, between Alexandria and Gibraltar, in every kind and size of watercraft. Some of these had leaked, a few had foundered, but at no more than a stately cruising speed, and one always had the chance of swimming or paddling away from wreckage in the water. It had been a natural decision that he would never board an aeroplane. Once he'd lost his own vessel in the waters off Mallorca, Gerald had been effectively marooned. In the absence of convenient alternatives, he made one round-trip journey by air between Mallorca and London in 1979 for Aegina's wedding. It had surely been the freakish unreality attending every aspect of the reissue of his book that had flattered and sufficiently unmoored him into agreeing to fly to London for what was in fact no more than a cocktail party at the British Museum. Had they told him he would have to fly in an aeroplane to see his book in print and pick up his fifteen thousand pounds, he might not have agreed. He would have recognized it as a chimerical Siren lure.

"Perhaps we won't get on," he said, hopefully.

Aegina smiled at him. "We've got tickets, we'll get on." She wrapped her arm around his. "Don't worry, you'll live. We'll go have a coffee and a *bocadillo* after we check in."

Two

Lulu *had arranged* numerous birthday presents for herself. No one knew what she wanted as well as she did. The first was a hot, flaky, sugar-powdered *ensaïmada*, the spiral-shaped Mallorcan pastry, for breakfast. She rarely ate them, but they looked so lovely and retained an allure (usually dispelled on eating more than one) because of the infrequency of her indulgence. One, every now and then, was satisfactory and sufficient.

Floriana was another birthday present, though this was simply an addition to the normal weekly routine. The strong, silent, Indian-featured Brazilian woman came at four to give Lulu a massage. They were not friends. Floriana said, *"Bon dia, señora,"* and got on with it. She oiled, kneaded, swept her strong hands over the long, still quite tautly fleshed, lissome body on her table with some kind of dowser's absorption of the secrets summoned from the nerves and muscles beneath Lulu's skin, until Lulu felt herself falling and letting go any shards of tension, any disagreeable thoughts.

She had her big present planned for later.

Luc *woke from* his siesta to the chatter of voices, the clinking of plates outside the closed shutters. He'd arrived late last night and he'd drunk too much wine at lunch. The room was noticeably cooler, the light softer than the stabbing hard-edged bars that had shimmered beneath the louvers when he'd fallen asleep. A gentle flower-scented breeze played across his face and chest; he heard the wind in the pines outside.

He rose from the bed, naked, walked to the window, and cracked open the shutters. Below, in the wide courtyard beneath the wrack-boughed canopy of pines, the catering crew hired for his mother's birthday party— young, dark-haired Mallorcan men and women in tight black trousers, black trainers, and white shirts—were laying the tables. The massive, enigmatic Bronwyn, in baggy shorts, a vast T-shirt not concealing the roll of her breasts and belly, was briefing the crew grouped around her.

Luc's eye rested on one of the crew. She was tall; he could only see her back, a narrow but well-rounded ass in tight black pants, dark tightly waving hair pulled back. A billowy white shirt that told him nothing about what it covered. She turned, and he saw that she had a pronounced high-bridged, hooked nose. He watched her as she listened to Bronwyn with her mouth attentively open, until she walked quickly toward the kitchen and out of sight.

Luc closed the shutters. He was staying in the end room in the two-story addition to the main house, which contained most of the guest rooms. The barracks, his mother called it: a long rectangular building, white, tile-roofed, its windows framed with shutters painted the same sage green as the shutters on the main house. Its looming monolithic shape had softened over the decades as Cape honeysuckle, bougainvillea, palms and geraniums had grown and spread around its base and walls. Other than during the brief period at the beginning of his life when his father had been married to his mother, Luc had never had a permanent room of his own in his mother's home. Out of season, or when there were few guests, and he'd stayed in a small room in the main house. In his teen years, before the barracks had been built in 1970, he'd fashioned a lair inside a terra-cotta block-and-stucco hut near the back wall of the property, one of several rude original outbuildings used for gardening tools, perhaps at one time for animals. He'd fixed it up himself with a mattress on boards and bricks, a string to hang clothes on, shelves for books, and an electric wire run from the house whose two exposed ends he twisted around the screws in a lightbulb socket to read by. It was the size of a small solitary cell, but Luc felt at home in it. It was as far as possible from the house and the bar and the other guests and, most of all, his mother. He could come and go by the path to the garage without seeing anybody or being seen. He could live a secret life. People forgot about him for hours, sometimes days, at a time. Between his long summers in Mallorca, when Luc was back at school in Paris, living in his father's high-ceilinged, tall-windowed apartment in the sixth arrondissement, the walls inside his toolshed grew black with mold and had to be repainted white. He arrived every July to his newly painted hovel, holed up with books, with immense plans for sex, and lived through the season at the Rocks in a background corner like a watchful spider. But his little bunkhouse and the other outbuildings had been torn down to make room for the barracks, and since that time Luc had always occupied one or other of the rooms—wherever a guest was not—in the new building.

He saw himself in the mirror on the wall and pulled in his stomach. Still okay for mid-forties. He put on a bathing suit, a T-shirt, grabbed a towel, and padded barefoot down the tiled stairs. He walked around the tables and the caterers, heading across the courtyard toward the gate to the road.

"Hello, Lukey, darling!" a guest called from the bar across the patio.

"Hi," he said, waving.

He found April across the road, on the narrow ledge of rocks above the sea. She was lying faceup on a towel, topless. She had just come out of the water. Drops of seawater beaded on her pale, oiled skin.

"Hi," he said. "How are you doing?"

"Oh, hi." She put her hand to her eyes and squinted up at him. "I'm doing great. Are you going in? The water's, like, incredible."

"I might," said Luc. He spread his towel beside her and sat down on it. He didn't feel like going into the water, getting wet, jolting his still sleep-warm body awake. April had removed her hand from her face and lay with her eyes closed.

"Aren't you going to get burned out here?" he said.

"Uh-uh. I'm covered with bulletproof sunblock."

April was in her mid-twenties. She'd been cast in the film she had just wrapped, which Luc had written, for her ethereal, almost translucent milk-white skin, strawberry-blond hair (above and below). The sets and locations were monochromatic in tone: an urban wasteland of apartment towers in Paris's banlieues; the movie was shot almost entirely during the crepuscular hours of dawn and dusk. The exposed film had been desaturated of most of its color, so the girl (April), stalked by her obsessive former boyfriend, could blend or vanish into concrete wherever she went, and drive him insane. The unreal, liminal effect of her character was heightened by the fact that before shooting, Luc and the director had decided to cut most of April's dialogue and have the rest dubbed in breathy whispers to avoid the shattering effect of her San Fernando Valley accent on even the most monosyllabic French.

She looked healthier now. Her skin, faintly freckled up close, was alive—light goose bumps rose on her arms; the peach-pink areolae around her nipples had contracted and puckered as the salt water evaporated off her in the light sea breeze. Luc bent forward and placed his mouth over her cool, wet nipple, licking salty drops—

April flinched, pulling away. *"Don't!"* she said.

"Why not?"

"Someone might see you."

"There's no one here."

"Well, I'm not comfortable with you doing that in public."

"Whatever makes you comfortable, then."

Luc pulled his knees up to his chest. He looked out over the flat blue sea at a gigantic insect-shaped motor yacht steaming inshore to round the easternmost point of the island on its way perhaps from Palma to Pollença, or to drop its anchor off the plush Hotel Formentor.

"So, okay," said April, her eyes still closed, "I want to talk about your mother."

"Okay."

"Well. She's very beautiful."

"That's nice."

"I mean, like, I can't believe she's *seventy*!" she said, ending forcefully, as if Luc had been deceiving her about his mother's age for months.

"You think she looks younger."

April made a sharp exhalation. "Yeah! Like, *forty? Maybe?* And she has a really—I don't know—is that an upper-class English accent?"

"That's what it sounds like now. It's what used to be called RP, or Received Pronunciation. It was the way some people in England spoke about ninety years ago. You hear it in old newsreels where they talk about the Suez 'Ca-nell.'"

"Then how come you have sort of an American accent when you speak English?"

"Because I am an American. I told you, my father was American. When I spoke English, I spoke with him."

April was silent but cogitative in the sun for a moment. "So what happened with your mother and father? How come they split up?"

"Why does anyone break up? They didn't get on."

"So, does she, like, have a boyfriend?"

"Not in the way you think of it."

"What do you mean?"

"She's had friends. And visitors. Friends who fly down for a few days."

"You mean they come down to see her and they have sex?"

"Yes."

"Oh, wow. That's different. Does she know to use protection?"

"You know what, April sweetheart? I don't go there."

"Well, she's from an older generation, and she's, you know, out there."

"I leave those things to her. It's sweet of you to concern yourself, though. Are you coming in soon?"

"In a while. I'm just, like, it's so peaceful here."

"Take your time."

Luc stood up and walked back across the road.

T *here you are*," said Lulu, gliding across the patio between the bar and the main house. Their paths crossed.

"Hello, Mother. Are you having a nice birthday?"

"Yes, I am, darling. Come inside and have tea with me."

Luc followed his mother into the house.

"I'll have my tea now, Bronwyn," Lulu called as they passed the kitchen door. "And will you bring a cup for Luc?"

"Right!" came the reply, in stolid Estuary English.

They went into the living room that looked out over the shaded front patio, over the bougainvillea that obscured the dirt road but revealed the Jerusalem stone–colored rocks and the sea. Lulu arranged herself on the pale blue slipcovered sofa. Luc sprawled in a battered leather club chair opposite her.

"She's very lovely, your April."

Ah yes, he thought, here it comes. "She is."

"And is she any good?"

"What?"

"Is she a good actress?"

"Oh. She's not bad. You know. She's just starting out. She did well, as far as it went. She looked right—"

"And are you pleased with this film? Are you hopeful?"

"Well, it's not going to be *Lawrence of Arabia*." Luc's favorite movie, the benchmark for what films once were, against which he measured the subsequent impoverishment of cinema.

"Why not, darling?"

Luc smiled indulgently. "It's small, Mother. An indie film. A sort of noirish thriller. But it's edgy. I think I did a good job with what they gave me. Depending how well it turns out, if it gets some good reviews, has some legs, then my stock will go up; if it doesn't, or if it disappears, then I'm none the worse off, it's been a reasonable payday, and I'm on to the next."

"And what decides how well it turns out?"

"How it all cuts together. What the performances are like. What they—"

"Who are *they*, darling?"

"The director, the editor, the producer—"

"I thought you were going to produce your next film."

He laughed good-humoredly. "Well, I'm trying. It's not that easy. *Lawrence of Arabia* may be the greatest film ever made, but it couldn't get made today—"

"You told me yourself—you've complained for years, in fact—that the writer has no power. You're a hireling. But if you produce it, you're the boss. You get the right people and tell them how you want it done, and you have control of the end result."

"Yes, but—"

"But you have to come up with your own project, right?"

"Yes, Mother. That's right. And the money. And that's what I'm trying to do. I've told you. I'm writing stuff, I'm always reading, looking at properties, talking with people—"

"Now you sound like a schoolboy making excuses about your homework. Luc, you're forty-five. You can't be a beginner forever. You're treading water. You'll be none the worse off if this film drops into a black hole because nobody's ever heard of you. What happened to that novel you were going to write? It sounded wonderful. Why don't you write that?"

"I did write it, Mother. You read it. You thought it was rubbish. Evidently, you were right, because no one wanted to publish it."

"You were going to write a better one. I'm talking about *that* wonderful novel. Why don't you write it? Look at the rubbish that sells. You're a better writer than that. Write a *good* book."

"That's a great idea. I hadn't thought of that—"

"I can't stand to see you wallowing in failure."

"Mother—" Luc took a deep breath. He smiled. "I've written four films and made some money. I own a nice apartment in Paris—"

"Your father's apartment."

"Never mind, it's mine now, and I *own* it. It's worth a fortune. I work. I have friends. A nice life. Where, exactly, is the failure part of that?"

"You're throwing yourself away on dross. And look at this one—this girl you've brought down. She's *pretty*, sweet—extremely *simple*—but is she the girl for you? I mean, what *are* you doing, darling?"

"Listen to you: *this one*, she says," Luc said more irritably than he'd wished. "I mean, what about you? When's the last time you tried having a relationship with someone?"

"Darling, I have many dear friends, as you know. I don't *do relationships*, like taking the waters at Baden-Baden."

"I know. You're completely self-sufficient, apart from regular servicing. I, on the other hand, try to engage with the human race now and then. I try to have relationships. They're difficult, but at least I try. I'd still even like to have children someday. I should think you'd be pleased that I bring someone down, but you're not. Instead you're—I mean, what *are* you talking about, Mother?"

Lulu looked at him steadily. "I'm talking about the joke you once told me, about the position of the writer in the film industry."

"Which of the many jokes was that?"

"The one about the starlet who's so stupid that she sleeps with the writer."

"Ah." Luc looked at his watch—his father's old stainless steel Rolex—as if reminded of an appointment. He stood up. "Well, I'm going to have a shower before I dress."

Bronwyn came in with a tray.

"I've got your tea," she said to Luc. "Do you want to take it with you?"

"No, thanks, Bronwyn." He left the room.

Outside, Luc started toward the barracks, then changed his mind, swerved left, and walked across the patio.

"Hallo!" said the cheerful blonde behind the bar. Lulu's staff were always British girls, usually very young and fantastically thrilled to spend a season in Mallorca for very little pay. Luc hadn't met this one. She was wearing a loose sarong.

"Hi. A San Miguel, please. I'll just have it in the bottle."

"Sure. You're Luc, aren't you, Lulu's son?"

"Yes. And you are?"

"Sally! Hi!" She stretched her hand across the bar and Luc shook it.

"Of course you are," he said.

"You're the film producer!"

"Just a screenwriter."

"Oh, brilliant!"

Another cretin.

"No, no, Luc, her name *really is Sally*!" said an elderly man sitting on a nearby barstool. He appeared to be naked, except for the salami-sized cigar in one hand, and all but the rear strip of his tiny Speedo concealed by a large belly. "This Sally's a *Sally*!"

For most of the 1960s, the Rocks' universally beloved bartender had been a plump, pretty, effusive English blonde named Sally. The regular annual guests had thereafter called all successive bartenders Sally.

Sally pulled a San Miguel from the thick-doored icebox-style fridge with the handle that clicked shut, and placed the bottle, immediately frosting with condensation, on top of the bar.

"I'll try to remember," said Luc. "How are you, Richard?"

"I'm well, old bean," said the man with the cigar. "And how are you? Arabella's jolly excited to see you. And to meet your friend."

"I'm looking forward to seeing her," said Luc. "You can put it on my tab," he told Sally.

"Brilliant!" she said.

Peripherally, Luc noticed the younger couple at the bar smiling broadly at him. He could tell, a prickling in his skin, that they were just about to say to him, with a rapid and thrilled rise in inflection, "Oh, do you work in *films*, then?" He turned quickly away.

Luc took the beer and walked across the courtyard and sat at a table that had not yet been laid for dinner. He raised the icy bottle to his lips. His first San Miguel this year. It had been Luc's first alcoholic drink, 1965, the summer he turned fifteen. The first one had been too bitter, but a few days later he'd had another and soon they began to taste just right. Those bubbles on the roof of his mouth and the clean, hoppy flavor. Every year since, the first San Miguel became his madeleine. As he drank it, scenes from all those summers spent at the Rocks and around Cala Marsopa rose up whole and three-dimensional before him with all their hopes, intrigues, and desires that had somehow never been slaked.

He drank half the bottle immediately while it was as cold as possible. Of course, if he did make *Lawrence of Arabia*, it wouldn't be good enough for his mother (she had only seen the film once and found "all that desert excruciatingly boring"). Her job as a mother, which she took seriously, had always been to goad him with his complacent wallowing in mediocrity. His persistent nonarrival. The little triumphs—a César nomination for one of his screenplays—were heard, when he mentioned them, pronounced "how nice for you, darling," and never mentioned again. The success and good fortune of managing to get jobs, make money, were ignored. The two years he'd spent in Los Angeles developing a screenplay that went nowhere, but for which he'd made good money, was an opportunity to offer sympathy over yet more failure. "I know you wanted it, darling, but I do think it's as well nothing came of it. It was such absolute rubbish." Trouble was, he agreed with her: when was he going to make it—*really* make it? When was he going to be more than an also-ran? At forty-five, could there still be something big ahead, or was this it? Small movies, made for not a franc more than the anticipated box office of German, French, and middle-European territories, ennobled by the appellation *noirish*, destined for certain oblivion; enough money to live less than another year on; and the perks of per diems, good hotel rooms, and someone like April Gressens?

The old, cold horror gripped him: was he fated to hack his way through mediocrity?

"*Perdó.*"

He looked up. It was the catering girl with the hooked nose.

She'd spoken reflexively in *mallorquí*, but now she said in Spanish, "*Perdóneme*"—her hands were full of plates, cutlery—"*tengo que*—"

"Yes, of course," Luc answered in fluent Spanish. "I'm in your way." He started to rise.

"No, you can sit," she said, "if I won't disturb you. I have to lay the table."

She worked efficiently around him. Now he saw that she was impressively ugly. A gargoyle on the wall of an Egyptian crypt. Large black eyes, a low brow, a wide full mouth, everything asymmetrical, and that nose, like a Tintin villain. Everything else, though, was pretty good: the thick dark Spanish hair, a dancer's body.

"You're *mallorquina?*" he asked.

"My ancestors are from here. I live in Barcelona but I've come here to Mallorca every summer of my life."

"Ah, like me, except for the ancestors," said Luc. "What are you called?"

"Montserrat," she said.

"I'm called Luc—Lluc in Catalan."

"Yes, I know," she said. She smiled at him suddenly, as if she knew something he didn't that amused her intensely. "Pleased to meet you."

"And you," he said. "This what you do?"

"No. This is work for the summer. I'm studying art history, religious iconography, at the University of Barcelona."

The best university in Spain. Not just an asymmetrical face, then. "Are you religious?"

"When I need to be." She grinned. Sharp white teeth in wine red gums. "Nice to meet you—at last." She went off to set another table.

At last? What's that all about?

Now he couldn't take his eyes off her. *Montserrat.* Her ancestors, easily discerned, were Roman, Moorish, Catalan. She was the highly evolved product of all of Mediterranean history and cultures. Luc understood her immediately as he would never fathom the opaque shallows of the homogenized April from California. Intelligence poured off her. She was quick, knowing (she knew more than he did about something, apparently), and funny. She would understand him too, he knew it absolutely. He sipped his beer, watching Montserrat swing her lean thighs and narrow hips around a table. Her quick eyes and hands adroitly covering a table. She had strong hands. Her genetic makeup contained eons of domestic skills. She could probably herd goats just as well, with children on her hip. He imagined her in Paris. Reading a book on religious iconography in the Luxembourg Garden. In his apartment. He imagined the view from just above the knees upward between Montserrat's thighs. Maybe she could transfer to the Sorbonne.

He'd got her all wrong, he realized. She wasn't ugly at all. Her face was a Picasso.

His mother was, of course, right again: What was he doing with April? Like a good Californian, she was skilled in bed, but with a rote avidity that smacked more of conscious performance than lust, and was, not astonishingly, beginning to bore him. He would undoubtedly bore her too before long, with his frame of reference that might as well be allusions to the Upanishads for all that April understood at any given moment what he might be on about. He ought to find someone like Montserrat, warm, real, unconcerned about his mother's sexual protection. Like old Gerald had done: married a local woman who'd given him a child and stuck to him, and devoted herself to him until she'd dropped. He imagined the children he and Montserrat would make together: dark-haired, beautiful, artistic, extraordinary, asymmetrical. They would all be Picassos—

"Hey!" said April.

Luc tensed reflexively as she dropped into his lap with a proprietorial heedlessness.

"Look. What. Your. Mother. Gave me," she said, her voice full of amazed reverence. "Aren't they just, like, incredibly beautiful?"

"They are," he agreed.

They were straps of braided gold yarn containing glinting metallic filaments. They looked exotic, fabled, Levantine. They had the burnished golden hue of ancient coins.

"You wear them on the top of your feet," she said, raising her bare foot.

"I know. I've seen them before."

April didn't seem to hear him. "You put this loop around the second toe, like this, and then they go over the top of the foot and then around the ankle and fasten like this." She put the pair on her feet, which were like a child's feet: pale, unveined, undistorted by ill-fitting footwear, now dressed as if for a toga party.

"Your mother just, like, floated over to me when I came in and gave them to me. To keep!"

"She's taken a shine to you."

"Really? Aw. She is totally beautiful. Look, what do you think?" She lifted her legs, pivoting them for angled views of her adorned feet, unaware (or perhaps not) of the way her buttocks ground into Luc's lap.

He looked over her scissoring legs at Montserrat, who had moved off to a more distant table.

"Aren't they amazing?" said April. "You wear them on bare feet, without shoes."

"Yes, they're amazing. They were made in the sixties by someone who lived here. A friend of mine."

"I'm going to wear them tonight."

April rubbed her gilded foot along Luc's leg. She moved her buttocks again, consciously now. "Mmm. What's this?"

Only his body's brainless response; Luc wasn't interested in pursuing it. "Nothing much."

April got up and stood beside Luc. She raised her leg, stretching her foot aloft balletically, and then brought it down onto Luc's lap, pushing into him.

"Hey," he said.

April gazed at her feet. "These things are making me feel, like . . . I don't know . . ." She raised her arms and began to sway. She'd shown him her belly-dance technique several times. That's what's coming, he realized. He stood up as the towel around April's hips began to twitch and her gold-topped feet darted toward him. Again, he looked at Montserrat, across the patio.

"Okay," he said. He took her hand and tried to lead her toward the barracks, but April, gyrating slowly, pulled her arm away. He turned and walked on quickly toward the barracks. He leapt up the stairs toward his room.

Three

L ate in the afternoon, Charlie rode his bike down the rutted dirt driveway from C'an Cabrer, his grandfather's farm. It was another kilometer along the paved road into Cala Marsopa. He met Bianca at the English and German bookshop and café off the plaza. They bussed each other on both cheeks and walked, Charlie pushing his bike, through town to the port.

"Ho-laaa," Rafaela, the pale, lightly mustached, dark-haired woman who owned the Bar-Restaurante Marítimo, greeted them both with affection.

"Hola," Charlie replied, with a smile, "cómo estás?" He'd been brought to this restaurant overlooking the port as an infant in a basket, and he'd come back every summer of his life. Rafaela always knew him. It wasn't so everywhere in Cala Marsopa. A week ago, buying a bag of hot churros from the gnarled vendor whom Charlie had known since toddlerhood and remembered like an uncle who always had a treat for him, the old man had looked at him—now a six-foot youth—without recognition, and asked him for "fünfundzwanzig pesetas," and Charlie had been cut to the quick.

Rafaela led them to a table on the terrace overlooking the yachts and the fishing boats in the harbor. They ordered hamburguesas, papas fritas, and Cokes. Before the food arrived, Sylvestre, Natalie, and Marie joined them. Rafaela had known them for years too: the children of children of foreign residents who had lived on or come back to the island since Rafaela had been a child herself. They ordered calamari.

"*On va tout le monde à l'anniversaire de Lulu au Rocks?*" asked Sylvestre.

"Yeah. I'm going to be the DJ," said Charlie.

"*Ahhh, non!*" said Marie, expectorating the first word with exasperation. "*Putain, j'en ai marre de cette musi-i-i-que.*"

"No, it's cool," said Charlie agreeably. "Anyway, it's what Lulu wants."

After they'd eaten, Sylvestre and the two French girls walked back through town.

The sea breeze had died. It was hot near the stucco apartment buildings and concrete walls that had replaced the shade of bent pines and crumbles of limestone that defined the edges of the old fishing harbor that still appeared in postcards of Cala Marsopa. Charlie and Bianca climbed the steps to the top of the breakwater and walked out to the blinking light at the far end where they sat in the shadow of its structure, out of the flash. It was cooler above the water.

They kissed wetly, hungrily, like people eating steadily under a time constraint. Charlie put his hand inside Bianca's shirt and slipped her precocious breasts free of her bra. She threw her legs over his lap and let her hand rest on Charlie's thigh. Charlie's own crossed legs prevented, he hoped, Bianca feeling his erection pulsing spasmodically beneath her. As a child, Bianca had been skinny. When Charlie saw her the summer they were both twelve, she'd become softer. At thirteen, she was heavier. This year, at fifteen, Charlie's age, that heaviness had concentrated in her sizable breasts, and her hips. Now he thought of Bianca ceaselessly when he masturbated, but they'd been playmates since they were children and he didn't want to spoil their friendship. Sex had come over them, and they played with it nicely like friends playing dolls. They went no further. By unspoken agreement, they'd settled on this decent plateau of intimacy. Charlie liked Bianca too much to make her uncomfortable.

After a bit, he looked at his watch and said, "I better get going."

At the bottom of the steps, Charlie got on his bike. Bianca sat on the crossbar and he pedaled them down the quay. He dropped her close to the plaza and she said, "*À toute à l'heure,*" as he pedaled away.

Five minutes later, he swung into the small driveway off the alley and laid his bike against the wall outside the kitchen.

At seven, with the tables set, dinner being prepared, most of the Rocks' guests were in their rooms, bathing, dressing, or still taking a siesta. A few were sitting at the bar in bathing suits. Charlie walked across the patio toward the bar, past two middle-aged men hunched over a backgammon board. Dominick Cleland, even hunched, was tall and thin, with a thatch of straight gray-blond hair that made him look like a dissolute version of a well-known British cabinet minister. He was wearing a royal blue Turnbull & Asser shirt over Speedo briefs. His long, hairless legs, shapeless and knobbed as a giraffe's, entwined around themselves, ended in long sockless feet and white Gucci loafers. He had written pulp novels about the misbehavior of the British upper classes, but his subject no longer held the public's interest and he hadn't published a book in twenty years. With a small annuity left to him by an uncle, he lived most of the year in a tiny flat in South Kensington, and spent his summers at the Rocks. He felt at home there. If he was near the phone in the bar when it rang, Dominick liked to answer it by shouting into the receiver, *"Los Roques! Dígame?"* regardless of the fact that no one but Anglophones ever telephoned the Rocks.

His opponent, and physiological opposite, Cassian Ollorenshaw, resembled, even in his youth, the actor Edward G. Robinson at his most toadlike and implacable. Now, his face blotchy red from inflamed rosacea, he peered at the board through small, round, yellow-lensed glasses. His body below his large head was inconsequential, swallowed in a voluminous white T-shirt and skirt-sized swimming trunks. They played fast and silently. They'd been there, playing backgammon at a table on the patio, every summer—except a couple of years when Cassian had been in prison—since Charlie's father had first brought him to the Rocks as an infant. They'd been there when he played in the pool as a child with the children of guests, and with those same children when they returned as teenagers. They were more familiar to him than most of his relatives. Cassian looked up now and said, with a small smile, "Hallo, Charlie."

"Hi, Cassian."

"Hallo, Charlie," said Sally, as he approached the bar. "I'm supposed to give you whatever you want to drink tonight."

"A Coke, please. Just the bottle'll be great, thanks."

He took his Coke into the small room off the bar that once housed the gas bottles. It was no wider than its two glass doors. Inside stood a chair and a table that supported a turntable. Charlie set his Coke down on the table and began going through the vinyl albums that filled a wall of shelves.

Lulu came out of the house, gliding across the patio in a gauzy linen djellaba that billowed behind her. She smiled serenely.

"Lulu, *darling*," Dominick Cleland greeted her loudly, while shaking a cup of dice. "Are you having the most *wonderful* birthday *ever*, my love?"

"I am, thank you, Dominick. So happy you're here to share it with me."

Lulu didn't break her pace. Dominick threw the dice.

The guests at the bar wished Lulu a happy birthday. "Thank you," she said, her smile raking them as she swept by. She went into the small music room.

"Charlie," she said.

"Oh, hi, Lulu. Happy birthday."

She hugged him. "I have a present for you."

"For me?"

"Yes, darling."

She handed him a small black bundle of cloth. It fell open in his hands. He held it up. It was a long black shirt without a collar, opening halfway down the chest with lots of small buttons close together.

"It's from Morocco. It's old but it's never been worn. I want you to have it. I think it will look very good on you."

"Thanks, Lulu."

"Put it on."

"What, now?"

"Yes, sweetheart. It's your uniform for this evening. I want to see how it looks on you. Take off your shirt and put it on."

She sounded like a mother, affectionately, matter-of-factly in charge. Charlie unhesitatingly pulled off his white T-shirt. He pulled the black Moroccan shirt over his head.

"Marvelous," she said. She ran a hand over the shirt, smoothing it down his chest. "Do you like it?"

"Oh, yeah," said Charlie. "It's really—"

"It is a man's shirt. Don't worry."

"No, I like it, it's great."

"You look very good in it, Charlie. Now you remember what we discussed about the music?"

"Yeah. Quiet and gentle, Noël Coward, Al Bowlly, Charles Trenet, Sinatra for dinner—"

"Not only."

"No, no, I know, mix it up. And then Beatles and sixties stuff, Tijuana Brass, Motown afterward."

"That's it," said Lulu, looking very happy. "You know, I'm so pleased it's you here to do this for me, Charlie. It's so very sweet of you. Thank you." She smiled at him.

"I'm happy to do it, Lulu. It's fun."

She leaned forward and kissed his cheek. "See you later."

Four

"Are you ready, Papa?" Aegina called. "We'll leave in five minutes."

It was so odd to have her father here and Charlie far away at C'an Cabrer in Mallorca. Even when Charlie spent a night or two at his father Fergus's flat in Chelsea, he was nearby. He always spent the summer holidays with her in Mallorca. Now he was there—she knew he'd be all right with Penny and François—and it was a strange, sweet comfort to have her father here with her at home in London. He seemed almost like a son, downstairs in Charlie's room, getting ready for his big night out. He was far more helpless than Charlie, at sea in the world beyond Mallorca and the Mediterranean.

He would never come to London again after this trip. She had to make it fun for both of them. She had to remember it.

"I'm ready now," Gerald called up.

He was sitting on the bed in Charlie's room, looking through *The Way to Ithaca*. He didn't want to *read* aloud—it would feel too pompous. He wanted simply to talk, briefly, about how he had come to write the book, but he feared drying up if he tried to waffle along without preparation. He'd decided he would abbreviate and paraphrase the first part of the introduction, which he had rewritten for this new edition. He'd made pencil marks against the paragraphs he thought might sound sufficiently logical in thrust yet conversational if run together. He could glance down at these and tell a brief story.

He closed the book, got up, and left the room. He walked through the kitchen into the large studio living room.

"I'm ready," he said again, in case she hadn't heard him.

"I'll be down in a minute," Aegina called from her bathroom upstairs.

The large room was full of paintings. Several big ones by an artist who painted people in the vivid colors that might have lain beneath the covering of their skin: organ purples, blood reds, veiny blues, bone whites, pus yellows, slashed across their bodies to delineate light and shadow—and possibly, it occurred to Gerald, character. Were they supposed to be bilious, bloody people? Otherwise, what was the point? They were quite valuable, Aegina had told him. Another artist's landscapes—or that was what they suggested to Gerald: layers of topography perhaps, in a narrow range of bog hues—filled in most of the other wall spaces. Hardly any of Aegina's own work, except the portraits of himself and Charlie for which they'd sat impatiently in the living room and on the terrace in Mallorca. And her painting of her mother, his wife, Paloma, from an old photograph.

Sunlight poured through high northern windows. "I'll wait outside," Gerald called upstairs.

He walked out to the courtyard where Aegina's little Renault was parked, and smoked a Ducados—his hand shaking, he noticed, as he lit it. It was six o'clock but as sunny and warm as midafternoon. After so many years in the Mediterranean, he'd forgotten the long, light summer evenings at the northern latitude of London. He remembered a perpetual twilight along the Thames Embankment on so many evenings early in the war.

He looked at the other studios surrounding the courtyard, the glass atriums, the spiral staircases. She'd been awfully clever, Aegina. With several other artists, she'd purchased a former women's prison, a quadrangle of brick buildings with courtyard and garden space between two streets in Fulham, not far from Bishop's Park on the Thames. The core purchasers had sold off sections of the prison, now called Burlington Lodge, as artist's studios, at considerable profit. Odyssey, Aegina's shops of imported clothes and fabrics—now with branches in Manchester, York, Birmingham, Bath, Norwich, Falmouth, Plymouth, Southampton, as well as the original in Covent Garden and elsewhere in London—had made her rich (or so it seemed to Gerald); but she'd done as well buying and selling property. Yet she wasn't painting much anymore, which made Gerald sad. She'd taken him to lunch at the Chelsea Arts Club, small rooms crammed with paintings where all the arty-looking members knew her. "No, he's a writer," she said, beaming, when she introduced her father and they asked if he too was a painter. "He's got a book coming out tomorrow. The publishing party's at the British Museum." Gerald had smiled wanly in embarrassment.

"Papa, you look fantastic!" Aegina said, as she came out of her studio into the courtyard. She'd also taken her father to Harrods to look for clothes suitable for an author at his book launch party. They chose a navy blue linen blazer, pale khaki trousers, dark blue socks, brown loafers. Gerald had bought some cotton briefs too, which looked better than those he usually found in Mallorca. Aegina tried to pay for everything but Gerald wouldn't hear of it with his thousands of pounds idling in the bank. The bill was £435, more, he was certain, than he had cumulatively spent on clothes in his entire life. It made him feel absurdly grand, but Aegina saw that he enjoyed it. He'd brought his Tonbridge School tie to London, which she'd sponged clean.

"I mean, look at you," she said. "You're slim and tan. *Very* well dressed. Totally dishy!"

"Anybody would look good alongside you," he said. "Well, no one would notice anyone else, for a start."

She was wearing a sleeveless, brick-red, long narrow cotton dress that showed off her dark hair and eyes, her Mediterranean complexion, lithe brown arms and calves.

Gerald's face softened. "Of course, you always remind me of your mother."

Aegina smiled. "That's a compliment, thank you." She took a small disposable Kodak camera from her bag. "Now, stand there by my front door."

"Oh, come on," pleaded Gerald.

"No, this is a treat for me, having you here. Please. Don't look so grim!"

Gerald moved to her door and tried various squinting smiles. Aegina clicked. "Nineteen ninety-five," she said, looking through the lens, "Papa came to London for his publishing party."

In the car, Aegina swung them quickly out of the courtyard into the street and they tore away.

Gerald had once known London well—up in the holidays from school and again with friends from university, leave during the war; the thrilling sense of limitless possibility awaiting one in the greatest of all cites, even (especially) as it was being bombed . . . and then he'd gone away and spent his life on a small island and never come back. He recognized most of the route up Fulham Road, through the edges of Knightsbridge and Belgravia, but then he became disoriented by new buildings and the one-way system, and finally, though he knew approximately where they must be on the map of London in his head, he was lost. But Aegina was marvelously sure and wove through traffic with what seemed a rally driver's expertise. She was so astonishingly accomplished, he thought. All from her mother, of course.

"Do you see much of Fergus?" he asked her.

"Sometimes. When he comes to pick up Charlie, or I drop him off. School events."

"And do you get on?"

"Oh, sure. I mean, as far as we need to. We agree pretty much about all things Charlie."

"And how is Charlie with you both? Does he get on with Fergus?"

"Oh yes," said Aegina, flicking glances right and left, into the mirror, shifting down, shifting lanes. "He's navigated between us and through the divorce with some kind of fish instinct. Always swimming smoothly around anything that might catch him up. He doesn't talk about it much, or about either of us to the other. I think he's all right. He's happy."

"Good," said Gerald. He was silent for a minute. "And are you happy?"

"Yes, I am."

"Good," said Gerald. "Do you have . . . you know . . . anybody?"

"Not right now."

"Not ever, then?"

"Well, Papa, of course." She shot him a quick look between checking three mirrors and hurtling around a double-parked car. "What do you want me to tell you?"

Well, not *too much*. But he wanted Aegina to be happy. She was certainly successful. Pity his sister Billie was dead, he thought. She could have told him more. Aegina had gone to school in England after her mother died, and she'd stayed with Billie at half-terms and other times during the school year. They'd become close—Billie not quite a surrogate mother, but more than an aunt—and she'd come to know details of Aegina's life that Gerald had missed.

He still had a great sense of having failed Aegina. She'd run wild in Mallorca and he'd shipped her off to Billie. And look at her. She had turned out unarguably well—the divorce from Fergus was surely not a bad thing—but he still asked himself if he should have kept her at home, or, God forbid, moved back with her to England somehow himself . . .

"Just that you're happy," said Gerald.

"I'm happy," she said firmly. She looked at him quickly again, smiling beautifully. "I'm *very* happy about you and your brilliant book."

G erald!" A thin, broadly grinning, frizzy-haired woman with round steel-rim glasses, black tube dress, bore toward him from a group standing before an enormous marbled statue of an ancient Greek the size of King Kong who appeared to be lying in a deck chair. "I'm Kate! Gosh, you're *handsome*! Damn, we should have had you properly photographed! May I kiss you?"

She'd already done so as Gerald said, "Certainly." Over her shoulder, he saw a group of smiling people opening toward them.

"You must be Aegina!" said Kate Smythe. "How wonderful to finally meet you both! We're *so* pleased with the book—it's getting the most fantastic buzz! Don't fill up on the hors d'oeuvres, we're taking you out to dinner after the party. Gerald, come and meet everybody."

Nicky, Ruth, Claire, William—Gerald had spoken with them all on the telephone while gazing at his olive oil in the larder. He'd forgotten now who did what, but Kate was tagging them again, "publicity . . . foreign rights . . . art direction . . . editorial." Their fulsome display of affection for him, a total stranger, was unnerving.

Then Kate took his arm and steered him to other people: Doughty authors, editors of the *Guardian Review, The Sunday Times,* the *London Review of Books,* buyers from Waterstones, Foyles.

"I love your book!" everyone said. *"Adore* your book!"

They chattered and milled in clusters that broke and regrouped beneath the giant friezes and marble figures of mostly reclining, glaze-eyed, superbly muscled figures looted from the Parthenon and lining the long, austere, Zen space of the Duveen Gallery. Gerald held tightly on to a glass of Champagne as people spoke to him. He barely drank.

They didn't, in fact, want to talk about his book. Apart from the Doughties, as they called themselves, no one appeared to have actually read it. They wanted to tell Gerald what they were doing and how his book somehow related to that and how timely and amazing that was. Gerald smiled as if he understood, or could hear, and looked at their hair and spectacles and skin and wondered how old they were and how they lived. It didn't seem to matter what he said.

"—thinking of doing an article about how much things have changed in the Greek islands since you were there on your little boat—well, indeed, since Homer's time—"

"—a rapidly expanding niche—"

"—on the front page next Sunday—"

"—we're doing a little sidebar about what books people have on their bedside tables, if you'd—"

"—might do some reviewing for us?"

"—spend any time in the Solent? We've got a Nicholson thirty-two we keep in Lymington—"

"—my card—"

"—brilliant!"

"—aren't there a lot of Germans there?"

As Aegina stood beneath the great Selene horse, watching her father in his moment of success, a man slipped toward her around the horse's flank; she was not aware of him until he stood at her side. Tony Watkins had written a series of best-selling and serialized memoirs exposing himself as a corrupt rake who'd done appalling things while holding a mid-level appointment in the Heath and Thatcher governments. He was grinning at her as if they shared some intimate understanding.

"Aegina. And here I thought your father was some goatherd in Spain. You've been hiding him under a bushel. How clever of you. I'd love to meet him properly."

"Well, there he is, go say hello to him," said Aegina.

"No, I was thinking why don't you both come round for dinner tomorrow night? I'll invite someone for your father. How about Edwina Porboys? She'd certainly like him. Just the four of us. Edwina will bring some Ecstasy. Has your father tried it?"

"You're repellent. Go away."

Over his shoulder she saw her father. He looked happy.

"That's what I love about you, you see," said Watkins. "Something in you knows me so well."

"Fuck off," said Aegina.

As she walked toward her father, Kate began tapping a glass and the party grew quiet. She spoke of the fortuitous rediscovery of Gerald's "small, understated masterpiece of vernacular history and travel," of its distinction and authority in an age of navel-gazing memoirs of house-building and eating in foreign places, and how thrilled she and everyone at Doughty were to be able to launch a new edition of what would undoubtedly prove an enduring classic.

"—so I give you Doughty Books' thrilling new publication *The Way to Ithaca* and its author, Gerald Rutledge."

Gerald saw them all grouped around him, smiling, clapping, vividly recalling his nightmare of an intellectual Scylla. He opened his mouth, waiting for a moment when he could start.

Aegina was aware of her racing heart and a roaring in her ears.

"Thank you so much, Kate," Gerald began. "And all of you at Doughty Books. And the rest of you, who apparently have nothing better to do with yourselves." This brought a generous laugh, under the cover of which Gerald cleared his throat at extensive length.

"I too am thrilled, as you can imagine, to see my foundling book plucked from obscurity and given new life again in so fine an edition. Perhaps it's not unlike getting a really good face-lift: you begin to feel your old self again."

Everyone laughed again—Aegina with them, astonished; where had he come up with that one? She began, almost, to feel relieved.

The noise of their laughter affected Gerald like the sudden infusion of a drug. He looked down at his book in his hands. He saw the pencil-marked paragraphs in his mind's eye and realized that he knew it all by heart, he'd known the story for most of his life, and wouldn't need to open the book at all.

"I won't bore you for long, but I thought I'd tell you something of how I came to write the book. I spent most of World War Two aboard British Navy vessels in the Mediterranean. At one point, we were anchored on Skerki Bank west of Sicily. This is a remote reef between Sicily and Tunisia that rises from the sea floor to only a foot or so beneath the surface. Four thousand years of shipping has navigated, successfully and otherwise, around this unmarked reef. It was hot and, along with some of the crew, I went swimming. There was no land in sight, but we discovered that we could wade calf-deep in the water. We had no swimming masks as everyone has today, but we could see that the reef was littered with ancient amphorae, the two-handled pots in which Greeks like King Agamemnon and his armies that fought the Trojan War carried wine, olive oil, almonds, dates, honey, and, of course, gold and valuables, aboard their ships. We had no breathing apparatus either, of course, yet simply by shallow diving, we brought eight or ten of these barnacle-encrusted amphorae to the surface—archaeological looting it would probably be called today. Some of the amphorae were almost intact after who knew how many hundreds, perhaps thousands, of years they'd spent underwater. What, we wondered, was inside them?"

Gerald's audience had become as still as the surrounding ancient Greeks. Kate looked enthralled, as if she hadn't yet read what he was going to say and couldn't wait to hear it.

Gerald smiled. "Thick, ageless sludge. No gold. No honey or almonds either, to augment His Majesty's naval rations."

Titters, happy smiles.

"But seeing these old jars coming up out of the sea, breaking the surface into the light of present day—breaking through the membrane of history, as it were—gripped me quite powerfully. During that one afternoon on Skerki Bank, all the tales of ancient Greece became real for me. Here was proof."

Aegina stared at her father. Before her eyes, he had transformed into an instinctual storyteller—or, he was living it all again: he was back there now, on that reef.

Gerald went on. "Throughout the war, and afterward, during the years I spent cruising the Mediterranean in an old, twenty-four-foot gaff cutter, I read again and again passages in my old green, tattered, salt-stained edition of A. T. Murray's prose translation of *The Odyssey*. Two volumes, published by the Loeb Classical Library. I also read many volumes of British Admiralty sailing directions for the Mediterranean Sea. These were not literature, usually written in very dry prose, but occasionally the men who penned the descriptions of harbors and coastlines—not scholars, but one could detect a certain level of education in their idiom and references—managed to get past their editors"—more, knowing laughs—"the suggestion that many of the islands, harbors, headlands I was seeing might well stand as the factual locations of various episodes from *The Odyssey*. Some of this was obvious. If there *were* a factual geography to *The Odyssey*, the whirlpool of Charybdis could hardly have been anywhere but the Strait of Messina, which, at the wrong state of the tide, could spin a corvette in circles. The cliffs where Odysseus was ambushed by the boulder-throwing Laestrygonians might well have been—I can't think of any other location—the entrance to the Corsican harbor of Bonifacio. And there is a cave . . ." Gerald's attention, and then his voice, momentarily faltered ". . . where I believe Odysseus found the cunning to outwit Polyphemus, the Cyclops. . . ." He fell silent, gazing at the marble frieze on the opposite wall.

Aegina had never seen her father in such a state. He was transported.

At the moment when his pause became conspicuous, Gerald collected himself and started up again. "Well, why shouldn't *The Odyssey* be a real story? I thought. We know that Troy was real, that a great battle was fought there, and that Schliemann and others, only a hundred or so years ago, armed with a copy of *The Iliad*, went to a mound of rock and grass in Asia Minor and found the city, and the proof of war. Descriptions of place fill *The Odyssey*, often as detailed and accurate as the particulars of a property listed by an estate agent. Over time, sailing these same seas and coastlines, propelled by the same winds that pushed Odysseus's ships, *The Odyssey* acquired for me the weight of truth. I began to think that Homer, whether he was blind or not, had heard detailed descriptions of these places, or perhaps even seen them for himself. Eventually, I became determined to sail my own small boat from Troy to Ithaca, using *The Odyssey* for sailing directions, as Schliemann had used *The Iliad* to find Troy, to discover the true geographic route of Odysseus's long, treacherous voyage home from the Trojan War. In time, in one vessel or another, I sailed the whole route. *The Way to Ithaca* describes his voyage, and mine alongside it."

Gerald stopped, suddenly spent. He looked at the expectant faces. He felt he had stopped too abruptly; he needed to say something more. "The title of my book, of course, comes from Cavafy's poem 'Ithaka.' I like his suggestion that it wasn't reaching Ithaca that mattered so much, as what happened to one along the way. Thank you all, so very much."

The noise of applause and chatter rose in the gallery and echoed around the splendid marbles. Aegina clapped and watched her father. He had gone somewhere while talking and not all of him had come back.

Then the yachtsman, the chap with the boat in Lymington, asked: "How long a trip was that, actually, Gerald, to sail from Troy to Ithaca? Not as long as it took Odysseus, I hope?" He chortled knowingly. "Could one do it in a season?"

Gerald had to think for a moment. He spoke quietly, as if remembering out loud. "I didn't do it all at once. Over a number of years I traveled every leg, in my own yacht, or aboard British naval vessels during the war, but not in the order in which I set out the route in my book, Troy to Ithaca. I was going to do it . . ." He stopped.

Aegina stepped forward. Something was happening to him. In his brain or heart.

Gerald's hand rose hesitantly to his throat. His face contorted. His eyes rose to the marble figures on the far wall.

"Oh dear," said Kate. "Do you need some water?"

Aegina swept quickly past her. She reached Gerald and held both his arms, partially shielding him, as he began to weep.

Five

As everyone *sat down* to dinner, Lulu rose.

"Thank you all for being here for my birthday. I consider myself incredibly fortunate to have such dear and faithful friends. Most of you have come back here to the Rocks year after year, for decades—some of you as long as I've been here—what on earth are you thinking?"

Adoring laughter.

"You've given me lovely birthday gifts—after I told you not to—but you are, each of you, all the gift I want. I wanted to get something for you too. Just baubles."

At each place setting on the five tables was a name card for the guest and a wrapped gift. Well, this was Lulu, wasn't it? She was being truthful: her greatest joy was her friends, and she was the best friend anyone present had ever known. Some of them, at difficult moments in their lives, had come down for a few weeks in the summer, occupied rooms, ate the Rocks' food, children in tow even, to find that Lulu refused to accept a penny from them. Cassian Ollorenshaw had become a fixture at the Rocks for at least six months of the year after his spell in Pentonville prison. (He wasn't a *bad* man, of course, but a trusted friend to Lulu and others, and he'd made a number of people, Lulu included, quite a lot of money.) Everyone here had seen Lulu, at the drop of a hat, drive anybody all over the island; give them books, clothing, paintings; pull whatever she had from her closets, off her walls, out of her fridge; give whatever she had to her friends when Lulu knew before they did that it was exactly what they needed at that moment.

"Tokens of my love and gratitude to each one of you. And I want those of you—that's most of you, of course—who remember our *dear* Tom and Milly, whom we loved so very much"—she turned briefly to Cassian, and then looked again around the tables—"to remember them now too. Happy birthday to all of us!"

Lulu raised a glass of Champagne. Everyone clapped and drank. A man rose to make a toast but Lulu interrupted him briskly. "Roddy, darling, you're sweet, but let's eat our lovely dinner that Bronwyn's made for us, and we can talk some more later."

There was an excited buzz, a Christmas sound of everyone's packages being torn open. Lulu had bought them Swatch watches, necklaces and bracelets from Morocco and New Mexico, embroidered slippers, scarves, Montblanc pens, Filofaxes; gifts that were useful and would see a long life.

"Can you believe this?" April said, raising an Hermès scarf to her cheek, looking around and seeing tears and delight on the faces of the other guests. "Look, Luc! Lookit this stuff! Lookit how all these people *love* her! My God, do you, like, know how lucky you are to have such a mother?"

"The best mummy in the world," said Luc, watching Montserrat weave through the tables carrying a tray laden with plates heaped with food.

Dominick Cleland had noticed April the day before, as soon as she and Luc had arrived. Partly, naturally, because she was with Luc, which rendered her an immediate curiosity, and because she was fantastic-looking, with that incredible complexion—he could see in his mind's eye the apricot dusting and flesh of her pubis as clearly as if he were standing inches from an impastoed painting. Dominick admired Luc's consistency. He always managed to turn up with some tasty bint. Never held on to them from one year to the next, but he rarely came down empty-handed. Once he'd arrived with a yacht full of people; a little adventure that had turned out very nicely for Dominick. Generally they were young and still undemanding, grateful, curious, and interested in making a career in the arts—ideal fodder for Dominick's well-oiled mix of elevated conversation and carnal suggestion. It must be the films, he supposed, the endless supply of hopeful supplicants grabbing at anything for a way in. It couldn't be Luc himself, who would never have what a man needed—power, or the illusion of it, confidence, an inherent disregard for a woman's tenderer feelings—to hook the sort of woman he was still delusionally looking for. Dominick had long ago rid himself of the desire for such thoroughbreds. They ate a man up faster than cancer. Now all he wanted was a bit of a chase, a delicious conquest (wasn't that really the finest moment?) culminating in a fuck, preferably delectable, but any fuck at all would do—it was like Chinese dinners: he'd never really had a bad one—a dalliance of no more than a week or so, after which one of them, he or the girl but not together, would hopefully get onto an airplane.

After dinner, when they cleared a dancing floor on the patio, Dominick went directly to their table and asked April to dance. She seemed flattered.

"Go ahead," Luc said to her, smiling as beatifically as his mother.

Dominick, now in pink shirt and white slacks above the white Guccis, still had the moves: the Hully Gully, the Pony, the Watusi and the Mashed Potato. They'd worked at Annabel's a hundred years ago and the girls still seemed to go for it. Anyway, it made them laugh, especially if he really cranked it up, and it was amazing how he could work a kind of snake charmer routine on them: fix them with a smile, laugh at himself, pour good Champagne down them, make it dribble from their lips. He could see them reappraising him as the evening went on: he wasn't *that* old, they began to think—he was certainly fit. He was jolly good fun. He liked women, they could tell; and they could tell that he knew what they wanted. Most evenings, by a certain point, if they were still there, he was home.

He wasn't trying to seduce Luc's little playmate. Not now anyway, but you never knew when you might meet one of them again—as he had, several times, in London, and by then, introductions and Mallorca behind them, he could find the situation marvelously well along.

Luc was relieved. He knew April wanted to dance—she wanted to show off her shimmy and flick her golden feet between someone's legs. None better than Dominick. They were made for each other. He didn't give a toss if Dominick managed to get her phone number.

Luc got up and wandered into the house, into the kitchen. A number of the caterers were washing the dishes, drying glasses in the scullery in back of the main kitchen. Montserrat was not in sight.

"Like the dinner?" Bronwyn asked. She was sitting at the kitchen table, a bottle of Laphroaig and three fingers in a large crystal glass in front of her, smoking a small cigar. She wore a generalissimo-sized chef's jacket, heavily stained with food and wine, a linen napkin tied around her head like a bandanna.

"Great," said Luc. "Loved the blood orange sorbet."

"It was good, wasn't it? Want a drink?"

"Sure." Luc got a glass, sat down, and poured himself a shot from Bronwyn's bottle.

"Down for long?" she asked.

"A week maybe. If I can stick it out."

"Well, you're a good boy, coming down for your mummy's birthday. She's very pleased."

"Hardly. I'm the fly in her Yves Saint Laurent body lotion."

"Don't be silly. She loves you. She means well. She talks about you all the time."

"Yes, in terms of unfailing disappointment. Like a bad bet she can't get over."

"Oh, rubbish. You know she loves you. You can hear it whenever she mentions your name. You may be forty-whatever-it-is but you're still her little boy, you know. She says you're coming down, and you can hear how much it means to her."

Luc drank half his glass. "Where'd you get the caterers?"

"Which one?"

He looked round again. "Not here now. The nose."

"Montserrat."

"That's right. Montserrat."

"She worked in the kitchen at the Fonda when Javier was the cook. She's a Llobet."

"What, as in Juan Llobet?"

The name that loomed over Cala Marsopa like the permanently shuttered Llobet house hulking above the town on the road to the lighthouse, a severe, forbidding, Stalinist-era mansion that might have been designed for Lavrentiy Beria's house parties that included assassinations. Juan Llobet, the reclusive billionaire, Barbary Coast smuggler in his criminal infancy before World War I, later Franco crony, banker to the Nacionalistas of the Spanish Civil War, Mallorca's oligarchic Boo Radley; dead decades ago. Everyone coming into town drove along Carretera Juan Llobet, and most did some business, if just at the ATM, with Banco Llobet. At one point, Luc's mother had known a Llobet, one of the old boy's sons, who came to Cala Marsopa with his family every summer, but that association seemed to have faded years ago. *Montserrat Llobet.* It didn't surprise him. She was Mediterranean aristocracy, albeit from a dark, bent strain, like having Barbarossa for a grandfather.

"Yes, sweetheart. Some offshoot of the family. She's gorgeous, isn't she? Good luck."

"No, you know, I was just curious. I was talking to her earlier. She seemed interesting. Studying at the University of Barcelona."

"Yeah, she's interesting. Intelligent and ambitious. She sent Javier out of his mind."

"What's she doing waiting tables here, then?"

"Her father makes her work through the summers, even though he's filthy rich. She's good with food. Got a good work ethic. She's into art history. She'll probably end up running Christie's in Madrid."

Luc saw Montserrat Llobet's life unfolding like a spread in *Paris Match*. The yachts, the villas on Cap Ferrat, the gorgeous children—someone else's Picassos. Why the fuck can't I get a woman like that, and have such a life? But he knew. You were either born into it, a Llobet or a Grimaldi, or were positioned through the immense crimes, laundered in the oblivion of time, of a previous generation. Or you made it really big in the movies—you became Sam Spiegel or Alexander Korda—and you met someone like Montserrat Llobet at a party on a yacht at Cannes. And the world was yours.

Or you were someone who wrote French B movies that went straight to video and you got April Gressens from Tarzana.

Luc emptied his glass. "Great dinner, Bronwyn."

"Thanks, sweetie."

He got up and went outside. "Je T'Aime . . . Moi Non Plus" was coming out of the patio speakers. He'd heard it from inside the kitchen, but the crest of the time warp didn't hit him until he set foot on the patio. Then he remembered everything, or the feeling of everything, of the summer of 1969. The way the world felt then and what he thought would happen to his life.

He walked to the music room. Inside, Charlie was flipping through stacks of records; on a barstool sat his rather ripe-looking *petite amie*, a girl Luc had seen around, holding a glass of Coke. They looked like a shot from *Vanity Fair*'s party page.

"Oh, hiya!" said Charlie, breaking into a huge grin as he saw Luc. "I saw you out there at dinner. I was going to come out and say hi, but Lulu gave me the job of DJ and I gotta stay on it."

Luc was staring at him oddly, his eyes ranging up and down between Charlie's neck and hips. "Nice shirt," he said after a moment.

"Oh, yeah. Actually, your mum gave it to me. It's Moroccan, apparently. I think it's quite old."

Luc continued looking at the shirt, smiling. "Nice of her. Yeah, it's from Marrakech. It's about twenty-five years old—I remember when she got it."

He looked at Charlie in the shirt. What a sweet kid Charlie is, Luc thought. He seems genuinely pleased to see me. Evidently, he knows nothing, about the shirt's provenance, or anything else. Looks just like his mother.

"Cool! Um, Luc, this is Bianca. Bianca, Luc."

"Hi," said Bianca.

"Hi."

They shook hands.

"How're the films going?" asked Charlie.

"Good. Just wrapped a movie."

"Fantastic. What's it called? Who's in it?"

"Probably no one you've heard of, or will ever hear of. It's called *Perdu*. Lost. It'll be out in about eight or ten months. I think."

"Oh, I bet it's great. I loved *L'Autre*! I've told you that. It was really great."

"Thank you, Charlie. I'd forgotten that you'd seen it."

"You down for long?"

"About a week. You?"

"The summer, as usual. Hang on—" "Je T'Aime . . . Moi Non Plus" was ending, and Charlie started looking through the albums in his hand.

"I'll leave you to it, Charlie. It's nice to see you."

"Thanks. It's really good to see you, Luc. Take care."

"You too." And to Bianca, Luc said, "Nice to meet you."

Luc walked to the bar. Charlie had put on "A Taste of Honey" by the Tijuana Brass, blasting away the plangent intravenous melancholy of Serge Gainsbourg. Dominick was frugging vigorously around April, who was laughing as she wove her own sinuous, smoldering thrusts toward him.

His mother, in flowing white shirt and trousers, was dancing affectionately with Cassian, her arms stretched out and resting on his shoulders, while he talked to her about something that clearly meant a lot to both of them, perhaps the Footsie 100.

Luc turned away and went through the gate and crossed the road to the rocks. Here, the music was not so insistent, or pungent with memory, and he heard the sound of the waves slapping and sucking at the rocks somewhere below his feet, and he remembered jumping into the water, long ago, right here, unwillingly, at exactly this time of the night—

A tiny red glow indicated someone sitting nearby on the ledge over the sea, smoking a cigarette. A dark slender shape with hair diffusing the lights of the port.

"*Hola*," she said.

A great electric charge passed through Luc. "Montserrat," he said.

"Yes."

"It's me, Luc. We spoke—"

"Of course. I know it's you."

He walked toward her. He could see her face now, his eyes adjusting to the dark, and she had turned so that her strong features caught the light from across the road. He couldn't understand how he hadn't seen it immediately: it was the most beautiful face he'd ever seen.

He said, "I liked talking with you earlier."

"Yes, me too. It was nice, finally, after all these years."

"What do you mean?"

"Well"—she laughed—"I was in love with you for years."

Luc's Spanish was fluent, so he knew he hadn't misunderstood her. He'd imagined it, then. So clearly too. "What?" he said.

She laughed, her teeth bluish in the dim light like the wavecrests appearing out of the dark running toward the rocks around them. "Yes, for many years I was in love with you."

Tripping over a rock but catching himself, Luc sat down beside her.

"When did we meet?" he said.

She was amused by his utter confusion. "We have never met. But I've known you for many years."

"How? We have friends in common?"

"No. Years ago—fifteen years ago maybe—you had a motorcycle. For many summers. Right? I used to see you everywhere on that motorcycle. You looked incredible. Like *Easy Rider*, you know? So American—you are American or English?"

"American."

"I thought so. Or I wanted to think so. You were my dream guy. Sometimes you had girls on the back of your bike, and oh, my God, I wanted to be on the back of your motorcycle with you. You have no idea."

"I don't remember seeing you—"

"No, of course not. I was ten years old, twelve, thirteen. And ugly—aie! I was just an ugly little girl, and you were this cool American guy on a motorcycle." Incredibly, she reached up and touched his hair at the side of his head, pulling it gently. "Your hair was long then. Oh, I was so in love with you!" She laughed again, looking at him with such dumbfounding pleasure.

He stopped himself from kissing her—he wanted to feel those teeth with his lips and tongue so badly—but he'd wait, he'd prolong this sublime moment just a little longer. He grinned back at her. "If you were ever ugly, that's not the case now."

"Well, now it's not so bad as it was. And you're older, but still the cool-looking guy. More European I think now, no? It's interesting, after all this time, to talk with you."

"I could talk with you for . . ." He looked at her wide, beautiful mouth, the dark gums, the white teeth, her amused eyes. So beautiful, and now so ready—

Headlights from the road lit them both, not directly, but Luc saw her eyes going to the car. She stood up.

A black BMW 318i, stopped. Montserrat smiled at the car, then turned to Luc, leaned forward, and kissed both his cheeks with amused affection. "See you later, Easy Rider," she said. She got into the car. Luc caught a glimpse of a young man, Spanish, masses of black hair, white teeth, lean planes of face. He and Montserrat threw their heads together for a more than perfunctory kiss, and she slammed the door and the car drove off. A cloud of dirt rose and swirled behind it, smearing the lights of the port.

He had no idea how long he sat there. After a while he heard the sea breaking on the rocks below, withdrawing in long heartfelt sighs, breaking again.

He stood up and walked back across the road. The music was quieter. Several couples were still dancing. The whole album of *Revolver* was playing. Some woman was making John Lennon feel like he'd never been born. Luc knew how he felt.

He went into the garage and stamped on the kick-starter of his old Rieju motorcycle. "Thank you, Vicente, hombre," he said when it started up on the second kick. His mother's gardener always filled the tank and cleaned the carburetor and plugs when Luc was expected for a visit.

He tore out of town. The warm night air blew his shirt open and felt cool on his chest, a sensation he remembered from so many long ago nights in Mallorca, on his way to where he believed some answer might be found—as now.

They would hear the whine getting louder, so he only drove halfway up the long drive. He got off and laid the bike against a carob tree. But the house was dark as he approached. There was no car. He could see from below that the doors to the terrace were closed. He walked up the steps. Still no sound or light. He tried the kitchen door and it was locked. But Charlie was here; she must be too.

He knocked.

Then he called. "Aegina?"

He walked through the scrub around the house looking up at the closed windows.

"*Aegina!*" he yelled up at the empty house. "*Aeginaahhhh! I'm sorry!*"

A*fter parking the motorcycle* back in the garage, Luc walked around the house and across the patio to the bar. It was deserted, no Sally. While he helped himself to a bottle of Perrier from the fridge, he became aware of a woman grunting, straining, as if pushing a boulder up a hill or having a despairingly difficult bowel movement . . . then a man sounding as if he was urging on a reluctant horse . . . Fucking. It wasn't loud, but it was oddly clear. Luc couldn't make out where it was coming from. Not the barracks, too far away; not the house. Then he remembered that Bronwyn was always saying there was this strange St. Paul's Cathedral effect: from her room she could hear everything that was being said in the bar at a conversational tone. The fucking was coming from Bronwyn's room, along the wall, up by the pool. "Come on! *Come on!*" the man was exhorting now. Luc recognized Dominick's voice. It made perfect sense. Solace where you find it. Or as Somerset Maugham had written about impromptu sex: you can dine every night if you're willing to eat turnips.

He took the bottle of Perrier and went up to his room. April was lying with her back on the floor, her feet raised against the wall above her, toes aimed at the ceiling.

"Where have you been?" she complained, in perfect counterpoint to her balanced pose. "I looked everywhere for you."

"I went for a ride on my motorcycle. Are you okay?"

She didn't answer.

"What?" said Luc.

"I just got off the phone with Aaron."

"Ah."

"He really wants me back."

"He always did, didn't he? I thought it was you who broke up with him."

"It was."

"But now you're going back to him."

With exquisite yogic abdominal muscle control, April lowered her legs, swiveled on her buttocks, then rose into an erect-backed lotus position, pulling her feet onto her thighs.

"You see, the way you say that," she said, "I don't think you care about me at all. I mean, like, I get the feeling if I said that—I'm going back to Aaron—you'd just say okay. I don't think you'd even want to talk about it. I think you'd prefer to just go to bed and read a book."

Luc sat down on the bed, stretched his legs out, and looked at April. "But you did just say that, didn't you?"

C*harlie and Bianca* had danced too. They revolved slowly on the dance floor, their bodies pushed closely together. When he changed the records, she came into the music room with him and they kissed.

At midnight, she said, "I've got to go." They kissed again, as if they hadn't been doing it all night.

"I should probably stay until Lulu says I can go," said Charlie. He was staying at Bianca's house while his mother and grandfather were in London. "See you later . . . well"—he grinned—"in the morning anyway." And Bianca left for the short walk home.

Twenty minutes later, Lulu came into the music room and said: "Leave that on, and come with me. I have something else for you."

She held Charlie's hand and led him back across the patio into the house, through the living room, around a corner, down a hall, into her bedroom. Charlie had often been in the house, but never here. The first thing he noticed was the large portrait of Lulu over the bed. She was reclining full-length in a red dress. Charlie knew right away it was a bad painting. His mother's portraits always looked right. Not absolutely correct, like a photograph, but strokes of paint, loosely arranged, that ended up looking just like the person you *knew*, but better than any photograph could possibly represent that person. It was probably the time it took to paint a portrait. A photo caught less than a second of someone, whereas he'd seen how people came to his mother's studio to sit for days and weeks, and she got to know them during that time, the way they laughed, the things they thought and talked about with her as she worked. All that, the whole person, somehow came through in his mother's portraits. He'd always supposed all portraits were like that, so he'd been surprised when he went to see her pictures hung at the Royal Society of Portrait Painters show, at how bad the other exhibited paintings were: minutely detailed with expert techniques, their subjects looking stiff, unnatural, the hands in at least half of them looking like a mannequin's. He didn't know the people in the portraits, but he knew the paintings were badly done and the people didn't really look like that at all. This was what he thought of Lulu's portrait now. The face was recognizably hers but not right. She was sort of staring, unfocused, looking slightly off to one side. Her neck was too long and bent at the wrong angle. The colors were too bright. The body showed beneath the dress as though the material was thinner than it must have really been, but it wasn't her body at all.

"I want to pay you, sweetheart. Five thousand pesetas we said, right?"

"Yes, Lulu. Thanks *so* much. I hope you had a lovely birthday."

"I did, dear Charlie. It's been marvelous."

She went to her dressing table, opened a drawer, and took out her wallet. She counted out five large beautiful bills and gave them to him. Charlie stuffed them into his jeans pocket.

"Look," said Lulu. She put her hands on his waist and turned him until he faced the full-length mirror lying against a wall at a slight angle. Its gold-painted frame was peeling, the silvering splotched and corroded, and Charlie knew that it was beautiful. He saw the pitted image of them both, like a couple in an old black-and-white photograph. He was black, his hair, jeans, the Moroccan shirt, dark complexion, and Lulu, her hair and clothes, all white.

She pulled him toward her and lifted her face to his. She was as close to him as he'd been with Bianca for much of the night. He saw what he had never noticed before: the white line of a small scar at the bottom of Lulu's chin. "Now do me a little favor before you go, will you?"

"Sure," said Charlie. He felt terribly grateful for the job, the shirt, Lulu's kindness to him. He'd do anything for her. He thought she might want a crate moved in the kitchen.

She sat down on a leather-topped brass stool. She reached for a bottle of lotion, handed it to Charlie and swiveled on the stool until her back was presented to him. "Be a dear and rub some of this into my neck and shoulders. They ache so." She reached back and pulled her braided ponytail over her shoulder. Then she shrugged her shoulders on each side in a swaying motion and her gauzy shirt slipped off and dropped to her waist.

Charlie looked in the mirror and immediately looked away. He'd seen lots of women's breasts because everybody went topless at the beaches and swimming pools in Mallorca. He might have seen Lulu's breasts too at some point, but he didn't remember. He hadn't thought about her like that, as he had about some of his mum's friends when he'd seen them on the beach.

He squeezed some lotion onto his hands and rubbed. The skin was smooth and tight and warm, so that the lotion became immediately viscous and slippery.

"That's lovely, darling," Lulu said. "Do keep going."

Charlie was so pleased that she liked it. Lulu really liked him.

Her head dropped. Now Charlie glanced in the mirror. Her forearms were lightly crossed. He saw her small breasts either side of the cord of white hair that she held against the middle of her chest. They were very small, like a girl's breasts, but they had pronounced dark nipples that were as thick as his fingertips. His erection, sustained for much of the night by pressing into Bianca, now revived, achingly.

"Mmm. . . ." Lulu hummed.

Charlie felt heat rise off her skin. He felt it on his chest and stomach through the black shirt. Lulu was breathing deeply now, through her nose, the way he'd seen women breathe while doing yoga on the patio at the Rocks. He wondered if Lulu was falling asleep and he made a small noise in his throat. Her hand rose to his on her shoulder and she patted it. He thought she meant that was enough, fine thank you so much Charlie, time for him to go, but she held on to Charlie's hand and stood and turned and pulled the hem of his Moroccan shirt up to his chest and hugged him. He felt her nipples against his stomach.

"You don't mind, do you, darling?"

"No."

"Do you want to hug me?"

"Sure," he said affably. It was her birthday, after all. He put his arms around her, his palms on her warm back between her shoulder blades. She was half the volume of Bianca, sinewy, yet soft and warm.

Lulu began to move against him. Her head nuzzled into his chest. Her groin pressed into his, and it was impossible to conceal himself. Her hands playing across his back moved down inside his jeans onto his buttocks.

"Charlie," she crooned softly. "You have such lovely, lovely smooth skin. Come."

She released him, but held his hands firmly and led him to the bed and pushed him down on his back. She knelt over him, running her hands across his stomach.

"*Such* lovely, lovely smooth skin." She lowered her head and brushed her mouth back and forth across Charlie's stomach. He felt her hands on his jeans undoing the button, the fly.

"You don't mind, do you, darling?"

The nerves across his stomach twitched like a horse's flank. "No," he said.

Then he felt her hands on him, pulling him right out of his jeans and underpants, squeezing gently.

Lulu's head lifted and she looked into his face. "Are you a virgin, Charlie?"

"Yes." He wondered if he should have lied. Maybe she would stop now.

"Then this will be a beautiful birthday present for both of us. You're sure you don't mind?"

He didn't want to hurt her feelings. And he didn't want her to stop. "No. It's all right. Happy birthday, Lulu."

She laughed. Then she kissed him on the mouth. Her lips were thinner than Bianca's, her tongue more confident. Then she moved her head down across his stomach again.

Charlie thought he knew what she was going to do now. He looked up at the dark beams on the ceiling.

He was right.

Six

Gerald *had brightened* and become restless in the car as they drove the last few kilometers into Cala Marsopa. He was looking at the trees. "We need rain," he said.

From the car window, Gerald caught intermittent glimpses of the landscape: the drooping, desiccated, midsummer carob pods; the flaring red, orange, and yellow blush of Indian fig prickly pears. Lemon trees, almond trees, olive trees, interspersed with scattershot Doppler echoes of their car flashing past beige stone walls, beige stone houses. He was impatient to see his own olive and lemon trees—what was left of them. He pictured himself among them on the slope above the house in the light of late afternoon. If he turned, there, in his mind's eye, he would see the contours and ridgelines of surrounding hills which were imprinted in his brain as much as the lines in Aegina's paintings on the walls in his house. Through his olive trees, he saw the blue sea he had sailed over, and then he rose and flew over the sea and saw, in small scale, the whole of the Mediterranean, and Alexandria and the dust of Egypt in the war, and the books he had read then and afterward and the history he had come to know through them, the line threading through all these pictures to the present time and place.

Then, as the road descended toward the sea, Gerald's eyes fixed on Los Olivos, the clustered development of townhomes that bulked on the hill above his property.

Aegina could feel her father tensing.

"Abomination," grumbled Gerald. "Christ, why couldn't I have got this book money years ago? Then I wouldn't have sold my olive groves to that—" He stopped abruptly.

"Because things don't happen like that, Papa, when we want them to. You're lucky it's all happened the way it has. Even that—" She stabbed a finger at the gaudy, stuccoed, arched entrance and paved road to Los Olivos rising up the hillside. "It wasn't what we wanted, but it helped—didn't it?" She shot him a look. "Everything could have been a lot worse, you know. If you were living in England, who knows what sort of life you'd've had. You could be an old-age pensioner in some council flat, shuffling off to the high street supermarket with a string bag and nearly run down by a double-decker bus every time you wanted to cross the street. I mean, look where you live, Papa. The way you live. What you've managed to do. And what's just happened. It's not too shabby, is it?"

"Well . . ."

Aegina glanced at her father again and saw his eyes raised, looking out the window now for the first sight of C'an Cabrer.

"I'm very proud of you, Papa. Charlie will be too. He'll read your book someday, and he'll become curious about you. He'll ask me questions, like I've asked you, and I'll be able to tell him what an unusual life his grandfather lived."

Gerald snorted.

"I'm still not sure, though, why you didn't go off to Greece when you could have, why you stayed in Mallorca."

"Well, I met your mother."

"But that's not true, is it? The timing's off. You met her after you'd been here for three years. Come on, why didn't you go before that? You can tell me."

"I lost *Nereid*. You know that."

"That was three years before you met Mama. You still could have gone to Greece. It was probably cheaper to live there than in Spain. You could have got another boat when you published your book the first time. You decided to stay."

"Oh, it's all ancient history," said Gerald, striving for vagueness. "I can't remember what happened when. I met your mother, that was the reason. Lucky for you."

She let it go. "Yes." Aegina grabbed her father's hand and squeezed it. "I'm glad you did."

T wo days later, Aegina climbed the stairs to the "tower," Charlie's room on the second floor of C'an Cabrer. It had once been a feed loft. Years ago, Aegina had paid to have it expanded and a bathroom added. She didn't come up the stairs often. She heard music on the other side of the door. She knocked.

"Yeah?" came Charlie's voice through the door.

"Can I come in?"

"Sure."

He was lying on the floor beside what appeared to be a woman's small red leatherette vanity case. It was open, the two halves held together by small hinges; a turntable in one half, a speaker in the other. Old LPs and 45s were scattered on the carpet.

"My God, where did you find all that?" asked Aegina. "I haven't seen this since I was your age."

"Downstairs."

She sat down beside him and looked through the album covers. Charlie, she noticed, was staring at the 45 rpm record revolving on the turntable. When the song came to an end, he lifted the stylus and turned the record player off.

"I loved that song—I still do," Aegina said.

"Yeah. Me too," said Charlie.

Aegina looked at him. "Aren't you going into town tonight?"

"No. I think I'll stay here."

"Charlie, are you all right?"

He didn't answer.

"You've hardly left your room since we got back. Has anything happened between you and Bianca?"

Big pause. "Not really."

"Do you want to tell me?"

Charlie was quiet.

"Did something happen at Lulu's party?"

"Sort of."

"Can you tell me?"

She waited. She knew when to wait.

"The party was good. I did the music. Bianca left around midnight, but it was still going a bit." Charlie stopped, picked up a record and put it down again. "I did it . . . sex . . . with a woman there."

"Oh," said Aegina, as evenly as she could. "Oh," she said again, as she thought of what to say, discarding most of it. "Well . . . was it . . . all right? Was she nice to you?"

"Yes."

"Did you use a condom?"

"No."

"Oh, Charlie. If you're going to have sex, you must. It can be danger-ous, you know. You know that, you've read about AIDS—"

"I know."

"Have you and Bianca—"

"No."

"So this was your first time?"

"Yes."

Aegina picked up Charlie's hand and squeezed it. She looked at it, his beautiful, now almost fully grown hand, and felt sad. Of course, everyone always said it goes by fast, the days long but the years like blinks, yet still . . . it was too fast. "Does Bianca know about this woman?"

"No."

"Are you going to tell her?"

"I don't know. What do you think?"

Now he looked at her. And she was supposed to be wise.

Aegina took a moment. "Well, that's difficult. I mean, you don't want to lie to her—right? That's *not* good," she said emphatically. "But it would hurt her. You can tell her, if you feel you should . . . I guess you have to think about what your relationship with Bianca is, where it's going—and whether you're going to do this again, with this woman. Are you?"

"No. She doesn't want to."

"She was probably using you. I mean, I'm sure she liked you—you're beautiful—but it wasn't very thoughtful, or nice, of her. Do you have feelings for her?"

"I think I love her, but I know she doesn't love me. She's a bit older."

"Oh, Charlie." Aegina reached out and gently pushed some of Charlie's hair aside and left her hand on his forehead. "I know how you feel. I remember feeling like you do now. I know what you feel."

He looked at her with sudden interest. "Really? And did he then not want to be with you again? What an idiot."

"Well, it was sort of different. But I had the same feelings. All of them, I promise you."

Charlie pushed idly at the records on the floor. He looked up at his mother. "Are you upset with me?"

"No, darling!" Aegina hugged him. "Oh, sweet Charlie boy, you've done nothing wrong." They hugged for a minute. "But Charlie. Please. Use a condom next time." She released him and looked at him. "Do you have any?"

He smiled thinly. "No."

"Right. Well, we'll get you some. And if you do have—if you make love with Bianca, you must use them. With anybody. Do you promise me?"

Charlie nodded.

She released him. "Thank you for telling me. You can always tell me anything. You know that, don't you?"

"Yes, Mum. Thanks."

"Are you coming down for dinner?"

"Yes."

Aegina stood. "Ten minutes, okay?"

Charlie nodded.

Aegina turned to leave. She stopped. She walked across the room and picked up the shirt that lay on a chair. Aegina held it up, looked closely at the embroidering, the stitching . . . she rubbed her fingers against the cloth.

"Where did you get this?"

Charlie looked at the shirt and at his mother. "She gave it to me."

Aegina stared at the shirt, and then at Charlie. "Who gave it to you?"

"The woman." said Charlie. "It's from Morocco. It's old."

Aegina looked down at the shirt for a moment, then placed it—as if it were an exhibit—carefully back on the chair.

She left the room.

Charlie turned the knob on the record player and the 45 began spinning around again. He lifted the stylus and placed it on the record, "Everyone's Gone to the Moon."

1983

In Turnaround

One

The steady hornet sound grew louder, angrier.

"*Voilà!*" said François Duhamel. He smiled around the kitchen at C'an Cabrer, sweeping an arm with a grandiloquent air toward the noise coming from the open door to the terrace. "*Je vous présente* Señor Gómez, and his *fearful* Lambretta. Are you ready for our ramble through the campo, gentlemen?"

"*Absolutely*," said Fergus Maitland. He was tall, incipiently flabby, his curly hair wet but drying, still partly plastered down in long waves; small but cheerfully expressive features in a fleshy face. He was dressed not for a walk in the Mediterranean landscape but in his all-purpose summer holiday wear: Lacoste swimming briefs, a short-sleeved rose-colored shirt, black loafers, black socks, Panama hat by Herbert Johnson of Bond Street. "Aegina, my love, Charlie me darling," he said, "have fun at the beach." He walked to the kitchen table, where Aegina was giving three-year-old Charlie his breakfast, and kissed his wife and son.

Gerald looked moodily out a kitchen window, opposite the terrace door, at the sloping hillside of lemon trees.

"Be careful at the *playa*," said François. He was a skinny, floppy-haired man in his early thirties. His wife, Penny, and their daughter, Bianca, were also seated at the kitchen table. "The wind is calm, but the sea is still agitated today. There will be waves out at Cala Espasa, *soyez prudent avec les enfants*, okay?"

"Of course we will," said Penny.

François walked outside onto the terrace that overlooked the long uphill driveway. Fergus and Gerald—Gerald last, slowly, reluctantly—followed him. They looked down at Señor Gómez coming up the hill ahead of a large plume of greasy blue smoke.

"Christ," said Fergus, "he really is on a fucking motor scooter. What's wrong with a car? Wouldn't a builder want to give some sense of solidity?"

François smiled. "Oh, he does. You'll see."

The muffler on the Lambretta was unavailing. The 150 cc engine's whine reached a nostalgic authenticity as it crested the top of the drive and suddenly subsided to a relatively quiet purr. Señor Gómez killed the engine and looked up at the three men looking down at him.

"*Buenos días,*" he said with grave formality. He stepped off his machine and pulled it back on its stand.

"*Salud, amigo,*" said François. "*Venimos abajo.*"

They descended the steps to the driveway. Señor Gómez was dressed like a peasant: blue cotton shirt faded from many launderings, threadbare darker blue trousers, old tennis shoes. He removed a small, battered, narrow-brimmed coarsely woven straw trilby, revealing a forehead so pale and gray above his sunburned face that the skin looked corpselike. The deep creases on either side of his mouth and around his eyes, and the lattice of lines along the back of his neck, were engrained in black, like the ineradicable soiling of a miner's skin. Señor Gómez was short, about five-foot-five. He had a Buddha-like composure.

François made the introductions with some flourish. "*Señor Rutledge, el propietario. Señor Maitland, nuestro banquero. Señor Gómez, constructor.*" Gómez shook hands with the three men. Gerald felt the keratinous calluses of the builder's hand.

"Very old!" said Fergus, smiling jovially, pointing to the ancient Lambretta. It had two separate saddle seats and a crazed, yellowed acrylic windshield. "*Antiquo!*"

"*Ah, sí,*" said Gómez, impassive yet betraying a scintilla of pride. "*Modelo cincuenta y ocho. Veinticinco años.*"

"*Bueno,*" said François. "*Pues, vámonos?*"

"*Sí,*" said Señor Gómez.

François led them around the house to the hillside Gerald had gazed at so glumly through his kitchen window. They climbed a short distance through groves of lemon and almond trees. Tinder-dry leaves, almond shells, twigs crackled underfoot. François lunged ahead with long strides, bobbing over his thighs. Fergus moved awkwardly, picking his way, and was soon out of breath. Gómez walked with short, sure, deliberate steps, like a donkey. Gerald seemed to amble, even uphill, familiar with the ground; but he dawdled in the rear, picking up fallen branches, fruit, dropping them thoughtfully to one side as if grooming a fairway. They reached a path and followed it horizontally around the slope. Soon the house behind them was obscured by the contour of the hill. The land in front of them now fell away and the lemon and almond groves gave way to neat rows of olive trees. Through the trees they could see the town, the lighthouse, the sea.

François stopped. "*Bueno,* here we are," he said. He turned toward Señor Gómez and Fergus, and spoke to both of them. "*Aquí está la parcela.* Here's the parcel. From here, *desde aquí*—" He raised his arms, gesturing downhill, then at right angles across the slope, back toward the town. Then, his hands and arms aiding him more figuratively, François spoke in Spanish of hectares, numbers of units, an access road, the running of power, telephone, water, and sewer lines.

"*Fantastico!*" Fergus interjected at moments when he thought he caught the gist of a vision of the completed project. In his four years of visiting Mallorca as Aegina's husband, he'd discovered the convenient fact that with the simple addition of an *o*, many English words became their Spanish counterpart. Others did not, but the continental effect usually carried the day.

Señor Gómez's face, beneath the straw hat, remained inscrutable. His narrowed eyes flicked across the land as François spoke.

Gerald looked in the same direction, at the peaceful, sloping olive grove. Olive trees could live for two thousand years. They showed their age: the twisted, misshapen boles had erupted—over centuries—with lumps like the warts on a cartoon crone's nose, limbs were deformed and articulated as if ravaged by rickets—but these were all the healthy survivors, older than most European states, and they were still producing. Gerald had never thought of himself as owning these trees. He had husbanded, pruned, ministered to them for thirty years, mindful always that he was only a caretaker for a brief duration. And they had fed him in return.

He'd never imagined cutting them down.

W*ell, he has to*," said Aegina, her eyes on Charlie as he shrieked, turned, and ran screaming up the sand toward his mother. A wave rose, curled, and broke with a roar behind him. He wasn't going to make it, Aegina saw, but that was Charlie's game. His eyes locked on to hers and she laughed and made a face of mock terror. The sweeping cataract overtook him, reaching as high as his upper thighs, splashing his chest, and Charlie ran on, squealing, eyes popping at the water snatching at his legs like maddened puppies.

It was sunny and almost windless on Mallorca, but somewhere across the Mediterranean, inclement weather, perhaps a mistral in the Golfe du Lion, had produced waves that now swept around the eastern end of the island to provide Charlie and everyone else with a rare day of real surf at Cala Espasa, the normally sheltered cove north of town. He ran ceaselessly in and out of the water, fleeing the waves that unfailingly caught him. The first few times he fell and was completely submerged, and rose gasping for breath, Aegina had rushed for him, her hands playing across his face and head, smoothing the salty water away from his eyes. But Charlie was only thrilled and turned and staggered seaward toward the retreating water. Again and again, untiringly, like a dog after a bone.

Bianca was less enthralled. "Uh-oh," said Penny, seeing what was going to happen a second before Bianca tripped in the surf and the water buried her. She jumped up and ran, reaching her daughter as she rose spluttering out of the subsiding froth. Bianca was trying to keep up with Charlie but she'd fallen too much and now she started crying. "Oh, sweetheart," said Penny, scooping her up. She brought her back to their spot on the dry sand beneath the umbrella, wrapped Bianca in a towel, and hugged her. Then she said, "Is he really broke?"

"Practically. He used to have a very small income from an aunt—you know, like people in old novels: three hundred pounds a year, on which they'd live genteelly in Dorset or something. But he spent that capital once he bought C'an Cabrer, and since then he's lived off what he's been able to produce and sell. But you can't make a living now from selling olives and lemons and almonds. Not the way he did. It's all big supermarkets now, HiperSol and SuperSol, and they buy from large-scale suppliers. The little *comestibles*, like Calix, and restaurants, that wanted thirty liters of olive oil and a few tubs of lemons—well, you know, you've seen it—they're all gone, or going, or buying from the same big suppliers. They're paying a lot less per kilo, and they only want to buy by the ton. And now the town's put the property taxes up."

"It's so sad," said Penny. Bianca heard her and looked up at her mother and made a sad face. "It's all changed now, isn't it?"

"Yes. It is sad," said Aegina, her eyes following Charlie in the water. "It's breaking his heart—it breaks mine too—but he's got to sell something. He sold two parcels of land down at the bottom of the drive years ago, but they didn't pay much, not what they'd fetch now. I've suggested he sell the whole place and move into a smaller house in town, but he says he'd hate that and I probably would too. He's lucky he's got François to do it with."

"François thinks they'll do very well. And it should be nice. I mean, they're really nice houses, and not too many of them. François says you won't see them from your house."

"Well, it's the trees, Penny, that he's really upset about. He's been looking after them ever since he's lived here, they're like his friends. But there's nothing else for it. He can either do this, with François, and have some say in it, or sell the whole place to someone else and then it would be a lot worse. I mean, look what's happened to Mallorca, just since you've been here."

"I know. Though of course, it's not been bad for François. He's done awfully well with his developments. It's great that he and Fergus can make this happen together, for Gerald."

"Yes, it's great," said Aegina.

Charlie ran screaming with laughter up to them, dripping salt water, to get Bianca, but she was alarmed and burrowed into her mother. He ran off into the waves.

"Fergus goes to the Rocks quite a bit, doesn't he?"

"Yes."

"You don't mind?"

"No, of course not," said Aegina. "The guests are all English. He's comfortable there. Really, I'm glad he's found a place he likes here, somewhere to go and have a drink. I don't have to go there, and he doesn't mind that either. I think he enjoys getting away from us for a few hours. And now he's got this project, it'll keep him busy. It works out well."

"Gerald never goes there?"

"No. He used to walk or drive by when he thought no one would notice. I remember driving past the Rocks in the car when I was a child—when it was the long way home—and he would slow down."

"What do you think he feels about Lulu?"

Aegina shook her head slowly. "I'm not sure. He was obsessed at one point—my mother had to give him a proper bollocking about it."

"And you still don't know what happened between them? Luc never told you?"

"No."

Charlie came running up again. "I'm hungry!" he said.

"*Bueno*," said Aegina. "*Bocadillos.*"

She and Penny opened baskets and laid a lunch out on their towels. The children nibbled on giant sandwiches.

When they returned to the house from the olive groves, François spread blueprints on the dining room table before Señor Gómez. They showed elevations and construction details for four different designs of two-story villas of approximately the same size and footprint. Each had four bedrooms (or three bedrooms and a study), three bathrooms, an open-plan ground floor with a kitchen and living room flowing toward a terrace. Each house had its own pool. Each design showed slight variations in exterior details and use of interior space. The villas would be oriented toward a view of the sea while not conforming to a uniform relation to each other or the access road. They were similar to but larger than the houses at Los Piños, the small development François had built along the road to Cala Espasa. That project had been a success, all houses sold, but François had found his builder, who lived half an hour away in Artà, merely adequate and was unwilling to expand into a larger project with him. He wanted someone now who could produce a finer finish, with experience of a greater number of units and more difficult terrain, who lived near enough to guarantee a consistent presence. Gómez and another Cala Marsopa builder, Roig, were the only contenders. François wanted Gómez.

"*Bueno,*" said Señor Gómez. He declined François's invitation to lunch. He had to look in at a job, he said, though François believed he was simply uncomfortable at the idea of any kind of convivial social intimacy. The builder rolled up the blueprints and tucked them under an arm. He would be in touch in a few days. They shook his horny hand again and watched him putter away down the drive on his Lambretta.

"It's a wonder he's still alive," said Fergus, as they climbed the steps from the drive. "Trundling around on that thing holding on to a set of blueprints at the same time. He's a proper crank. Is he interested, do you think? And do we want him?"

"Yes, we want him," said François. "And at this moment, this is what he wants, I believe. He's doing a very nice job down at Porto Colom, but this is something different. Quite a big job, but rather nice, you know. A little more cachet. A development of pretty houses in a beautiful setting, on a lovely hill, well made. A showpiece. Yes, he's interested. Yes, we want Señor Gómez."

"Should we see that fellow Roig again?"

Gerald went out onto the terrace. He stood in the shade and lit a Ducados. He pictured the village of tourists on the hill above his house, playing music late into the night, their screeching cars, screaming drunken laughter, barking dogs, rubbish thrown down the hill onto his property, the quiet of his olive groves gone forever.

Fergus came out onto the terrace. "Gerald, I'm taking us all to lunch. Shall we go to the Fonda?"

"What about the Marítimo?" said Gerald.

Fergus loathed the Marítimo, with its greasy calamari and its plebeian clientele of fishermen and the horribly naff tourists from the blocks of flats above the harbor. "Yes, absolutely. Is that okay with you, François? The Marítimo?"

"I shall be very happy at the Marítimo."

Gerald went into the larder and pulled two plastic HiperSol bags from the basket hanging on a nail. He filled them with lemons from the plastic tub on the floor.

They drove to town in Fergus's boxy Range Rover, which seemed to glide and sway like an alpine cable car down Gerald's steep driveway. The leather interior cosseted one with an upholstered comfort Gerald could only recall from a first-class railway carriage of long ago, but he believed the car's center of gravity was too high, capsizable, and it made him nervous on corners. He felt the same way about Fergus, and his massive, cheerful confidence. But his son-in-law was looking after Aegina undeniably well—in addition to what she was now making from her shop in Covent Garden—and Gerald was no longer anxious that she wouldn't be provided for. "He's amusing and he makes me feel safe," Aegina had said of Fergus before they married. Gerald had not made his daughter feel safe, he had come to realize, a little bitterly. On the contrary, he knew she felt increasingly responsible for him in his impecunious fastness atop a hill in Mallorca, with a dwindling subsistence income, no provision for her beyond the dubious potential of his moldering property's value, and the uncertainty of his own old age and inevitably advancing decrepitude. Fergus's scheme was irresistible to Gerald as a father. Didn't mean he had to like it, however.

The Marítimo was a concrete two-story building at the head of the port. The restaurant sat on the upper level, above the road. From the terrace, diners could look over the breakwater at the sea.

Gerald was embraced by the proprietor, a square-shaped man, pale skinned, with areas of white fuzz below his jaw that he had missed with his razor. Gerald handed him the two bags full of lemons, which the man received with solemn appreciation.

"¡Gerald, viejo amigo!" he said warmly. "¿Cómo estás? Demasiado tiempo, hombre." He was about Gerald's age, but looked older and unwell. He moved with difficulty.

"Bien, Rafael. Y tu?"

Rafael Soler shrugged and emitted a series of fatalistic grunts. "El hígado. El reumatismo. ¿Qué se puede hacer?" He shook hands with Fergus and François, whom he had met before in Gerald's company and therefore accorded a fulsome courtesy.

Rafael's pretty, dark-eyed teenage granddaughter, Rafaela, followed them out onto the terrace as her father sat them at his best table, under the awning, overlooking the port, asking them if the location was agreeable.

"Estupendo," said François.

"Posseeblay sangria, por favor?" said Fergus, grinning at the girl.

"Sí," said Rafaela, promptly turning back into the bar.

Rafael remained beside Gerald's chair and put a hand on Gerald's shoulder, as if to support himself, as they exchanged recent news. Fergus's Spanish was a rudimentary holiday boilerplate, acquired over the last four years, but he caught a few words about boats and fish, couched in tones of fatalistic disappointment. Rafael gazed out at the port, wheezing and shaking his head. Here it comes, thought Fergus, the workingman's inexorable disgruntlement with the improvement of his lot. This one, for instance, bloated from lack of exercise and overeating, whose father no doubt worked eighteen hours a day and dropped from disease. François was nodding in commiseration while Gerald politely translated for Fergus as Rafael told them of the small size and scarcity of the fish everywhere in the Mediterranean, the reduction of the local fishing fleet, their berths increasingly taken over by yachts that never left port.

"Jolly sad, isn't it," said Fergus, sympathetically.

"Homer called it the 'fish-infested' sea," said Gerald. "No longer."

Rafael recommended the gazpacho, wished them *"Buen provecho,"* and shuffled off.

"Ah, finally we have a little breeze," said François.

The salt- and moisture-laden air shimmered, refracting sunlight. Gerald looked out at the sea as if through a filmy membrane and saw himself in a little white boat beating into Cala Marsopa for the first time, rounding the old breakwater, coming alongside the quay below the old Bar Marítimo, when he knew nothing of this place and had no intention of staying beyond a change of wind.

"It's still an infested sea," said Fergus.

François looked at him. "How do you mean?"

"Well," Fergus said, throwing a hand out over the port. "Look at all these bloody boats. Like our good friend says, they didn't use to be here, did they?"

Nereid had been the only yacht in the harbor in May 1948. Then the tubby, flaring hulls of fishing boats, perhaps fifteen of them, some painted with an unblinking Egyptian eye in the bow, filled the tiny inner port. Black nets had lain across the stone quay; fishermen, faces creased like walnuts, sat on them in the sun, knitting with giant wooden fids.

"All these yachts are full of people spending money," said Fergus. "They come and eat at his restaurant, don't they?"

"Yes," said Gerald. "But the Spain that they come here for, that's disappearing."

"I'm not sure about that, Gerald," said Fergus. "It's always disappearing, and getting replaced by something else—usually better. I should think most people wouldn't miss the old Spain—squatting toilets and no telephones. The tourists come here for sun and sand and paella and tapas. Tits and bums on the beach. They're coming from Sheffield and Düsseldorf. They've never seen anything so fantastic, and it's cheaper than staying at home. And the locals, they're on an incredible roll, aren't they? Look at the improvement in their lifestyle."

François laughed. "The Spaniards used to believe all non-Catholics still had vestigial tails under their clothes."

"What nonsense," said Gerald.

"Who knows," said François. "But Gerald, here I must agree with your son-in-law, *nuestro banquero.* Eight years ago, before Franco died, all the women in Spain were dressed in black and riding around on donkeys. Now, glory of glories, they're all topless on the beaches, wearing nothing but a thong, and driving SEATs and Renaults. It was more picturesque, but so was Europe before the industrial revolution, when everyone had bubonic plague. The Spaniards don't want the old postcard, the crumbling walls, the donkeys. Ask Señor Gómez. He wouldn't want the old days. He's getting rich."

Rafaela brought out a tray with a basket of bread, glasses, a large pitcher of wine, oranges, and lemons.

Gerald said: *"Rafaela, prefiero un vaso de agua con gas, por favor."*

"Sí, Gerald," she said, and went away.

"This place," said Fergus, "the Marítimo, how old is this structure, then? It looks brand-new. Where'd the money for that come from?"

"They rebuilt this end of the port and extended the breakwater about ten years ago, after a winter storm damaged the original structure and the old fishermen's buildings," said Gerald. "I think insurance helped them."

"Right. And look at your mate in there, glued to the telly in the bar. He's doing a lot better now with a business twice the size of the old one. He says he doesn't like the yachts filling up his lovely old harbor, but he's the first stop for every boat in Europe pulling into the dock right below us."

Rafaela came out with large bowls of gazpacho.

"*Estupendo*," said François.

She asked what else they would eat.

"*Hamburguesa, por favor*," said Fergus, in execrable Spanish. François and Gerald ordered grilled sardines.

"Shall we talk about what Gerald shall be paid for his beautiful hillside?" said François, persistently cheery. "I've gone over it with him, but you're better with the numbers, Fergus."

"Yes, let's," said Fergus, pouring each of them a glass of sangria. Gerald pushed his away. "Right! Gerald! Rather than buying your land outright for what we could scrape together right now, which would not reflect a proper market value or potential, my group wants to make you a partner, and bring you along with us as we go into profit, and make you more money."

"That's very good of you, Fergus," said Gerald. "Why would you do that?"

"I'll be perfectly honest with you, Gerald. I'm doing it for love. You're Aegina's father, Charlie's grandfather. I want what's good for them, which happens, in this instance, to be what's good for you. With this deal you'll make enough to see yourself through what we all hope is a prolonged and graceful old age, in your own home. I know you've got Sanitas to pay the basic medical bills, but now you'll have enough for extras, you know, whatever you might need. Then, in the fullness of time, you'll have an inheritance to pass on to Aegina and Charlie. I mean, I'm not going to pretend the money isn't a factor. Of course it is. We'd never get it off the ground otherwise. But what makes good financial sense here, is good for Aegina and Charlie, and you too, down the road. See?" Fergus quaffed half a glass of sangria. "*Fantastico!*"

Gerald's eyes flicked across the table to François, who smiled back at him confidently. "*Alors*, it is a win-win, *non?*" François said.

Fergus poured more sangria, and went on. "We've drawn up a partnership. Down payment on the land to you, Gerald: twenty-five thousand pounds. Solid. In four payments spread out over the first year. Then we build as we sell. Build a few houses, sell them, build a few more, till we sell out phase one. Five properties. Then phase two. Another five, selling for more money. You'll get fifteen percent of partnership profits on each house. That's how you're going to make real money. After ten houses—after phase one, the way you live—you'll be set for life."

"Let me see," said Gerald. "You get my land, bulldoze my olive grove, for six and a quarter thousand pounds, right?"

"To begin with, yes. But look, my investors are putting in half a million. I'm investing myself—I'm going to buy one of the phase two houses for Aegina and Charlie. We'll be forking out from the beginning, but you're getting money up front, Gerald, and thereafter fifteen percent of everything we make."

"Of profit. You said the profit of each house. At what point do you declare profit? On the sale of each house, or after your investors have recouped their half a million, or whatever your overall expenses will have amounted to?"

"Well, it's structured, you see, so you can't put it like that. We can do the numbers anytime you like, and you can see. But the principle is clear. Ten properties selling on a sliding scale starting at four hundred thousand pounds, the earlier sales going for the smaller price to get us rolling, the later properties going for more. Overall gross will be about six to eight million, minimum. Of which about half will be profit. Bit of tax, which we should be able to shelter most of for you, and your cut will be close to three quarters of a million pounds, Gerald. In about two years. In Switzerland, if you like. How's that, then?"

"Who are your investors?" asked Gerald.

"A group I work with in London. They like the holiday market down here for exactly the reasons I've just said to you. They're not interested in the Costa del Sol, with all those condo developments. Mallorca's more villagey. We think Mallorca has prospects for the sort of mini estate developments we're talking about here. Minimum impact on the landscape—you'll hardly be able to see it from the road—you won't see it at all from your place, Gerald. Twenty cars maximum, at full capacity, plus a few visitors going in and out. Each property has a pool. Elegant. Good neighbors for you. They'll invite you to their parties."

"And this group of investors is quite solid?"

"Safe as houses—actually, they're *safer* than houses. Most of them are Lloyd's Names. Mutually insured. They're solider than acts of God. You can't do better than that. And we're ready to go. Today."

Gerald knew that, on paper, Fergus could prove any assertion, show him figures to assuage any doubts. Such assurances meant nothing to him. For himself, Gerald would eat olives, almonds, carobs, and drink well water laced with lemons. But Fergus made Aegina feel safe, she'd said. And now Gerald could do this for her.

Rafaela brought out three plates.

"Sauso tomato, *por favor*," said Fergus. "So what do you say, Gerald? I'd like to tell my people as soon as possible. This is a go project, with Mr. Motor Scooter or the other bloke, the moment you sign."

Fergus and François both looked expectantly at Gerald. He was staring out over the breakwater.

What's his problem? thought Fergus. He always seems disappointed, haunted by something. Here he was doing Gerald the biggest favor of his miserable life, offering him security for himself and his family, and he seems put out. Joyless old bugger. Worse luck, he'd passed that on to Aegina, for whom nothing was ever quite right. Both of them, haunted and disappointed, never satisfied.

"Do you need to think about it some more, old boy?" asked Fergus. He looked at François and rolled his eyes. Then back at Gerald. "Earth to Gerald."

Gerald pulled his gaze from the sea and looked back at them both. Fergus's condescending "old boy," from an arriviste property developer half his age, was offensive to him, but amusing too. Fergus was a buffoon. "No. I don't need to think about it any further. I'll sign whenever you like."

"Excellent!" said Fergus. "After lunch, then. I'll write you a check at the same time. Six grand in your hand today, Gerald. How's that then?"

Gerald didn't seem to hear. He was looking seaward again, quite focused.

The other two turned their heads in the direction of his gaze.

A large yacht, shaped and decorated like a sleek pirate galleon with an elevated poop deck, a square sail billowing from a yard on its foremast, was rolling in the light breeze, approaching the port.

T*he two men* stood barefoot on the teak deck at the forwardmost point on the yacht *Dolphin's* bow.

"That's my mother's house, there," said Luc, pointing at the house above the rocks. "The sage-colored shutters."

"*Mais c'est fabuleux!*" said Gábor Szabó. "Such an extraordinarily beautiful island. But why is it still so unknown?"

"Well, it's not, really. Robert Graves lives up on the north end of the island. You know"—Luc was never sure about movie people, what one could assume about their frame of reference, and this was particularly so with Szabó—"*I, Claudius?*"

"But of course. Superb. He's a TV writer?"

"He wrote the book from which the BBC series was adapted." Luc moved quickly on. "Joan Miró lives here—the painter—outside Palma. Then, of course, George Sand, the French writer—the nom de plume for a woman, as you know—spent a winter on the island with her consumptive lover, Frédéric Chopin. He hated it. She wrote a book about it. *A Winter in Mallorca.*"

"Yes, I've heard of it. I thought it was a novel. Like *The Mysterious Island* by Jules Verne. Like Lilliput."

"No. Quite real."

"But no one talks about Mallorca. No one goes to Mallorca. And look—it's incredibly beautiful. *Formidable!*"

Szabó was entranced. He had voyaged by square-rigged ship from a distant place (Monte Carlo) to find this terra incognita: a discoverer of unknown lands, a Bougainville, a Cook, a da Gama. He wore a blue Tahitian sarong beneath a billowing, long-tailed white linen shirt from India. Across his back, a pointillist stippling of blood and wider broth-hued patches of plasma and pus had seeped and diffused into the fine weave.

He clapped a heavy arm across Luc's shoulder. *"Mais c'est fabuleux! We have reached Ultima Thule! We will break new ground here, Luc."*

Two

The group lay on their mats beneath the pines at the far end of the Rocks' walled garden, above the pool. Overhead the light breeze soughed the breath of multitudes through the needled branches. They were five, including Lulu: Sarah Bavister, a regular Rocks guest, down for two weeks without her husband, with the children and a nanny who were presently at the beach at Son Moll, which was more sheltered from the unusual waves; Dominick Cleland, enchanted by the novelty of Lulu's sudden yoga enthusiasm and the contortions of the attendees; and two people off the yacht *Dolphin* that had come into port earlier in the afternoon: Gábor Szabó's French wife, Véronique, and her sister, Mireille.

Fergus sat at the table in the corner of the patio near the bar, watching Cassian Ollorenshaw play backgammon with the Hungarian film producer off the yacht. After lunch, Fergus had driven François and Gerald back up the hill to C'an Cabrer, and written Gerald a check for six thousand two hundred fifty pounds, a quarter of the down payment for the transfer of ownership of five and a half hectares of Gerald's land of designated coordinates in the town of Cala Marsopa to the Mallorca Ventures Company. Gerald had signed the document Fergus had prepared. Done.

Now Fergus was absorbed by the mood at the table. It had something of the repressed excitement of an auction room.

Cassian, in swimming trunks and a long-sleeved shirt, sat hunched, still, gnomelike, peering yellow-lensed at the board. His longish red hair was slicked back in an old-fashioned manner with some sort of pomade, curls escaping regimentation at the back of his neck, forehead slathered with zinc oxide which had run into the hair at his temples. Not a vain man. A red box of king-sized Dunhills and a gold crosshatch Dunhill lighter sat on the table beside his left elbow. Released from Her Majesty's Pentonville prison in North London in April, he had spent most of his time since then sitting at this table in the corner of the patio. It had become his office. The bar's phone, its extension line snaking along the tiles and disappearing behind the bar's counter, sat on the table beside his cigarettes.

"I'll simply pay the entire phone bill," Cassian had told Lulu. "It'll be easier than sorting out how much is mine, yours, whomsoever's. Most of it will be mine." He was usually on the phone all day. Snatching it up whenever it rang, he therefore took most of the Rocks' incoming calls and had soon filled the reservations book with the bulk of the forthcoming season's bookings. He was efficient at solving overlapping room conflicts, which Lulu, happy to accommodate room requests and leave time for people who were unsure of how long they wanted to stay, not good at dealing with the odd days of empty rooms, had never managed so adroitly. "It's a much quieter room," Cassian frequently advised a caller. "Otherwise you'll be kept awake all night by the music from Ses Rotges up the road and awoken by the gardener and his boy at seven. But you must be out by the fourteenth."

Szabó, lounging in a chair across the table, still in a sarong but wearing a clean, pale blue cotton shirt, was losing the game. He didn't mind. He savored the engagement with an opponent of such great skill. It was like playing against an Arab in a souk. He had played Luc aboard the yacht, but Luc was an indifferent backgammon player, their games usually a foregone conclusion, and Szabó had been bored. Nor had they played for money. Cassian was taking real money off him.

"I hear you're going to be building up on the hill," Cassian said to Fergus.

"Oh. Yes." Fergus was surprised but not displeased to be the subject of deal-making news. He assumed someone Aegina or François knew had spoken about it to someone else. "We've just signed, in fact."

"I know Johnny Barton," said Cassian.

"Oh do you? Yes, he's one of our investors. How do you know Johnny?"

"We were at Eton together."

"Oh, right."

"What are you building, if you don't mind my asking you?" asked Szabó.

"No, not at all," said Fergus. He outlined the scheme for two phases of tasteful villas occupying an unparalleled site overlooking the town with views over a wide swath of sea to the south and east and, on exceptionally clear days, even of Minorca.

"Where is the location?" asked Szabó.

"Just outside town, a kilometer from where we sit."

"Are you fully subscribed?"

"You mean—"

"Have you already sold off all your lots?"

"Oh, no. No, not quite. We have some interest, people I know in London have put in, but yes, still room to get in."

"And must you build all your houses to plan," asked Szabó, "or could one purchase several lots from you and build something larger?"

"Ah. Well, I'm sure that could happen. As long as the house and the grounds were in keeping with the style of the surrounding development. Which is certainly extremely attractive. More like something you'd see on the Côte d'Azur."

"It sounds marvelous. Could you show me the site?"

"Absolutely," said Fergus. "Whenever you like."

"Tomorrow morning? Ten o'clock?"

"Certainly. I'll pick you up at your boat."

"*Fabuleux,*" said Szabó. He briefly glanced down at the board again, threw the dice, moved, then looked up toward the yoga group under the pines. He found Lulu a compelling sight. They had been introduced before the session began and over the last hour he had watched her work through a sequence of repeating yet continually evolving movements, like the ringing of changes with church bells. He was mesmerized by Lulu's astonishing flexibility, evidently verging on double-jointedness, and her slim, tautly muscled form, smooth brown skin that began to glisten as the class went on, the thick cord of white hair worn in a long braid bound loosely at her neck, the strongly etched dark eyebrows that contrasted with her white hair, her fluidity of motion, her liquid calm. An extraordinary woman. How odd, surprising, that she, this radiant graceful creature, so English, so old world in accent and affect, of such a distinct physical presence, was the mother of the insecure and twitchy Luc, who spoke French with fluent argot.

Lulu liked to finish her yoga sessions with short philosophical readings. She had lately been thumbing through an apposite-seeming volume titled *The Awakening of Intelligence*, by Jiddu Krishnamurti, left by a guest in one of the rooms. She found much of it incontrovertibly silly, but she liked the author's name and the promise of the title. The cover photograph of the author, however, gave her pause. Krishnamurti was undoubtedly holy-looking, undeniably attractive in that Indian way that she herself frankly couldn't bear but others were so impressed by, a sort of Beatle Gandhi. But if he was so enlightened, why the elaborate, swirling comb-over (unquestionably molded and controlled with hair spray) to conceal his obvious baldness? What a *bald* admission of self-consciousness and insecurity placed like a beacon of contradiction on the cover of a book touting inner truth or whatever it was. But the readings struck, she thought, the right note, forming a suitable bridge between the stirring and release of physical and spiritual energy and a subsequent gin and tonic.

While her acolytes lay flat on their mats, breathing with the trees sighing delicately above them, Lulu opened the book at a dog-eared page and began to read in her clear voice that carried across the pool and the patio to the bar with the modulation and accent of old radio clips:

"'The old culture is almost dead and yet we are clinging to it.... Unless there is a deep psychological revolution, mere reformation on the periphery will have little effect. This psychological revolution ... is possible through meditation....'"

Soon the yoga practitioners came down to the patio with their mats and bags, breathing and stepping like dancers, glowing with perspiration and inner radiance. They settled at several tables. Dominick played bartender and brought them drinks.

Szabó stood, graciously thanking Cassian for such sport. "You will take a check tomorrow, I hope?" He had lost twelve hundred pounds to the Englishman.

"Sure," said Cassian. "Unless you sail off first."

Szabó laughed appreciatively. He crossed the patio and joined his wife, her sister, and Lulu and the other woman at their table. He arranged the sarong neatly about his legs as he sat down. "And how did you all enjoy the yoga?"

"Very pleasant," said Véronique Szabó stonily.

"So it appeared," said Szabó. "It's a rare spot you have here, Lulu. Your own little Alhambra."

"Hardly that," said Lulu, "but it has become an enclave of sorts. One feels one can leave the world outside, to some extent."

"Thank God!" said Sarah Bavister. She was standing, pulling back her hair. She was shaped like a pouter pigeon, small and delicate but with disproportionately large breasts on top of a protuberant chest. "I've been coming here for years. The rest of the world becomes more and more horrible, but here it's always exactly the same. Just like Lulu."

"Darling Sarah," said Lulu.

"Do you take outside guests for meals?" asked Szabó. "Because we would love to join you for dinner tonight. We are four, including your brilliant son."

"We'd be very happy to have you," said Lulu. "I'll tell the cook."

"And will you please be our guests for lunch aboard *Dolphin* tomorrow?" Szabó looked around the table.

"Ooh, yes, please!" said Sarah. "It's such a fantastic-looking boat. I'm dying to come aboard and have a look."

"Yes, thank you," said Dominick.

"All of you, yes?" Szabó's gaze stopped at Lulu.

"It's very kind of you," she said, smiling pleasantly, standing up. "Now I must go see Claire about dinner. We sit down at nine."

Szabó watched her for a moment as she padded away on bare feet. Then he turned around in his chair to face the two men still at the corner table by the bar. "Gentlemen, you'll come to lunch with us tomorrow aboard the yacht, I hope?"

"Thank you! Love to," said Fergus.

Cassian simply smiled, thinly, acknowledging the invitation.

Szabó and his group finished their drinks and left to walk back to the port along the sea.

Fergus remained at Cassian's table.

"Do you play?" asked Cassian, setting up the board.

Fergus laughed. "Not in your league."

"Oh, don't worry about that," said Cassian. "We can play a game for fun."

It didn't sound like fun to Fergus. "Actually, I should push off pretty soon too." But he sat and toyed with his drink. He'd heard of course that Ollorenshaw had been in prison for financial irregularities at a rarefied level. It was practically a credential. Fergus was intrigued by him.

"Your property plan sounds good," said Cassian, arranging the backgammon pieces.

"Yes, I think so," Fergus said cheerfully. "Should do jolly well."

"Do you think you could have gone for a denser development of the property?"

Cassian was gazing at him like a lizard with heavy-lidded eyes through the yellow lenses of his glasses.

"Well, of course, we talked about it. It would have meant a lot more work. More money up front. And then a much bigger impact on the surrounding properties. Quite frankly, I don't think we'd have got the go-ahead from old Gerald if we were looking to do anything more ambitious."

"I see," said Cassian. He rattled the dice in the cup and threw them down onto the board. A three and a one.

"Can't tempt you?"

"Oh, all right," said Fergus. "Just one game, then. I have to get into town pretty soon."

L*uc didn't hang around* after walking Szabó and his wife and her sister along the shore road to the Rocks and making introductions, pecking his mother's cheek. He went into the garage and wheeled the old tinny Rieju Jaca out into the dusty street and jumped on the kick-starter. The bike fired right away. *Gracias*, Vicente. A thousand pesetas when I see you, *amigo*.

Luc cruised back to the port to pick up Gaspard, *Dolphin*'s Guadeloupean Creole chef, who needed to replenish the ship's stores. He drove through Cala Marsopa with Gaspard on the back of the bike, pointing out the fruit and vegetable markets. He dropped him at the new supermarket behind the plaza.

"They'll deliver to the boat," Luc told him. "Most of the *mercados* too. Or they can call you a taxi to take you back to the port. The taxis will drive down along the quay to the boat."

"*Formidable*," said Gaspard. He cut an exotic figure among the doughy white European tourists in department store summer wear. Six-foot-four, skinny, café-au-lait complexion with pouting lips, enormous and frankly inquisitive, frankly gay blue eyes, kinky black ponytail. He wore a billowing white linen shirt and red capri pants, a tasseled Moroccan Berber satchel slung over his shoulders. "*Merci, mon cher*," he said, blowing Luc a kiss and waving him away.

Luc idled the bike through town. The streets, now mostly macadamized, built up, newly fronted and sidewalked, still took him, by no matter what route, along inexorable azimuths backward into the past. He looked as always for a certain head, hair, body shape, general aspects that he wished or feared would suddenly shift and lock into vivid particularity. Most of all he wanted to see her face.

He stopped at the *tabacos* near the port, once a dark hole-in-the-wall selling cigarettes and *lotería* tickets with toothless fishermen sitting on chairs outside, now a smart glass-windowed retail space that also sold olivewood chessboards, botas, castanets, small felt-covered bulls, and bullfight posters. The fishermen and their chairs were gone. He bought a pack of Gitanes, and said *bona tarda* to the aged crone who no longer recognized him.

She was standing outside, looking at the Rieju, a little boy holding her hand, when he came out.

"It is yours," said Aegina, "I thought so."

She looked at him calmly, a small smile—he could read nothing else. The kid was dark-haired, olive-skinned, like Aegina, gazing up at him with large brown eyes.

"And this is yours?" Luc asked.

The kid moved behind Aegina when he saw Luc looking at him.

"Yes. This is Charlie. Charlie, will you say hello to Luc? He's an old friend of mine."

The little boy remained behind his mother, clutching her thigh.

"He's beautiful, what I can see of him. Which is that he looks like you."

"Luc, I'm so sorry about your father," she said. Earlier in the year, Luc had sent her a letter, addressed to C'an Cabrer in Mallorca because he didn't know her London address, telling her that his father had died of metastasized prostate cancer, a day before his sixty-first birthday. "I liked him very much when we met in Paris. I'm so sorry."

"He liked you too," Luc said. "And you heard about Teddy?" One of their cohort of childhood friends whose parents lived in or returned seasonally to Mallorca, whom they'd known and played with most summers as long as they could remember, Teddy Trelawney had overdosed on smack and died in New York that winter.

"Yes, I heard," said Aegina, glancing down at Charlie, who started pulling his mother's arm, holding on to her hand with both of his. "I can't believe that, how he got to such a place. Teddy had a such a sweet and beautiful nature."

"I'm sure he was sweet to the end," said Luc. Her hair was shorter, shoulder length now, still deeply dark, black except in the sun, and otherwise she looked much as she had the last time he'd seen her, like this on the street four years ago—better, he decided: there was more of her in that face now. "You look good," he said.

"You do too. You look thinner."

"I've been running. I ran a marathon in April."

"I can't imagine that."

Charlie was now tugging hard. "Wait a minute, Charlie," she said. "Are you still in Paris?"

"Yeah."

Her arm was stretched sideways, Charlie was leaning perilously away from her. "I want to go," he said.

"Yes, we're going, Charlie," said Aegina. She looked at Luc, the kind of look that conveyed in less than a second an acknowledgment of the bildungsroman of their shared history.

"It's good to see you. Bye."

"Bye," he said, feeling something like a bowling ball in his chest. He watched them walk away down the checker-textured sidewalk. Charlie had let her hand go, but now Luc saw Aegina's hand and the boy's move toward each other reflexively until they clasped.

Luc stuffed the cigarettes into his shirt pocket and climbed aboard the Rieju and rode away. It was after five, people were coming off the beaches. The streets were mobbed with strangers, British, Scandinavian, German tourists familiar with the town, owning it as if it were now theirs as it had once been his.

Three

A man named Block traveling with his wife steps off a train while it's stopped in a station somewhere in Europe. He enters the station café to buy a newspaper. Inside, an elderly woman stumbles. Block catches her, she clings to him, saying something he can't quite hear. People in the bar crowd around them to help. Block tries to get away—his train is leaving—but now the elderly woman is clutching fiercely at his lapels, babbling something into his ear with feverish insistence. Others support the woman, lay her down, and Block pulls free. He runs outside into pelting rain, but his train pulls away without him.

Soaking wet, he goes into the station, asks the woman in the ticket booth if he can get word to his wife on the train. She shrugs, she doesn't think so. Block asks when the next train leaves. Not for another two hours. He walks back into the café. The old woman has died—she lies on the ground, quiet and still. People have pulled back, buzzing about what has happened, waiting for the police, ambulance. Block orders a coffee. As he drinks it, shivering in his wet clothes, a man appears at his elbow to thank him for trying to help the old woman. He did nothing, says Block, he was simply there when she stumbled. The man sees Block is cold and wet and buys him a Cognac. Gratefully, Block sips it. She appeared to be saying something to you, says the man who bought him the Cognac. I wasn't listening, says Block, I was trying to get back out to my train. You must have heard something, the man says. Now Block looks at him, sensing, for the first time, something other than friendliness—

"But really, come on, Luc. We need to know," Szabó said. "The whole movie turns on this, what she says to him. We don't need to know this?"

"Gábor, we *will* know—*eventually*. Yes, of course we need to know," Luc said carefully, respectfully. "But this is kind of the point: it doesn't really matter what the old woman says. He doesn't know, we don't know—that's good: tension, suspense. All we, and he, know is that these other guys *think* he knows, so they come after him. It's the MacGuffin. I thought you liked that, the fact that we don't know."

"Yes, yes, of course I like it. *I* like it. I *love* it. But will the audience like it? Will my distributors like it? Will *they* understand that this is a piece of movie cleverness that they must accept? I'm not so sure."

"But it's also what's existential about this story, Gábor. It plunges Block into a labyrinth of meaningless detail and confusion—I mean, there's a logic behind it all for Yatsevich and his thugs and we make that clear—but it's so wild and confusing for Block that he begins to question the structure and meaning of everything in his life. That's why he changes."

"And he gets the girl," said Szabó.

"Yes. But that's not the change," said Luc, gently. "However, *as* he changes, she increasingly believes in Block, so she *reflects* his new view of himself."

Szabó laughed. "It's not that complicated. Is not his new view of himself that she likes. Is his cock."

They'd started in Paris, meeting in Szabó's home, in cafés, over dinners at Brasserie Balzar, where Szabó and Véronique liked to eat several nights a week. Szabó's wife was nearly always there during their talks, a silent, uninvolved presence who would concentrate on her food or read a book, apparently as unengaged in their discussions as a dog—until she spoke.

The screenplay was tight before Szabó ever saw it. Luc had struggled to make it work like a watch. There were no extraneous parts. It moved fast from the station bar to the second train, where Block meets the girl and they jump on a bus eluding the man who bought him the Cognac, to the house on the lake and the long rowboat ride through the fog and finally the dingy office and the photographs of the old woman as a young girl holding hands with the man, the industrialist, who was her father. Luc had made the locations purposely vague, bland, unidentifiable—like the chilly Clermont-Ferrand of Éric Rohmer's *Ma Nuit chez Maud* that Luc loved so much. Apart from suggesting that this could happen any-where to anyone, it also meant the film could be made wherever a pro-ducer decided to shoot it, wherever he could make his deals and wanted to spend his money. This pragmatic approach had informed every deci-sion Luc had made in constructing his story. This one would get made.

Szabó loved it. He raved about it. He *got* it: the existential odyssey that propels Block toward an understanding of the hollowness of his life and a move toward a more authentic one. He had bought an eighteen-month option on the screenplay with an option to renew for a further eighteen months. They talked about cast.

"I see Roy Scheider," said Szabó, early on, peering sharply at Luc to convey the acuity of his vision. As they discussed the screenplay, Szabó started calling Block "Roy," describing how Roy steals a car from the sta-tion parking lot at night—

"But Block doesn't steal a car," Luc said. "Block wouldn't do that. He wouldn't know *how* to steal a car. That's not his character. They take the bus—"

"Luc, Luc." Szabó waved a forked morsel of veal, smiling indulgently, paternally. They were eating dinner at Balzar. "Roy Scheider doesn't take the bus. Who takes the bus in the movies? You have to wait in line with women who are bringing home chickens for dinner. With school-children. The action stops. No. It's impossible. Roy Scheider can't stop to wait for a bus."

"What if it's not Roy Scheider?" The actor's hard, angular features were not what Luc had imagined for his softer, more physically vulnera-ble protagonist, a man with a face that could illuminate doubt and fear.

"Who, then?"

"Well," carefully now, "I don't know . . . how about Albert Finney?"

"Albert Finney? Albert Finney doesn't open a movie. I don't get my distributors with Albert Finney. Who knows Albert Finney?"

"He's a great actor. He's got a human face."

"Luc. Albert Finney—who is this? English character actor, good for five minutes in the whole movie, eight seconds at a time, as bureaucrat or heavy, to give a note of class. Everybody in the world knows Roy Scheider. *The French Connection. Jaws.* For this, they know Roy Scheider in Finland, in Africa, in the jungle towns in Borneo where every week they paint the movie posters badly by hand as mural on the cinema wall and you see this great big Roy Scheider with eyes popping out of his head like a squid being chased by a giant shark. And guess what"—Szabó pushed the forkful of veal into his mouth and smiled knowingly, openmouthed, at Luc as he chewed, audibly grinding the meat to pulp with his molars—"Roy's cheap. I talk to his agent. He wants his own movie. He doesn't want to be Gene Hackman's buddy or second violin to the shark. He wants to be a star all by himself. To get the *girl*, not the fish! And I guarantee to you that he will read your screenplay and see that it is tailor-made for him, with a few changes. Like he doesn't sit and wait for a bus. Nobody takes a bus."

"Cary Grant took a bus in *North by Northwest.*"

"You put Cary Grant in a wheelbarrow and everything in the movie looks fantastic. Not Roy Scheider. He needs a fast car and Raquel Welch in the passenger seat. Then you got a movie."

"Raquel Welch?"

Szabó laughed affectionately. "My dear Luc. Who were you thinking for the girl?"

"I don't know. Isabelle Huppert—"

"Roy Scheider never would go to bed with such a girl. Too neurotic, talking talking all the time—"

"She has terrible freckles," said Véronique, without looking up from a thick, atlas-sized magazine, *Yacht*, with boats the size and shape of buildings on its cover.

"It's true," said Szabó. "They are not running through the jungles of Asia, driving on the highways in America, for Isabelle Huppert covered with freckles, talking, having depressions. My distributors never buy this film with such a girl."

Szabó chartered a yacht in Monaco for six weeks. Full crew, chef, plenty of cabins. A quiet cruise along the Riviera with his wife and her sister, very beautiful girl. Luc must come along, Szabó insisted. They would work every day and make a few changes and have the completed draft by the end of the cruise.

"Um . . ." It sounded like true arrival: cruise the Riviera on a yacht with a film producer, women, write a screenplay. But even after a meal with Szabó and Véronique, Luc couldn't wait to get away from them and clear his head. ". . . Well, I—"

"Graham Greene wrote *The Third Man* on Alexander Korda's yacht on a cruise in the Mediterranean," said Szabó, raising bushy eyebrows at Luc.

Luc hadn't known this, but he thought *The Third Man* an exemplar of the power of withholding information from the audience. "I love *The Third Man*—"

"So what does she say to him?" asked Szabó. "If we don't hear what the old woman says to Block, we have the audience wondering what is going on."

"But Gábor. Don't we *want* the audience to wonder what's going on? To *not* know? Like in *The Third Man*."

"No. If they don't know, they don't care. *The Third Man* opened very bad. Now is a classic, then was a big disappointment for Sandy. *Casablanca*, it's the letters of transit. You know this immediately. That's your MacGuffin, but we know what it is. Everybody is running around looking for the letters of transit. Whoever gets them, gets out of Casablanca. Simple. Here, Block doesn't know what he's looking for. He looks stupid. We don't care, nobody cares. We must hear what the old woman tells him in the ear in the station."

"But the *whole movie* is him *finding out* what she whispered. Who

she is, what Yatsevich is looking for. And what the movie's *really* about
is how Block finds meaning in his life by doing something right. *That's*
the mystery, and people will find that more interesting than—"

"Doesn't work. My distributors will be saying, 'What it's about?' I
can't tell them it's about Roy Scheider running around looking for himself to find out who he is. They will think it's a hippie story and they will
say no. Roy Scheider knows who he is. He's a tough guy. He's a man. So
I have to say to them, it's about a man finding the paintings taken by the
Nazis, that only the old woman whose father took them knows where
they are and she tells Roy Scheider, and he goes to find them and kills the
bad guys who are chasing him and he gets the girl. *That's* a *movie.*"

Luc had always believed he would be successful and make money as a
writer. His father, Bernard Franklin, of Walpole, Massachusetts, was a
longtime Paris-based journalist with the *Herald Tribune* who had written books about French exceptionalism and Anglo-European interests.
Luc had seen his father write them, one after another, published only to
vanish into the black holes of bookshops, never to be seen again. Luc
found his father's books dull—nobody read them on airplanes or in
cafés—and they made almost no money at all. Luc wanted to write novels. Like Hemingway and Steinbeck and Fitzgerald, and later like Ker-
ouac, that would sell better than his father's earnest efforts and be made
into movies.

When the novel he'd written at twenty-seven had been turned down
by every publisher he'd sent it to, he sank into prolonged shock. He
started writing another but, sundered by doubt, put it aside. One day in
Paris he met a friend at Le Select who was having a drink with a film
producer named Claude. Luc's friend introduced him to the producer,
describing him as a writer. Claude talked about a story he'd read in a
newspaper about a refugee who had tried to swim from an outlying Albanian island to the heel of Italy, a distance of fifty miles. He'd been picked
up at sea close to the Italian coast, with no sign of a boat or raft nearby,
and taken back to Albania. "Can you imagine?" said Claude, looking at
them both. "The dream, the bravery, the *disappointment!*" Luc mentioned

the John Cheever story "The Swimmer." Claude remembered the movie, which he had loved. *"Ah, Burt Longcastaire."* He hadn't known it was adapted from the Cheever story. He called Luc the next day, and they met and talked again about the story of an Albanian trying to swim to Italy. Was it possible, Claude wondered, that anyone could stay afloat for so long? Luc told him about the high salinity of the Mediterranean, which would help any swimmer, and how he himself had spent much of his childhood swimming around Mallorca. Claude offered Luc twenty thousand francs—about five thousand dollars—if he would write the screenplay of the story they would outline together. Luc agreed. Claude gave him a book of screenplays written by Jean-Claude Carrière to show him how they were written. Luc wrote the screenplay in a month. Then Claude became wrapped up making another film, but Luc had been paid to write a screenplay. He was a screenwriter. He was hired to write more. Since he was bilingual, he could write screenplays in French or English— he wrote several in both languages so producers could show a property to both French and American distributors. He wrote spec screenplays to offer for sale—people in Hollywood were making fantastic sums selling spec screenplays; Luc even thought of going to Los Angeles, to the Mountaintop—and for several years went with a producer to the Cannes Film Festival. Eventually, little by little, nothing happened. He was thirty. The creeping sense of disjunction between what was supposed to happen in his life and what was actually happening, began to terrify him. He saw himself sinking into oblivion.

Szabó looked like a life raft.

The Szabós, with Véronique's sister, boarded the yacht in Monaco. Luc was to join them two weeks later. Since his plane ticket was to Nice, Szabó told him to meet the yacht in the little port of St.-Jean-Cap-Ferrat, between Nice and Monaco. Although he'd never been there, Luc knew of it: it was where Somerset Maugham had bought a fabulous villa and lived much of his long life.

The yacht was not there when he arrived by taxi in midafternoon— they would be out sailing during the day, Szabó had told him over the phone, back in port by sunset. Luc left his bag at the *capitainerie*, and walked uphill along the narrow lanes of the Cap, between high hedges of pine and cypress and dense bulwark copses of flowers that allowed only partial views of the great pastel-hued, frosted, and crenellated villas. These were the homes of the rich and the not famous: disenfranchised European nobility; Nazi profiteers; modern industrialists; and some genuine, unimpeachable strains of old money. Not writers.

He was looking for Maugham's Villa Mauresque. He'd read Maugham's novel *The Razor's Edge*, the story of a young man seeking truth amid the trappings of European luxury, many times. Just as many times he'd seen the glossy black-and-white 1946 Oscar-nominated movie adaptation, starring Tyrone Power and Gene Tierney—whose nipples visibly harden beneath her gossamer-sheer silk blouse in the final climactic scene as she parts from her lost love, played by Tyrone Power, for the last time—in a villa on the French Riviera.

With his millions made from writing, Somerset Maugham bought the Villa Mauresque, and lived out his days there in luxury, writing in the mornings, playing bridge through the afternoons, entertaining some very fortunate guests. One of them, Luc read in some biography of the writer, had walked through the house and gardens, marveling: "All of it from writing!"

He finally found the entrance to the Villa Mauresque. Maugham had been dead for almost twenty years, but the Moorish symbol he had adopted to ward off the evil eye, monogrammed into the cover of all his hardcover books, was still engraved in stone at the entrance to the villa's driveway.

They worked mornings in a quiet spot on the forward deck of the yacht, sitting in folding teak director's chairs with their coffee, while the crew prepared breakfast, and Mireille, Véronique's sister, slept late in the aft cabin. As they talked, Véronique stood behind Szabó, a tray beside her, squeezing and lancing and wiping with alcohol and cotton balls the dense new crop of acne cysts that had boiled up through the skin across Szabó's back and shoulders during the night. It took her at least half an hour every morning. Szabó ignored her as he would a manicurist and concentrated on their story. Luc tried not to look at the pile of blood-and-pus-soaked cotton balls mounting on the tray.

Since fleeing Hungary as a documentary filmmaker after the 1956 uprising, Szabó's attenuated commercial instincts had been honed by producing soft-core pornography for the German and Scandinavian markets, before moving successfully into increasingly less lurid mainstream features. As they pulled apart and reconstructed Luc's story to reflect the requirements of his distributors, Szabó's tone, his approach to the project, shifted. Before, he had been confident, amused by Luc's naiveté, but respectful of his ideas, his story. Now, he became visibly less happy. "I don't know," he began to say, clicking his tongue in his mouth as he worried a gap in his molars, "we're losing focus." Their morning work sessions grew irregular. Szabó, a chronic insomniac, always up early to work and chase away nocturnal demons, began to appear late. Or to sit in the yacht's teak-paneled saloon, sipping coffee and looking distractedly at the charts of the nearby coasts. He grew bored.

The wide square sail, emblazoned with a coat of arms that incorporated a leaping *delphinus*, was rarely used. The engine propelled the yacht, and the generator ran all day and most of the night. They motored to Antibes and ate dinner at Chez Félix in the old town. Szabó had heard that Graham Greene dined there every night and he hoped to meet him. He had greatly admired Greene's brief performance as a film distributor in Truffaut's film *La Nuit Américaine*, but they failed to spot the elusive author on two consecutive nights.

"I want to sail in the sea," Szabó told the yacht's captain, Tony Clement, a weathered, laconic Englishman with a good accent, dressed in white shirt and shorts. "Not this back-and-forth between boat parking lots. I want to sail across the sea to another country. I want a *voyage*."

"Quite right too," said Tony agreeably.

"Where can we go?"

Tony spread a chart of the western Mediterranean across the saloon table. "Well, Corsica—"

"How long?" cut in Szabó.

"Calvi in a day—"

"Farther," said Szabó. "A *voyage*. Out of sight of land. Sailing all night. Across the sea."

"How about the Balearics?" said Luc to no one in particular.

"Where?" asked Szabó.

Luc touched the chart, more than a foot across the paper below the French coast.

"What is there?"

"Islands belonging to Spain," said Tony. "A day and a night and a day perhaps to get there."

"Do they have charm?"

"Well, it's not the Côte d'Azur."

"Actually," said Luc, "I more or less grew up there."

Szabó looked at him in surprise. "Where?"

Luc placed his finger on the chart again. "Right there. The east end of Mallorca. My mother has a small hotel there."

"Really? Is it charming?" said Szabó.

Luc was suddenly full of inspiration again. "It's beautiful," he said.

Four

L uc *slept aboard* the yacht, but rode his motorcycle early to the Rocks to catch his mother at breakfast.

"Darling, I don't go aboard boats," said Lulu, "except ferries. You know that."

Yes, yes, he knew. So she always said, and he couldn't recall her aboard a boat in all the years they'd lived beside the sea and a port full of yachts and friends who came and went in them. But Szabó was taken with her. She had impressed him, and Szabó wanted to impress her back in his own arena aboard his fancy rented ship. People had been impressed by Luc's mother all his life and he knew the power of her reflected glory.

"Mother, the boat's not leaving port. It's the size of a building. You won't feel any movement—"

"I don't get seasick. I just don't go aboard yachts," said Lulu emphatically. "You know that."

"I know," said Luc. "But Gábor keeps going on about you. I think he's arranged the whole lunch just to see you again."

"I can't help that. He can come here if he wants to see me."

"It's just a lunch."

"It's a boat."

"Oh, for fuck's sake!" said Luc. "Just because you had a rotten time with your first husband on some little boat a hundred years ago, what's that got to do with life now?"

"That won't help, darling."

"I know. You don't do what you don't want to do. I know that. What an idiot I am to think you'd make an exception for me."

Abruptly, he left and zoomed off on his motorcycle.

She was immune too to the cajoling of Sarah Bavister. "Oh, Lulu, you've *got* to! Look at that bloody boat! Come on, we've *got* to go see it. Really, don't you want to?"

"No, I don't."

After breakfast Lulu pulled on gloves and picked up secateurs and climbed the steps to the garden above the pool. Yesterday's light breeze was gone. What remained, barely felt on the skin, produced a sound like gentle exhalation overhead in the canopy of the pines that shaded much of the garden. She snipped at the rosebushes planted along the back wall. They were doing awfully well. She'd sprinkled Tom's and Milly's ashes in the rose beds in May. They had died in a small plane crash on the way to a fishing holiday in Scotland—just when they'd become wonderfully rich from all those strawberry punnets. Cassian had brought them down from London in two large Horlicks bottles. Tom and Milly had rented Villa Los Roques during the summers after the war. They'd invited Lulu down, and then loaned her the money to buy the place. "We'll keep it in the family!" they said.

Dear Milly. Was she was being fanciful to imagine that the roses had never looked better? Snip . . . snip . . .

Luc was intelligent, of course, but she was no longer sure of his talent. She had read his prose—the beginnings of abandoned novels, the one he had finished which she thought poor and which had been roundly re-jected by publishers. He'd talked about another novel, a story of a jour-nalist in Paris during the occupation. That at least sounded commercial because it had Nazis in it. Then he had started writing screenplays instead. Snip . . . snip. She had to admit he had some sort of facility for film writing. She saw the scenes he wrote clearly, but she wondered why anyone would go to see such films, full of aimless people with a knack for self-destruction. She disliked recognizing Luc in these characters—they all seemed pathetic, and therefore quite believable. Snip . . . At least he was making a little money. She'd helped him out a number of times, but it was always disappointing to give money to a grown man.

Snip . . . snip . . .

This ludicrous film producer obviously liked him. He'd invited Luc on holiday. He had money. He was full of praise for Luc's work. He might actually make the film.

Snip. Miss you so, Milly, darling. What do you think?

Later, as she came down the steps from the garden, she found Sarah beside the pool.

"I will come to lunch with you," announced Lulu.

"Oh, darling Lulu, how wonderful!" said Sarah.

"What time do we have to be there?"

"One, I think."

"We'll go in my car."

She went into the house to change.

"I'm so glad Lulu's coming!" Sarah said.

"I'm surprised," said Dominick, who lay nearby, eyes closed, glistening with oil in the noonday sun. "Lulu doesn't do boats, you know."

"You're coming, aren't you?" asked Sarah.

"Oh yes," said Dominick. "I want to see inside that boat. I bet it's got a fuck nest the size of the Great Bed of Ware."

F ergus's *Range Rover* purred along the quay just before ten. He parked beside the yacht. *Dolphin*'s deck was five or six feet above him and he could see no one aboard. Gingerly, holding its rope rail, he mounted the narrow, unsteady, aluminum gangplank thingy.

"Hello," he said when a crewman, polishing a brass thingy, came into view. Then he saw the film producer farther away on the foredeck, his shirt off, his wife doing something to his back. He could tell the man had forgotten.

"Hallo!" said Fergus again. "Did you still want to see our property?"

"Of course! I am coming."

Five minutes later, Fergus was driving him through town. "Are you in fact looking for property?"

"Always," said Szabó. "The Côte d'Azur, the Cinque Terre, all too crowded now. Not peaceful. So I look around anywhere. I would like a villa in a quiet place near the sea in the sun. Not a long flight from Paris. There is an airport here, yes?"

"Oh, absolutely," said Fergus. "Palma, an hour and a half away. Flights all over Europe. Probably two hours to Paris. Four hours door to door. That wouldn't be bad, eh?"

G erald was pruning the olive trees—trees that were no longer his, technically, though he was unsure of the exact demarcation between his land and the lot he had now officially sold to Fergus and his cabal of developers. Hopefully they wouldn't chop them all down, even those on their parcel, but build their villas to blend into the landscape and preserve as much of it as possible—as Fergus had assured him was their intention. It had even occurred to Gerald that they might not be able to sell their lots and the development might come to nothing in the end. So until some villa-owning holidaymaker told him to clear off out of his front garden, Gerald would continue to prune and look after as many trees as were left standing.

Now he heard Fergus's voice in the nearly still morning air. That breezy, chummy, confident waffle, though he couldn't make out the words. Gerald immediately grabbed his small pruning saw and the large, worn straw basket he'd brought with him, and scuttled away, his espadrilles making no sound in the brush. He moved upslope out of the line of sight that Fergus, and whoever was with him, would have across the property toward the town and the sea view. He was well up the hill among the prickly pear and the cork oak when he saw them below:

Fergus, in Panama hat, and a large man wearing a blue shirt the size of a bedspread. Gerald crouched and watched. They continued a short distance and stopped. Fergus pointed and gestured around him with expansive enthusiasm. Gerald could see from his stolid posture and cursory glances around him that the man in the shirt was unimpressed. Good. He made only a few comments before turning away, leaving Fergus to follow him back the way they'd come, still chattering.

Gerald moved along the hill above them, keeping them in view until they disappeared below the house. He waited until he heard the Range Rover moving down the drive.

He found Aegina painting in her studio off the kitchen.

"Who was Fergus with?" Gerald asked. Rivulets of sweat marked the dust along his temples and neck.

"Some film producer off a yacht in the port. He was showing him the land. Did you talk to them?"

"No. I went to ground."

Aegina laughed. "Of course you did."

Gerald looked at the canvas on her easel. It was a view of where he had just come from: the olive trees, the land falling away to the sea, the distant ridgeline to the north. Aegina had taped a color photograph of the scene to the easel above the canvas. "It's beautiful," he said.

Aegina turned to him. "You'll always have it to look at."

Gerald leaned over and kissed his daughter. Then he said, "Where's Charlie?"

"Penny came and took him to the beach with Bianca. I have a free morning."

Gerald went back outside. He picked up his basket and pruning saw and walked back around the hill to the olive grove. He continued pruning, shaping the trees for how he would want to see them and pick their fruit in fifty years' time. He knelt and held the small trimmed branches against his thighs and cut them into shorter lengths for the basket. He would burn them in the fireplace over the winter.

A*s she painted* her picture of her father's olive grove, Aegina listened to her father's records. He liked the pastoral music of the late-nineteenth- and early-twentieth-century English composers: Vaughan Williams, Elgar, Butterworth, Holst, Finzi, Alwyn, Bantock, Parry, Bridge, Delius, Moeran. Gerald liked to read the novels of Thomas Hardy, Arnold Bennett, Anthony Powell, while listening to a stack of his LPs on the old HMV record player. He imagined, Aegina knew, the landscapes of Dorset, the Lake District, and the fen country, London, and the Five Towns in Victorian gaslight, as he read. To Aegina, however, it was all indigenous Mallorcan music—the music she'd listened to growing up. When she heard it she saw the landscape around C'an Cabrer, all the pictures that rose up from her life in Mallorca.

Seeing Luc in town had disassembled her. They had imprinted themselves upon each other in the way babies and animals do with life's earliest emotional and olfactory associations. It would always be Luc, and then everyone else. Would Charlie and Bianca also grow up with a sense of fated inevitability about each other? Naked together at the beach with fat little hands sharing clumps of sand, naked later with hands exploring each other's bodies? Would their whole hermetic world, built of the idea of each other, also rupture and be lost?

In some now unrecallable way, Fergus had seemed the correct antidote to Luc. Stable, cheerful, amusing, massively self-confident, unneurotic, presentable, tall, clean, wearer of suits. A property developer, not an artist or a dreamer. Not her type at all. An odd, incongruent presence at a party seven years earlier at the Sydney Close studio of one of her Chelsea School of Art instructors, Jonquil Thorn, R.A. Half a head taller than everyone else at the party, his pinstripe weaving through a sea of denim and leather.

Fergus had chatted her up as soon as she'd arrived.

"Are you one of Jonquil's students?"

"I was," said Aegina. "I work now."

"Ah. But you're an artist?"

"Yes."

"I don't know a thing about art," he said blissfully.

"Why are you here?"

"Jonquil tells me what to buy. I've bought some of her big abstract thingies. What sort of stuff do you do?"

"Not abstract."

"Like what?"

"Oh, landscapes, drawings, portraits. Very boring."

"Actually, I need some landscapes."

The next evening he appeared at the door to Aegina's small basement flat off Gloucester Road.

"How did you know where I live?" she asked.

"I found your address in Jonquil's Filofax. Can I come in and see your stuff?"

She was offended and flattered. "Does she know?"

"Doubt it."

"Well, since you're here."

He had to stoop through the doorway.

"I like this one," Fergus said, picking up a dark, smudged-looking riverscape, one of Aegina's attempts at a Whistler "nocturne" of the Thames. "It's awfully good—isn't it?"

She was involuntarily charmed that he admitted he didn't know (or affected that he didn't) and asked her, the artist. "Well, it's never as good as one wants it to be—"

"Do you want to sell it? How much do you want for it?"

That was the other thing about Fergus: money.

"I have no idea," she said. He was interested for the wrong reasons. It was embarrassing.

"Two hundred pounds?"

"It's certainly not worth that. You can get a decent nineteenth-century landscape at Christie's for two hundred pounds."

"Well, I like it."

"You don't know a thing about art. You said so yourself." She nodded at her painting in his hand. "QED."

"What's not good about it, then?" Fergus persisted. "What would Jonquil say about it?"

"You'd better ask her—"

"I did. Not about this, obviously, but about you—as an artist. She thinks you're good. Two hundred sounds reasonable, then. You've seen the rubbish out there for ten times that. Right?"

He made her nervous and she wanted him to go away. But she was broke too—always—it infected the way you thought about everything; it weakened resolve. "If you insist."

"I do. Have you eaten?"

It seemed churlish to refuse him. She was even more uncomfortable now. But also hungry.

On the Fulham Road, they were engulfed by a flock of pigeons taking to the air, and Fergus quickly threw his arm around her. He placed himself between her and the pigeons.

He took her to San Frediano. The food and wine were good. Fergus told her about a pigeon he had found and kept for a few days in his dormitory at boarding school. "It shat all over Matron, in her starched white uniform, when she discovered it. I got into terrible trouble."

Aegina laughed. "What happened?"

"Six of the best!"

"What do you mean?"

"A jolly good caning! Six strokes, well laid on."

"You mean they beat you for that?" She saw him as a little boy, hit repeatedly with a bamboo cane.

He asked her out again. She was flattered but not interested. He was ten years older. He was the sort of businessman type she felt she had nothing in common with. He was almost too tall. She put him off, several times.

In late spring, Fergus knocked at the door to her flat.

"You've been gone," he said.

"I was in Morocco." She explained that she'd flown to Morocco and bought some shirts and other clothing and brought them back to sell at various shops, a small but profitable excursion she'd made several years in a row that had helped put her through art school.

"Will you come to dinner? San Fred all right?"

She was off guard, unprepared to think of a good excuse. She was exhausted but, again, hungry, and remembered the food. And he suddenly seemed . . . likable. "All right. But not late, if that's okay with you."

At dinner he told her about the converted barn he'd just bought in Dorset. It needed paintings. There was an auction of British and European nineteenth-century paintings coming up at Christie's, and he wondered if she'd come with him sometime in the next few days and help him pick out a few things.

"I thought you liked modern art," she said.

"I don't know that I like it at all, but one ought to have some of it. I want the older stuff for the barn. You know, cows and hay wains, that sort of thing. Oh, come on."

They went to a viewing on the Thursday before the auction. Aegina recommended a pair of oils of the Bay of Naples by Arthur Meadows: they were good and she believed they would prove good investments.

He drove her home by a circuitous route. "Can I use your fantastic eye for something else?"

He took her to a block of older flats in Fulham. "I've just bought the building." They climbed stairs to a flat on the second floor. "Look, you can just get a view of the river and Wandsworth out this window. What do you think of that molding? I can knock down a few walls and make larger flats of several of these, put an extra bathroom in each. Big open-plan kitchen. Got to put in a lift. What do you think?"

"They'd be fantastic flats," said Aegina, seeing her version of what he saw.

"I'm going down to my barn this weekend. Why don't you come?"

Automatically, but graciously, she declined.

"Oh, come on," he said. "What are you planning on doing otherwise?"

"I'm going to paint. Go for a walk in the park."

"Well, you can paint in the barn. Bring down whatever you need. Walk along the Dorset cliffs. Pretty nice, actually—have you read *The French Lieutenant's Woman?* That part of the world. I've got masses of work to do. We'll only see each other for meals. Your own bedroom and bathroom, of course. Fireplace in your bedroom. Nice pub. I'll just be too busy to spend any time with you, that's all."

"If you're that busy, why should I come?" But she had already begun to think about it.

"Well, I can make time for you if you insist. But I really want you to see it and tell me what sort of things you think I should get for it."

In the country Fergus wore Levi's. He didn't work that weekend, she didn't paint. He proved to be an indefatigable lover. Friday night, Saturday morning, Saturday night, Sunday morning. On the drive back up to London, he suggested they stop for dinner at San Frediano. It had been a lovely weekend, she said, but she just needed to go home to her flat.

The next day her vagina was red and inflamed. Not surprising, she thought, but a day later it was worse. She went to her doctor. A yeast infection, he pronounced, often the result of activity after a hiatus; might that be a possibility? Yes, said Aegina. She asked if the man might now have it too. Very possibly, her doctor said; he suggested she inform her friend that if he did have anything, it wasn't serious.

Mortified, she rang Fergus.

"I've got a vaginal yeast infection. It's nothing bad, it's not VD, but you might get it or have it too. I'm sorry."

"No, don't be sorry—*I'm* so sorry—did I give it to you?"

"No, probably not. Don't worry about it. It just happens. You're okay, then?"

"Tip-top, when I last looked. But Aegina, I'm so sorry you're unwell. What can I do for you? Can I take you out to dinner?"

"I'm fine. I'm not unwell, really. I think I'll stay in, though, thank you anyway."

But Fergus was launched on a trajectory of gallant solicitude. He brought flowers and food—a cooked chicken, soup, asparagus, and trifle, from Foxtrot Oscar, a cold bottle of Pouilly-Fuissé—round to her flat. "I'm not inviting myself in," he said. "This is just for you. I'll leave. Please ring me when you need anything." He turned to go, but of course she asked him to stay to help her eat (there was more than enough, it happened, for two). A few days later she brought food to his flat and made them dinner. He had a huge kitchen full of professional equipment.

He wasn't Mr. Right. She knew that absolutely. They were so different. But she began to stop resisting him. Fergus was fun, unexpectedly amusing. Light. Generous. Dependable. This is what a man should be like, she thought, even if he wasn't her sort. But what was her sort? What, actually, was missing? She felt looked after. She liked him—a lot, she decided. He wasn't exactly good-looking, but attractive—a large part of it that incredible self-confidence. There was no drama. She worried that this was because she didn't like him enough.

Then he was knocked down by a taxi outside the Michelin building on Sloane Avenue and when she went to see him in hospital, his face was bruised and he looked so pleased to see her that she felt a surge of emotion that seemed true. She looked after him when he went home. She met his mother, a pleasant woman, when she came up from Basingstoke after the accident. . . .

T*he music had stopped.* Aegina became aware of the solitary sound of her brush on the canvas.

Somehow she always knew when Luc was in town, but she'd managed to avoid him for years. They had seemingly excised each other, like an amputation. But now she could feel the phantom limb; it still itched or stung but it felt like a natural part of her. In its place, Fergus was some sort of efficient prosthesis.

Five

L uc watched his mother's SEAT 600—the Rocks' car, in practice, the way she let everyone use it—come down the quay. The sun blazed off the windshield, he couldn't see who was inside.

After leaving her at breakfast, full of anger, he'd turned away from the coast, tooling the motorcycle inland along back roads all the way to the nowhere village of Ruberts, almost at the center of the island, a sinuous route remembered from visits to a friend who'd once owned a house there. Far enough to ensure he wouldn't return to the yacht before the lunch. He didn't want to tell Szabó that his mother wasn't coming.

When he stepped aboard *Dolphin* just before one o'clock, Fergus was the only guest, sitting around the wide cockpit table talking with Szabó, Véronique, and Mireille.

"Ah, Luc!" Szabó seemed overjoyed to see him.

No doubt, Luc thought, he was becoming fatigued by Fergus's relentless bonhomie, though the two women were laughing and appeared to be enjoying Aegina's husband. Mireille particularly. Szabó's sister-in-law, a small creature with a muscular, almost simian build and a chronic poker face, had seemed catatonic to Luc so far, beyond the minimal energy she summoned for sunbathing, reading, and eating. "Véronique's sister will be with us," Szabó had said in Paris when outlining the cruise, working his eyebrows with the apparent suggestion of an intrigue. "She's very attractive. Véronique has told her all about you." The advance praise seemed to have worked against him. Luc found Mireille to be devoid of the remotest interest in him, almost to the point of aversion. She resolutely ignored him, or responded to his attempts to engage her in conversation with the polite sufferance accorded an overtalkative tradesman. Yet now, demonstrating unsuspected reserves of personality and humor, she was smiling, tittering, rocking in her seat with amusement, attending to every word Fergus was saying. It seemed like a miraculous medical recovery.

The abiding mystery of Fergus. Luc had seen him frequently during the last few summers at the Rocks. An English sort Luc understood by the term "Hooray Henry," a loud, shallow twit, though evidently successful at business. Money, Luc knew only too well, effected the most extraordinary alchemy on most women, but even so, he couldn't put Fergus and Aegina together. He didn't see how she could have made that work. The Aegina who could make a life with Fergus was as unsuspected as the suddenly effervescent Mireille.

"*Salut*," said Luc, choosing French, his own way of cutting Fergus.

"Where are your mother and the others from the Rocks?" Szabó asked him plaintively, in English.

"I guess they'll be along soon." Averting his eyes, he looked down the quay, and then saw the little SEAT. "Actually, here they are."

The car parked beside the yacht. Out came Sarah; Dominick's long legs; then, incredibly, his mother. She glanced up and her eyes found him, and she smiled at him. Luc felt an unaccustomed rush of love for her.

"Thank you, Mum," he whispered, embracing her as she stepped from the aluminum passerelle onto the deck.

"Just for you," Lulu said quietly.

Luc felt Szabó behind him and stepped aside as the producer swept forward across the deck like a grandee.

"My dear lady," said Szabó, beaming at Lulu, dipping forward twice with decorous precision, his large lips grazing each of her cheeks. He turned graciously to Sarah. "Hello," he said, kissing her only a shade more perfunctorily, "and . . ."

"Dominick," said Dominick.

Szabó shook his hand. "Thank you for coming. Are there no more of you?"

"Just us," said Sarah.

"*Fabuleux*," Szabó said. He gestured across the deck to where Fergus, Véronique, and Mireille were now standing. "Your friend Fergus is already with us. Will you have a glass of Champagne?"

Roger, a deeply tanned, ponytailed young crewman in white T-shirt, white shorts, deck shoes, approached with a tray of fizzing golden flutes. Szabó passed them out to his guests.

"What a fantastic yacht!" said Sarah.

Szabó shrugged ineffably. "She is incredible," he said simply.

"Can we have a look inside?" asked Dominick.

Even Mireille, who had been bored to death in every cubic foot of the boat, went below immediately ahead of Fergus as Szabó led his guests on a tour of the yacht's interior.

"Ooh, love-lee! Could I have a bath after lunch, please, Gábor?" said Sarah, when she came into the master bathroom. The bathtub, capacious enough for two, was made of vertical, inward-curving teak staving locked together with steel bands, resembling a large, shallow, elliptical barrel cut in half. Something pirates might have frolicked in with ladies of the night in old Port Royal.

"Certainly," said Szabó. "You may all have a bath."

Outside the bathroom, in the aft master cabin, Dominick gazed at the bed. It was strewn with white pillows and extended almost the full width of the ship, which tapered toward the large, asymmetrical, mullioned windows set across the stern, at the head of the bed, in the manner of an eighteenth-century galleon.

"A swashbuckling fuck," Dominick commented sotto voce to Lulu.

"Completely silly," Lulu quietly responded. "From the little I know of being at sea, one would roll about in this bed like a ball bearing and right out one of those cottage windows."

"Yes, but most boats like this never go to sea. They sit in marinas for years on end."

Lulu felt claustrophobic. "I'm going up on deck," she said, heading for the stairs.

Szabó said, "Is everyone ready for lunch? I've prepared a little surprise for you."

When they returned to the deck, the large cockpit table was covered with a linen cloth and set for lunch, with baskets of bread, ice buckets of white and rosé wines, bottles of Pellegrino. They sat around the table on royal blue cushions atop teak benches and deck chairs. Directly overhead, stretched taut on thin wire but appearing to float above them, hung a flat trapezoidal awning of royal blue canvas, casting a deep and comforting shadow across the cockpit.

Two young crewmen appeared with bowls of salad. They poured wine for the guests. They went below and reappeared, each carrying a tray laden with plates of food. Gaspard followed them out. Véronique introduced the chef, who described the meal as the plates were handed out: cold grilled quail with a reduced fig sauce, tiny warm new potatoes, avocado halves filled with pomegranate seeds, plates of toast with pâté de foie gras.

As the plates were set before them, Lulu felt the deck beneath her feet and the ship around her tremble.

She turned to Szabó. "You've turned on the engine. You're not taking us out?"

"It's the generator, dear lady," said Szabó. "It goes on and off all day. Now, please, dear Lulu, tell me how long you have owned your fabulous Rocks, and when did you come to Mallorca?"

"I came down from London in 1947 to cook for friends who were renting the house that's now the main building. Eventually I bought it—"

Lulu's eyes flicked from Szabó's wide beaming face, which he had planted in front of her in an attempt to obscure most of her field of vision, to the long breakwater mole with the blinking-white-light structure at the end of it. Its relation to the yacht was changing. She looked toward the bow and saw that the long uptilted white bowsprit and wire forestay were slowly swinging across the view of the rocky shoreline on the other side of the harbor.

"Why are we moving?" said Lulu sharply.

Szabó's face twinkled with a wonderful secret. He turned and nodded at the ponytailed crewman, who stood twenty feet forward on the deck at the foot of the mainmast. Roger quickly untied a line wrapped around a cleat. At the same moment, two crewmen on either side of the deck began hauling on lines, pulling with all their weight.

No, thought Luc. He turned his head quickly aft to the large spoked wooden wheel, where he had learned that Tony, the captain, would be found during any significant maneuver of the yacht. Tony was now spinning the wheel.

The guests were startled by a swishing, slipping sound of cloth on cloth overhead which quickly became a rumble as a heavy curtain of white translucent sailcloth dropped from the wide horizontal spar halfway up the mast. A tremor went through the ship. Slowly, the cloth ballooned outward; the coat of arms and leaping *delphinus* rippled and then became still, restrained by lines at its bottom corners, as the great square sail filled with the light breeze and tugged at its restraints; and now the yacht began to glide purposefully away from the quay toward the open end of the port.

Lulu stood abruptly. "Put me ashore. I am not going anywhere on this boat."

"My dear Lulu," said Szabó, clasping his hands in front of him, "I am only taking you away for a hour, to glide upon the sea as you eat your lunch. It is my whim, my wish. Please indulge me."

He smiled at her, certain of the irresistible spell of his mischief.

"Fantastic!" said Sarah.

Dominick's eyes fastened on Lulu.

"Gábor," said Luc, also standing, "we must put her ashore. She won't—"

"Luc, it's my gift to your mother and your friends," Szabó said, now opening his arms toward the group around the table. "It is my pleasure." (Even in his consternation, Luc briefly registered the echo of the same words, spoken in the same tone of magisterial grandeur, by Anthony Quinn, playing Auda abu Tayi of the Howeitat in *Lawrence of Arabia*, to

Lawrence and his band of Arabs who have appeared miraculously out of the Nefud to enlist the Howeitat in an effort to attack Aqaba. "It is my pleasure," Auda says, as he hosts a great feast in Wadi Rum.)

Lulu turned from them and walked quickly aft along the deck to the stern, the part of the angled yacht closest to the receding shore. With a sudden movement, she flung her handbag away from her. It soared across twenty feet of water and landed on the concrete quay. She took off her espadrilles and threw them both after the bag. Then she stepped balletically up onto the raised bulwark and leapt overboard.

Luc was still following her down the deck. He watched her plummet feetfirst into the water slipping by below. A moment later Lulu's head broke the surface in the yacht's wake, and she started swimming toward the concrete steps indented into the quay.

Everyone from the table was standing at the rail, watching. They saw Lulu reach the steps and rise gracefully out of the water, as if she went swimming in the harbor with her clothes on every day. She didn't look back but walked to her handbag and shoes, picked them up, and strode on to her car, dripping elegantly.

"Golly," said Fergus.

"Ah," said Dominick, grinning with admiration, "Lulu."

Szabó, astounded, turned to Luc. "But why, Luc? What happened?"

"She doesn't go out on boats, Gábor. She only came because she thought we were staying in port."

"Lulu!" shouted Sarah. "You all right?"

Beside the car, Lulu turned and smiled. "Yes, thank you," she called clearly and pleasantly. She tilted her head and squeezed water from her thick ponytail.

"See you later, darling!" Sarah called back, waving. "We won't be long!"

They watched her get into the SEAT and drive away down the quay.

Szabó masked his disappointment and barked out a laugh. "*Mais elle est superbe!*" he said. "An extraordinary woman, your mother, Luc."

"Yes," said Luc. And you're no Auda abu Tayi of the Howeitat. Suddenly he missed his mother. He wished he could jump overboard and swim away from Szabó and his ship of fools and spend the afternoon with her. He would have if he hadn't pinned his movie hopes on Szabó's pleasure.

"*Mais elle est dingue, cette femme,*" Véronique muttered to Mireille, with a Gallic shrug of contempt.

Szabó turned to his remaining guests with a determined smile. "Well, let us return to our splendid lunch."

Dolphin sailed on into the small slopping waves outside the port, pulled apparently by its large-bellied square sail, and the now set staysail and mizzen sail. But beneath its kitschy galleon glamour labored a heavy, ponderous tub propelled, in fact, by its thumping GM 671 diesel.

Six

Kneeling on the larder floor, Gerald worked a small plunger to transfer his olive oil from the large demijohns, in which it came from the press, to liter bottles.

He paused. From the small ventilation brick high in the wall, came the angry insect whine of a chain saw. Gerald set the bottle and plunger down on a sheet of newspaper on the tile floor.

Outside the kitchen door, he heard the chain saw below the carob trees, somewhere down near the road—undoubtedly on his land. The whine dropped to a low buzz for a moment and behind it Gerald heard the snorting of a diesel engine engaged in some fitful, grinding effort. He walked quickly downhill toward the noise.

The whining and groaning became louder, more insistent. Gerald felt the machines eating into him. He began to run through the trees. Ahead something large was moving, leaping in spurts, snapping wood and trees like a maddened rhino. Something yellow.

The woods opened up. On the slope leading down to the road, a tumble of felled trees and ripped limbs lay beside a wide, ragged swath of red-brown dirt that swept fifty yards uphill. At the bottom, twenty feet of the slumbering beige stone wall running beside the road had been breached, the rocks pushed in and swept aside. At the top of the torn gash in the hillside lurched a snorting yellow bulldozer. Gerald recognized the compact shape of Señor Gómez, the builder, in the driver's seat. He wore a scarred white hard hat. His muscular brown arms worked two long control levers, driving the caterpillar tracks forward in bursts that pawed at the earth beneath them.

Another man in a hard hat—younger, small like Gómez though beefier, his son perhaps—was scything his way up the slope above the bulldozer with the chain saw. The trees dropped as if slaughtered, limbs pawing skyward as they fell. The bulldozer came behind him, the blade uprooting the raw stumps, pushing everything into tangled heaps to the side of the chewed dirt wake stretching down to the road. The two men were progressing uphill at a walking pace. The air was filmy with the noxious particulate of diesel exhaust and the chain saw's greasy blue smoke.

Gómez, his eyes darting everywhere as he worked, noticed Gerald staring at them. Gómez flicked his head upward in greeting. Gerald's eyes found his. The Englishman looked dazed. He seemed not to comprehend what the two men were doing. Gómez rested the bulldozer for a moment.

"¡La carretera!" he shouted. He chopped a hand in front of him, uphill, then away to the right, indicating the path of the access road that would lead to the development in the olive grove. Then his hands returned to the levers and the bulldozer snorted and jolted ahead.

Gerald remembered the road now. It was to start down at the main road and loop around the hill above his house and he'd never see it or hear it, Fergus had said. There would have to be a road of course, not only for the owners to reach their wretched villas, but up which cement mixers and lorries with building materials would rumble for months, years perhaps.

Here it was—already. Gerald had pictured only the little suburb of villas depicted in the artist's impression on the prospectus that Fergus had shown him. In that flat and literal ink and pastel illustration, a smudgily suggested but mature landscape surrounded the orange Spanishy houses with tile roofs and terraces and alternating window placements to distinguish one model from another. A tidy scene that could have been anywhere. Gerald—foolishly, he now realized—hadn't thought about the wide borders of destruction that such a modest Eden would inflict on the edges of his remaining property. He hadn't anticipated the noise. He was shocked by the suddenness of its arrival—for some reason, he'd imagined all this would start after the summer—and the vivid reality of what he had agreed to—all for six thousand pounds, to begin with.

He watched for a few minutes as Gómez and his man continued on up the hill. He was stunned by their speed and brutal efficiency—they would surely hack a broad scar up and around the hill all the way to the olive grove in a matter of a day or two.

Gerald looked at the sawn trunks, limbs, and torn, uprooted trees scattered across the hill like a slain army. Numbly, he turned and tramped back through the carobs toward the house.

I've made the most terrible mistake.

Seven

L uc was sick of sailing. It was the most excruciating pastime he'd ever encountered. Going, essentially, nowhere, indirectly, uncomfortably, and agonizingly slowly. At the same time he was a prisoner, forced to endure and negotiate Szabó's notions about plot and story and what would please a distributor, and the bludgeoning monotoneity of his poodle wife and her lobotomized (until today) sister. All through lunch, and afterward, as the boat lurched and turned and drifted slowly farther from the land that remained tantalizingly in view, Luc kept seeing his mother leaping overboard, a sublime act of defiance and independence that he admired and envied increasingly as the hours dragged by. He saw himself in the sea, swimming away from the yacht, its noise and foolishness diminishing over the waves.

During lunch, he became invisible. He said little, then nothing. Nobody paid any attention to him. He was a known commodity to the group on the boat and to the guests from the Rocks, but they were new meat to one another and, evidently, mutually fascinated. After lunch he went below to his cool cabin to lie on his bunk and read.

L uc awoke disoriented. It was light; for a moment he thought it was morning. Then he heard the voices on deck, indistinctly, and remembered who was aboard.

It was oddly quiet. After a moment he realized the engine was off. The yacht was rising and falling gently, and rolling slowly from side to side. Through the small porthole beside his bunk he could see that the light outside had softened, hitting the water at a more oblique angle, the sky was bluer, past the shattering white heat of the middle of the day.

He lay on his bunk for a while, lulled by the peaceful motion of the boat and the disinclination to get up and go on deck and talk with anybody. He wanted to get off the boat and have dinner with his mother. He looked at his watch: almost five o'clock. They must be sailing back to port on a favorable wind, close to arrival. He sat up.

When he came on deck and looked forward over the bow he saw only the sea. He finally found Mallorca low on the horizon and far away—eight miles, he guessed from the distances he'd learned to estimate on the cruise so far. He was confused: the big square sail had been rolled up like a windowshade, the mainsail set and hove flat amidships in a way that Luc had come to understand was meant not for propulsion but to steady the rolling of the yacht.

Sarah's voice, edged with stridency, came from the cockpit: "Any news, Luc?"

He turned. Sarah, Dominick, Fergus, and Mireille sat in the cockpit, presenting a strange tableau. Except for Mireille, they looked like people in a station waiting for a train. Mireille, topless, sat beside Fergus, one leg raised, with her foot planted on the teak bench, the other stretched out with its foot on the table, her bikinied crotch getting a good airing. Luc had never seen her drunk but she looked it now.

"When are we going back?" Luc asked.

Sarah made a face of theatrical chagrin and reached for a wineglass on the table.

Mireille giggled.

"Well, that's the sixty-four-thousand-peseta question right now," said Dominick.

"What do you mean?" said Luc.

"THE ENGINE'S CONKED OUT!" Sarah shouted. "Where have you *been*?" She was red with sunburn in the face and across her shoulders and Pouter pigeon bosom above her small bikini top.

Now Mireille laughed loudly.

"It's not funny!" Sarah snapped. "I've got children waiting for me. They'll be wondering where I am."

"Yes, me too, but at least they know we're all right," said Fergus consolingly. "We've been in sight of the Rocks the whole time—"

"Then they must be going out of their bloody minds wondering why we're just *sitting* here!" said Sarah. "My *God*, I wish I'd jumped overboard with Lulu! She *knew*! She bloody well *knew*!"

"She didn't know," said Luc. "She just doesn't go out on boats."

"Well, now I know why! My *God*—"

Luc went below and found the engine room door open. Inside the cramped compartment, filled with pipes, hoses, wires, dials, valves, Tony was sitting on a small milk crate beside the engine. Parts of it were unbolted, rubber hoses unclamped, oily bits and pieces sat in a red plastic tub at his feet. He was bolting or unbolting something with a socket wrench worked by a clicking ratchet. Roger, the ponytailed crewman, was squatting nearby, holding tools like a nurse beside a surgeon.

"Hi," said Luc.

"Hiya," Tony said pleasantly. He didn't quite look at Luc, inclining his head toward the door, his eyes alighting briefly on a pipe near Luc's head.

"I missed all the excitement, I guess. I've been asleep. What happened?"

"Nothing too exciting," said Tony. "Engine overheated. Had to shut it down. We sucked a bag or something up into the seawater heat exchanger. Got through the strainer plate in the hull. Blocked the water to the impeller, which burned out and broke into pieces. Got a spare impeller, of course, but I've got to clear the system of whatever the obstruction was, and burned bits of impeller and what have you."

"How long do you suppose it'll take to fix?"

"Dunno," said Tony, as if it were an intriguing philosophical conundrum, suddenly presented and greatly worth pondering. His face looked unusually thoughtful for a moment. "Done when it's done, is my best guess," he concluded cheerfully, looking down at the engine as if it were a naughty child. Then he turned to Roger with a knowing look and said: "At least it's not a Volvo Penta." Roger laughed, catching some tacit witticism, but Tony merely smiled complacently.

Luc had noted Tony's serene, Buddhistic detachment in the course of their cruise. Perhaps from long exposure to the whims of charterers and the vagaries of mechanical or marine problems, the captain was blithely unruffled by changes of plan, contradictory orders, disappointments such as no dock space at Portofino, tension or moods, adversity of any kind. He kept to himself, either near the helm on the aft deck when under way, or unobtrusively going about ship's business, listening to weather forecasts on the radio, navigating, tightening or adjusting the odd bit of gear, instructing his crew with very few words. He was not a front-of-house captain or a raconteur who entertained guests with sea stories or salty charm. He was peripherally ever present, his eyes generally fixed either on the horizon or some piece of boat, a vague, low-wattage stoner smile deflecting any invitation to chat or intimacy.

"Right," said Luc.

He started to turn away, and Fergus appeared beside him, stooping to push his head into the engine room.

"How's it going?" Fergus asked with forced cheeriness.

"Yes, coming along," said Tony, lifting his head for a moment, with a pleasant smile.

"Oh good!" said Fergus, with relief. "Be on our way soon, will we?"

"Ah. That I can't tell you," said Tony genially.

"Oh. Right. Well . . . Look, can we get in touch with somebody ashore? We'd like to let them know we're all right and when we'll be back. Do you have some sort of radio thingy we might call the Rocks on?"

"Yes, of course," said Tony. "Roger can do that for you up at the nav station. Rodge, try the Real Club Náutico on two-one-eight-two. They can probably patch you through to a telephone ashore. Would that help?"

"That would be super," said Fergus.

Roger laid his tools down, wiped his hands on a cloth, and came out of the engine room. Fergus followed him.

Luc went into the galley to get a beer. Véronique and Gaspard were going through the fridge and freezer, taking smoking packages out and re-storing them, talking at a fierce argumentative pitch, gesticulating emphatically, snorting with disgust, but agreeing absolutely, about the threat of Danish butter to the European Economic Community. They paid no attention to Luc as he crept between them and reached into the fridge.

"Where's Gábor?" he asked.

"Don't disturb him," said Véronique. "He's lying down. He's completely stressed with all these people with their problems."

"What problems?"

"They want to go home! What can he do?"

"I'm sure no one thinks it's his fault."

"Of course it's not his fault!" said Véronique.

Luc took his beer outside, passing through the navigation cubbyhole as Roger was saying, "Real Club Náutico, yacht *Dolphin*, over . . . Real Club Náutico . . ." into the radio, while Fergus looked on.

Outside, the unhappy captives looked expectantly at Luc as he came on deck. Mireille had disappeared.

"What's the word on the engine?" asked Dominick. Strands of his normally slicked-back hair were hanging down on either side of his forehead, signs of spillage stained his shirt. Much of the detritus of lunch had been cleared away, but their half-filled wineglasses still sat on the table. A bottle bobbed with the motion of the yacht in a silver bucket of melted ice.

"I don't know," said Luc. "They're working on it."

"But this is ridiculous, Luc!" said Sarah. "I mean, how long are we going to sit here, drifting out to sea? I mean, *look!* We're bloody miles away now! Jessica and the others will be *frantic!*"

"Fergus is trying to call the Rocks now."

"Luc, what about the dinghy?" said Dominick, pointing to the large rubber Zodiac dinghy with an outboard motor hanging from davits over the stern. "Can't they run us ashore in that thing?"

"I don't know," said Luc. It was the yacht's tender, used in every port or anchorage to run the guests to and from shore. It was fast, stable, and sped across the water like a commando boat used to storm a beach. He looked forward and noticed Tim and Ian, *Dolphin*'s other two crewmen, sitting up in the bow, smoking.

"Could you *please* go find out, Luc?" Sarah implored.

"Yeah, sure."

"Thank you!"

Rather than run it by the blissed-out Tony down in the engine room, Luc walked forward to the two crewmen in the bow. Both were English lads, perhaps working through a gap year.

"Hi," said Luc as he approached.

"Oh, hi, Luc," said both Tim and Ian.

Luc smiled at them pleasantly. "Could you run a few of us back ashore in the Zodiac?" He inclined his head aft. "They've got to get back to their kids."

"Oh . . ." Tim frowned for maximum effect, conveying a convincing middle ground between tremendous willingness and expert doubt. "I dunno. It's quite a ways now. I mean, we're at least six miles offshore. You'd better ask Tony, I think."

"Could you ask him while I get our group ready? We really have to go."

"Sure," said Tim, throwing his cigarette overboard and loping gamely down the deck.

"Great. Thanks," said Luc, coming behind him.

In the cockpit, Sarah and Dominick sat up and looked expectantly at Luc.

"Tim's going to go see about it," he said brightly.

"*Brilliant!* Thank you *so much*, Luc!" said Sarah. She and Dominick stood up, as if their train was approaching.

Fergus came out on deck. "They can't seem to get through on the blower for some reason—"

"Never mind," said Sarah, "we're going back in the rubber boat. Luc arranged it."

"Oh, fantastic," said Fergus, nodding to Luc across the chasm of their mutual acquaintance. "Well done."

Tim appeared. "I'm afraid Tony says it's too far to go in the Zodiac."

"What?" said Sarah, indignantly. She turned to Luc. "I thought you said we could go?"

"Well, I thought we could. I just asked Tim if he could ask the captain."

"It really is too far, actually, to go in a dinghy," said Tim. He frowned again, tremendously sympathetically. "It could be quite dangerous over such a distance."

Fergus addressed Tim. "Why aren't we sailing back right now? You've got the sails, at least. Why are we simply floating here? Can't you work on the engine while we sail back? Or sail us back and work on it tomorrow? I mean, we've got obligations ashore, you know. The engine's not our concern. Will you go tell that to your captain, please?"

"Yeah, I will, absolutely," said Tim. But he stood in place, bobbing slightly, hesitantly. "The thing is, we *would* of course sail back if we could, but there's not much wind right now, and what there is, is coming off the land, actually blowing us away from Mallorca, and the yacht's very heavy, so we couldn't actually get anywhere under sail alone, at least in that direction. Right now we're sort of hove to so we don't drift even farther away. So, unless there's a change in the weather, we can't really get back to shore until they fix the engine."

"But that's ridiculous!" said Sarah, appealing to them all. "We can't just sit here and drift all over the bloody Mediterranean! We've got obligations—I've got *children* waiting for me ashore! I mean, it's all right for Gábor, who's obviously gone to bed or something, but *we* didn't sign on for a bloody cruise, did we? We came for *lunch*! I mean, it's just *not on!*"

"Absolutely," said Tim, now bobbing with sympathetic concurrence. "Look, I'll just go get Tony, shall I? You can talk to him about it."

Unhesitatingly, he disappeared into the saloon.

Dominick lifted the dripping wine bottle out of its bucket. "Anybody fancy a top-up?"

Sarah snatched a glass off the table and shoved it toward him. "I do!"

Eight

After she'd showered off the salty, slightly oily residue of her swim in the port, Lulu put on white cotton shorts and a large white linen shirt and told Claire that she would have a salad beneath the leafy trellis out on her front terrace that overlooked the rocks and the sea and was not used by guests.

As she ate her salad, she could see *Dolphin* rolling slowly in the light breeze about a mile offshore, its sails billowing. How picturesque—that fatuous man!—but she was happy to see the yacht, off in the distance like that, because it made her intensely glad she was not aboard.

Her body convulsed with an involuntary shiver.

She'd tried for Luc's sake—he had no idea what concessions she'd made to herself—but it had been a mistake. She'd broken a rule and look what had happened. She would never set foot on a boat again, not for any reason.

After lunch, Lulu took her siesta. She woke at four and swam fifty slow laps in the pool. She showered again. It was cool finally in the house. She put on a cotton djellaba with nothing underneath and went into the kitchen. Claire was preparing dinner: *merluza con samfaina*, a Mediterranean fish sautéed with tomatoes, peppers, aubergines; a cobbler made with gooseberries Judy Plumley had just brought down from England; and Claire's homemade peach ice cream.

"Perfect, Claire," said Lulu.

"Lulu?"

Cassian stood in the kitchen doorway. In one hand a silver cocktail shaker that dripped with condensation, in the other two crystal glasses half full of olives. "Martini?"

"You don't know how much."

They went out onto the front terrace. Lulu arranged herself on the wide white sofa; Cassian sat in a large wicker armchair. He poured their drinks, passed a glass to Lulu, and put his feet up on an ottoman upholstered with a threadbare piece of kilim. "You didn't go out with the others, I see," he said.

"No. I escaped."

"I thought you might have."

"And thank God too." She peered out at the sea. "They've disappeared. They've either sunk or gone round the corner somewhere. God knows how anyone can stick it for hours at a time, floating so near to where you want to go but not getting there—as often as not on purpose. It must be a very particular enthusiasm, like Morris dancing. Torture if you ask me."

"That's because you need to be the captain of your own ship, Lulu."

"Bless you, darling. Someone understands." Lulu sipped her martini. "Perfection. Your sainted father taught you well. The trouble with most Englishmen is that they learn to drink in pubs, where a properly prepared cocktail is a mystery on the order of turning mercury into gold."

Cassian smiled. "When was the last time you were in a pub, Lulu?"

"I don't go to pubs, darling."

"I didn't think so."

"I was in one during the war. It was horrible," she said, in the tone people use when referring to distressing wartime experiences best forgotten. "*Salud.*"

They sipped.

"Did you know that Gerald Rutledge doesn't have a telephone up at his house?" asked Cassian.

"I'm not surprised. Why do you ask?"

"Because Fergus Maitland has given out your number here for people to contact him."

"Yes, darling, everyone does. I don't mind."

"No, quite."

They sipped.

Cassian said, "Have you heard of El Niño?"

"No. What is he, a bullfighter?"

"Possibly. The one I'm talking about is a periodic weather phenomenon occurring in the Pacific Ocean, which brings unusually warm water to the west coast of South America. It makes more rain on the land. It happened this last winter. There were catastrophic floods in Paraguay."

"Poor Paraguay."

"Actually, it changes the weather all over the world. Australia got less rain than usual, and had lots of fires instead. Drought in Africa."

"Poor old Australia. Africa's always been completely ruined."

"The thing is, last winter's El Niño caused billions of pounds of damage in Paraguay and Brazil and Australia and lots of other places."

"What rotten luck," said Lulu, sipping her martini.

"Yes. Not only to those places and millions of their benighted inhabitants but to their insurers. If you're a Name at Lloyd's—if you're personally liable for all that insurance—right now you're rather wishing you weren't."

"I see. You're about to make a stunning point of all this."

"Yes." Cassian smiled. "If you're a Name at Lloyd's, this has been a bad week. The numbers for worldwide damage caused by last winter's El Niño and the resultant liability are in."

"Well, darling, I'm awfully sorry for everybody, for Lloyd's, for the whole world. Is there anything I can do?"

"There is, in fact. You know my friend Johnny Barton."

"I've heard you speak of him."

"Johnny's been calling here all day for Fergus Maitland. He's in with Fergus on this property they're developing on the land they've just bought from Gerald Rutledge."

"Ah," said Lulu. She put her glass down on the coffee table. Then she picked at and rearranged the djellaba around her crossed legs.

"You know about it?" asked Cassian.

"Just the little I've heard here and there," said Lulu. "Holiday villas. Is that it?"

"That *was* it. Johnny represents the majority of Fergus's partners. Most of them are Lloyd's Names. They want out."

"He wants new partners?"

"No. Not at all. They want to sell the land. They bought it on extremely favorable terms—just yesterday, I gather. Today, they want to dump it. They'll probably offer it back to Gerald if they can't get rid of it."

"How extraordinary. The disasters of the world come home to roost in our back garden. What do you have in mind?"

"I'm thinking of taking it off Johnny, but doing something different with it. What Fergus was planning—separate villas with gardens— underutilizes the land. Many more units could be put on it, for a lot more profit. Like those condominiums down in Porto Cristo. Do you want to come in with me?"

"You mean build an entire village of those semidetached hovels? How revolting."

"It made their developers a lot of money."

Cassian lit a king-sized Dunhill.

Lulu knew the small eyes behind the thick yellow lenses. "You've thought it through, then."

"Yes," said Cassian.

"How much?"

"About a hundred thousand pounds. I'll put up the same. We'll use your lawyer, Beltran, to draw up a partnership. We'd get a couple of models up and then sell the rest to be built on contract."

"I don't think I've got a hundred thousand pounds, darling."

"I think you'll find you do, actually. More than that, with your share of Mummy's estate."

"Oh. Would *we* make a lot of money?"

"I reckon three to four times our outlay at the end of two years. A lot more in the following two years. We could run all the purchases through an offshore company. Use my bank, the Butterfield, in Bermuda."

"Who else have you asked?"

"Nobody. This would be just you and me. I won't bother if you're not interested. It can go back to Gerald."

Lulu picked up her drink from the table.

"What about Fergus? Does he come with it?"

"No. He's a shareholder only with Johnny's group. He can't stop the sale. He's finished, out."

"Could Gerald stop us building what we want?"

"Not a chance. But we need to move quickly. I want to tell Johnny today or tomorrow—preferably before Fergus comes back on that boat, calls Johnny, and goes home to talk it over with Gerald."

Lulu looked away, out over the rocks to the sea.

Nine

Charlie *woke at seven* in the evening. His afternoon nap, which in London began at one or half-past, didn't start until three or four in Mallorca where, with all the beach-going and playing with Bianca and helping his grandfather with the lemons and olives, he slept longer hours.

He could tell it was evening. His room was dim, the color gone out of it. Through the open window he could see the fading pale blue sky over the green leaves of the lemon trees.

He knew where he would find everyone beyond the door of his room. Grandpa would be in the living room, smoking his smelly cigarettes, listening to the radio that called itself the BBC World Service and told Grandpa what was happening in the world. There was always a disaster somewhere and when the BBC World Service told him about it, Grandpa would blow his smoke toward the ceiling and say, *"Plus ça change."* Mummy and Daddy would be on the terrace having their drinkies. Charlie liked lying in bed, knowing where everyone was and that he could go be with them as soon as he decided to get up.

I will get out of bed very soon, he thought.

He waited as long as he could, which was about seven seconds, and then he got up and went to the door.

He heard the radio as he came out of his room.

"Ah, Charlie, there you are," said his grandfather, standing up as Charlie came into the room. "How are you?"

"Good," said Charlie. He walked sturdily through the room and out onto the terrace. No one there. He turned around. His grandfather was behind him.

"Where's Mummy and Daddy?"

"Yes, they're not here right now," said Grandpa cheerfully. "Daddy went for a boat ride, and Mummy's gone into town to see when he'll return. She'll be back any minute."

Charlie walked past his grandfather and into the kitchen. No one there either.

"Would you like some TriNaranjus, Charlie? Orange drinky?" Grandpa was smiling in a very big way at him.

"Where's my mummy and daddy?" Charlie's voice rose to a squeak and he began to cry.

"Now, don't worry," said Grandpa. He picked Charlie up. "They'll all be back soon. It's all right, Charlie boy." Grandpa kissed his forehead.

Charlie bawled and pushed away from the stinky cigarette smell.

Grandpa carried him into the living room and put him down on the sofa. "Shall we play a game, Charlie? What about noughts and crosses?" They'd been playing that recently and Charlie had won all the games. "Or shall I read you a story?"

Charlie jumped to the floor and ran out to the terrace. He reached the rail and cried out over the drive below. *"Mum-myyyy!"*

Grandpa caught him and lifted Charlie into the air and they moved away from the rail and back into the living room. "Everyone'll be back soon, Charlie, don't you worry," said Grandpa, bouncing him up and down and pretending to laugh. Charlie didn't want to hear it. He placed his hands on his grandfather's chest and pushed strongly. He wailed.

"I'll tell you what." Grandpa held him out and looked into Charlie's face. "Shall we go look for them?"

"Yes," said Charlie. He stopped crying and was still.

"Right. We'll go into town. I know where they'll be. One of two places. We'll go look at both, shall we?"

Charlie nodded. This made sense.

"All right, then. Well, let's get something on your feet."

Grandpa carried Charlie back into his room, where they found his little blue espadrilles. He slipped them onto Charlie's feet and said, "Mummy's got my car, and your daddy's got his car, so we'll go on Grandpa's moped. Okay?"

"Yes, Grandpa," said Charlie.

Now it was almost dark outside. Down on the drive, Grandpa started the moped and sat on it. Charlie was suddenly afraid Grandpa was going to leave without him and his face began to crumple, but Grandpa lifted him up and set him down on the seat in front of him, almost in his lap, with Charlie's legs out either side between Grandpa's legs. The machine throbbed beneath them.

"Now you hold on, with your hands on my arms, like that. Hold on tight to my arms or my shirt. Got it? That's it. Hold on tight, Charlie. This way you can't fall sideways or go forward and I'm right behind you. All right? Off we go."

The moped whined, wobbled, and plunged down the steep drive. They appeared to be falling. Charlie shrieked. Somehow they didn't fall, but continued swooping down the drive like a bird.

At the bottom of the hill where the drive met the road, they stopped. Grandpa looked around and said, "Off we go. Hold on tight!" The moped buzzed loudly and trembled beneath Charlie's legs and then it leapt ahead. Charlie laughed a squeal of delight. The stone walls at the sides of the road blurred. A small patch of yellow light bounced in front of them as they tore through the dark beneath an indigo sky. The warm air buffeted Charlie's face, his thick dark hair flew around his head.

"This is fun!" he shouted.

"It is, isn't it!" agreed Grandpa.

The dark fell away as they came into town. Shops liquid with light pouring out of them and car headlights streaked past. Charlie was thrown backward into Grandpa's chest, and forward, grabbing onto Grandpa's arms, with the moped's sudden fits of fast and slow. They flew through town, weaving miraculously through traffic, down dusty side streets, turning, slowing, and zooming through the dark. It felt dangerous but

Charlie knew he was safe, so it was fun. The moped whined louder and picked up speed and they were racing through the port with the lights of the town streaming across the water beside them. Charlie suddenly heard another moped beside them, but it was only the breakwater wall close by as they sped down the long quay toward the blinking white light at the end. They slowed and stopped, the moped puttering softly beneath them.

"There's Daddy's car, you see?" said Grandpa. And so it was: the familiar boxy Range Rover shape all by itself on the long quay. "Well, he's not back yet. He went for a boat ride and they're late."

Charlie started to worry about this, until Grandpa said, "I expect they'll be back shortly. Shall we go find Mummy, then?"

Charlie nodded. "Yes."

The engine grumbled beneath Charlie, Grandpa turned the moped, and they sped back down the quay. They whizzed around the port until Charlie found he could tell where Grandpa was going.

"The Rocks, Grandpa!" he shouted. His father had taken him there a few times, to have a TriNaranjus while his father had drinkies with his friends. Charlie liked the Rocks.

"That's right," said Grandpa.

They slowed and stopped outside a large house beside the sea. Grandpa turned off the moped and carried Charlie through the gate into the open area inside where all the grown-ups had their drinkies. People turned and looked at them.

"Any news from the yacht?" Grandpa asked.

"No," several people said.

A man with red hair and yellow glasses approached them. He spoke to Grandpa in a very quiet grown-up voice: "Gerald, I think it would be better if you go home. We've heard nothing. If we hear anything, we'll send someone up."

Charlie could see that Grandpa was looking around everywhere for Mummy and Daddy, but the red-haired man put his hand on Grandpa's shoulder and led them back outside. "We'll let you know," he said again.

"But then where's Mummy?" Charlie asked as Grandpa started the moped again. He began to cry. "Where's Mummy?" he wailed.

"She'll probably be back home by the time we get there, Charlie boy," said Grandpa.

The moped leapt ahead and trundled on down the bumpy road. Soon they were grinding slowly up the long driveway. Eventually they reached the top, and, the best thing in the world, Grandpa's car was there. She'd heard them coming and was waiting for them on the steps.

"Mummy!" Charlie yelled.

She took him in her arms and hugged him. Over Charlie's head, she looked at her father.

"Where have you been?" she asked.

Ten

When twilight was quite gone, the sea and the sky became fathomlessly dark. There was no moon, the stars were faint, the air opaque with humidity. Mallorca lay below the horizon to the north beneath patches of sulfurous loom. Closer, at indeterminate distances, hovered the lights of fishing boats hung with incandescent lamps to attract fish, each surrounded by a diffuse glow on the black vinyl sea. Low on the water, the fishing boats disappeared and reappeared like fireflies.

The guests aboard *Dolphin* were stunned into quiescence. Fergus and Sarah sat in the intimate light of the electric brass lanterns that the young crewmen, Tim and Ian, had fixed above them in the cockpit. Sarah had been mumbling to herself for some time, and Fergus—after a few polite, unanswered assays of "I'm sorry?" and "What did you say?"—ignored her. Inside the saloon, Dominick sprawled on a settee, leafing through copies of *Paris Match*, *Vogue*, *L'Express*, his eyes following whoever was moving through the yacht. Now and then Véronique thudded barefoot quickly back and forth across the saloon carpet, between the galley and the master suite aft where Szabó had retired and remained cloistered since shortly after the engine had conked out and the first mutterings of dismay and complaint had arisen.

Véronique was resolutely disinterested in the situation and condition of the luncheon guests who had—she didn't care whose fault it was—long overstayed their welcome. She shot resentful glances at Dominick as she passed, and he smiled imperturbably back at her. When the mood on deck had become too unpleasant and boring, Mireille too had vanished below somewhere.

In Szabó's absence and Véronique's dismissal of the tedious passengers, Luc had felt obliged, for a time, to play host to the Rocks contingent—his mother's friends, after all, and he the connection that had resulted in Szabó's invitation. He'd brought them more drinks, olives, tried chatting encouragingly with amusing stories of the boats full of Rocks guests that had been late or presumed missing or even sunk, over the years, but all of which had eventually reappeared with no more harm than excessive sunburn and the odd pregnancy—

"Are these stories of yours supposed to *help?*" Sarah snapped at him.

"I dunno," said Luc. "I thought they might. I mean, it could be worse. There are certainly less comfortable boats—"

"Are you saying this happens all the time?"

"Well, not all the time, but it happens. People are always getting into trouble on boats—"

"As Lulu *bloody well knew*! She might have *told us!*"

"You can't say she didn't give us a hint," said Dominick with a malicious grin.

"Oh shut up!" Sarah threw an olive across the cockpit table at Dominick. That was when he went into the saloon and started reading magazines.

A*t nine o'clock,* Szabó appeared at the door of the engine room. He had bathed and appeared fresh in billowing white linen shirt and trousers, at some counterpoint to the greasy disassembled chunks of engine and the oil-smeared hands and features of Tony and Roger, who were laughing.

"You are having fun, Tony, yes?" said Szabó.

"Oh, yes. Happy in my work, always."

"Good. We are about to have dinner, so get the other boys to bring you in something if you want to eat."

"Thank you, sir, we'll do that," said Tony.

"And how is it coming, the engine?"

"Splendidly. I've got the heat exchanger off and the lines—"

"No, no, no." Szabó waved a fat hand. "Means nothing to me, engines. Just tell me how long you think it takes."

"We'll have you all back ashore by breakfast, Mr. Szabó."

"Very good."

Szabó climbed the few steps to the saloon, where Dominick smiled cheerfully at him from the settee.

"How are you?" asked Szabó.

"Marvelous, thank you so much. I wouldn't want to be anywhere else in the world," said Dominick.

"Good. We are eating dinner soon. You'll join us?"

"Oh absolutely. Very good of you to look after us so well."

"Of course. You are my guest."

Szabó went out on deck.

Mireille had reappeared, wearing an oversized faded blue T-shirt with the white words GO HIKE THE CANYON across the back. She and Fergus were helping Tim and Ian set the cockpit table. Luc was saying something to Sarah, who was staring dully at the table.

"Good evening," said Szabó. "How is everyone?"

"All right, thank you," said Fergus. "Any news on the engine?"

"It's coming along," said Szabó. "Luc, let's have a little chat."

Szabó walked forward along the deck with legs splayed sturdily against the slight motion of the boat. Luc followed. He'd heard everything in that "let's have a little chat."

Szabó stopped on the foredeck where they usually worked. Their deck chairs were gone. He held on to the bar-taut forestay and looked out across the dark sea at the few bobbing lights. Then he turned to Luc.

"We've done wonderful work together, Luc."

As bad as that.

"You have integrity, Luc," Szabó went on. He put a hand on Luc's shoulder. "You have taught me something about that. All the time I am seeing this Roy Scheider movie. Roy does this, Roy does that. Until I realize"—his face beaming with sincere epiphany—"you didn't write a Roy Scheider movie!"

"Well, I mean, it could—"

"No, no. It's true. Perhaps an Albert Finney movie, I don't know—but a work of *art*. Of psychology, deep meanings. What I loved—immediately, when I first read it—was your story—*your* story—of this man, this nothing man—*a guy who takes a bus!* My God, when do you ever see this? And then he enters this crazy world, and he finds in himself, this nothing little guy, character! It's fantastic. He's *not* Roy Scheider. I see him now—"

"Well, he could be—"

"No, no, no—you are right. Albert Finney, Alan Bates, Tom Courtenay. An *actor*. Someone we forget he's a movie star and we see this man that you write. And the world he discovers for himself. It's a character piece, not a thriller."

"Well, a sort of noirish—"

"I can't make that movie, Luc. I want to *see* it, go to the cinema and *see* it, *very much*, that film with those kind of actors, but I never get the money from my distributors to make it. Meanwhile, we are ruining the beautiful story that you write."

"So . . . you're giving up the option?"

"No, no, no. I still own the option until expiration of option period. This is a good thing for both of us. I put it into turnaround. When I get back to Paris, I find someone who will make this film—*your* story. I know some English producers, in particular I am thinking of one from Scotland. The right kind of independent producers. They make the little English films. I sell it to them. I become executive producer. They make the movie. It's quality. Everybody is happy. You get a BAFTA award. Then everyone wants you to write their screenplay. It's very good for you."

"You mean, you're going to sell the option to someone else?"

"Exactly. Much better for you."

"What if they want to do something else? Like make it a romantic comedy and bring in another writer."

"No, no, no. I sell it only to the right people. Good people. The people who want to make this sort of film, who will respect you. Perhaps they ask you to direct. Like Bill Forsyth. This is auteur sort of film. This will be perfect for you."

"It's nice of you to be so concerned for me, Gábor," said Luc.

Szabó clapped his arm across Luc's shoulder. "You are my friend, Luc. Come, we eat dinner. We drink some good wine and talk of the fun we have had together," he said, reminding Luc of Paul Scofield as the dissembling KGB officer in *Scorpio*, saying to rogue CIA operative Burt Lancaster, shortly before Scofield tries to assassinate Lancaster: Come, we will drink vodka together and talk of old times, and cry.

The others were already seated around the cockpit table. Gaspard was holding a wide dish of purple-black pasta. "*Alors. Le tagliatelle à l'encre de seiche,*" he said, "*avec,*" nodding at the dishes Tim and Ian were placing on the table, "*une ratatouille, une omelette aux fines herbes, une salade.*" He shrugged. "It's what we 'ave. It's the best I can do."

"*Parfait!*" said Véronique, with a loud clap. "*Parfait, parfait.*"

"*Merci,*" Gaspard said mournfully, and he withdrew.

In a discernably resentful tone, Véronique said, "Gaspard has been trying to make something from very little what we have on the boat. We were not prepared, you know."

"It's *very* kind of you to look after us so well," said Dominick. He was sitting next to Sarah, who was partially slumped against him.

"Well, we can't put you off the yacht," Véronique said seriously, shrugging, apparently having considered it.

"Looks jolly good!" said Fergus. "The black, um, thingy, what's that?"

"Pasta," said Véronique.

"Squid ink?" asked Dominick.

"Yes."

"Wonderful."

Véronique served her husband and then herself and passed the dish to her sister. Mireille, sitting beside Fergus, heaped the black pasta onto his plate.

"Oh, thank you," he said. As she brought her arms forward, Fergus gazed down the wide drooping neck of her GO HIKE THE CANYON T-shirt.

Szabó filled the meal with campaign stories, and reminiscences of his great friend, the late actor Stephen Boyd, and their adventures making movies in Yugoslavia. "Stephen! Such a funny man. Loves the practical jokes. A beautiful man."

As they ate and Szabó talked, a breeze came across the water, unnoticed by the diners. Fitful at first, rattling the slack mainsail overhead, it steadied into a serviceable wind, putting the restless canvas to sleep. Roger appeared on deck. Wordlessly directing Tim and Ian, they adjusted the mainsheet, allowing the sail to belly out, and raised the staysail. The diners heard the whispering rustle of rope through blocks, the fast clicking of winch pawls. The yacht ceased rolling; it leaned and steadied and became quieter than it had been for hours, the only sound the rhythmic whooshing of small waves moving alongside the hull like a gentle but powerful respiration.

"We're moving," said Dominick.

Roger went aft to the wheel and set a new course on the autopilot. The yacht was now pointing closer to the loom of Mallorca on the horizon.

After dinner Szabó excused himself saying he had much work to do.

Luc helped Véronique, Tim, and Ian to clear the table, taking plates and dishes below to the galley.

At the table, Sarah whimpered to Dominick about her dreadful sunburn. He applied lotion soothingly and ever so lightly across her enflamed breasts, while Sarah exhaled small cries of pain and relief and despair.

Fergus lit the cigar Szabó had given him and stood at the rail at the edge of the deck. Mireille joined him, and barked and convulsed at his comments.

Back in his cabin, Luc tried reading, but he could only think about who might pick up the option on his screenplay. He tried to decide if this was a good or bad development. It might go to someone with taste. Or Szabó might refuse to sell it unless he got some deal he was looking for that no one would want to give him.

Or nothing might happen.

All this time wasted thinking about Roy Scheider. Getting into Roy Scheider's skin, imbuing him with a sensitivity and empathy that would mesh with survival driving, a simmering brutality, and not too much talking.

Luc couldn't read. He couldn't possibly sleep. He got out of his bunk and left his cabin barefoot.

On deck, the yacht was moving slowly but steadily. The sea surface was still flat but now stippled with breeze. The wind was southerly and warm—from Morocco maybe. Luc walked forward, on the windward side of the taut staysail, the deck beneath him so stable that he didn't need to hold on to anything.

He stopped at the very apex of the bow beside the long bowsprit that projected twelve feet over the water forward of the hull. It was an exposed position: the wire handrail that ran along the edge of the deck stopped six feet behind him for ease of sail handling at this concentrated spot; for security he held onto the staysail's wire forestay that rose from the deck to the mast crosstrees. This was his favorite place on the boat. Here, on a small triangle of teak planking, the water below rushing past him on both sides, he seemed to be flying at bird height and speed over the sea. He was almost off the boat; Szabó and all his crappy ideas and his rude wife and sister-in-law were all behind him, in another world, encapsulated in their solipsistic bickering and holidaymaking, while he rode ahead of them, in the clear breeze, as detached as a ship's figurehead.

Against the many small noises made by a yacht at sea—the tumbling, hissing, or burbling of water; the high- or low-pitched whistle or moan of the wind through the almost countless ropes and wires that make up the complicated architecture of a sailing rig; the creak, stretch, hum of the warp and weft of so much mechanical gear; waves of vibration at the upper and lower range of human aural sensitivity, all of which becomes the quotidian ambient voice of the world afloat, in a very short time ignored and unheard by those used to it—against that, Luc now heard something else.

It was rhythmic, irregular, escalating, not boat or sea—human . . . grunting. Luc leaned forward and craned his head around the forestay and saw, in the dim shadowless shade beneath the staysail, the message GO HIKE THE CANYON swaying astride a pair of long, pale, twitching legs—

Luc recoiled. Twisting awkwardly in an effort at noiseless retreat, his toe caught beneath the bowsprit. He exhaled sharply through a wide-open mouth to make no sound, his knee buckling and he squatted, spatial orientation thrown for a second, falling back until he knew they'd hear him when he hit the rail or the deck, but he hit nothing. He dropped with great surprise through the air into the gently curling bow wave.

His mouth, still open, filled with water—warm, salty. He exhaled sharply, coughing, clamping his lips closed against inhalation. He tumbled underwater, still disoriented, kicking, hands out. He couldn't tell which way was up. Eyes open, he saw dim phosphorescence. He bumped against something hard, the hull. His hands found it, slick and moving fast. He pushed away, afraid of the propeller, then remembered about the engine. He came up, sucked air, and was pulled down again. Now he knew where the surface and the boat were. He clawed up, and away from the boat, so the propeller, even if it wasn't moving, wouldn't catch him, hold him down, or hit him in the head. But he had to shout and let them know. He came up again. He was still forward of *Dolphin*'s stern.

"Help!" he spluttered. It wasn't loud enough. He sucked in air, getting water too, gagged, coughed. "Help!" he tried again.

The boat kept going, not fast it seemed, but the stern was passing him now. It was a perfect movie shot. The POV of someone in the water with a sailboat sliding past and leaving him behind.

"Help! Stop! I've fallen overboard! Hellllp!"

Now the yacht was past, moving away. *Dolphin* looked beautiful, heeled slightly, the sails filled out into pale parabolas—finally it looked like its brochure. No one coming to the stern rail, though. The lights on in the aft cabin, where Szabó was right now. He couldn't see if the windows were open.

"Help! Gáborr! He-e-e-lllp!"

It sounded loud enough.

"Hell—"

A small wave from the wake slopped into his face and filled his mouth.

He shouted some more. Nobody came to the rail. Kicking hard, he tried to get his head up and cupped his hands around his mouth and screamed.

"He-e-e-e-e-lllllllllllllllllllllllllllllllllll—"

He went under. Flailing, he rose above the surface again. Heart beating, gasping for air, Luc turned all his attention to staying afloat and catching his breath. For a moment he could no longer see the yacht. Then he found it. By sleight of perspective—Luc's eyes were at literal sea level, the horizon only ten or twenty feet distant—*Dolphin* was disappearing fast, already hull down from his fish-eye POV, the rig slipping below the waves. In less than a minute it was impossibly far away, diminished in perspective, its lights fading.

"H-e-e-e-e-e-llllllllllllllllllp!"

Gone.

Luc dog-paddled, revolving slowly, to see what else might be around him. Only the foreshortened circle of small waves. No lights, but in one direction, the north he thought, the loom of Mallorca far away in the sky. Part of him was stunned, unable to think or imagine, refusing to grasp what had just happened.

In another part of himself, an inner voice said clearly: "You're dead, pal."

Luc had spent half his life in the water, around boats and swimming off rocks along the shore. He'd done a lot of snorkeling—he could hold his breath for maybe two minutes—he was completely at home and relaxed in the water. But he'd never been much of a swimmer. Swimming was the way you got from boat to shore or water-ski to the rocks, a couple of hundred yards. He could always manage that. He'd never tried for more.

He was about eight or ten miles south of the east end of Mallorca. There were no rocks or islands to head for.

Unless someone on board *Dolphin* missed him pretty soon and they came back and found him—but even then, Luc knew, there was only one way that could work. The way it had happened with the Clutterbucks, Malcolm and Pansy, friends of his mother's, and their fifteen-year-old daughter, Cobina, sailing their yacht *Vagabond* years ago off the southern coast of Spain toward Gibraltar in a *levante* gale at night. Pansy had just come up into the cockpit, clutching two mugs of hot chocolate, prepared below with epic difficulty on a single paraffin burner, for herself and Malcolm. As she stepped aft toward Malcolm at the wheel, the boat lurched on a wave and Pansy, more mindful, she said later, of the hot chocolate than of herself, flew overboard into the sea, still carefully clutching both mugs. The yacht, tearing along under a press of sail, was instantly past her. There was nothing to be seen of Pansy in the frothing wake astern.

"Well, darling, if you'd been Malcolm, sitting there at the wheel waiting for your hot chockies, and suddenly there it goes, me with it, shot into the dark like one of those people out of a cannon at the circus, instantly buried in enormous waves, what would you have done?" Pansy liked to ask. "Well, thank God, he did the only sensible thing. He sat there for several minutes thinking it all through. Didn't move a spoke of the wheel, let go a sheet, or in any way check the yacht's progress. Off he went over the horizon, thinking jolly hard, with me already a quarter of a mile astern. Eventually he rang the bell we had there in the cockpit to wake Cobina. As you know, it can be difficult to wake a teenager, no matter where she is. Malcolm rang and rang the bell, and eventually Cobina appeared at the hatch. 'Mum's gone overboard, a little way back,' he said to her. 'Go below and pull on your oilskins, and come back up here and take the helm.' Off she goes. Back up into the cockpit a few minutes later. Boat's still cracking along on course. 'Take the helm and keep her on this exact course, not a degree off,' Malcolm told her. Cobina took the wheel and Malcolm then went below. Down at the chart table, he works it all out: the yacht's course made good, allowing for set and drift made by the wind, current, what have you. Then *my* course made good, allowing for same, from the spot where I fell in, plotting both positions at a point another four minutes into the future—at that point a good fifteen minutes since I'd gone overboard. Where the yacht would be then, where I would be. Jolly clever. Then Malcolm draws a course from the yacht at that point to me at that point, adjusting again for wind, current, leeway made on the return course, and pencils it off on the compass rose. Comes back into the cockpit, takes the wheel from Cobina—who's completely nonplussed, darling, because she's still half asleep—and continues counting to himself until the four minutes have elapsed. Then he brings the yacht about—a jibe in that wind—and begins beating back, directly into the wind, along the new course he's just worked out.

"Well, I was perfectly calm and content. I knew that was it. There was nothing to be done. Not a chance—not the *slightest* chance, darling— of being found and rescued in a gale, at sea, at night. I accepted it completely. I thought it a pity, but there it was. I thought about all sorts of things—growing up, summers in Cornwall, my old boarding school Benenden even, I can't imagine why—that I loved, what an absolutely *marvelous* life Malcolm and I had had, what a glory Cobina had become, what a fabulous woman she would be. That sort of thing. I wasn't in a hurry to end it. I wasn't trying to swim anywhere. I was just going up and down on the waves, having fun thinking about it all. And I decided that's what I would do: just go up and down and think about how *marvelous* everything had been, until I sort of fell asleep, or whatever it is that happens to one. I might as well have been plummeting to earth out of an airplane without a parachute for all that I had the *remotest* thought of coming out of it somehow. Tremendously peaceful.

"Well, about, I don't know, twenty minutes later, I saw a light. I thought, Hallo, what's that? It didn't occur to me that it could possibly be *Vagabond*. I didn't know what it was, how far off, nothing. A fishing boat or a ferry miles away was my first thought. Then I saw it going up and down, pitching with the sea, and I realized it *was Vagabond*, and they were getting close. At that moment, I can tell you, I became scared to death—what if they didn't find me? I now thought. I almost wished they'd go away! Then, in moments, the yacht was alongside, and Malcolm was on deck shining a ruddy great torch into my face, saying, 'Ah, there you are,' as if I were a missing sock. Well, he got me aboard, and I went below and made some more hot chocolate."

That wasn't going to happen here. *Dolphin* had no Malcolm Clutterbuck, no one had seen Luc go overboard to mark a position and do all that clever navigation so they could go back and find him. No one had heard him go—the care he'd taken so Mireille and her lover wouldn't hear anything.

Luc tried to remember what he had seen. Just her GO HIKE THE CANYON T-shirt on top of the white legs beneath her. Could have been Dominick, the presumptive ever-ready lech. But he'd been too absorbed by and quite far along with Sarah's broiled *poitrine* to squander his energies elsewhere. Dominick had some unerring instinct that enabled him to detect and tumble the unlikeliest quarries. Luc had noticed his solicitous attention to Sarah in the aftermath of the engine failure. Undoubtedly, he'd soon find a cabin, if he hadn't already, where he could look after her properly until repairs had been effected.

Not Tim or Ian or Roger. Mireille had been as determinedly unaware of their existence as she'd been of Luc's.

Fergus, then.

Luc should have spotted that the moment he came aboard at noon and saw that Fergus, wittingly or otherwise, had ignited unsuspected responses to wit and male company in Mireille's neurasthenic personality—

Cheating on Aegina, the fucker. Luc had always known Fergus wasn't worthy of her. He felt vindicated, and angry. And now he couldn't tell her. Well, he wouldn't have told her; she'd figure it out for herself if she hadn't already. She'd get rid of Fergus someday. He'd always believed that.

But by then—well, by tomorrow morning probably—he, Luc, would be dead. No getting back together, then. He'd always wondered if she'd thought of that as much as he had. Not that he'd wanted to necessarily, but there had always been Aegina first and then everyone else. He compared all women to Aegina and he'd never been able to get past her or leave her behind. She had imprinted herself on him like a tattoo.

Had she really left him behind? Embraced *Fergus* as the future?

How funny to think that she now would live a long time without him; in ten, twenty, thirty years she would remember (hopefully) the last time she'd seen him: on his motorcycle outside the *tabacos*. Thirty-three years old. What would she remember—the good stuff or the bad? He'd always thought there was more to come between them.

The water wasn't so warm now. Vertical, Luc swept his hands before him in a faint breaststroke, his feet moving slowly beneath him, not going anywhere—pointless swimming—but treading water to stay afloat.

That's all he'd ever done. He felt he hadn't started his life yet. He hadn't become successful, or made any money, or fallen in love with someone—else. It was always going to happen after he'd finished whatever he was doing and did the next thing. It was the next thing that was going to work.

He paddled in a circle, just looking around casually as you would anywhere you found yourself stuck for a while.

How do you drown? Do you get so tired that you just can't stay up? Since he wasn't swimming, he wasn't exhausted, yet. He was sure he could float like this for another ten or twenty minutes, maybe longer . . . he had no idea. Maybe he could float until daylight and then some yacht would see him. It was always possible. Conserve heat and energy—or should he expend energy, swim a little, to stay warm? That would burn calories, and soon he'd run out of whatever energy he still had.

It didn't matter. Nobody was going to find him. This was it.

You're dead, pal.

He didn't have a watch. How long had it been? Ten minutes, maybe? Half an hour? He looked up at the stars. They were clearer than earlier, when the sky had been hazier. Cold and distant.

He wished he could read—something by Maugham—or Nevil Shute. He'd meant to read more Nevil Shute after *The Chequer Board* and *Round the Bend* and *A Town Like Alice*—he loved Nevil Shute. Read until he fell asleep. Drift off into those worlds that had more shape, made more sense, than his own ever had.

Water filled his mouth. He spat it out, jolted and suddenly afraid, kicking and splashing, as if it had been some animal nipping at him. Was it a little wave or had he sunk under for a moment?

Jesus, was it going to be a sordid struggle, full of fear and pain? A tiny, meaningless struggle under the stars like some roadkill rabbit convulsively kicking by the side of the road long after the car that had run it over had disappeared?

Should he get it over with? Go down and suck water? How do you do that?

He wasn't hopeful—hope doesn't spring eternal, Pansy Clutterbuck knew better—but he wasn't ready to stop thinking. He still had a lot to think about.

That cunt, Fergus. She was bound to leave him eventually—but then what? Would she actually find someone else—someone she loved?

That was Luc's problem: he loved only Aegina. He'd known he'd never love anyone else, not like he loved her—well, he needn't worry about that now.

Luc thought of his mother. He saw her diving overboard again, and his heart swelled with admiration.

How would she take it? What would she do?

Then he realized what she would do.

Eleven

It was a three-minute drive in Fergus's Range Rover from the port to the Rocks. After jilling about offshore going nowhere for so many hours, it seemed too sudden an arrival.

Szabó, in the front passenger seat, got out first. He waited as Tony, *Dolphin*'s captain, and his haggard and sunburned guests, Fergus, Dominick, and Sarah all climbed out into the mid-morning heat. No one said anything. Szabó turned and led them solemnly through the gate like a defeated general.

From his corner table beside the bar, Cassian saw them trail in. He lowered the book he was reading, *The Rise and Fall of the Third Reich* by William Shirer. Hallo, he thought, here blows an ill wind. Szabó's eyes quickly found him.

"Good morning," Szabó said, his face and voice wooden. "Is Lulu here?"

"I'll see," said Cassian. He rose and crossed the patio and went into the house.

A moment later Lulu walked out to meet them. Cassian stood close behind her to one side, as if to take an elbow. She glanced over them briefly. "Where is Luc?" she said.

"I am sorry to say that we are not sure," said Szabó. "He was not on board the yacht this morning. We do not know when or how he left us. This is Captain Clement. He can tell you what is being done."

Tony was brisk. "I've notified the Salvamento Marítimo and they're making a search. I've given them accurate coordinates of our position, but the problem is we don't know when, therefore where exactly, Luc went overboard. We only know he wasn't aboard at breakfast. We did a search of the immediate area—"

"I don't understand," said Lulu. "You only noticed him gone this morning? Then what have you been doing out there since yesterday?"

"Our engine broke down," explained Tony. "We spent the night repairing it. We got a little breeze around midnight and have been tacking up toward the island ever since, and then got the engine going at about four this morning. We didn't miss Luc until around eight o'clock. I started a search back along our track, but he might have been anywhere—"

"Do you mean you've *left him out there?*"

Sarah began to sob.

"We looked this morning, Lulu," Dominick said. "But we'd no idea when he'd gone, you see. We were almost back here when we discovered Luc wasn't aboard."

Tony said, "The Salvamento Marítimo should be out there pretty soon."

"My dear lady—" Szabó's voice was brimful with solicitude and gravitas.

"Oh, *shut up*, ridiculous man!" said Lulu. She waved dismissively at Szabó and Tony. "Go away." She gripped Cassian's arm, looked at him and at Dominick. "I need you both to come with me, please." Lulu turned and walked quickly around the house toward the garage. Cassian and Dominick followed her.

"I reckon we need to make a report to the police," said Tony to the remainder of the group.

"Yes, of course," said Szabó, "but you are the captain, it is you who makes the report. I am now going to return to the yacht."

"Well, the police'll probably want everyone's name," said Tony. "I should get those from all of you."

"Right," said Fergus thoughtfully. "But I mean, it doesn't really have anything to do with us, though, does it? If we'd been on a ferryboat or something, we'd just be passengers, wouldn't we?"

"We're not a ferryboat," said Tony. "I shall need your names."

Lulu drove fast, dust whirling behind them along the road above the rocks. They were soon at the port. She drove the SEAT right down to the water and stopped abruptly at the edge of the pontoons where the fishing boats, motor boats, and smaller sailing yachts were moored. She jumped out of the car. Cassian and Dominick followed her as she walked quickly down the pontoon dock.

People were crawling over boats, lying in the sun on their decks, lifting aboard coolers, children, parents-in-law. Motorboats pulled away from the pontoons and grumbled toward the fuel dock.

"What do you want to do, Lulu?" said Cassian.

"We need a boat. Something that goes fast, obviously. Dominick, that's your department."

"Lulu, the coast guard, the Salvamentos—" he began.

"They're as pathetic as the Guardia Civil," Lulu snapped. "We can't leave it up to them. We've got to go get him ourselves. Nobody else will."

Dominick looked briefly at Cassian, who looked back in tacit confirmation.

"Right," said Dominick. While not the yachting sort, uninterested in boats, per se, he liked to rent speedboats to take girls water-skiing. He could tell fast boats from slow boats and he knew how to make them go. "Well, it's short notice—"

"Just find the boat, Dominick," said Lulu peremptorily. "Obviously one with someone on it. What about that one?" She stabbed a finger toward a squat, hulking concretion of scoured white fiberglass, wide in the back, sharp in front, the shape of an arrowhead, enlivened around the sooty exhaust holes in the stern by decals depicting orange flames.

A blond man and woman, both deeply bronzed, slim, and tautly muscled, sat in the sun in the cockpit close to the dock.

"Looks fast," said Dominick.

Lulu walked to the edge of the dock, three feet from the couple in the boat. "Do you speak English?" she asked them.

"Yes, of course," said the man, with a German accent. He smiled.

"My son has fallen off a boat out at sea. I'd like to hire your boat to go look for him."

"Oh," said the German. He and wife exchanged a look and then he looked back to Lulu. "I'm sorry. This is not possible for us. We are waiting for our friends. You should tell the police. They can help you—"

"I'll pay you five thousand pesetas an hour. Or whatever you want," said Lulu.

"We don't need your pesetas," said the German, his smile vanishing.

Dominick called from down the dock. "Come on!" He was waving at them. Lulu and Cassian ran toward him. As they approached, a deep, barely silenced roar overwhelmed every noise around them, and a cloud of blue smoke rose from the water and swirled around Dominick. A small wiry man in swimming trunks was already throwing dock lines off a long, narrow, gray, cigarette boat with the profile of an upturned blade of a scimitar. The roar had subsided into a rumbling that sounded as if it came from the inside of a large cave.

"This is Jorge," said Dominick. "He knows me. I've rented boats from Manuel, the man who owns this. He'll take us out."

"*Venga, venga,*" said Jorge, fully alive to the urgency of their task. He took Lulu's hand and led her across a flat space of fiberglass shell to the small, deep cockpit. Cassian followed her. Dominick threw off the dock lines and began crawling forward to the cockpit. Jorge touched a brace of throttles. A roar burst out of a deep cave somewhere beneath them again.

As they passed the end of the breakwater, Jorge's hands closed over the throttles again. He pushed them steadily all the way forward and the long boat leapt as if out of a gate. It seemed to fly over the sea as it planed at fifty knots away from the coast.

Lulu yelled something at Dominick.

"What?" Dominick tried to say, but his mouth filled with wind as he opened it.

Lulu clutched his arm for support and turned her face to him. *"Well done!"* she shouted into his ear.

Twelve

After dropping *Szabó and Tony* back at the port, Fergus drove out of town to C'an Cabrer. Naturally, with Gerald's resistance to installing a phone—ridiculous—he hadn't been able to call Aegina yet to tell her he was all right. Though, from the terrace, she or Gerald might have seen the yacht heading toward port earlier in the morning. She must have been awfully worried about him. Presumably they'd told little Charlie some story so he wouldn't fret. Poor little fellow.

Apart from the fuck on the foredeck engineered entirely by that randy little tart Mireille, it had been excruciatingly tedious. Absolutely the worst thing about it was simply not being able to get off when one wanted to. Fergus couldn't think of another situation where one couldn't say at some point, Thanks, I'm off now. An airplane flight, that was the only other experience he could think of where you couldn't get out of it, get a taxi, a train, plane, whatever was necessary at whatever price, and go home. Now he thoroughly understood Lulu's aversion to going out on boats. They might have been out there for fucking days.

He turned into the drive and engaged the Range Rover's four-wheel drive and shot up the hill fast—they'd hear him.

As the house came into view through the lemon trees, it occurred to him that Aegina might possibly be upset about Luc. They'd had some sort of a thing at some point. As far as he knew, they never saw each other now. Obviously they weren't close. A little shock perhaps, offset by the great relief of knowing that he, Fergus, was all right.

Yes, there they all were on the terrace, little Charlie too, waving at him as he powered up the last few yards. He tooted the horn, and turned into the flat parking area below the house and stopped.

"Hal-lo!" Fergus said breezily as he got out.

"Daddyyyyyy!" shouted Charlie.

"Hallo, little man! How are you?"

"Good!"

Up inside the house, Fergus lifted Charlie into the air as the boy raced to him.

"We were looking for you all night, Daddy!" Charlie was still full of the sense of freaky misadventure.

"I'm so *sorry*, my darling. The silly old boat broke down. We had to just sit there for hours. Jolly boring!"

"Thank God you're all right," Aegina said in a low emphatic voice. "We were worried."

"I'm sure you were."

"I went down to Rocks last night but no one knew anything. What happened?"

"Engine broke. Took them all night to fix it. Bloody boat can't sail a foot without it, apparently, at least not in the right direction."

"And everybody's okay?" asked Aegina.

"Luc went missing, somehow."

"What do you mean? Is he all right?"

"We don't know. He may not be all right, actually. He wasn't aboard when we got back."

Fergus was still holding Charlie. Aegina took him and lowered him until he stood on the floor. She looked at her father and said, "Charlie, take Grandpa into your room and show him some of your Legos."

"But I—"

"Charlie, I've got to do some pruning in the orchard," said Gerald. "Can you come and help me?"

"Yes, Grandpa."

Gerald took Charlie's hand and they left the house.

Aegina said, "Where is he, then?"

"Well, he went overboard, we think, at some point. We don't know when. We only know that he wasn't on board the boat this morning."

Yes, there it was: quite a shock, evidently. Her face suddenly very pale.

"You didn't find him?"

"Well, we looked for an hour or two, but the thing was, we'd no idea when he'd gone missing, so he could have been anywhere. The captain called the coast guard or somebody and—"

"Do you mean you *left* Luc *out there?*"

"Well, *I* didn't. It wasn't my call, darling. The captain thought—"

Aegina abruptly turned away from him and ran down the steps to her car. In a moment, she was hurtling down the drive at breakneck speed.

Obviously, quite a bit of a shock. He turned and went into the kitchen to see if there was anything to eat. He was famished.

L ater, when she returned from town, Aegina found Gerald in his toolshed. He was spraying an ancient pair of steel secateurs with WD-40.

Aegina stood in the doorway. Her eyes were shiny.

Gerald looked at her. "Were you able to find out anything?"

She shook her head. "There was a Guardia car at the yacht. The Salvamentos are looking for him. Nobody knows anything. What do you think, Papa? How long could someone stay afloat out there?"

"Well . . ." He wouldn't say what he knew. "It depends on things . . . the sea state—it's pretty calm now, and was last night—how strong the person is. A lot of chaps in the war floated about for quite a long time after their ships were torpedoed"—when they had something to hang on to—"anything's possible."

Gerald had known few such lucky men. He'd known many more who had drowned. Into his head now popped the long-ago page from *The*

Oxford Book of English Verse that always floated up before him when he heard of people drowning, or not drowning:

> *Obscurest night involved the sky,*
> *The Atlantic billows roared,*
> *When such a destined wretch as I,*
> *Washed headlong from on board,*
> *Of friends, of hope, of all bereft,*
> *His floating home for ever left.*

Cowper's "The Castaway." He didn't remember much of it—just the few lines he knew were the truest, if you were in the water:

> *He long survives, who lives an hour*
> *In ocean, self-upheld . . .*

Gerald put down his tools, wiped his hands, and hugged Aegina. He ran a callused hand over her head, down the thick hair. "Just have to wait and see."

She remained stiff and tight in his arms. They both knew there were no soothing words about untimely death.

Thirteen

I can't say . . . *exactly,*" Dominick said anxiously. He was looking at the distant land on the horizon, and then at the sea around him. It was all much of a muchness, the fucking sea, wasn't it? One bit of blue water just like the next—and then too it looked completely different in daylight. The green hills behind the coast that they couldn't have seen at night were now clearly visible. Unseen in the dark, with just the loom of coastal lights, the island had seemed farther away. "We were hereabouts . . . I think."

They'd been out on the cigarette boat for hours. They were sunburned. Their eyes hurt. The sea surface was still almost calm. The sun was high and dazzling and sprang harshly off the water in tiny broken facets. The boat was moving slowly, almost idling, its loud rumble no longer an exciting adrenaline rush but an excruciating, head-throbbing invitation to jump overboard, or scream, or go below into the tiny cabin and plunge one's head into a foam cushion but, of course, no one could do that.

"You were here," said Lulu with certainty. "I watched you floating off this way and kept seeing you all afternoon getting smaller and smaller. I couldn't understand why you weren't going anywhere or coming back."

The boat's track was meandering. Lulu turned and looked aft to Jorge at the wheel. He was dazed; he was losing the back-and-forth vectoring pattern Lulu had explained and insisted on. "*Oye!*" she called to him. "*Vamos a continuar lentamente adelante y atrás por aquí.*"

"*Sí, señora,*" answered Jorge. He turned the wheel, and the bow of the long boat swung away forty-five degrees.

"How are you doing, Lulu?" asked Cassian. He put a hand on Lulu's arm.

"I'm very angry at those people, that Hungarian and his stupid crew, for not being more careful. For leaving him here. What if they'd been halfway to Italy or somewhere? Who would have come out to look then? Of course, there's not a sign of the Salvamentos. No helicopters or airplanes. It's entirely up to us."

Cassian said gently, "Well, we'll do our best, Lulu. That's all we can do."

Dominick said: "It's been quite a while since he went into the water—"

"I know that!" Lulu said. "Don't you think I know that? Don't tell me what's obvious."

She looked over the wide, blue, relentlessly dull sea. No corners, no dips or holes or hills or different colors or identifying marks of any kind. Nowhere to stop and rest. Only a limitless blue opportunity to sink and die an unnatural, struggling death. She could hear the gentle, realistic entreaties in the tones of their voices, behind their words, to give up hope. She would not. Nobody else would find him. Nobody else would care. It was up to her. It was all up to her. It was the only way anything ever worked. You couldn't depend on anybody else. But she knew herself, so she knew what to do. Most people had no clue. They waited to see what would happen to them, and then they complained when it did.

"Luc will know that I'll come and look for him. So he'll hang on. So we're going to keep looking."

Dominick stopped himself from saying, Lulu, why would Luc think for a moment that you—you, mind you, darling, after diving off that fucking ship—would get into another boat and come out and look for him yourself?

She said, "Of course he'll know it!" so sharply that Dominick thought he must have spoken out loud.

Jorge and Dominick swapped looks. Jorge's said, *Pues, how much longer? I hate to say it, hombre, but it's . . .* and Dominick's said, *Never mind, just keep doing what she says.*

Sometime later, Lulu said, "Look, there he is." She pointed.

Two hundred yards away, they could all see a hand waving at them. They could even see right away that it was Luc.

"*Dios mío*," said Jorge. He spun the wheel, and the boat grumbled toward Luc like a suddenly energized mastiff. When it was close, Jorge turned it around and backed toward Luc as if into a parking space. Then he pushed the throttles ahead for a moment to all but stop the boat's drift, and pulled them back into neutral. He leapt onto the stern and lowered the hinged chromium ladder from the narrow diving platform close to the waterline. The stern drifted slowly to Luc. They all gathered on the platform. Jorge climbed down the ladder into the water. He reached out and took Luc's hand. He pulled him to the ladder.

"Hallo, Mum," said Luc. It came out as a croak. "Fancy seeing you here."

"*Tire, tire!*" Jorge said to those on the boat.

Cassian and Dominick took Luc's arms. Jorge put an arm around his waist. Luc's arms and legs still worked a bit. They pulled him up the ladder.

Lulu embraced him. Then she let him go. "You're all right now," she said.

They got him up across the rear deck into the cockpit, where he sat down on a molded, cushioned seat. His lips were cracked, his eyes were red.

"Got any water?" he croaked.

"*Sí, sí, sí,*" hissed Jorge. He hurried below into the boat's cabin.

"I don't believe it," said Dominick. He looked at all of them in amazement.

"How long have you been in the water?" Cassian asked him.

"I went in about midnight. What time is it?"

"Almost two. Fourteen hours."

Jorge reappeared with small bottles of Evian water. He pulled the top off one and handed it to Luc. Luc took it and drank slowly. He dribbled it onto his lips and licked them off. He poured it over his face.

"Fantastic," he said.

"It's just incredible. Luc, how did you stay afloat?" asked Dominick.

"Dunno," between dribbles of water. "Just hung about. I was on my back for a bit." More water, hardly seeming to swallow it, but letting it flow in and out of his mouth. "At first I was sure that was it. I knew they weren't coming back because they didn't see me go. But after a while, I knew you'd come out and look for me, Mum."

"Of course I did," said Lulu, almost indignantly. "What else would you expect?"

"Nothing." He smiled, then registered pain and put a hand to his cracked lips. "I realized that. So then, I just kind of hung around."

They took him below and wrapped him in towels.

At the wheel, Jorge turned the boat in a wide, slow sweep, pushed the throttles forward, and sped back toward the land at a gentle cruising speed. Now and then, he shook his head and looked around at the empty sea and mumbled: *"Increíble. Increíble."*

Fourteen

At the end of August, Aegina and Charlie and Fergus drove away in the Range Rover, back to London. Tourists and summer residents left the island. Villas were shuttered. Boats sailed away. Streets were quiet. Only the momentary insect whine of a moped interrupted the wind moving through the canopies of the pines that grew around houses all over Cala Marsopa.

There followed days in September that were just as hot and sunny as any day in August, the sea as blue and seductive as midsummer, the air as full of the electric tinnitus of cicadas in the noonday heat, but they were interspersed with brand-new days when cool winds blowing across the island from the Serra de Tramuntana along the north coast carried the trace of woodsmoke and the cool humidity of mountain clouds. The perceptible creep of autumn, the different air, and the aspect of the sea from C'an Cabrer, one day royal blue and faceted with sun, the next battleship gray and rolling like molten pewter, all these signs excited Gerald. Toward the end of September came cold, heavy drops of real rain, augurs of the equinoctial gales that would soon complete the change of season.

This was when Gerald most loved the island, when it resembled again the lush and peaceful backwater he had first come to know. He had lived in this same spot for thirty-five years, but much had altered around him; Aegina had grown up and gone away and brought Charlie back to the island. C'an Cabrer had metamorphosed (most noticeably in recent years with Aegina's money and ideas) from bare buildings that had housed goats and sheep into a rather nice Mediterranean home. And the seasons, as now, reliably made everything new again. He liked to remember Goethe's line: "A man can stand anything but a succession of ordinary days."

Once Aegina & co. had left and the house was quiet, Gerald attended to his tools. He laid his knives and scythes and saws and pruning gear out on the bench in his toolshed and set about sharpening and cleaning everything. He brought the Grundig shortwave radio from the house and listened to the BBC World Service as he worked. The eternally comforting rendition of "Lillibullero"—the recording by the Royal Marines band that he'd heard all through the war and almost daily through the years since—signaling the top of the hour followed by the GMT time tick, and the chimes of Big Ben. On Sunday mornings he listened to Alistair Cooke's *Letter from America*. On the third Sunday in September, Cooke spoke of the oak and maple leaves changing into their characteristic fall colors along the Merritt Parkway in Connecticut and how the parkway had been pushed into creation by the formidable Robert Moses, a city planner who had altered and stamped New York City as indelibly as Hausmann had made his mark on Paris. Then Cooke spoke of the current difficulty between the Reagan administration and the houses of Congress to instigate new public works on a scale vastly less ambitious than anything Moses had accomplished, and how such discussions were already contaminated by the Democrats' early jockeying to field an opponent to Ronald Reagan in the presidential election at the next turn of the leaves, just one year away. Gerald always enjoyed *Letter from America*; it might as well have been *Letter from Mars*, conjured up and dispatched by the urbanest of Englishmen, in the space of fifteen minutes. Then "Lillibullero" and Big Ben again.

On some days, Gerald could still be surprised to find himself living out the greater part of his life here. Not a location of classical antiquity—he'd never heard of Mallorca before finding it on his chart—though it did contain the same plants Homer put in the garden of Alcinous: the olive, the grapevine, pear, pomegranate, apple, and fig. Yet everything, including two wives and his daughter, had followed the chance putting into a convenient port—an accident of the wind—just as so much had been determined by capricious winds, or gods, in *The Odyssey*. But now he'd lived here for decades, most of that time alone, a kilometer from the woman who had kept him here, and hardly seen her in all that time. Twice, perhaps, in thirty-five years. Once on the street, sudden and electric; and again, a freak episode (though wasn't everything?) for a morning in a distant part of Spain. Gerald had been hollowed out by what had happened between them, but tissue had grown around the hollow and life had evolved out of that crook of accident. Not the one he'd imagined when he had first come here. But now . . . C'an Cabrer had become home, the genesis of his child. What he had made of his life.

On the last Monday in September, before Big Ben had chimed eight in the morning, Gerald heard heavy equipment through the lemon trees—not Gómez again, surely? The work had ceased after that first day, and Gómez had never reappeared. Fergus's visionary development had come a cropper, just as Gerald had hoped it might, notwithstanding his pecuniary need for its success. "Don't worry, no question of you returning the six grand," Fergus had assured him, "the deal's done, the money's absolutely yours to keep, old boy." "Who owns the land, then?" Gerald had asked him. "Well, my group right now. They'll probably offer it back to you for half price, then you can sell it again." Gerald knew he would never sell it again, he'd simply get by, with, for now, his windfall six thousand.

He didn't stop to turn off the radio. He loped downhill through the trees. He could hear more than one heavy-duty diesel revving in tandem with the dry snapping of tree limbs and the deeper muffled groaning of earth-moving efforts. Behind that, as Gerald got closer, rose the unsynchronous whine of many chain saws.

Gómez's work—fifty yards of bushwhacked trail cleared by the bulldozer and his man with a chain saw—had already been obliterated by the orange Komatsu backhoe and the Caterpillar wheel loader, each twice the size of Gómez's machine. Scattered across the hill above them were more men than Gerald could quickly count, clearing a highway-wide swath with chain saws, shovels, pickaxes. Gómez was not driving either machine.

"*Oiga!*" Gerald called up to the operator in the enclosed cab of the backhoe. The man couldn't hear him. He only noticed him when Gerald ran forward into his line of vision beside the plunging bucket. Then he burst out of the cab, yelled angrily at Gerald, waving him away. Gerald approached him.

"What are you doing?" he asked the operator.

"I'm doing my work! What are you doing? You crazy?"

"Do you work for Gómez?"

"Who? No. Jaime Serra. Now, keep away!" The backhoe operator climbed into his cab. Before he shut the door, Gerald yelled:

"Who is he? This Serra?"

The operator shouted, "Is a builder." Then he shut the door. He grabbed at the levers arrayed before his seat. The backhoe's bucket reared into the air and then plunged downward, its teeth burying in the earth beside the raw stump of a cedar. The bucket dug down, worrying at the root structure as if maddened. As Gerald watched, the stump trembled, then rose, torn out of the ground by the bucket. In quick, jerky movements, the bucket uprooted the stump and pushed it aside. Two men set upon it with chain saws, swiftly amputating the root tendrils. The backhoe's track jerked and the whole machine lunged forward.

Gerald watched the activity for a moment, the two great machines tearing at the earth, the men like ants carrying pieces away. They moved efficiently on up the hill.

He turned and hurried toward the house, already framing the irate letter to Fergus. It was clear they had sold the land. They were supposed to offer it back to him first.

Sold it to whom? And would they, whoever they were, build the same houses?

For once, Gerald wished he owned a telephone.

1970

The Phoenicians

One

I*t was cold* on the moonscape plain south of Mohammedia where they left the Atlantic coast and the hills of the Rif and headed inland on the two-lane N9. The Renault Quatrelle's heater wasn't working. Luc thought it was probably leaves in the air intake. He'd thought this for more than a year, but only in cold weather when he was in the car driving and unwilling to stop. He wished he'd thought of it before they left Paris, but then it didn't occur to him that it would be cold enough in Morocco in July to need a heater—the three previous nights in France and Spain had been warmer—and he didn't want to stop now either, in the middle of nowhere in the middle of the night. With its loose sliding windows and other misaligned openings, the Renault was as airtight as a tent. Luc was freezing, but Aegina, asleep in a blanket on the backseat, didn't seem to mind. She slept easily and deeply.

A sign hove into the dim yellow radius of the Renault's headlights: Arabic hieroglyphs, below them the words *Tensift–El Haouz*. Luc hoped it was a town. They'd eaten dinner west of Rabat, a good tagine royale with a bottle of Rif mountain rosé, though that was many hours ago and he was hungry again. And sleepy, but food would wake him up. Half an hour went by. No town. The landscape—what he could see of it beyond the headlights, loose in their housing, flickering like tallow candles in the cold filament pulse of starlight—stretched out as a barren sea floor littered with nubs of pale corals disappearing into the dark. The road was flat and straight, or nearly so, though the slight rises, dips, and contours gave Luc the sensation of driving through endless dark rooms that had no walls but constantly changed in size and shape.

"Aegina."

He'd said it several times, she realized. She came slowly up to the surface and opened her eyes. The car was slowing down. It was, she felt, far into the night. She lay still and watched the light on the inside of the car's roof and on Luc's face growing lighter as he peered ahead.

"Aegina—" He glanced back, his eyes met hers briefly, then he looked forward as the car came to a stop. He turned in his seat again and looked at her. "Hungry?"

She sat up. Ahead, a bus—one of those ancient smoking Moroccan buses that carried whole families and chickens on the roof—was stopped, engine running, headlights boring a tunnel through the smoky dark ahead.

Beside the bus, two men and a boy squatted at the edge of the road around a brazier filled with glowing coals over which they held sticks like short fishing rods. No dwelling or shed, no truck or animal. Just a gas lamp, the brazier, the men, and the boy beside the road in the middle of nowhere, and several of the bus's passengers taking the sticks rising from the coals. Aegina smelled burning meat.

"I'm famished," she said. "Is that food?"

"Smells like it."

"Where are we?"

"No idea," said Luc. "About halfway, I think, between the coast and Marrakech. Probably get there at midday. I might need to sleep for a couple of hours at some point."

"I'll drive after we eat."

They got out and walked toward the small oasis of food and light. The sticks were skewers of lamb. Aegina smelled rosemary and coriander. As they reached the brazier, one of the squatting men produced out of the dark a small, round, flat loaf of bread, sliced and open. He held up fingers: *Un? Deux? Trois?*

"*Deux, s'il vous plaît,*" said Aegina.

He picked two skewers off the brazier and laid them on the open bread. He threw salt and spices over the sizzling meat, closed the bread around it, and pulled out the bare skewers. Luc got three skewers in his bread.

"*Vingt-cinq dirham*," came the guttural French.

Luc paid with crushed dirty notes from his pocket.

The bus pulled away leaving the faces of the three Moroccans hovering above the brazier coals. A single red ember on the dark plain beneath the neon pinprick of stars.

Luc and Aegina walked back to the Renault and ate their Moroccan sandwiches, leaning against an engine-warmed front panel. Aegina tasted everything as it uncorked in her mouth and spritzed beneath her tongue: the hot meat, the salt, the spices, the warm fat and grease soaking into the bread.

"I've never tasted anything more delicious in my life," she said. She looked at the three figures huddled beside the brazier, and into the impenetrable circle of dark surrounding them, and back at Luc. "Luc—can you believe we're here?"

"More amazing," he said, chewing, looking at her, "is being here with you."

"Yes. It's fun." She smiled—her mouth full, cheeks distended, lips unable to close over teeth and sandwich—she smiled at him with more than fun. "I'll drive now. I'd like to."

He wanted to kiss her greasy lips, but while he was thinking if he should, Aegina got into the driver's seat. Luc got into the back. He lay down and pulled the blanket over his legs. Soon the car was swinging and lurching down the road.

"You're good?" Luc asked.

"Fantastic," said Aegina.

He looked up at the mass of her dark head, tilted slightly forward, alert, arms stretched forward to the wheel, the side of her face, jaw still working on the meal, in the glow of the faint headlights.

He felt happy.

Two

Since her mother's death in 1966, when Aegina was fourteen, she'd gone to boarding school in England. On long weekends and at the beginning and end of term, she stayed with her aunt Billie, Gerald's unmarried elder sister, who lived in a converted chicken coop, called the Chicken Coop, near the edge of Knole Park, in Sevenoaks, an hour by train south of London. It had been a lifesaving arrangement for all three of them, though Aegina and her father had missed each other badly during the first year while she was in England. But the arrangement had forced upon Billie—a woman of distinct tastes and habits with no wish to adapt them to the constraints of a relationship with a partner— a charge and imperative that stitched together her scattered life. Billie lived on a tiny income from translating French academic articles, supplemented with the infrequent sale of her Middle-earth–looking ceramic ware, grew fruit and vegetables in her garden, and foraged for what she didn't grow. She eschewed owning a motor car in favor of a retired Automobile Association BSA motorcycle and sidecar. After Aegina's arrival, the bike presented a problem only at the beginning and end of each school term when Aegina went to and from St. Hilary's School for Girls, eleven miles away, with her regulation trunk and tuck box. However, they managed the whole three-wheeled ferrying challenge with rope and careful cornering.

At the end of this summer term, her last at St. Hilary's, Aegina had spent the first few days of the holiday staying with her best school friend, Penny, in London. They went to parties, and Aegina shopped for clothes to take to Mallorca. Then she took the train down to Sevenoaks. Billie was waiting in front of the Railway and Bicycle when Aegina came out of the station.

"Did you have a nice time in town, pumpkin? How's Penny?"

"Great, thanks, Billie. Penny sends love." Aegina pulled on her helmet and goggles. In all weathers, and despite the flap and barrier of protective gear and clothing, their companionable side-by-side positions on the bike meant that they were used to conversing in an ordinary way, though at volume, on the road. As Billie tore up Mount Harry Road with a snorting rise to the note of the exhaust, Aegina shouted: "GUESS WHAT? I'M THINKING OF GOING TO MOROCCO, BILLIE."

"REALLY?" Billie shrilled.

"I FOUND A SHIRT AT THIS SHOP ON THE KING'S ROAD. IT'S FROM MARRAKECH IN MOROCCO. I'M SURE I COULD SELL MORE LIKE IT IN MALLORCA—AND IN LONDON TOO. I DON'T WANT TO MAKE ANY MORE SANDALS. SO I WANT TO GO BUY SOME SHIRTS. I NEED THE MONEY FOR ART SCHOOL. WHAT DO YOU THINK?"

"AN INTERESTING IDEA, PUMPKIN," Billie shouted noncommittally.

At home, Billie piled and fastened the long braid of her waist-length gray hair on the top of her head and laid out lunch—nettle soup, homemade granary bread, various cheeses, with their sine qua non accompaniment, Branston pickle, a Mackeson stout for herself, and a weak Rose's lime cordial for Aegina—while Aegina showed Billie the black Moroccan shirt she'd found at a shop called Granny Takes a Trip, on the King's Road, and talked about her plan.

Over the last few years, her father had been forced to sell two small parcels of his land, down on the road, to pay for Aegina's school fees and costs, but he didn't have enough money for her to go on to art school. She'd applied for a scholarship, but even if she got that, she was going to have to find some sort of job to make more money. During the previous few summers she'd made a little money selling small foot thongs she'd woven out of gold-colored hemp to some of the shops in Cala Marsopa, and to guests at the Rocks, but their novelty was done and she was tired of them. She had saved almost a hundred pounds. There were return flights to Morocco for under thirty pounds. If she went down and bought sixty or seventy shirts—the girl in the shop whose boyfriend had bought them in Marrakech thought they had cost no more than a pound each—and sold each for five pounds, she could clear over two hundred pounds; enough, perhaps, with a scholarship, to get through a year at art school. And if it worked out, perhaps she could do it again in the holidays next year.

"But you're not thinking of going alone, pumpkin?" said Billie.

"I knew you'd say that. I've been thinking of who I could ask. Trouble is, everybody's got plans. Do you think I should ask Dennis?"

Dennis was Aegina's nominal local boyfriend. He'd been a pupil at Sevenoaks School but had also just taken his A levels and would be going on to university. They'd met just before last Christmas at an end-of-term dance engagement organized by St. Hilary's and Sevenoaks School—neither school being coed—to get the boys and girls together to refine their social skills. Dennis had taken her out at the beginning and end of each term since they'd met. He was sweet, Dennis, and musical, sort of: he played the five-string banjo with some school friends in a bluegrass band called the Ide Hill Boys. Aegina had gone with him to watch them play at the Feathers in Tonbridge. Dennis stood in the back behind the fiddle and the mandolin players, his teeth bared with palpable effort, as if he were running behind them in a road race and trying to catch up. On the last few occasions they'd seen each other, they'd kissed. Aegina had liked that all right—she found Dennis attractive enough, tall and thin with curly black hair and amazingly long eyelashes—but she hadn't wanted to go any further. She'd realized she found him a little boring.

"Do you want to go with Dennis?" asked Billie.

"Not really. He'd be all right, but I think *I'd* be looking after *him*."

"Probably. But it's good to be seen with somebody. I'm pretty sure your father will feel the same. I mean, I have no idea what Morocco's like—do you? Is it safe?"

"I'm eighteen now, though. I can go where I want, can't I?"

"Well, you're just eighteen, but that's not the point if we're being sensible. Your father and I will both be worried about you, Aegina, and I think with good reason. Going off to Africa? I really think you've got to get somebody to go with you. It needn't be a boy. What about Penny?"

"She wanted to go, but they're all going to Scotland and she's signed up for a sort of Swallows and Amazons sailing course for half the summer." Aegina could feel the clammy hands of reason strangling her wonderful idea. She was determined to go but she didn't want to fight Billie over it. Beneath her loving support, Billie was obdurate when she believed she was right. Billie would win.

Billie had some of the same hesitation to disagree with Aegina. She had the authority but Aegina was very independent—a wild trait, Billie thought, from her mother—and she could be fiercely willful if she thought her cause was just.

Billie brought their drinks to the table and sat down and took a long draft of her Mackeson. "Well, it's a jolly good idea, pumpkin—very enterprising. Don't let it go. We just need to find someone to go with you. What about your friends in Paris?"

"I'm sure they're all going down to Mallorca."

"Well, so are you. But they might like a little trip beforehand. Why don't you ring a few of them after lunch?"

Three

On her second morning in Paris, Aegina dressed quickly, wrote a note for Florence, and left the house. She didn't like Passy. It was too quiet and bourgeois and Right Bank and full of money and made her feel poor and disenfranchised. She preferred the Left Bank, where she'd stayed with Sylvie on her earlier trips to Paris, but Sylvie and her family were already in Mallorca.

"*Maroc! Bien sûr je viens avec toi!*" Florence had shrieked down the phone two days ago. "*Viens immédiatement!*" But once Aegina had arrived in Paris, things were different. Florence's parents were adamant. Two girls alone in Morocco? *Mais vous êtes folles?* Absolutely not—unless one of their male friends would go with them.

Pas de problème, said Florence. She phoned Natalie and Aymar and François—all friends from summers in Cala Marsopa—and they met at the Café Flore. Aymar was leaving the next day for two weeks at Éric Tabarly's *école maritime* in Brittany. Skinny, floppy-haired François was going down to the Vaucluse to cycle the Mont Ventoux section of the Tour de France course, hoping for a place as a *domestique* on next year's La Vache Qui Rit team. Serge and Alain too were already in Mallorca.

Et quoi de Luc? Aegina asked with perfect nonchalance. On the train to Dover, on the ferry across the Channel, on the train again all the way to the Gare du Nord, she'd found herself thinking about Luc. She hadn't seen him for four years. Not since the horrible summer.

"Luc?" said Florence. She shrugged and looked around the table.

They hardly saw him anymore, even in Paris, she said. Sylvie thought he'd gone to New York. No, said Aymar, he'd seen Luc a few weeks ago: he thought he was going to Rome to work on a movie for the summer.

Don't worry, said Florence, we'll get someone. She couldn't go anyway until after the Doors concert; she'd already scored tickets for next week.

A egina took the Métro, full of early-morning commuters, to Cluny–La Sorbonne and walked up boul' Mich. She bought a croissant at a café on place Edmond-Rostand and walked into the Luxembourg Garden. Billie would be livid if she went on her own. Her father would be frightened, and full of silent rebuke that would find her in the middle of the Sahara. Besides, they were probably right: it would be better to go with someone.

She felt the threat of defeat. Always the horrible, stunting gap between dream and desire and practicality. If she didn't go to Morocco, what would she do? Go to Mallorca, try to sell more of her foot thongs, wait to hear from art schools—*wait, wait, wait.* Wait for life.

She finished her croissant, buttery, flaky, beside the *verger*, the little enclosed orchard bordering rue Auguste-Comte. Out on the street, through the railing, people in dark coats walked furiously by on their way to work, but on the sandy paths between the grass contours and around the ruminative busts of Baudelaire and Sainte-Beuve, it was quiet. She watched the uniformed gardeners snipping at the long espaliers of pear and apple trained to spread their limbs like set designs for a ballet.

She looked in her worn canvas handbag for the napkin on which Aymar had scribbled Luc's number. Actually, it was his father's apartment but Luc was still living there, Aymar said.

He was probably off somewhere, like they'd said, Rome or New York. She wondered if he'd even talk to her.

Out on rue d'Assas, she found a telephone. "*Allo, oui?*" She recognized his voice.

T*hey met* at the café Saint-Médard in the fifth, on the edge of the Quartier Latin, where the tumbling rue Mouffetard and other streets debouched like streams into the small-scale square Saint-Médard.

Luc had in fact gone to Rome. Through Fabio, a friend and classmate at the American University of Paris, he had an incredible summer job lined up, he'd thought, on a Fellini movie shooting at Cinecittà, but the job had fallen through. He'd stayed with Fabio at his parents' apartment in Prati, going out to the studio daily, hoping something else would turn up, but it hadn't and he'd felt in the way at the apartment and finally returned to Paris. He was going down to Mallorca at some point over the summer, but later. Lulu had had a building she called the barracks built beyond the pool in the back of the property—in the process, knocking down the toolshed in which Luc had made his home at the Rocks for the last ten years—and everything was still a mess. Luc could imagine his mother barking at workmen and at him too, roping him in somehow. He didn't want to go down until the middle of August at the earliest. He was at a loose end. And then Aegina had turned up with her Moroccan shirt caper.

He'd always felt this strange, not altogether pleasant, but intimate connection between them because their parents had briefly been each other's first spouse. As if he and Aegina were sort of step-siblings by a near miss. Luc had always liked Gerald, the little he'd seen of him; he was pleasant to Luc. His mother never spoke of Gerald, her first husband. It had been a very short marriage before her only slightly longer marriage to her second husband, Luc's father. When Luc had tried asking her about Gerald she would only say dismissively that it had been a *colossal* mistake, and nothing more. He wondered what Aegina knew.

She looked unbelievable. Dark as dark hair could be without being black, the olive Spanish complexion. Tight blue jeans, a loose red-embroidered blouse from Cochabamba. He hadn't seen her for years (he'd been away, she'd avoided him) since Cala Marsopa, the summer she was fourteen. How much of that did she remember? He remembered all of it.

"I don't have a lot of money," he said, hedging.

"Nor have I," said Aegina. "I've got enough for the shirts, and I want to stay in just the most incredibly cheap pensions. We could get student train fares. It shouldn't be too much."

She sounded so English now.

"Actually," Luc said, "we could take my car. It's pretty old, but it doesn't use much petrol."

"What, drive from here to Morocco? And back?"

"Yeah. I'm sure it would make it. And we could sleep in the car."

That image settled on both of them.

"I mean, we could take turns driving," Luc said. "One of us could always drive while the other slept. It would be cheap and we wouldn't have to stop."

"No, right. Yeah. That would be good."

"Yes. You know, I'm not . . ." How to say this, exactly? "I'm not suggesting anything. I have a, sort of, girlfriend."

"Oh, good!" said Aegina. "I have a boyfriend. That's all right, then."

"Great," said Luc.

They sipped their coffees.

"How come he couldn't come with you?" asked Luc.

"Oh, he's busy. He's a musician. He's got—he's playing music somewhere."

"Ah."

"Who's your girlfriend?"

"Oh, she's an actress. Well, she's just done a few things."

"Fantastic. What's her name?"

"Sophie. What's your boyfriend's name?"

Aegina raised her coffee cup and sipped. "Dennis," she said from behind the cup.

"What instrument does he play?"

"The banjo."

L uc's father took them both to dinner at his favorite restaurant, Chez René. He asked about the trip, the route, the plan. It sounded like a wonderful adventure, he said. He knew of a journalist in Tangier if they needed local help. He asked Aegina how she liked school in England. He didn't ask her about her father at all. Then he gave Luc five thousand francs in case of an emergency.

Four

L uc was driving again when the first light crept into the mirror, navy blue against the black ahead through the windshield. The light encircled the horizon until he could make out the silhouette of the Atlas Mountains ahead and to the left.

The road, a gray line trending away over the shallowly contoured plain like a road in a children's book, gained elevation as they approached Marrakech. They entered the Département de l'Haut Atlas and the land became greener, hillier, supporting small farms and vineyards, resembling the backcountry of Andalusia in southern Spain, which they had driven through before reaching Algeciras. They navigated with the Michelin map of Maroc. At a bookseller in the rue de l'Odéon, Luc had found a guidebook *Marrakech et Sa Région*, eight years old, published by Guides Pol; *édition 1962*; thirty-one pages and a town map. The center of the town, and its most undoubted attraction, assured the guide, was the great central square, the Djemaa El-Fna, one of the busiest market squares in Africa, around which spread the labyrinthine streets and alleys of the vast souk, the largest market in Morocco. Inside the medina, or old town, of convenient access to the Djemaa El-Fna and the souk, would be found a number of riads, large old houses converted to guest accommodations with rooms around a central courtyard.

They passed through the walls of the medina. The streets immediately grew narrow and crowded with people. Luc followed the few signs for the Djemaa El-Fna until the signs stopped and the serpentine streets, lined with wavy-sided, outward-leaning brown walls pocked with irregular doorways and small windows, twisted away into an unnavigable maze. He turned, trying to follow a fading sense of direction, and was soon lost.

"Look," said Aegina, who had the guidebook open on her knees. "A riad. Al Hamoun. It's in the book. Shall we try it?"

Ah, oui, bien sûr," said the shyly smiling, lightly bearded concierge/ maître d'hôtel.

He led them to the second floor, where a balcony landing wrapped around a courtyard garden and gurgling fountain. The room was spacious. White walls, the long narrow French window framed with a wide strip of royal blue. A large double bed with a thin mattress, sagging in the center but covered with inviting-looking clean white sheets. Aegina went to the window, opened it inward, and pushed out the louvered shutters. There was a view of an alley, rooftops, some green palms beyond a wall.

Aegina turned to Luc, grinning with excitement. "I don't think I want a nap now. I want to go explore."

After the press of narrow streets between contiguous ragged-walled cinnamon buildings, an inward-toppling adobe pueblo continuum, the Djemaa El-Fna opened before them like a stadium-sized flea market. Rows of stalls shaded with cloth; idle donkeys; carts, tables covered with beads, necklaces, gems, fossils, dates, pistachios; orange juice stalls; snake charmers; chained Barbary apes; dervish dancers with wrist cymbals; drummers; beriberied beggars; bent pretzel-twisted snot-streaming emaciated blind cripples extending palms to the high floating clouds; water sellers dressed like London's Beefeaters with brass cups and bulging, darkly sweating goatskins full of water.

Like a swarm of gnats, packs of feral boys in ragged shorts and T-shirts found them and tugged at their arms.

"Hippie! Hippie! What you want?"

"Come, hippie! Just for look!"

"You want kif?"

Cheerful grinning boys with glaucoma-clouded eyes, tooth-gapped scurvied gums, pellagra lesions.

"Berber bag!"

"Amber necklace! Silver!"

"I guide, I guide you, hippie!"

Shedding the boys, they found the entrance to the souk, a street that quickly devolved into a rutted path that led between buildings and descended in crooked tacks beneath sagging strips of canvas strung overhead, throwing bars of sun and shadow below. Stall-sized shops, filling narrow alleys between stuccoed walls lit with bare hanging bulbs, lined both sides of the path. Alleys of carpets and kilims, alleys of djellabas, leather bags, saddles, belts, alleys of sorbet-hued leather Berber slippers with pointed upturned toes. In almost every shop a transistor radio sat on a shelf or the floor, with a crude wire antenna snaking toward the low ceiling. Out blared Moroccan torch songs: ululant waves of female lamentation.

"Shirts!" said Aegina, grabbing Luc's arm.

They'd reached shirt alley. Shop after shop filled with shelves of soft cotton shirts, shirts on hangers in front of each little retail space. Several styles and colors were displayed but the predominant shirt was white, with a round collarless opening to mid-chest, fastened with multiple small thread buttons.

Aegina fingered a white shirt hanging out in the alley. The proprietor, a short, plump, clean-shaven man wearing a white djellaba and yellow slippers, quickly plucked the hanger from aloft and laid the shirt out across his arm before her.

"Best quality," he said, looking up from the shirt to Luc and Aegina with limpid eyes, as if proffering his firstborn for consideration of a scholarship at a music conservatory.

"That's what you're looking for, right?" said Luc. "It's like yours?"

"Sort of," she said. "But this material around the collar is really a piece of trim sewn around the edge—"

"Very fine," said the proprietor. "Best-quality stitching."

"Yes," said Aegina, smiling at the man. She pulled her black shirt out of her bag. "I want it like this, do you see? The fancywork, whatever it's called, round the collar, is embroidered into the shirt material, not stitched on afterward."

"Yes, yes, yes, I understand," said the proprietor, hanging the shirt up. "Come." He beckoned them to follow him with a quick repetitive downward motion of his hand. "Come, I show you."

"Do you have black shirts?" Aegina asked him.

A brief, tolerant exhalation. "Of course. Plenty black."

They followed him into the back of his shop, the small space overstuffed to the ceiling with piles of shirts. He pushed through mounds with practiced bursts of force. He rooted through cardboard boxes. He turned and held a black shirt up before Aegina. "Especial shirt," said the proprietor. With fat fingers he drew their attention to the embroidery around the collar, at the hem, the cuffs. "All make by hand. No machine. Especial. Very best quality. Much time."

"Right, that's more like it," said Aegina. "Do you see, Luc?"

"Yeah."

"I want to buy a hundred," Aegina said to the proprietor. "How much per shirt for one hundred?"

"One hundred shirt?" said the man. "You want one hundred?"

"Yes."

"This is fifty dirham shirt."

"Fifty dirham?" said Aegina, clearly surprised.

"Of course. One person working, by hand, very careful, all day. Sometime two day."

She looked at Luc. "That's about six pounds. I can't do that."

"For one hundred shirt I make best price, thirty dirham one shirt. Three thousand dirham, one hundred shirt," said the man.

"I'm sorry, it's just nowhere near what I can pay."

"How much you pay?"

"I'm looking for shirts for no more than ten dirham," said Aegina.

The man carefully folded and smoothed the valuable black shirt, gaz-ing down at it, smiling. "I have shirt for you for ten dirham." He placed the black shirt down and moved toward the front of his shop. He pulled another black shirt from a pile and held it up to Aegina. "Very fine qual-ity. One shirt, ten dirham. One hundred shirt, I make best price, six hun-dred dirham."

Aegina looked at the shirt, and glanced at Luc. "See, it's like the white shirt. All the trim is sewn on."

"But black thread," the proprietor noted sagely.

"Black thread?" said Luc.

"Of course." He pantomimed trying to rip the trim off, conveying that it was practically riveted to the shirt and would never come off. "Strong."

"Black thread is strong?"

"Stronger."

A t sunset they emerged from the souk, exhausted, disoriented, as if out of a circus tent, into the Djemaa El-Fna. They'd heard the sound of it inside the alleys as they drew closer, like the ocean approached through buffering dunes. The number of people in the square had increased many times since they had passed through it in the afternoon. Countless men were drumming and clashing cymbals to a single aggre-gate rhythm. Smoke from braziers, from oil drums, mixed with spice and savory particulate, hung in oily blue wreaths over the crowd. Crippled dogs loped in skewed diagonals.

"I've got to sit down," said Aegina.

"Are you hungry?"

"Yes."

"Me too."

They climbed steps to the second-story balcony of the Café des Pal-miers, which overlooked the square. The tables on the balcony, bathed in the light of sunset, were all taken.

A deep, heavily accented, recently familiar voice penetrated the ambient din, in English:

"The little Renault people."

A man, seated with a woman at one of the tables, stood up and drew out two empty chairs. "Eat with us."

He was in his mid-thirties, medium height bolstered by Spanish boots to not quite six feet, studiedly dressed as a Barbary pirate: beneath an embroidered blue Berber vest, his cream linen djellaba glowed pink in the crepuscular light, a tasseled leather satchel of genuine antiquity hung from a strap across his chest like a bandolier. Sheaves of long blond hair hung below the folds of the black cloth he had wound around his head into a turban. A red walrus mustache obliterated his mouth.

The woman smiled radiantly and stood to greet them. She was about ten years younger than the pirate, and taller in white espadrilles. She too wore a turban, more loosely wrapped than his, of rust-colored silk, the same color as her hair. A long plain white shirt hung over white dhoti trousers gathered at her slim ankles.

"Hello!" she said warmly, as they approached. She stood and embraced Aegina and kissed both her cheeks, and then did the same to Luc. Her hair, pungent and slick with some oil, flopped against his face and mouth.

They had drunk beer together on the ferry from Algeciras to Tangier. Rolf, a German, was shopping for Moroccan merchandise for his boutique in Munich. He'd introduced Minka as his Yugoslavian girlfriend. "I'm Montenegrin," she'd said in nearly accentless English. She looked more like a Pre-Raphaelite muse, with mahogany-red hair, large green eyes, and long milk-white, blue-veined neck. They spoke English, also the lingua franca between Rolf and Minka, who did not appear to speak much German.

When they'd returned to their cars on the ferry, Luc and Aegina to their stonewashed Renault, Rolf and Minka to his mud-flecked black Jaguar sedan, Rolf had admired their pluck at heading for the hinterland of Africa in their meringue of an automobile. "You are braver than me to drive this little Renault," he said, with a suggestion of mirth somewhere beneath his inscrutable mustache. Rolf's every statement sounded as if it were enunciated in unison with a Berlitz language course record.

Now he said, "So you make it in the little Renault?"

"Yeah, it was great," said Luc.

"Did you find any shirts yet?" asked Minka.

"No," said Aegina. "We just spent hours looking in the souk. We'll go back tomorrow. It wasn't encouraging."

"Of course," said Rolf. "They show you the tourist shirt with the tourist price. You have to find the manufacturer."

"That's what we'll try to do tomorrow," said Luc, irritated by Rolf's implication that they were witless rubes who would be taken for every dirham. Luc knew that already.

"It's incredible, Marrakech, no?" said Minka, tossing her hair and gleaming at them both. "Did you get here last night?"

"No, this morning," said Aegina.

"Look!" She waved a hand toward the balcony. "The Djemaa El-Fna! It's the most amazing scene, isn't it? Like a fairy tale."

"You drive all night?" said Rolf.

"Yes. One of us drove while the other slept," said Luc.

Rolf said: "We spend the night in Tétouan. We make it in four hours straight today. Now we got a fantastic room at the Mamounia. Winston Churchill's room. He always come here."

"I'm so glad we found you," said Minka, briefly touching Aegina's arm, and looking at Luc. "I missed you both after we left Tangier."

They ate couscous and tagine and dense unbleached Moroccan bread and drank two cold bottles of white Moroccan wine. After the sun dropped below the minareted backdrop, Rolf pulled a small wood and brass pipe from his satchel and lit it. A cloud of sweet smoke rose over the table and then flattened in the light breeze and drifted away.

"It's cool to smoke dope here?" asked Luc.

"I think it's cool, man," said Rolf. He passed the pipe to Luc, who took a drag and held it out to Aegina. She sucked gently and passed it to Minka.

"Is it Moroccan?" asked Luc.

"Of course. Kif from the Rif. I always buy from my dealer in Tétouan when we come through. It's fresh, just the tip of the leaves. No stalk."

They were all tired from the driving and soon fell into a sleepy, giggling stupor.

"We're going to go," said Luc, as Aegina's head fell onto his shoulder.

"Please come have dinner with us tomorrow at the Mamounia," said Minka.

T hey behaved as easily as step-siblings when they got back to their room, although they'd shared only the Renault until now.

Each went to the bathroom down the hall in turn. Aegina returned smelling of toothpaste and got into one side of the bed wearing a T-shirt and underpants. The light in the room was poor, and Luc turned it out. He undressed to his underwear and got in the other side of the bed. The dim ambient light of the nighttime street came through the shutter louvers.

"Luc?"

"Yes?"

"Thank you so much for coming with me."

"Oh, well . . ." He groped for a suitable reply, something neither too casual or enthusiastic, rather than tell her it was already the most exciting thing he'd ever done in his life. "It's fun."

Very tentatively, he put his hand on her shoulder. Her move now. Then he heard her breathing: she was asleep.

It took him longer.

Five

S hirts?" *said their concierge* the next morning after he'd asked them what they were looking for in the souk.

"Yes." Aegina opened her bag and pulled out the black shirt. She held it up. "I want to buy shirts like this one. Do you know where we can find them?"

His head lolled backward and he emitted a high quavering note, a private giggle of sorts. "How many shirts you want to buy?"

"Maybe a hundred. It depends on the price," said Aegina.

"One hundred shirts?"

"Yes."

The hotelier motioned with his hand for them to sit at the table by the fountain in the courtyard. "In twenty minutes I will have someone take you to the shirts. Sit, I bring you tea."

"We've been through the souk and seen most of the shirts there," said Aegina.

The hotelier waved a finger and clicked his tongue on the roof of his mouth. "Not souk. You will see."

Fifteen minutes later, he reappeared with a boy of about twelve. Not a scrofulous street urchin but healthy and clean, neatly dressed in blue shorts and a white short-sleeved shirt that looked like a school uniform. "This is Yusef. He is my son. He will take you to see shirts."

"Thank you so much," said Aegina.

Yusef, shy but full of the gravity of his mission, nodded at them. They followed him outside.

The boy led them along indistinguishable streets, away from the Djemaa El-Fna. He walked steadily ahead, looking over his shoulder occasionally to see that his charges were following him. When Luc and Aegina tried to come alongside him, he walked faster. They reached a district that was not the souk, not picturesque: trash-strewn lots filled with carts, oil drums, toppling shanty sheds cobbled together from scraps of wood, corrugated leftovers; carpenters' shops drifted up with sawdust; upholsterers' yards windblown with cotton flotsam; sheds housing iron-works, stacks of rusted plate.

"Luc," said Aegina, tugging at his sleeve, "it's the *polígono*." The Spanish word for the industrial park at the edge of large towns in Spain. As a child, Aegina had often gone with her father to the *polígono* at Manacor when Gerald took some broken piece of mechanical contrivance to be welded or bought paper bags full of nails or galvanized screws.

"I guess," said Luc. He'd not been much of a *polígono*-goer himself.

Yusef, following his nose as unerringly as a dog padding home to din-ner, led them through a warren of smaller alleys. They passed long sheds holding bolts of cloth, poles draped with dripping bundles of vegetable-dyed variegated yarn. Luc and Aegina trotted, almost stumbling with distraction, after him.

The boy slowed and stepped into the doorway of an unmarked shop-front. They followed him into a room that might once have been a small travel agency. Pinned to the walls were sunbleached TWA posters: one showing the Liberty Bell, *PHILADELPHIA* above, *FLY TWA* below; in another, cartoon saguaro cacti and golf clubs erupting out of a fat, cartoon cowboy boot, with the legend: *ARIZONA—FLY TWA*. Small models of Air France jets and Royal Air Maroc DC-3s sat on the room's single desk.

Yusef spoke with the woman wearing a head scarf and a long, primly buttoned gray robe, who sat behind the desk. She looked briefly at Luc and Aegina, then rose and went through a back door.

A man came into the room, followed by the woman. Luc thought he looked like Ernest Hemingway's younger brother. Large-framed, pepper-and-salt-bearded, his mostly white hair crew cut, his intelligent face set in repose. He and Yusef formally shook hands, and then the boy spoke to him. He shook hands with Luc, touching his hand to his breast afterward. He didn't shake Aegina's hand, though he nodded to her with courtly acknowledgment.

"*Je m'appelle Rachid,*" he said.

Luc and Aegina gave their names.

Rachid and Yusef spoke in Arabic for several minutes, Rachid glancing occasionally, with polite brevity, at Luc and Aegina. He questioned Yusef with close interest, the boy responding with assurances and a great deal of knowledgeable information, Rachid nodding at possibilities.

"What on earth can they be saying?" said Aegina quietly.

Rachid turned to them and said, "What is it that you are looking for?"

Aegina produced her shirt. Rachid took it and examined it closely, the cloth, the hems, the embroidery at the neck. He handed it back to her without expression. "Only black, you want?" he asked.

"I'd like to see white too."

"Come."

They followed him through the back door. On through a dark, hot storage room full of wrapped bundles and cardboard boxes. Through another door.

They emerged into a long shed, with a low corrugated roof, brightly lit by windows and white fluorescent tubes hanging from the ceiling beneath trails of electrical wire. About twenty people, from children to withered husks—they might have been four generations of an extended family—sat at tables and on the carpeted floor. Most were sewing. Four men were cutting cloth with heavy shears at long shiny tables. It was hot, fans blew at the ends of the room and at strategic points between.

"It is my factory," said Rachid. He led them to a pile of white shirts on a table and picked one up. It was similar to the shirts they had seen in the souk, with the trim sewn on in long strips, but the cloth was finer, and the work neater.

"It's very nice," said Aegina. "But I'm looking for shirts that are embroidered around the neck"—she held up her black shirt again— "like this."

"Of course," said Rachid. He led them to the other end of a shed where four middle-aged women, all wearing diving mask–sized bifocal glasses, sat on the floor. Their voluminous robes were indistinct from the piles of cushions they sat on, so that they appeared to be shapeless bean- bags with bespectacled faces atop swathed mounds of cloth. A large fan was blowing across the group, producing a soft breeze humid with rank body odor and a miasma of cheap perfumes. The women smiled shyly at Luc and Aegina. They smiled back. Rachid picked up a mauve garment and showed it to Aegina. It was a long shirt, the sleeves and hem finely embroidered with a dark purple thread. The work was intricate, in a pat- tern of tight interlocking complexity, like lace.

"This is beautiful," said Aegina.

Rachid raised his eyebrows and said simply, "Yes."

"Would you be able to do this around the neck of a shirt"—she held up her black shirt once more—"like this?"

"Yes," said Rachid. Then he added kindly: "But it will be better than this. Please, leave your shirt with me, and you will come back tomorrow."

Six

The Renault cruised for a parking spot among the sleek monochrome Peugeot, Citroën, and Mercedes sedans parked beneath silvery palms in the moonlight beside the Mamounia hotel.

"I don't see the Jag," said Luc. "Maybe they've forgotten."

"After three hours?"

They'd run into Rolf and Minka again in the souk, and Minka had again invited them for dinner at their hotel.

"I think they're a couple of space cadets, those two. Dressed for a Claude Lelouch movie."

They parked and walked toward the softly floodlit entrance to the hotel. The tall ochre façade loomed like a fort with embrasured parapets, surrounded by palms, a castle-sized Moorish entrance. Its elegance and remove from the busy souk and the blistered, ravaged, beautiful old town made it seem inauthentic, more like the Alhambra by Disney.

Aegina stopped near the entrance and faced Luc. "Do I look okay?"

Her dark hair, washed and glossy after she'd run olive-oiled fingers through it, was parted in the middle, broke on her shoulders and fell far down her back. Her large eyes and her teeth shone. She wore no bra and the oblique light from the hotel picked out her small breasts pushing against the fabric.

"Aegina, you look incredible."

"Thank you." She looked him over, his thin white cheesecloth shirt, Levi's. "You too."

"Too bad Dennis and Sophie aren't here to see us."

Aegina pinched his waist through his shirt.

We're going to make love tonight, he thought.

They walked inside.

Rolf and Minka were sitting at a table in the bar. Fingering their drinks, smoking, staring at remote extremities of the room, not talking. Minka saw them first; she smiled and waved. Rolf turned his head, fixed his eyes on Luc and Aegina as they approached and made a remark to Minka. She didn't seem to hear. She stood up and leaned forward to hug and kiss both as they reached the table.

"So glad you came to have dinner with us!" Minka said.

"You found the shirts, yeah?" Rolf said as they sat down.

"Possibly," said Aegina. "The man we met, a sort of shirt factory owner, is running up a model to show us tomorrow."

"What about the price?" asked Rolf.

"He wouldn't talk price until we see what he's making."

"*Ja, ja,* then he makes the strike. Once you like it, he gets you like this." Rolf suddenly grabbed air as if catching a fleeing chicken by the neck.

"And then, if you like it, what happens?" asked Minka.

"Well, if we can agree on a price, then we see what he can give us and how long it will take."

Rolf and Minka told them what they'd found for his boutique in Munich. Leather Berber satchels, Berber slippers, carpets, hookahs, shirts and vests; how much they paid, how it would be shipped back to Germany. At nine, a liveried waiter materialized to tell them that their table in the dining room was ready. They rose and followed him.

The dining room was full of beautiful and tanned Europeans weighted down with Moroccan accessories. They gazed languidly at the new arrivals.

A cadre of waiters pulled out their chairs and seated them.

"We didn't see your car out there," said Luc.

As if glad to be asked, Rolf said, "*Ja,* we rent an *auto à louer.* Some Peugeot piece of shit. Always I have the Jag serviced when I come to

Marrakech. It's a fucking long drive from Germany. There is a good mechanic here. I give him the car for a few days and he makes a racing tune."

"Must take a lot of petrol from Germany to here," said Luc.

"*Ja*, masses," said Rolf. "Many thousand of franc, peseta, dirham. Got to make it worthwhile." He talked about the many trips he'd made through Morocco, to the Rif and the Atlas Mountains, to Al Hoceima on the Mediterranean coast, and how everything was becoming ruined by hippie tourism. "You are coming to the tables after dinner?" he asked Luc.

"Oh!" Minka said with guttural disgust. "He likes the gambling. You will lose all your money!"

"No, I don't think so," said Luc.

"Always I have good luck," said Rolf. "It's because I am a Syltsman. A man from the island of Sylt."

"Oh no. Please," said Minka.

"*Ja, ich bin ein Syltsmann.*"

Minka said again: "Don't start with that."

"You don't like my beautiful song?" asked Rolf.

"What song?" said Aegina.

"No! Now he will sing it," said Minka, with real or mock unhappiness.

"*Ich bin ein Syltsmann,*" said Rolf. "The most successful pop song ever to come from the island of Sylt. You don't know it?"

Minka tried to clap her hand over Aegina's mouth. "I don't think so," said Aegina, pulling away, laughing.

"It was German second place for the Eurovision Song Contest in 1964. In Sylt I was number one for a year."

Minka looked at Luc and Aegina, her eyes rolling upward.

Rolf leaned back against the bloodred upholstered banquette. His eyes stared into the distance and he started to sing in a deep, melodic, unabashed voice, "*Ich bin ein Syltsmann, ich bin ein Syltsmann, mein Zuhause ist neben dem Meer . . .*"

Minka's head fell against Aegina's shoulder as if she'd been clubbed, her mouth dropped open. Aegina laughed, watching Rolf sing.

"*Mein Vater und sein Vater, und ihre Väter vor ihnen . . .*" Rolf's eyes closed. "*Waren Seeleute.*"

L uc was dizzy. They'd drunk too much wine and smoked more dope in the Mamounia's garden. He lay in bed in the dark, waiting for Aegina to return from the bathroom.

Last night she'd fallen asleep beside him. How far were they going to take this respectful almost-step-sibling business? Was she so relaxed with him because she'd bought completely into that Dennis–Sophie gambit, or was she in love with this Dennis the banjo player? Was she really as comfortable with him as a sister? Wasn't she attracted to him? She had been once—or maybe not: maybe that was more about what was going on with her that summer than anything to do with him. With anyone else, he'd have made a move already, but now he had an instinct that he should not rush it. This was Aegina—at last—not some fling. He decided he would let happen what would happen, however slowly.

Did people make money playing the banjo?

He must have fallen asleep. She was getting into bed. He felt a T-shirt next to him. He felt her warmth flooding beneath the single sheet that covered them. Aegina didn't wear scent, but she had a smell—he didn't know what it was or what it smelled like except that it was hers and he now lived to breathe it. He closed his eyes, angled his head, and inhaled as he had never inhaled before. There was a dampness to the musky warmth that poured off her . . .

I t was light through the louvers when she woke. Now she knew they were going to make love. She wanted to and she knew he did too. She'd fallen asleep the first night, and he'd fallen asleep last night. He was being so sweetly respectful. But he would wake and she would start it.

She could feel she was wet. She slipped out of bed, gliding silently to the door.

In the bathroom, she checked on things—it was approaching but not quite time for her period. No sign, just wet, ready for him. She peed. After she flushed the toilet, she splashed water from the small hand basin between her legs, cleaning and dabbing herself with toilet paper. Then she washed her face and rinsed her mouth.

When she got back to the room, Luc was dressed, standing at the window. The shutters were open and he was looking out into the street.

He turned to her. "Hi," he said. "How are you?"

"I'm good," said Aegina.

"I'll go downstairs and get some coffee, and you can take your time. How's that?"

"Lovely. Thanks."

Seven

Rachid showed them into a small room at the rear of the long sewing shed. It appeared unused, a formal setting, with cushions on the carpeted floor. A single faded color photograph in a frame hung on one wall: a swirling multitude of bearded men dressed in white robes filling an enormous square.

"Please, sit," said Rachid, indicating the cushions.

As Luc and Aegina sat down, a girl entered the room carrying a brass tray with a silver teapot and three small glasses. She placed the tray on the floor and left the room. Rachid sat down. "You will take tea?"

"Thank you," said Luc. He turned and smiled at Aegina.

Rachid poured, raising the teapot dramatically, eighteen inches up and down again, as the trajectory of thin steaming green liquid perfectly filled each small glass. He placed a glass in front of Luc and Aegina and then picked up his own. "Please," he said. He waited until they drank a sip of the hot, very sweet mint tea before he took a sip himself.

"Please, one moment," he said. He rose and left the room.

"Better drink it all up," Luc said to Aegina. "Manners." He liked the Moroccan mint tea that was served everywhere, but Aegina found it too sweet and undrinkable.

"And then he'll pour me more," she said.

Rachid came back into the room. He carried two shirts, one black, one white, on wire hangers. He separated them and laid them on cushions in front of Luc and Aegina and resumed his seat.

"Please. Look," said Rachid.

Aegina picked up the black one. The collar, hem, and sleeve edges were all minutely blanket-stitched, not bound with trim or appliqué. She looked closely at the embroidery around the neck, at the small buttons sewn down the opening at the chest. She held the shirt up before her. The black cotton was finely woven, light, silky, not quite transparent, and produced a velvetlike sheen where it broke into folds. The dense black-upon-black embroidery stood out like lace over a sheerer fabric.

"It's beautiful," Aegina said quietly. She turned big brown eyes on Luc. "Really beautiful. This is it."

"Do you like the white?" asked Rachid.

Aegina passed the black shirt to Luc and picked up the white one from the cushion in front of her. The cloth was as fine and lightweight as the other. The embroidery did not stand out as visibly as on the black shirt, but there was more of it. It imbued the shirt with a suggestion of a fine, muted brocade.

"This is exquisite," said Aegina, again in English. And then in French for Rachid: "These are very fine. Very beautiful."

He nodded his head. "It is what you are looking for?" he asked.

"Oh yes. But more beautiful than I had imagined."

"Good." Rachid smiled, and nodded. "What are you going to do with the shirts? They are not for you only to wear?"

"No, I want to sell them," said Aegina.

"This is what I thought," said Rachid. He lifted his glass and took a noisy, slurping sip that cooled the tea between glass and mouth. He put the glass down and licked his lips. "Where do you sell them?"

"In Spain. Perhaps London," said Aegina. "I know several people with small shops where they sell shirts and clothing for men and women. I will see if they will buy these shirts, or sell them for me. I'm not really sure."

"And you would like now to buy one hundred shirts?" said Rachid.

"That depends on the price. But these shirts—your shirts—are very beautiful. They are the best I've seen. Yes, I would like to buy one hundred if we can agree on a price."

"And if you sell all the shirts, one hundred shirts," said Rachid, "what will you do?"

"If I can sell them for a good price—enough, you know, to make it worth the trip here to Marrakech—then I'd like to come back and buy more from you. Perhaps many more."

Rachid nodded seriously. He lifted his glass and took another noisy sip of tea, licking his lips again. He looked across the room at the photograph on the wall. Then he looked at Aegina.

"For one hundred shirts I will sell to you for"—he lifted a hand and stuck up fingers one by one—"four dirham for each shirt. For one hundred shirts, four hundred dirham." He gazed at them both.

Aegina looked briefly at Luc, her face void of expression though he could see something like a klaxon going off in her eyes. Then she looked at the shirts, and then at Rachid. "Four dirham for each shirt?" she said.

"Yes," said Rachid. "Is very good price, I think you know. This price for one time. I would like to help you to make your business to sell my shirts in London. You will be able to sell for much more money, I think."

"I think so, yes," Aegina said carefully.

"If you return to Marrakech to buy more shirts"—he waggled his head slightly, once to each side—"I will ask you to pay a little more. Five or six dirham for each shirt. It will depend. But now, one time, you can take one hundred shirts to London for this price and see if you can make business."

Rachid raised his glass again and slurped noisily.

They walked away through the unpretty streets of the Moroccan *polígono* quickly, as if they'd been shoplifting.

"I can't believe it!" said Aegina. She alternately tugged at Luc's arm, skipped ahead, went back and pulled him on. "That's about *ten shillings* a shirt! And they're a *lot* nicer than the shirt I bought. I'm *sure* I can sell them. And make some money, and then come back and buy a lot more.

It's fantastic! Why is Rachid being so nice? We didn't even bargain with him."

"Maybe you should have."

"I think he went beyond that immediately. Do you remember the prices in the souk? This is really wholesale. He can't be making much at four dirham per shirt."

"Well, I'm sure he's not giving them to you at a loss, but obviously he's interested in what you're doing. He's investing in you."

"Yes. He is. Why?"

"Because it could open up a whole new market for him. Who knows where this could go? He looks at you and he sees what you're doing. He's a good businessman. He believes in you."

Aegina leapt skyward and whooped. She spun and wrapped her arms around Luc's neck and pulled herself close into him. She lifted her face and kissed him. Abruptly, she pulled away, grabbed his arm and pulled.

"Let's go have a wonderful lunch somewhere."

T*he little Renault people."*

Rolf's monotone rolled out of the lowering windows of a large sleek silver Peugeot that slowed and stopped in the middle of an intersection they were approaching on foot.

"Hi!" Minka waved out the passenger window. Then she jumped out of the car, heedless of the small vans, bicycles, pedestrians in the intersection. "Come and have lunch with us!" cried Minka. "We're going to have lunch by the sea! In such a beautiful place! You must come with us!"

Luc and Aegina looked at each other through their sunglasses. Aegina grinned. "Somewhere beautiful? Sure!"

Minka clutched their arms and pulled them toward the Peugeot.

Eight

R*olf drove* with the accelerator on the floor across the hazy beige plain. Luc sat in the passenger seat trying to ignore Minka's long legs folded up against the back of his seat as she rocked and laughed with Aegina.

"I thought Marrakech was a long way from the sea," he said.

"*Ja*, in a little Renault!" said Rolf. "No, man, we be there in an hour."

The speedometer needle quivered at 180 kph.

"But back in Marrakech by dinner, right?" said Luc. As the kilometers accrued, he began to feel abducted.

"Yes, but you have to see Essaouira beach," said Minka. "It's incredible. You won't believe it. It goes forever."

"Not like the little beaches in Mallorca," said Rolf. "I can't believe you guys like that place. It's fucked, no?"

"Depends where you go," said Luc.

"A guy on a yacht, a real sailor who came across the Atlantic, he was telling me the Azores are cool, man," said Rolf. "No one goes there, except the Portuguese. And not easy to get to, like Mallorca. You fly halfway to America. Too far for the package holiday tourist. The Med is fucking finished, man."

"The coast of Yugoslavia is still completely unspoiled," said Minka.

"Yugoslavia, Yugoslavia," said Rolf. "Everyone is going to Yugoslavia now. Or to Turkey, the new Greece. The moment you hear this, it's already too late. All those places are fucked, man."

Aegina's head lay on the seat back close to the fully opened window, the air blasting over her. She turned and said above the wind to the blond Teutonic head rising from the seat in front of her: "Half the tourists in Mallorca now are German."

"*Ja*, I know. Fuck all tourists, man, the Germans too," said Rolf. "They are everywhere now. I hope they don't come to the Azores. Probably they are going to Yugoslavia now. You will get tired of Mallorca too, man. There are better places."

"My mother was *mallorquina*," said Aegina. "My family was on that island before the Romans got there. Before there were any Germans anywhere."

"*Ja*, but you are an English girl. I can hear it. You are not *spanisch* or *mallorkisch*. I have a good ear for accents. And it's better for you this way, so you are not a peasant."

Abruptly, Aegina let loose a torrent of colloquial *mallorquí*, some of which Luc understood. As she spoke, Aegina was amazingly transformed into an authentic Mediterranean peasant woman, tossing her head and thrusting her chin toward Rolf.

"Yes, he's a pig, this Syltsman," said Minka, seriously.

I*t was an hour and a half*, almost midafternoon, before they reached the coast. Rolf turned left and drove past the beckoning rampart walls of Essaouira's ancient medina. Beach and ocean appeared on the right, stretching away to the south for miles. A vast, uncontoured expanse of shimmering heat, lovely as a runway, disappearing into haze. Squat, blockhouse hotels and apartment buildings sat across the road. After five minutes drive along the shore, Rolf slowed the car alongside the low, dust-blown vegetation and swung the Peugeot down a sandy track to a squat concrete building on the sand. A thatch-covered terrace looked out over the beach and the sea. Across a whitewashed wall, large, roughly painted blue letters spelled BONGO BAR.

"Bongo Bar," said Rolf, with immense satisfaction. "The best seafood in the whole of fucking Morocco, man. Fresh from the Atlantic."

He parked in a sandy, poorly defined parking space strewn with smaller cars. They got out, squinting in the intense glare of sand and sea.

Rolf stopped before the entrance to the bar, blocking the way. He faced the sea. "Only a Syltsman—or a Phoenician—can tell you why Essaouira is here since prehistoric times. The town is already old before the Roman Empire. Why do you think?"

"I give up," said Luc, who was thirsty.

"Protection, man," said Rolf. He swept his hands toward the long isthmus north of the town that ended in a stone quay projecting far into the Atlantic. "Here there are always the northerly winds. They make the big waves out there." He turned to face them and held up a finger. "Except when the winds come from the south." Like a conjuror, he moved his finger portentously across their line of sight, so they dutifully followed it, until it pointed to a small brown island almost a mile offshore. "And there is the island of Mogador, to stop the seas from the south. So you have the best anchorage and the oldest African town on the Atlantic coast."

"Fantastic," said Luc. "Let's get a drink." He took Aegina's arm and they walked past Rolf into the Bongo Bar.

At the table, Rolf continued his lecture: "The Phoenicians, man, they came here. The greatest traders in the world. They sail out of the Mediterranean three thousand years ago, they meet the wind in the north so they sail south to Essaouira. They stop right here. And they sail south again because they can't go back against the wind to the north. They sail on and on and on, until one day they look back and they see the sun coming up not on the left and moving to the right, what they see all their lives, but now it comes up on right, and north of where they are, and it moves to the left. Now they don't know where the fuck they are, man, so they keep going, always keeping the land in sight so they don't lose the world. And then the sun moves again from the left to the right, and they arrive back in Carthage, and they think they have gone around the world. But really they have gone all the way around Africa."

"They had the Suez Canal back then?" said Luc.

"Fuck, man, the Phoenicians didn't need the fucking Suez Canal."

A Moroccan approached their table. Rolf rose and embraced him. "Mustafa! *Mon vieux!*" he said. He seemed to cherish an epoch of warm memories. The man, middle-aged, short, dressed like a waiter in a white shirt and black trousers, allowed himself to be hugged and obligingly gave a tepid impression of acknowledging an acquaintanceship.

"*Poisson! Merluza, atún, calamars frites! Le meilleur!*" said Rolf.

Mustafa lifted his chin, made a noise with his tongue on the roof of his mouth. "*Poisson finis. Brochette d'agneau. Bifteck. Couscous.*"

"No fish?" said Rolf.

Mustafa made the noise with his tongue and his gaze slid away toward the back of the bar where a Moroccan man was whiningly berating a Moroccan woman. "*Brochette d'agneau, bifteck, couscous,*" he repeated, looking back at Rolf.

"Doesn't matter," Rolf told his companions. "It is the best in Essaouira." He looked across at a table of badly sunburned Dutch tourists who were yakking away in their strange tongue which sounded to Luc like fluent English spoken with a speech impediment, rendering utterances indecipherable except to those, like family members, long accustomed to making sense of them. "Good, *ja?*" said Rolf.

"*Ja, ja,*" said the Dutch table. "*Goed, goed.*"

A t five, as they stood up from the greasy ruin of their table, Rolf said, "So we stay for the night, okay? It's too late to drive back now."

"Absolutely not," said Aegina. "We've got to go back to Marrakech."

"Oh, man, it's too far. I don't want to drive. I need a siesta."

"No, Rolf!" said Minka. "I don't stay here in Essaouira for the night! Everything is in the room at the Mamounia. We must go back."

"Rolf," said Luc. "You said lunch, it was great, nice beach. But we're here on business. We have to get back. I'll be happy to drive."

"I drive, man."

They walked out to the big Peugeot and got in. Rolf drove north again toward the town. He slowed suddenly and turned into the fore-court of the Hotel Mogador, a new, unattractive building unenlivened by a repeating motif of ogee arches in the ground-floor doorways.

"I take a shit, man," said Rolf.

He stopped the car suddenly at a slant in front of the entrance and got out. Three squint-smiling bellboys of indeterminate age emerged from the cool shade of the lobby.

"*Caca,*" said Rolf, waving them away, walking into the hotel.

Twenty minutes later, Minka came back out to the car.

"I'm sorry. He's in a room. He's not coming out. He says he doesn't feel well. I'm really, really sorry! I don't want to be here."

Inside—a white Ali Baba ambience with daggers and fake Berber rifles on the walls—Luc asked the concierge when the next bus departed for Marrakech.

"*Six heures du matin.*"

"*C'est tout? Il n'y en a plus ce soir?*"

"*Ah, non.*" Smile, tone, and body language of well-exercised sympathy crossed with immutable fact. "There are only two buses per day for Marrakech. Six and fifteen hours."

A egina got up, staggering heavy-footed into the bathroom, and Luc came fully awake when he realized she was vomiting. Short barks, like powerful hiccups, soon followed by longer convulsions wrenched out of her like torture. They had both felt unwell when they went to bed and there had been only comforting cuddling.

Luc went into the bathroom and knelt behind her and put his hands lightly on her shoulders and her hips. Her long hair was falling around her face into the toilet bowl and he pulled it back as she retched with spasms that arched her back like a cat doing the same thing.

Then he stood quickly and lurched to the sink and spewed into it the viscous remains of the Bongo Bar lamb and couscous he'd eaten at lunch. Aegina, he now recalled, had only eaten salad.

When Luc finished, he ran the taps. Aegina lay curled up on the tile floor, her T-shirt soaked, face pale and glistening with sweat, eyes closed.

"Let me get you back into bed," Luc said, trying to help her up.

"No," she breathed. Then she quickly rose and pulled down her underpants, sat on the toilet and leaned forward across her knees and a gusher of liquid burst into the bowl beneath her.

"Sweetheart," said Luc. He knelt beside her. She still lay with her forehead on her forearms crossed over her knees. Luc put his arm across her back.

"You too?" she said hoarsely.

"Yeah. But I had the lamb."

"You had salad too. It was the salad."

"Can you get up from there now?"

"No."

Luc's bowels flopped inside him and his anus puckered with a burning sensation. He moved in a quick crouch to the bath and sat on his thighs with his bum over the edge and shat explosively into the tub. When he felt he could move, he reached for the tap and turned on the cold water. He threw cupped palms of cool water between his buttocks, and then he sloshed the water around the tub to clean it.

"Do you want to come back to bed?" he asked Aegina, who lay limply across her knees.

"No," she said. She reached for the toilet paper, flushed the toilet, and then lay down on the floor again.

Luc put a towel down beside her. "Lie on this."

He tried to move her onto the towel, but she said, "I can't." He rinsed a smaller towel under the cold tap in the sink and wrung it out. He sat down beside Aegina and wiped the clammy sweat off her body and then picked up the larger towel and draped it over her. He ran his hand back and forth over the towel.

"Aegina," Luc said.

"Unh . . ."

"I love you so much."

"Oh, sure," she said, her voice small and coming from beneath her. "Especially like this."

"Like this most of all."

Her hand moved across the wet tile and found Luc's foot and closed around it. Her fingers were cold. Luc put his hand over hers.

Nine

H e opened his eyes. The sun was up on the other side of the shutters. At some point in the night they had made it back to the bed and remained there. He looked at Aegina. Her dark hair across her face, olive complexion turned sallow. She appeared comatose. He lay down. He listened to Aegina's slow, deep breathing.

He couldn't sleep. He got up and went into the bathroom and closed the door. He rinsed in the shower. She was still asleep when he came back into the room. He pulled on his jeans, a T-shirt, sneakers. He went to the door, looked back at Aegina, and left the room.

S he was walking in the hard sand close to the water, djellaba billowing around her. She waved. They walked toward each other.

Minka hugged him closely as if meeting an old friend. "Where is Aegina? She is sick too?" she asked.

"Yes. Both of us. You?"

"Not me, thank God, but Rolf, aieeccch, both ends all night. Disgusting. I couldn't breathe. I had to get out. You are okay now?"

"Better anyway."

"Aegina?"

"She's sleeping."

"I'm so sorry! Rolf is a pig, making us all stay here. But he did get very sick." Minka turned to the clean sea. "It's beautiful, no? The edge of Africa."

The sea was bright beneath the sun, solid blue north and south.

"The sea is, yes," said Luc. "The beach is too big."

"Oh, I love it. But it's amazing, there is nobody on the beach now. Maybe they all got sick." She laughed, arching backward. "Shall we swim?"

"You go ahead. I don't have a towel or anything."

"Doesn't matter!"

"I just took a shower."

"Oh, come on, it's perfect. You will dry quickly. Look at the sea. Come on!" She began pulling him toward the water.

"No, you go. I'll just sit here."

"Och! No adventure!"

She pulled off her djellaba and threw it over his head. She was naked, of course. She ran into the waves. He watched her diving in and out of the waves like a seal. She ran back out of the water, ran fast toward him, and hugged him tightly—"Please, I'm cold!"—until he was completely wet.

"Now you have to come in!" She pulled at his shirt, lifting it up. Then she pulled at his Levi's.

"Okay, okay! I'll do it," Luc said. But she didn't stop, she was pulling at his jeans, and he couldn't help getting most of an erection. Then she pulled him, running into the sea.

In the water, she swam away from him into the sun in an effortless freestyle stroke. He followed slowly. She lay on her back and floated. She rose and fell and undulated like a long supple frond on the slight swell as the water rolled over her strawberry nipples and the sun caught the thatch of copper curls below her belly.

Luc got out first. He walked up to the dry sand and sat down hugging his knees.

Minka walked slowly out of the waves. She threw her head back, hair flying up scattering bright beads of water in the light. She smiled at him as she approached. "You are so slim. Rolf is like a bear. It looks good, the way you are." She lay down full-length on the sand next to him. She stretched, throwing her arms above her head, taking deep breaths. "My God, after that hotel room."

The water beaded across her body. Her skin had the lightest blush of pearl beneath the yellow sand that clung to her toes and thighs. Her nipples puckered and stood up. A wide but not dense swath of dark wet ringlets clustered below her hollow stomach, which rose and fell with her breathing.

She opened an eye and squinted up at him. "Oh, lie down in the sun. It feels so good."

He stretched out, keeping one knee, the nearest to her, raised. He closed his eyes.

"Feels good, no?" said Minka.

"Yes," said Luc, feeling the salt water evaporate with a sensation of tightening across his skin.

Minka lifted her head, twisted her shoulders into him, stretched her legs away, and laid her head, heavy, already warm through the damp hair, on his stomach. She turned her head until her cheek lay on the warm skin of his belly and she looked up into his face.

She rolled on her side until her other cheek lay on his belly. She put a cool hand around his cock which was straining from his groin like a dachshund on a leash.

"No, don't," he said. But remained still.

Minka raised her head and lowered it over him. Bands of hot and cool.

"Please stop," said Luc. He looked up at the small clouds passing slowly high above them. They had formed over the ocean and were gliding now into Africa. How insignificant he and Minka were, tiny, fretful, heedless animals far below. He raised his hand to pull her away but his hand found her waist and then moved up over the rise of her hip and across her buttock. "Stop," he said quietly. "Stop . . ."

She paused. "You want me to stop?"

"I love Aegina," he said to the clouds.

"Of course you do," said Minka. "She's adorable. I love her too." She sat up, looked around briefly, straddled Luc, and lowered herself onto him.

Ten

The cow was ambling slowly across the right lane as the Renault barreled around the corner.

"Jesus!" Luc pulled hard away from the cow, into the left lane.

The cow saw the car, paused, registered alarm with a toss of its head, and broke into a gallop continuing the way it had been going, into the left lane.

"Shit!" Luc's arms crossed as he swerved back for the right lane being vacated by the cow. But the cow, seeing the car change course a second time, abruptly made a hoof-skidding turn, bolted back in the direction of where it had once felt safe, and the Renault's left headlight and front fender impaled themselves on the animal's long right horn. The car shuddered to a stop.

"*Fuck!*" Luc shouted—because it expressed everything he was feeling up to that moment—and then also because the wheel had instantly become rigid in his hands in a way that told him they wouldn't be driving away from this. He looked over at Aegina, but she was already climbing out the door crying, "*Oh my God, my God!* The poor *thing!*"

"Don't touch it!" Luc yelled at her, getting out of the car, moving to intercept her. "It might hurt you."

"No, she won't. Poor thing!"

"It's a he—he's got a horn."

"Look!" She pointed fiercely.

He saw the udder, swaying heavily beneath the animal. The cow stood in the middle of the road, quivering, head down, a little above grazing height. The right horn had sheared off neatly at its base above the cow's brow. Not a drop of blood. Apparently the animal was no more than dazed.

Luc looked at the Renault. The front fender was smashed inward and down over the left front wheel. Yellow headlight glass glinted in the road.

A shout—a single-syllable wordless utterance, not outrage or reprimand, nothing more than an exclamation of sadness—came from the side of the road. A man with a straw hat, who looked like a scarecrow, was walking toward them. Other cows stood off the road near him. He kept his eyes on the cow as he came toward them.

"*Excusez-moi, monsieur. . . .*" said Luc. "There was nothing I could do. The cow was in the middle of the road. I tried to avoid it. . . ."

The cowherd muttered pained, wordless noises—"*Ehhhh . . . ohhhh . . .*"—that sounded sadder and sadder. Not a hint of recrimination aimed at the car or its occupants. Only sadness. "*Ohh-ohh . . . ehhh-eh-eh . . .*"

The cow ambled away, back toward the right side of the road where it had come from, toward its brethren creatures, who stood looking vacantly at the scene of the accident.

The cowherd looked at the Renault. He stepped toward it and pulled at something—the cow's horn, its base protruding from the crumpled housing of the headlight. He pulled it out—now an uncertain keratinous artifact, somewhere between a tusk and a small antler—and looked at it mournfully.

"I'm sorry," Luc began again. The man, no bigger than a boy, of rawhide-wizened middle age, looked up at him, looked down at the horn, turned, and walked slowly after the cow.

"Are you all right?" Luc asked Aegina.

"Yes," she said, "but that poor thing . . ."

"Well, the poor cow's already eating. Look." The creature, with its lone asymmetrical horn, had reached a small dusty bush at the side of the road and its lips were curling around what passed for small leaves. Luc turned back to the car. "The cow's fine. We're the ones who're completely fucked."

He approached the car and tentatively tried to pull the crumpled fender up off the wheel, to little effect. He sat in the driver's seat and tried to turn the wheel. "The wheel won't turn."

"Shall we try to get it off the road?" said Aegina.

Luc tried the engine, which started immediately. With the front wheels locked, the car could only move in a circle, but aiming off the road. It made a grinding noise from somewhere near the front axle. Luc kept going until the car sat on the dirt shoulder, and then turned off the engine. "That's it."

"Don't you think we can fix it?"

"Well, even if we could, it would probably cost more than the car's worth. And take forever. We've got to leave it."

"Right," said Aegina. She opened the side rear door and pulled out the large suitcase full of shirts and her own and Luc's small duffel bags. "Do you think we should hitchhike?"

"However we do it, I think we should get out of here as soon as possible. Somebody might get upset about the cow."

"It wasn't your fault."

"We should stop the first bus going in either direction. If it's going north it'll go to Tangier, or to Rabat or Casablanca or somewhere where we can get a bus to Tangier. If it's going south, we'll take it back to Marrakech and get the next Tangier bus or train. Okay?"

"That will be expensive."

"I've got money."

They'd come straight from Essaouira, collected the shirts, packed, and left Marrakech all in one day. They'd slept, tired, chastely, in the car while parked at a petrol station.

Aegina looked out across the dusty plain where the cows and their herder were already some distance away. "Poor cow."

"Hey, fuck the cow. And that fucking Moroccan cowboy who let it wander into the road. It's not even hurt, it'll probably grow another horn. We're the ones stuck in the middle of nowhere with a hundred shirts, and very possibly a tribe of angry Bedouins about to appear out of the desert wanting payback."

"Luc, I'm sorry about your car, but at least we're not hurt, and it really isn't your fault. I know it's all really unfortunate. But you've been in a bad mood ever since we left Essaouira, and this isn't helping you, I know."

"Can we stop talking about them, please?"

"We're not talking about them," she said. "I'm not anyway."

They had parted from Rolf and Minka in Marrakech on strained terms. Aegina had decided they weren't really a couple but were partnered in some more mysterious alliance.

She sat down on the large suitcase and took off her sunglasses, cleaned them on her cotton shirt, and put them back on. She looked studiously up and down the road.

North and south, the ends of the road dissolved into liquid distance. Cars materialized as indistinct nuggets of boiling atoms that soon resolved into dark approximate shapes and grew bigger—Luc thought of Omar Sharif's indelible first appearance in *Lawrence of Arabia*. But they came on like low-flying aircraft, the Moroccans sealed inside staring bug-eyed at the couple with the big suitcase beside the road as if they were Martians, before streaking past in a Doppler wavefront, leaving Luc and Aegina in a wake of wind and dust and filling quiet.

Yes, he was in a bad mood. He wanted to get out of Morocco, back to Spain, where he would feel steadier, where maybe they would be like they had been before Essaouira. He'd been speeding toward Spain and feeling better with every kilometer put behind them until they'd hit the cow.

Another molten speck emerged from the mirage across the road to the south. It grew clearer, larger, then low and sleek, and shiny black.

"Fuck," said Luc almost inaudibly. "I don't believe it."

Aegina stood up. She looked from the approaching car to Luc. "I don't want to go with them."

"Believe me, I don't want to either, but they *are* going in the right direction. And I really think we should get out of here."

The car approached, slowed, pulled off the road and stopped.

"Fuck, man. What happen to the little Renault?" said Rolf through Minka's open window. He and Minka got out, looking from the car to Luc and Aegina. "Are you all right?" Minka asked them.

"We hit a cow," said Aegina. She pointed at the small shambling herd now some distance away. "One of those."

Rolf and Minka looked from the cows to the crumpled car. "*Ja*, man, you are fucked. It is the end of the road for the little Renault."

He turned to them. "Well, we give you a ride, then. You're going still to Algeciras, *ja?*"

"Thanks, but you don't have room," said Aegina.

They had returned the Peugeot. The newly tuned and cleaned Jaguar Mark X carried two suitcases on its roof rack, and the interior looked filled with bundles. It rode low to the ground.

"No, man. We put your big case on the roof with ours. We get you in, with all your shirts."

R*olf drove more slowly* than he had in the Peugeot on the way to and from Essaouira, picking his way carefully and defensively through small towns. The Jaguar seemed to feel the weight of its new passengers.

Luc pretended to fall asleep in the backseat, while, beside him, Aegina chattered with Minka. Then he really fell asleep.

A*t Tangier*, Rolf drove the Jag onto the ferry, directed by the car deck crew. They got out and climbed the stairs up to the passenger decks.

"We see you in the bar, yes?" said Minka.

Aegina didn't answer. She pushed through the door leading onto the deck.

Luc followed her. She walked quickly ahead, focused on where she was going, as if she couldn't wait to get outside, as if unaware that he was behind her. At the edge of the deck, she stopped, placed her hands before her on the rail as if bracing for a wave, and looked out at the city beyond the port.

"Are you okay?" said Luc, leaning on the rail beside her.

She was breathing deeply. She didn't answer.

After a moment, he said, "What's the matter?"

She turned and aimed her suddenly inscrutable sunglasses at Luc. "So when did you fuck her? While I was passed out in our room?"

"What?"

"When did you fuck her?"

"What are you talking about?"

"I can tell."

"You can tell what?" Now even he could tell.

"She didn't look at you the entire time we were in the car. You both ignored each other—*I can just tell! I know!*"

He opened his mouth several times like a fish in the air. Aegina turned and walked away down the deck.

Luc walked after her. "Aegina—"

She turned and shrieked at him, *"Stay away from me!"*

People along the deck turned to look at them. Aegina spun and ran down the deck. Luc paused, then walked slowly after her. But he couldn't find her.

R*olf and Minka* reached the car first. Luc, who had been looking all over the ship without finding Aegina, came down the stairway with other passengers returning to their vehicles and saw the odd group beside the Jaguar. Aegina, sullen, stood away from the car, three car-deck crewmen standing around her, effectively trapping her, one of them straddling the large suitcase full of shirts, which had been removed from the car's roof rack. Luc heard the crewmen as he approached: "Is this your suitcase?"

"It's okay," said Rolf. He appeared uncharacteristically alert, focusing his attention on the three crewmen. "She is with us. It's my car."

In fluent Spanish, Luc said to the three crewmen, "What's the problem?"

"*El problema es que los pasajeros—*"

Aegina interrupted, in English to Luc: "I came down to get my suitcase. I'm getting off by myself." She repeated this in fast, angry Spanish to the crewmen.

One of the crewmen, looking implacably at Luc, said, "Passengers who boarded the ferry in cars must disembark in the cars, with all their luggage in the cars. She cannot walk off the ferry."

"*Bueno,*" said Rolf to the crewmen. He turned to Luc and Aegina. "We all get back in the fucking car now. We don't fuck around with these guys anymore." He unlocked the car, then grabbed the suitcase and threw it up onto the roof rack. "Get in the fucking car now," he said quietly. He pulled the rubber spider lashing over the suitcase, anchoring it atop the other cases.

"Aegina—" said Luc.

Silently she pulled open a rear door and got into the car.

"*Todo bien?*" said the crewman who had been their spokesman.

"*Todo* completely *bien*, man, okay, okay," said Rolf.

The crewmen walked away.

When they were all in the car, and Rolf had started the engine, Aegina said: "I'm getting out as soon as we're ashore."

Rolf—a brand-new, electrified Rolf—turned around and looked at her. "You don't get out of the car until we are through the port and into Algeciras. Then, don't worry, I throw you and your fucking bag, all of you, out of my car—"

"Hey—" began Luc.

"Fuck you, man." Rolf thrust an index finger into Luc's face. Then at Aegina. "You be still. You sit and you be quiet."

For the first time in hours, Luc glanced at Minka. She was looking ahead; her face was gray.

Rolf turned and looked forward and pulled the gear into drive. The Jaguar followed other cars off the boat into the line that moved fitfully toward passport control and customs.

T wenty *minutes later,* they stood mutely around the Jaguar as the *aduana* agents removed the door panels and pulled out the first plastic-wrapped bundles of kif.

"Oh, *Scheisse,* man," Rolf said to a customs agent. "I had the car serviced in Marrakech. Fuck, I don't believe it. Look what my *mecánico* has done to me. I don't know anything about this."

Abruptly, Minka bent over and began to vomit onto the dusty tarmac. She collapsed onto her hands and knees. Spasms wracked her. Long viscous threads hung from her mouth; she tried to wipe them away and smeared vomit across her face. She began to weep.

Luc glanced at Aegina but she wouldn't meet his eyes. He looked at Rolf, who was regarding Minka with disgust and anger.

The agents stood back, as if in fear of being spattered, and watched her.

Luc walked to Minka and kneeled beside her. He tore the tail off his blue-and-white-check cheesecloth shirt and began to wipe her mouth. He couldn't help it: he put his hand on her shoulder.

Eleven

G erald *didn't spend* a moment thinking about going. He put down the telegram and thought only of what he might need to bring.

He got out an ancient blue sail bag. He rolled up and placed at the bottom of the bag a change of clothes, underwear. Then his blazer, a good shirt, and tie.

What else? In his old canvas rucksack he placed the deed and description of the property known as C'an Cabrer. His passport with Spanish residency stamp. Aegina's birth certificate. Some photographs.

Some impulse made him grab two bottles of his olive oil from the larder.

Gerald took the sail bag and rucksack down to his car, a tinny 1955 Simca Aronde Commerciale station wagon.

He drove into town and stopped in front of the Banco Santander. Inside, to the astonishment of Barbara, the teller, he withdrew twenty thousand pesetas in cash, almost all he had in his account. Barbara looked at him in alarm. Gray-blond hair windblown about his head, blue eyes dancing anxiously in his tanned face, glancing at his watch. He appeared to be in flight.

"*¿Qué pasa, Señor Rutledge?*"

"*Todo está bien,*" said Gerald, smiling tightly, his callused hands stuffing the bundles of notes into his rucksack. "*Bien, bien.*"

"*¿Seguro?*"

"*Seguro. Gracias, Barbara.*"

He drove across the island to Palma. At 6:45 p.m. a *marinero* waved the Simca aboard the Alicante ferry. The ferry pulled away from the dock at eight p.m. It would reach Alicante at six the next morning. He would get to Algeciras sometime tomorrow.

Gerald watched as the huge stained-glass *ensaïmada* of a window in La Seu Cathedral, lit from within, bulking over the city in the old town, grew smaller and yellower and older as the ship rounded the breakwater and steamed, rolling and shuddering in periodic rhythm, out into the dusk over the purpling sea.

He was at sea again. Not often in the last twenty-two years. But here he was and he let himself look down at the water frothing past the steel hull of the ferry. He went with it, just for a moment, where he would once have gone: east and south around the boot, across the Ionian Sea, doubling Cythera and Malea's stormy cape, into the Aegean—

With a jolt, Gerald looked up from the water and around the deck at the other people standing by rail. Lulu would no doubt have been informed. She might even be on this ferry.

H e *slept restlessly,* aware all night that he was at sea, dreaming a cascade of disturbing dreams that tumbled away like a ship's wake. Once he left his cabin to go on deck and watch and hear the sea rushing alongside the hull. He saw the lights of fishing boats in many directions.

He came on deck again as shades of azure and deeper blues dimmed the stars above the ship's port quarter, and the mainland of Spain was a spotty line of radium against a black horizon ahead. He was curious to see this coast from the sea once more. He had sailed past here twice: bound for Malta on HMS *Furious* in the spring of 1942, rolling atrociously in a *leveche* gale, after a fueling stop at Gibraltar, and after the war, in 1947, considerably more slowly in the tiny engineless *Nereid.* In those days, the best landmarks, identified and ticked off on the chart one by one as the navigator passed them, were the round stone coastal *torres vigía,* small lookout towers often no higher than twenty feet, many erected by the Moors during their occupation of Spain, others built after the Reconquista, in the sixteenth and seventeenth centuries, to repel the Moors. As the sky lightened, Gerald recognized the dark silhouette of Monte Benacantil hulking above Alicante, and, closer, the Castillo Santa Bárbara turning pink across the mountain. But beneath it, Alicante was now a city. Serried rows of apartment blocks covered the narrow coastal plain below the mountain like a reforestation plan. The *torre* on the shore near the port, when he at last found it, was lost against a backdrop of shipping containers.

It took him eleven hours to cover the 670 kilometers to Algeciras, all of it on the A-7 Nacional within sight of the sea. He stopped in Motril and bought bread and cheese and water for his lunch and ate and drank while driving. The sea was flat, the wind just as he remembered along this coast in summer—too light, frustrating under sail—but ashore all was changed. The coast west of Málaga to beyond Marbella, which Gerald remembered as a dusty stretch of coastal hills as tawny as a lion's flank, was now an uninterrupted stretch of contiguous, densely clustered villa-and-golf developments.

Mostly he saw Aegina, always beyond the fly-spattered windscreen, incarcerated in a Guardia Civil jail.

The whole notion of going to Morocco to buy shirts had sounded very unlikely, dodgy even—he'd imagined camel-borne brigands and rapists—but he could see the appeal, the lure of the Moorish fountainhead, and his fears for Aegina had been marginally allayed by the fact that Luc would be with her. The money she said she hoped to make was very little, not enough to make much of a dent in what she'd need over the next few years in art school, and he'd been working on his own plan for that—he'd just sold another small parcel of his land near the bottom of the drive to a Spanish couple from the mainland—but it was admirable and enterprising of her to try to make some money on her own and that had persuaded him.

He reached Algeciras after dark. It felt as big as Palma, but not pretty, heavily industrial. He had no idea where she was being held. He drove on, immediately lost in the town and not seeing anywhere to stop.

Looming over the end of many streets floated the familiar anomalous marvel of the Rock of Gibraltar, which Gerald knew lay immediately south of the town across Algeciras Bay. He steered for that until, like a cygnet finding its way to water, he found himself in the commercial fishing port, on a street of decrepit pensions which conformed with his notion of the right sort of place to stay. The rates would be reasonable, and no one of sound mind would trouble with his Simca on the street.

Tired after the previous night and the long day, he slept better to begin with, but again he was awake early, now intent on finding Aegina and, however he could, helping her.

Twelve

Aegina *sat on her bunk* with her back pressed into the corner of her cell, reading. The position offered no privacy from the grid wire in the door, but she liked feeling the two walls at her back. She was on her second James Bond book, *From Russia with Love*.

Nobody would tell her anything. She'd tried asking the guards what they thought she had done, what was going to happen to her—and when—but they would only shrug.

Twice a day she was taken outside to a concrete-walled space for half an hour. She met the other women there, older, haggard-looking, chain-smoking. "What are you here for?" they asked her. She told them she didn't know. She'd been in a car coming off the ferry—

"*Aie,*" they said, shaking their heads, "*las drogas.*"

"No," Aegina said, "I had only shirts."

"Shirts!" cackled one of the women, and they all laughed.

She'd seen the way Rolf and Minka looked as the customs agents began going through the car. Then the *guardias* took them all into an office and immediately separated them.

One of the women offered her a cigarette. Aegina thanked her but she didn't smoke, she said. She asked the women why they were there. "Aie, this one!" they said, and laughed some more.

She was alone in her cell, although it had two beds, and a toilet without a seat behind a partition that shielded it from view through the wire in the door. She heard the other women in cells down the hall, talking and laughing; sometimes they talked long and quietly and she couldn't make out the words.

On the second morning, she asked the gangling young *guardia* who mopped the floors if there was anything to read, in either Spanish or English. He went away and come back with two Spanish *novelas* whose covers showed women with torn shirts running from, on one cover, a man on horseback, on another, a steam engine, and three books in English: *You Are All Sanpaku*, a book extolling the virtues of a macrobiotic brown rice diet, and two James Bond paperbacks. Aegina had heard girls talking about James Bond books in school. They weren't at all as she'd imagined. There was hardly any sex. Mostly it was traveling and killing and descriptions of watches, cars, train rides, the Bahamas, Istanbul. It took her out of the cell.

But it didn't stop her thinking about Luc for long. She'd believed him, as she was sick, vomiting, exploding with diarrhea, lying helpless on the floor, at her very worst, when he'd said, "I love you so much . . . Like this most of all." She'd believed him. At that moment, she'd loved him too.

And then she remembered how he had knelt down beside Minka when she was vomiting next to the car outside the customs building, and wiped her face with a piece of cloth he'd torn from his shirt. So, the way he'd been with Aegina—the sweetness toward someone who was being sick—was nothing special. A dog, sniffing smells, would have behaved the same.

Thirteen

O nce Lulu finished speaking with Luc on the phone, it had been impossible to get any more information from the Guardia Civil in Algeciras. Nobody knew anything, except, of course, that it was *muy grave*, very grave, *señora*, making it sound like murder.

She believed Luc when he said he and Aegina hadn't been foolish enough to try to smuggle drugs, but they'd been stupid enough to get a lift in a car whose panels had been filled with hashish. It was not a good time to be stopped with drugs. The Spanish newspapers were filled with lurid stories featuring the highly visible efforts of the Guardia Civil or the agents of the *aduana* at apprehending hippies who apparently couldn't go anywhere without kilos of marijuana. What smuggler wouldn't want to cloak himself with a pair of hapless children to give the appearance of a holidaymaking family? The silly fools.

Lulu knew, by instinct and preference, that she would get nowhere trying to deal with the authorities in Algeciras or enlisting lawyers either there or in Mallorca. She needed to go to the top, to someone with immense clout who, with a few words, or the correct conduit of pesetas, in the right quarter, would bring the matter to a speedy conclusion.

She knew such a person. She dialed a telephone number.

"Hello, Barty. How are you?"

"I am well, Lulu," replied the deep, cigar and single-malt voice that sounded inordinately pleased to hear from her. "How very charming it is to hear from you. How are you?" He spoke in fluent English, his *madrileño* accent barely apparent.

"I'm afraid I'm not ringing you about anything pleasant, Barty. I have a problem."

"I am sorry to hear it, *querida.*" Bartolomé Llobet's voice conveyed true sympathy. "What can I do?"

Lulu outlined the situation. Luc and a girl arrested getting off the ferry in Algeciras for being in a car packed with drugs—

"What drugs, *querida?*"

"You know, pot. Hashish, or kif, whatever it is that everyone gets caught with now."

"Nothing else? Not heroin?"

"Good lord no, certainly not that I've heard of. It wasn't theirs, they were simply being given a lift by the smugglers."

"Of course. When did this happen, Lulu?"

"Yesterday afternoon. I only got a call from Luc just now."

Llobet said: "Algeciras..." Bless him, Lulu could actually hear him writing down the details. "... and the ferry came from Tangier or Ceuta?"

"Tangier, Barty."

"*Bueno.* I will do what I can, *querida.* It should not be too bad if there are no other drugs involved. It depends of course, on the circumstances, who these other people are, what have you."

"Barty, you sound as if you know something about it."

"*Claro.* I have children, no?"

"They haven't been in trouble, not like this, have they? I've never heard anything."

The quick breeze of air through a forest of nostril hair in the phone's mouthpiece—an amused exhalation. "Exactly. *Bueno,* I will call you this afternoon."

"You're a lovely man, Barty."

"*Sí.* Well, I was once, no?"

"Of course, you still are."

He clicked off.

That should do it, thought Lulu.

O f course, you must absolutely go, Lulu," said Milly. "Tom and I will manage everything."

They were having breakfast on the terrace outside the sitting room. Milly was a large woman—six feet tall and built like a letter box—dressed in efficient English holiday mufti: Aertex shirt, cotton skirt, enormous plimsolls. Tom, sitting nearby with an old newspaper, looked like a scout-master. There was no question of their ability to manage the Rocks for a few days. India had been run for a hundred years by such people. Now they were doing perfectly well without an Empire. Bankrolled by Milly's inheritance, Tom had recently built a machine that popped out thousands of plastic punnets to package and protect fruits and vegetables. His company was now selling machines and punnets that had revolutionized the transport and sale of supermarket produce all over England, and he was getting rich. However, they always found the time to come down to Mallorca. There was no one else Lulu would have left in charge of the place.

"We'll keep the fires stoked, the animals fed," said Tom.

"Bless you," said Lulu. "I won't go yet, though. No point being there until Barty's done his job. Then I shall go and bring him home."

Fourteen

W e are conducting an investigation," Teniente Coronel Ruiz told the Englishman, making it sound like a procedure at the highest level of Interpol. "I cannot tell you what will happen to your daughter, Señor"—he looked down again at the sheet in front of him . . . the names of these English—"Señor Ruteleje. She will remain in custody for now, until such a time that the investigation is concluded, when she will face a trial or she will be freed, or fined perhaps, depending on the charges."

"I understand, Teniente Coronel," said the Rutledge. "So she has not yet been charged with any offense?"

Astonishingly, the inglés had correctly determined Ruiz's rank from the insignia of his epaulettes. "No. As I say, this is pending the outcome of the investigation. I can tell you, however," said Ruiz, looking balefully across his desk at the Rutledge, "that she and her friend, the American Franklin, crossed from Algeciras to Tangier on the same ferry as the owner of the car, the German Zenf, one week ago. Did you know this?"

"No," said the Rutledge, looking newly alarmed.

Ruiz shrugged. "It may be only a coincidence, but it could indicate a design, a plan." That was all he needed to say—normally something he would have enjoyed imparting—but for some reason he felt himself unbending. "It does appear however, that there is no previous connection between your daughter and Franklin and this Zenf and his companion, the Montenegrin woman"—he looked down again, another impossible name—"Kovačević, who have been traveling together for some time. On the face of it, their story that they were simply given a ride when their car met with an accident—we are checking with the Moroccan police for verification of this accident—sounds not entirely unreasonable. It will depend if the association is considered circumstantial rather than complicit. Probably it will be more a question of some proof that will appear, or not, to implicate them, rather than that they will have to prove their uninvolvement."

"I understand. Can I see my daughter?"

The Rutledge was even wearing a tie. A man of modest means, Ruiz realized, taking in the cloth and cut of his blazer, which appeared to be the sort of garment that sold for a few hundred pesetas at the Saturday market. "Of course. Cabo Primero." Ruiz instructed his corporal to take the *inglés* to the cells to visit his daughter.

"Thank you," said the Rutledge.

Very polite, respectful. Unlike the demanding and threatening Llobet, who had called again about the American Franklin, this time invoking the name and influence of a *senador* of the Junta de Andalucía if Ruiz could not provide details of any movement in the case. The Llobet did not seem aware of the Rutledge girl's being involved, or even the Zenf and the other woman or any of the basic facts of the apprehension. He just wanted results for the Franklin. Ruiz, like any proper official at his level, was a master of dissembling obfuscation, and assured the Llobet that he was pursuing every avenue of the furtherance of the case of the American Franklin.

On the third afternoon, Rutledge came in, nodded at Ruiz and said, "*Bona tarda,*" slipping, absentmindedly it seemed, into Catalan, instead of his usual *Buenas tardes.*

"*Bona tarda, Señor Ruteleje,*" Ruiz responded. "We have heard from the Moroccan police. They have found a vehicle, a Renault, with French license plates, severely damaged, inoperable. This conforms to statements made by your daughter and the American Franklin, and indeed the German and the Montenegrin woman. This could be seen as a corroboration of the innocence of your daughter and her friend."

"Wonderful," said Rutledge. "May I see my daughter?"

"Of course. Cabo Primero."

The corporal, normally at a desk in the adjoining room, did not respond. Ruiz craned his head to see through a door. He stood up. "I will take you up myself, Señor Ruteleje."

They climbed stairs to the second floor and walked down a linoleum-floored corridor to the holding cells. Ruiz instructed the *cabo* at the duty desk to bring the female prisoner Ruteleje to the visitor's room. He waited for a moment with the Englishman.

"Have you had much trouble with her?" Ruiz asked.

"My daughter? No, never. Nothing like this. She is an artist. Her interest is in painting."

The *cabo* returned with the prisoner. Ruiz had observed some of the interrogation of the Zenf but he had not encountered any of the others in the case. He was surprised to see that the sandy-haired Englishman's daughter looked absolutely Spanish. As dark as any local girl. When she saw the Rutledge, she said, "Hallo, Papa."

"This is your daughter?" asked Ruiz.

"Yes," said Gerald. "Aegina"—still speaking Spanish—"this is Teniente Coronel Ruiz. He was kind enough to bring me up to see you."

With her few simple words of thanks, Ruiz placed her accent—and now the Englishman's, which he had remarked several times but it had been harder with him. The nasally flattening of the vowels: Catalan from the Balearic Islands.

"*Pues, bona tarda,*" Ruiz said to both of them.

"*Bona tarda,*" said the girl pleasantly, acknowledging the shift to Catalan.

An hour later, when Gerald came downstairs, Ruiz said: "One would say that your daughter is absolutely Spanish." He held up Aegina's British passport, looking at the photograph and details in it. "She was born in Mallorca. She is truly your child?"

"Oh, yes," said Gerald. He set his rucksack on the floor and pulled out the envelope of papers he had brought from home. He knew from long experience the midlevel Latin official's pathological inquisitiveness and devotion to documentation which, when offered in the right circumstances, could particularize and humanize a subject under the power of such an authority. He now handed Aegina's birth certificate to Ruiz, who took it and scrutinized it intently. *Aegina María Rutledge y Puig*; Madre: *Paloma Teresa Puig y Froix*; Padre: *Gerald Desmond Anthony Rutledge*; Fecha: *13 mayo 1952*. Lugar: *Cala Marsopa, Mallorca, España*.

Gerald spread some photographs on the desk, and Ruiz looked through them with unguarded curiosity. Black-and-white with serrated borders, mostly of the little girl with her mother, a handsome woman, in whom Ruiz saw the daughter he had seen upstairs. Several of the three of them: the younger Englishman, stick thin, at a restaurant with the woman and the girl, now aged about five or six, their faces and the table-top overexposed with flash, a dark *bodega* in the background. Another photo showed them perched on rocks above the sea, a bottle and some bread around them. They looked happy.

"My family," said Gerald.

"Very attractive," said Ruiz. "The mother is *mallorquina*?"

"Yes. She was. She is dead."

Ruiz's face clouded. He looked at Gerald. "I am sorry for you."

"Thank you."

"And you still live in Mallorca?"

"Yes," said Gerald. He reached down and drew an unlabeled liter bottle of olive oil from his rucksack. He placed it on Ruiz's desk. "I have a small farm. I make olive oil. With your permission, I would like to give you this bottle.

"It is not necessary, Señor Ruteleje."

"I understand, but I would like you to have it. You've been very sympathetic. Besides, it's good. You will like it."

Fifteen

Y ou look seedy, Gerald," Lulu said, as she sat down at a nearby table. "The jacket and tie don't help, you know. They make you look like an indigent lining up for alms. How long have you been here?"

"A week. I got here the second day after they were arrested."

The café was the only one close to the Guardia Civil station; its awning over the outside tables was already necessary at nine a.m. Gerald had come here to sit and read the wretched but compelling *Diario del Pueblo* with his coffee every morning before visiting hours.

He opened his mouth to say something, but Lulu turned her attention to the waiter who was now standing raptly beside her.

"*Un café, por favor.*"

"*Muy bien, y algo—?*"

"*Nada más.*"

The waiter bobbed his head and spun away.

Gerald had been shocked to see her inside the Guardia station when he arrived at nine o'clock this morning—there would no visiting today, as Aegina and Luc were being released at eleven—and he left, embarrassed, when she began to harangue Teniente Coronel Ruiz about the delay in releasing her son.

Now she sat two meters away, gazing serenely at the stout Spanish women, genetically evolved by eons of domestic practice, moving stolidly like mules with their loaded baskets across the plaza from the large *mercado* building. Gerald couldn't take his eyes off her. Apart from a single accidental encounter outside Comestibles Calix a few years earlier, he hadn't been this close to her for twenty years. Her hair, which he had loved so very much, which had begun to gray before he met her, was now completely white except for a few tendrils of black at the nape of her slim neck beneath the gathered mass held aloft with some sort of spike. She was his age, forty-five, but her skin was taut across her face and beneath her jaw, and her figure, from what he could tell beneath the loose linen trousers and shirt, seemed more wiry than he had known it, the softness now muscle and sinew. He remembered her without the trousers and shirt.

Then he noticed the scar on her chin: so small now, a thin white curve, almost unseen unless you knew to look.

"Did you ever get the film—a roll of film—I gave Milly to give you?" Gerald asked. "You were supposed to develop it."

She ignored him, or didn't hear him, as the waiter returned with her coffee. She sipped.

"I lured them away, you know—"

She interrupted him. "And what have you been doing in Algeciras while I've been campaigning for their release?"

"I'm sorry . . . you've been what?"

"You know they're being released this morning?"

"Yes, I do."

"Do you have any idea why?"

"I think I do, actually."

"Well you don't seem very surprised. Or grateful."

"I'm very grateful to Coronel Ruiz, who's been quite sympathetic, as a matter of fact. More so than you may know. He's taken it off his own bat to look into their case and see that—"

"Gerald, you're an ignorant man. Do you actually think that uniform in there is letting them go because he's being *nice*? Done a good little policeman's job? I have asked friends, Gerald, people you couldn't possibly know or imagine, who, as a personal favor to me, have interceded at the highest level to effect my son's release, and, only incidentally, your daughter's. And what have you been doing? Sitting here for a week like a fly waiting for a window to be opened. Was that your plan?"

Gerald thought over what Lulu had said. Perhaps she was right, and she'd done it all. "I had no plan actually. Other than to be here for Aegina to do whatever I might for her. But, well, thank you, then, for your intercession, whatever you've done to help them out. Well done. Thank you." Gerald picked up his coffee cup and sipped. He looked down at his newspaper, but he saw instead the hulking cliffs of Sicily and felt a stab of acute shame.

"I lured them away, you know. Those—"

A man approached them. He stopped between their tables and looked at them both.

Abruptly, Lulu rose. She stared at the man, then at Gerald. "This is absurd," she said. She walked briskly away.

Gerald looked at him. He wore a dark gray suit. Older now, graying— his own age—but Gerald recognized him. The man with the baby along the road . . . eighteen, nineteen years before.

The man held out his hand. "Bernie Franklin. I'm Luc's father. You must be Gerald. I don't think we've ever met."

"No."

"Thanks for being here. I didn't know anything about it until yesterday. But they're releasing them today, right?"

"Yes."

"Can I join you?" asked Bernie.

"Of course."

They sat down. The waiter came out and they ordered more coffee. They talked about their kids.

At ten o'clock, Lulu, Gerald, and Bernie were sitting on steel chairs in the office. Gerald had hoped for another chance to speak to Lulu, but Bernie's presence stopped him. No one spoke. Then one of the *cabos* brought Luc and Aegina into the office.

Lulu stood up and strode to Luc. "Are you all right?" she said sharply.

"Yes, Mother," he said. "Sorry for the trouble."

Bernie walked forward and gripped Luc's arm. Aegina crossed the office quickly to embrace Gerald. She kept her eyes on her father.

Teniente Coronel Ruiz spoke: "I am sorry for the delay," he said, looking from Gerald to Lulu. "It was straightforward with these two. We did not believe they were part of the smuggling operation, but a member of the Senate and his friends chose to interest themselves in the matter and this official scrutiny delayed the release by several days." Ruiz indicated the baggage sitting on the floor before his desk. "This is everything that belongs to both of you?"

"Yes," said both Luc and Aegina.

"Collect your suitcases, then, please."

Luc and Aegina stepped forward. They each picked up their own small bag. Aegina took hold of the large suitcase full of shirts.

Luc knelt and opened his backpack, going through it. "I've got the original, the black shirt," he said.

"Keep it," said Aegina.

Gerald noticed her tone and that she was avoiding looking at Luc.

"Aegina, it's yours—"

"Keep it," said Lulu. "You drove her down in your car. You've done rather a lot for her. Come on, we've got the train to catch."

"When are you leaving?" Bernie asked her, but Lulu walked outside. Luc stared at Aegina. She still wouldn't look at him and took hold of the suitcase, and then Gerald moved to take it from her.

"Do come on, Luc!" Lulu called from outside. "I've got a taxi waiting for us!"

Sixteen

A week later, Luc rode up the dusty rocky drive to C'an Cabrer on his motorcycle. He knew the whine of the engine growing louder and louder would announce him before he reached the house.

At the top of the drive, he swung left and stopped behind the Simca. He turned off the motorcycle. The cicadas, silenced by the approaching blast of exhaust, now backfilled the unnatural stillness with the ambient, eternal sound of Mallorca.

Gerald appeared on the terrace above him.

"Good morning, Gerald. Is Aegina here?" Would she really not come out and talk to him?

"Hello, Luc. I'm sorry, she's in London."

"Oh."

Gerald saw the boy look down.

"I'm not sure when she'll be back. I think it will depend on how she does with the shirts."

Luc looked up at him again. "Right. Well, when you talk to her—you don't have a phone, do you?"

"No."

"Well, whenever you hear from her, will you please tell her . . . that I came by?"

Twenty-two years disappeared, and Gerald saw himself below, the devastated supplicant, banished, wanting to say so much and feeling the impossibility of conveying even the most reduced essence of it through an ill-informed, possibly unfriendly, gatekeeper. He felt keenly for the boy but he had no soothing bromide to offer. "I will," Gerald said. "I'll be sure to tell her."

"Thank you," said Luc. Then he stood and jumped on the kick-starter and the motorcycle noise drowned out the cicadas. Luc wheeled the bike around with short releases of the clutch and rumbled away back down the drive.

It burst from Gerald like an involuntary spasm of chorea, a Saint Vitus's bark:

"*Don't give up!*" he shouted.

But the bike was well down the drive, and Luc couldn't have heard. He didn't stop or slow or look around.

Gerald had startled himself. He was shaking. The motorcycle noise faded below. Soon he heard only the wind in the pines beside the house and the steady filling drone of the cicadas.

1966

Perfidia

One

Gerald and Aegina stood slumped against each other, watching the passengers coming through the opaque glass doors from the Customs Hall.

Gerald's face was haggard and gray, as if he had not slept or stepped outdoors for weeks. His right lower eyelid twitched spasmodically. Smoking—the whole normally unconscious business of fetching the pack from his shirt's breast pocket, shaking one loose, lighting it, raising his hand repeatedly to his mouth and lowering it again, sucking in and blowing out drafts of blue-gray smoke, flicking ash lightly away from his feet—was now a deliberate, meditative procedure offering long, drawn-out moments of relief. It gave him something to do, physical movement, a release of energy that partly masked the trembling of his whole body. And it was so blessedly ordinary.

Aegina wore large sunglasses; a baggy white T-shirt; small, tight jeans shorts. Her feet, in flip-flops, were black with dirt. She held on to her father's arm as if she feared gravity would soon cease and he alone could keep her from tumbling off into space.

"There she is," said Gerald.

His sister, Aegina's aunt Billie, wore a straw hat, a floral dress, and Clarks sandals. She carried a small navy blue canvas duffel bag. She saw them at once, and the thin lines of her mouth, open for air, clamped together into grim resolve as she strode toward them.

She dropped her bag and embraced them both. She held on to them tightly.

"Thank you for coming, Billie," Gerald said into her ear.

She shook her head slightly, dismissively. "Of course." She released them, looked at Aegina, and hugged her alone, tightly. Over Aegina's shoulder her eyes locked onto Gerald's.

"I'll go get the car," he said. "I'll meet you out there." He nodded in the direction of the exit.

"Right," said Billie. As Gerald sloped off, puffing clouds, she put her arm over Aegina's shoulder and pulled her close again and they walked slowly through the small terminal building. Billie's eyes ranged over the heads of the people crowding the terminal, as if to ward off further attack.

O utside, *a lanky man* in his thirties, with longish dark hair, was standing on the curb barking at passing taxis. *"Oiga . . . Oiga!"* He was unmissable in a robin's-egg-blue jacket, white pin-striped drainpipes, white loafers, but he was nowhere near the line where passengers were queuing for taxis and the taxis ignored him.

Gerald drove carefully around him and pulled up in the Simca.

The tall man glanced at them, then looked again, closely.

"A-gee-nah, isn't it?" he drawled.

She turned her large sunglasses toward him.

"It *is.*" He stepped forward, grinning at the three of them, then back at Aegina. "Gosh, you look awfully grown-up. What are you now, sixteen?"

"Fourteen," she said sullenly.

"Oh, well, that's jolly grown-up, then, isn't it? You must be Aegina's parents. I'm not sure we've met. Dominick Cleland. I come down to the Rocks every summer. Aegina and I are *old* friends, aren't we? I've bought quite a few of your foot thingies, haven't I?" He beamed at them. It was his manner, rather than intention, that suggested the freight of salacious double entendre that filled the air between them.

He saw at once he'd said the wrong thing. Polite, remote pain—the peculiarly English kind managed with tight half smiles and averted eyes—filled the faces before him. They *seemed* like a family the way they hung on to one another—though not English at all, actually, that sort of clingy behavior—and seeing her now, a little older, away from the Rocks, Aegina in fact looked like some local urchin.

"I'm Aegina's father," said Gerald. "This is my sister—"

"Billie Rutledge," said Billie. Not coldly, exactly, but Dominick felt a chill as he took the limp hand she lifted reluctantly to meet his. He shook hands with the father, a dry, brief squeeze. Then Dominick looked at the old Simca.

"I say, you're not headed to Cala Marsopa, are you? I couldn't possibly catch a lift with you? Lulu said someone might meet the plane, but there's no one here and it'll take forever to get a taxi."

Billie and Aegina were silent. They looked toward Gerald.

"We're—" Gerald began to say.

"I've just got the one bag. And a typewriter . . ." Dominick felt a pall settle over them. "But I'm sure I'll find a taxi—"

"We're going as far as Manacor," said Gerald. "We can drop you at the taxi rank there."

"That's on the way, isn't it? That would be fantastic. Are you sure?"

"Of course," said Gerald. He opened the hatchback and lifted Dominick's large, fat suitcase, which took up the entire footprint of the Simca's rear compartment. Dominick handed him the typewriter, a slim Olivetti Lettera. "Anywhere you like with this," he said cheerfully. "Unbreakable."

When they opened the doors, Dominick said, "No, I insist, I'll be fine in the back."

"No, you sit in the front," Billie said firmly.

"Are you sure?"

Billie got into the back with Aegina.

"I can't thank you enough," said Dominick feelingly as they drove away from the airport. "The taxis don't seem to be keeping up with the tourists. I was hoping to get to the Rocks in time for a bathe before drinks, and now I hope, I believe, I shall." He turned in his seat and grinned at Billie, who had slipped her sunglasses on. "We must have been on the same plane. Are you just down for your holiday?"

"Yes," said Billie. She looked at him briefly, then opened the sliding window so the air blew over her and stopped further conversation. She looked out at the windmills made of limestone towers and sailcloth.

Dominick craned his head farther round to see Aegina. She was expressionless. He couldn't see her eyes behind her sunglasses. She was looking forward, either at him or past him. "Have you broken up for the holiday, or are you still in school?"

"We've broken up," intoned Aegina.

"You've got the whole summer ahead of you. Marvelous! It seems endless when you're young, doesn't it?"

"Yes," said Aegina.

It was an hour to Manacor. Dominick noted the changes that were more apparent every year. The same Cézanney landscape he'd first seen in 1962, but every year the island became more built up. Urbanización Los Eucaliptos, Urbanización Las Almendras, square, unattractive *apartamientos* sprouting up around the inland towns serving the coastal resorts. More cars. Jerry everywhere now and nobody seeming to remember that they'd popped all those people into the ovens. Hardly saw anyone on a donkey anymore. But the heat, the swarthy peasants, the bright un-Englishness of it all, and the ancient-looking landscape, where it wasn't smothered by car hire or estate agent premises, still worked for Dominick. He felt as he always had when he came to Mallorca: he'd reached Shangri-la.

"I've been worried about development," he said, looking at Gerald and then around at the two in the backseat again, "but it's still *ineffably* beautiful, isn't it?"

They all looked ahead through the windscreen that was spattered with flies.

"It is, yes," agreed Gerald.

They dropped him beside the taxi rank at the bus station in Manacor.

"I can't thank you enough," said Dominick, as Gerald got out and opened the back of the Simca. An alert taxi driver was already out of his car and lifting Dominick's bag the moment Gerald set it down. "You will all come round to the Rocks and let me buy you a drink, won't you?" said Dominick. He bent and waved through the back window at Aegina. "Do come and see me!"

T hey *drove on* to the hospital and parked. Billie noticed grimly the way the staff smiled at Gerald and Aegina as they walked through the building.

In bed, there was little of Paloma visible to recognize. Her head was wrapped in a bandage. A ventilator tube was taped over her mouth, the noise of her respiration regular and overlaid with the machine that sounded like a bellows. Her eyes were shut, the lids dark as if sprinkled with kohl.

Approaching her bed, Gerald spoke to Paloma conversationally. "*Hola, querida. Billie está aquí. Va quedarse con nosotros un poco. Aegina está aquí también.*"

"Hallo, Paloma," said Billie almost cheerfully. She picked up Paloma's left hand, which lay on the thin blanket beside her thigh, and bent down and kissed it. Then she looked at the patient in bed. "Hallo," she said with less conviction.

Aegina sat on the other side of the bed and held her mother's right hand. Gerald pulled items from a straw bag—bread, small plastic bags of almonds and olives, a piece of Manchego cheese; a corked half-liter bottle of red wine; a tattered paperback, *The World of Odysseus*, by M. I. Finley—and arranged these on the table between the upholstered visitor's chair and Paloma's bed.

"I can stay now, if you like," Billie said.

"No, I'm fine," insisted Gerald. "Why don't you go home and relax. Come back later. Or when you like. It's wonderful that you're here now. You and Aegina can come and go, and you can leave me here."

"All right. Can we bring you anything else?"

"No. I'm all set for a bit, thanks."

"Aegina," said Billie. "Do you want to stay for a bit? I don't mind. I'm in no hurry to leave, we can stay as long as you like."

"No, it's all right," said Aegina. "We were here before we came to the airport." She stood up.

Billie looked at Gerald as he settled into the chair. "What, about seven or eight?"

"Yes. Fine. Don't wait dinner for me. Whenever you like after you eat."

*I*n the car, Aegina was silent.

"Sweetheart," Billie said, "you must tell me what I can do for you, and for your papa. Whatever you need at the shops. Whatever you both need me to do. It's what I'm here for. All right?"

"Okay." Aegina was gazing out the car window. Her limp body bumped and jostled like an abandoned marionette with the motion of the car. "Thank you."

Billie glanced at Aegina. That dreadful man was right: she certainly had grown in a year. She had her mother's small yet already womanly shape. Still staring through her enormous sunglasses out the window. Billie could think of nothing comforting to say—*Mummy may be brain-dead, sweetheart, but at least she's in no pain* wouldn't be helpful.

East of Manacor, the land showed less development. The road still ran beside the limestone walls of the terraced olive and citrus groves of small fincas. Above them rose hills covered with small pines and scrub oak.

"It is lovely here, isn't it?" said Billie. She immediately regretted her remark. It sounded trite and cheerful. "What I mean, sweetie, is that it's a beautiful land where your mother comes from, and that is a part of you."

Aegina's sunglasses swung toward Billie. "Thank you," she said.

Two

Arabella Squibb crouched on one foot on the lowermost rock ledge above the water, the other foot lifting the monoski in the air.

Luc gunned the engine and the speedboat leapt forward. Arabella tensed as the towline whipped up out of the fantail of foam behind the boat like something alive.

Yesterday, Arabella had spent the entire afternoon learning to let the towline pull her literally off her feet into midair to land on the rapidly deployed monoski without plunging face-first into the water. She could get up on one ski when pulled out of the water easily enough, but once she'd seen Lucy Valence plucked from a standstill off the rocks like a fly by the crack of a whip, Arabella was instantly determined to be able to do it. It was all about the little leap into the air you had to make at just the right moment. She'd got it, twice, yesterday, and then dreamt about it, that little push off into thin air, all night.

She pushed off—first time today—came down on the monoski, lurched forward from the waist before recovering and wobbling away across the water, precarious but upright, carving a trail of tight erratic curlicues on top of the boat's wake.

"Well done, darling!" shouted Richard Squibb. He had come across the road to watch his wife do this new water-ski trick she'd told him he simply *had* to come and see. He wore a much-creased Panama and a tiny, red man-bikini beneath his sunburned potbelly. He puffed at a fat Romeo y Julieta Belicoso and watched a moment longer, wreathed in blue smoke in the still air, before he turned and walked back across the road to the Rocks.

As the ski chattered and bounced beneath her like a runaway horse, Arabella slowly straightened her back until she found the position of relative equipoise she already knew from being pulled up out of the water on one ski. But the thrill of going from nought to flying off the rocks in a single moment with barely a splash to race across the surface of the sea after the boat had reinvented the experience.

She leaned back and dug in her right, rearmost heel and swooped to the right, with thrilling acceleration, across the speedboat's wake into the smooth water beyond. She heard a shout from ahead and looked up to see Luc turned in his seat looking back at her, his arm out, raising a thumb in the air, his sun-bleached hair flying about his head.

Darling Lukey. All of a sudden a *very* yummy sixteen. His father, an American whom nobody had ever seen who lived in Paris, had bought him the speedboat and engine so he could make some money for the summer. Five hundred pesetas a go, Lukey was charging the Rocks guests, and he'd been making thousands a day. Most of the guests were running a tab, but Arabella handed him the cash each time. Today she'd put a finger into his swimming costume and stuffed the bills into the waistband.

She zigzagged across the wake, leaning back and shooting off sideways and accelerating at what felt like incredible speed. Every time she turned and sped off in the other direction, Luc raised the Kodak Instamatic she'd given him to take pictures of her. Then he raised his thumb again and grinned. He made her feel that she was doing fabulously. Perhaps she was. At fleeting moments she felt graceful. She knew her body looked good. She skied for the camera—and for Luc. *Just for you, scrumptious darling.* He was looking at her the entire time through his sunglasses, glancing over his shoulder only now and then to see where they were headed. As the salt spray dried on her warm thighs and stomach and the thrumming vibration of the ski made itself felt in every muscle of her body, she felt tremendously sexy. She gazed steadily, despite the bumps, back at him.

Apart from the air on her face made by their skimming progress, the sea was mirror calm today, disturbed only by the surface-peeling wake of Luc's motorboat dispersing slowly like skywriting. The sea was sky-blue, the sky azure. Arabella felt she could water-ski all the way to Africa. She saw herself in one of those Italian films: water-skiing on the Bay of Naples, or off Portofino. The louche, tightly muscled boat boy, the blond version, staring at her through his sunglasses while he steered the boat with one arm cradled over the wheel. In the film she was supposed to let him take her to a fisherman's shack after water-skiing for a savage shagging, a classic symbiosis. Later her rich husband would tip the boy and thank him for giving his wife such a good time. Richard's tip, however, wouldn't be a good one. He was so awfully tight, despite being well-off. Poor Lukey, darling.

Abruptly she fell. When she came to the surface, Luc had turned the boat and was planing toward her. He throttled back and the boat slowed, settling lower into the sea, grumbling as it drew near. Luc bent overboard and picked up the floating monoski. Then he turned the wheel again, and the boat floated close to Arabella.

"You've lost your top," Luc said, scanning the water for the missing tendril of garment.

Arabella looked around for a moment, revolving in the water. "Never mind," she said.

Luc continued to peer intently into the water around the boat. The small ones, the sort Arabella had been wearing, made of cloth with no spongy filler, didn't always float on the surface. They could sink slowly and wrap themselves around the propeller.

"Sweet of you to worry, Lukey darling, but I've got a suitcase full of them. Can I get in?"

"You don't want to ski back?" He proffered the ski.

"I think I'll get out actually, darling, and dry off."

Luc hung the boarding ladder over the side and Arabella climbed up. She made no attempt to cover her breasts. She lowered her head, wrung out her hair with her hands, then threw her head up, arching her back with her chest pushed forward as she tossed her long, interesting if unnaturally dark hair back to splay out across her shoulders, splashing Luc's hot skin with cool drops. He handed her a blue Rocks bathing towel while politely though not overtly aiming his eyes elsewhere, but he caught a jolting peripheral impression of very dark nipples at the center of the triangles of pale skin surrounded by her deep tan. He had imagined just such a mishap with her mishap-suggestive bathing costume, the top of which seemed designed to come readily adrift, offering just such a view of Arabella's breasts, and they were better than he'd imagined. They were large, and though Arabella must be close to forty, he hadn't expected such a statuesque retention of their harnessed shape.

She sat beside him on the white and turquoise vinyl-upholstered seat as they flew smoothly at what felt like a hundred miles an hour above the surface of the sea toward the shore.

"Marvelous!" shouted Arabella. "Go, baby!"

She leaned back against Luc's arm, as if confusing it for the seat's backrest, and opened the towel to expose her goose-pimpled breasts to the sun. She moved again, settling herself more comfortably against him. The top of her head was level with his shoulder and he looked down on her breasts and the mound of her belly and its noticeable stretch marks rising above the tiny remnant of her bikini.

A moment later she said something he didn't catch.

"Sorry?"

"I said you're so polite, darling."

"Oh." Luc tried to remember what he'd said that was so polite. "Thank you."

They sped toward the shore. Luc felt every part of Arabella against him, almost a dead weight that heaved and lurched into him with the movement of the boat. Their thighs touched and bounced together, her skin was still cool from the water. He had a barely concealed erection and he hoped she would see it and touch it, but as far as he could tell, her eyes were closed. The boat tore on, jarred occasionally by an errant hillock of swell, and, for a moment, everything was in balance.

Luc recognized the tall figure waving at them from the rocks. "Dominick's arrived," he said.

Arabella sat up and looked ahead. "Dear Dominick. Such a silly old cunt. I can't imagine who reads those dreadful novels he writes or how he lives."

"Have you read them?" asked Luc. He was always meaning to but had been put off by their covers, which looked like dramatic renderings of the window displays of men's and women's fashions at Galeries Lafayette.

"I read part of one," said Arabella, as if only just now remembering. "It was *killingly* bad. But I do love him." She waved at Dominick.

"*Hal-lo, dar-ling!*" Dominick shouted. "Luc, you must tell me where you caught such a Siren."

Luc pulled the throttle to neutral and the boat wallowed closer to the shore.

"Darling, Dominick, how are you, silly old sausage?" Arabella said. She put a hand on Luc's thigh, squeezed it, and dove off the boat. She swam to the steel ladder Lulu'd had cemented into the rocks and climbed gracefully out of the water to where Dominick stood at the top, grinning at her.

"Good *God*," he said, staring at her breasts. "You come bearing gifts."

They kissed. "Give me your towel, you leering bastard," said Arabella.

She wrapped herself in the towel and turned toward Luc. "Thank you, Lukey, darling." She walked across the road to the Rocks.

Dominick watched her for a moment. Then he turned toward Luc. "Catch of the day?"

Luc smiled. "Ha-ha."

"Have you got time to take me out, or are you packing up now?"

"No, sure. Come on."

"Fan-*tastic!*" said Dominick. He dove into the sea.

Three

Arabella *was no different* from usual at dinner. But Luc understood now.

After the water-skiing and the sensational ride in the boat back to shore while she lay heavy and virtually naked against him, he was convinced that real, actual sex was in the offing. Arabella would give him some signal, arrange something, and it would finally happen. She'd always made him feel that she liked *him* particularly, that he alone understood her. For years, her eyes had swung to Luc's to let him—just him—know with a droll expression what she thought as someone beside the pool or at dinner was waffling on about Prime Minister Harold Wilson's ghastly teeth—"Why on *earth* doesn't the man go to a fucking dentist? Must he be so *insistently* the common prole?"—or the rising London property market. Last summer she'd told Luc he was turning into a "complete sexpot." From that day to reaching some sort of apotheosis this afternoon, he'd been engorged with fantasies of Arabella Squibb.

She bantered comfortably with Richard across the table, threw no more than normally conspiratorial looks at Luc, and at ten said she was tired, would forgo pudding and port, and stood up.

"I'm off to bed, my darlings," she said as she pushed back her chair and stood up.

"Are you really?" said Richard, squinting and blowing a dense blue stream of Cuban smoke upward toward the leafy overhead trellis.

"Really and truly. Thank you *so much*, Lukey darling, for such a lovely water-ski." She extended a hand toward him and moved her fingers as if caressing his cheek, though he was seven feet away.

"Anytime," said Luc.

And off she went.

This was it! A ruse—it had to be. Going to bed so early when Richard would stay up for hours more playing backgammon with either Cassian or Dominick now that he was here. Luc excused himself too, awkwardly, walking stiffly to his little toolshed along the wall.

He lit a candle and tidied his bed and then sat on it. He listened for noise without, and heard the chat of the diners still at the table, but no steps or rustlings along the path between his shed and the pool. After a few minutes he turned on the small, low-wattage electric lamp beside the bed and tried reading—he was on a Françoise Sagan jag, going through her little *livres de poche* in French, currently in the middle of *Les Merveil-leux Nuages*, but he couldn't get through a sentence. After twenty min-utes he turned out his light, blew out the candle, and wandered down to the bar. Richard and Dominick were playing backgammon at a table. Other guests were drinking at the bar. His mother was sitting at a table with Cassian and Tom and Milly.

Arabella had gone to bed.

L*uc rode his Rieju motorcycle* into town, parked it on the street out-side the Miravista, where the soft tones of Jackson Rale's electric guitar were floating over the walls like a vapor. He walked through the archway entrance, along the short path, and stopped at the top step over-looking the open dance floor beneath the tall pines. He scanned the dan-cers and the people at the tables. He knew half of them. Aegina wasn't there, unless she was in the loo.

Jackson Rale, a black American guitarist of indeterminate middle age, was playing "Bésame Mucho." When he stopped and took a sip of his drink, Luc approached him.

"Hey, Jackson." It was the way the American always greeted him, and Luc had started to say the same to Jackson.

"Hey, man," said Jackson. "What's cookin'?"

"Oh, nothing much," said Luc. He understood that Jackson wasn't really inquiring about anything, nor, probably, did he care what, if anything, was cooking, nor if there were a petroleum tanker fire blazing out on the street. Jackson exuded an immense if polite indifference to everything around him except his guitar and his Cuba libre. Mateo Pujols, the Miravista's owner, had obtained his services for the months of July and August through a booking agent in Palma. Jackson was a large man, not fat, but like one of those padded American football players gone to seed. He sat in the Miravista's patio under the pines beside the open-air dance floor and played short sets with his electric guitar. His technique didn't call attention to itself. He didn't play rock and roll or jazzy riffs, but steadily picked out an ancient repertoire of nightclub standards as soft filler between the longer and much louder sets of new and recent pop records that people came to the Miravista to dance to. Jackson's fingers were the size of pork sausages and looked far too large for the guitar's narrow fret board, yet he played smoothly and dependably, as if in his sleep. Luc particularly liked one song he played, a tune he'd heard before, maybe in a movie, but didn't know the name of, and he'd asked Jackson, a couple of weeks ago, what it was called.

"'Perfidia,'" said Jackson.

"I like it," said Luc.

"Yeah, it works," drawled Jackson. "Every time."

"Per . . ."

"'Perfidia,'" Jackson repeated. "An old Mexican song."

"Is it a woman's name?" asked Luc.

"Perfidia?" Jackson started to laugh, softly, rhythmically, a deep note of satisfaction, as he sat on a barstool beside his small amplifier under the trees, tuning his guitar, a dark-red-tinted Gretsch Chet Atkins Country Gentleman with considerable wear in the varnish below the strings. "It should be," he said, "heh, heh." He looked at Luc, his black face inscrutable and at the same time all-knowing. "It's a word for what some woman do to a man." Jackson looked away and raised his Cuba libre to his mouth.

In a second, Luc understood. "Oh. Yeah." Then he was incredibly grateful to Jackson for his man-to-man confidence. *Perfidia*: Mexican for blow job? And a song named for that? *Putain*, those Mexicans.

That's what he wanted from Arabella and had imagined until it ached: a *perfidia* out on his boat.

"Jackson, have you seen my friend Aegina? She's a little younger—"

"I know who you mean. Your little Spanish-looking girlfriend—"

"Well, she's not really my girlfriend, we're just friends."

"You better think that one through again," said Jackson. "But I ain't seen her, man. She ain't been in. Not tonight, so far."

"Okay, thanks." Luc scanned the crowd again, irresolute. Then he turned to leave. "See you, then, Jackson."

"Yep," said Jackson, with the enthusiasm of a mailman confirming the inevitability of the next day's visit. He put his drink down, returned his hand to his guitar. His thick fingers trembled lightly over the strings of the Gretsch and "Embraceable You" burbled out of his amplifier.

Luc walked back out to the street and started his motorcycle.

Four

Every evening at seven, a nun, Sor Victoria, came to Paloma's room. She smiled at Gerald but said nothing to him, except on the first occasion, when she came in and asked, "¿Permiso?" And Gerald, momentarily alarmed to see a sister of God, but quickly grateful, had nodded and said yes. Sor Victoria always sat on the edge of the bed and took Paloma's hand in her own and prayed quietly, raptly: "Dios, le ruego en el nombre de su hijo, Jesús Cristo . . ." When she was finished, she placed the limp hand over Paloma's heart and, with only a nod toward Gerald, withdrew.

After she was gone, Gerald usually turned off the noisy fan and opened the windows opposite Paloma's bed. Then the katabatic winds dropping from the pine-forested Serra de Tramuntana after sunset blew across the fertile midplain of the island, carrying spores of citrus and smoke and manure off the small farms of Mallorca, and the cool earthy breeze filled the room and diluted the pervasive hospital smell. The organic sounds outside the hospital—cars straining through streets sized for donkeys, glasses being set down and cleared off tables in cafés, women calling to children at great distances above the rising buzz and fade of mopeds and scooters—entered the room to dampen the insistent metronomic whoosh of the ventilator that sometimes, when the window was closed, seemed to grow so loud in the room that Gerald thought it must have engaged another gear or be forcing air into Paloma with greater effort, until he realized he was playing tricks on himself and he got up and went outside for a cigarette.

At eight, as Paloma's intravenous monomeal continued to drip from bags into her arm, Gerald put aside the book he'd been trying to read and broke out his oval slab of floury bread, hard cheese, olives, figs, uncorked his wine, and ate his dinner. Sitting beside her for two days, he had tried to read but found it difficult to concentrate. At moments, he'd talked to Paloma, on the chance that she could hear him, but he wasn't good at chatting inventively or cheerfully to her supine, vacant, huffing and puffing body. He was too aware of the magnitude of her absence, and he lapsed into grim, fidgety silences. He gave himself over completely to eating the food he'd brought with him. Like smoking, it gave him something distracting, physical, and ordinary to do. The small normal preparations and movements, even chewing and swallowing, comforted him. He'd heard on a BBC program that ants, suddenly exposed when a sheltering rock or rotting fallen tree limb is removed from above them, immediately stop to wash their faces, a familiar routine that reassures them against the stress and fear of sudden change. Gerald didn't know if this was true, but he understood it. Smoking and eating and other mechanical daily tasks made him feel better.

Billie appeared at nine. She was flustered.

"She's gone off and she didn't come back. Gerald, do you really think it's a good idea that she has a moped?"

Gerald looked toward Paloma. "Paloma did. She bought it for her. She thought it would be good for Aegina to be more independent. Able to go off and see her friends."

"But she's only fourteen. I mean, is it even legal? And she doesn't wear a helmet. Aren't you worried about her?"

"Yes, of course I'm worried about her. I worry about her when she's asleep in bed in the other room. I still get up in the middle of the night to see if she's breathing—"

"I mean about the moped."

"I know you do. It is legal, and nobody here wears a helmet. She wouldn't if I insisted. But that's the Spanish, they're much more rough-and-tumble than we are. Paloma would let Aegina wander off all over town when she was quite young, seven and eight. She thought it was good for her. I always see the specter of disaster, I imagine the worst vividly, terrible things. But her mother"—he looked down at the figure in the bed—"always thinks everything will be all right."

Billie sat down and stared at Paloma. "Can she hear us, do you think?"

"They say not. But"—Gerald swung his head and gazed at Paloma—"I don't know."

Billie looked at her brother. "Tell me again what happened."

When he'd gone to the post office two days ago to call his sister, Gerald had been brief. "Paloma's in the hospital, brain hemorrhage, she might not wake up," he'd told her. Now he said, "She was in the kitchen, ironing. I was making a pot of tea. She suddenly got a very bad headache. She said she had to sit down for a moment. She stood beside the ironing board and sort of tottered. I took her into the bedroom and made her lie down. She closed her eyes. I went back into the kitchen and made the tea. I brought it into the bedroom on a tray and she was asleep. I thought that was good. Then I saw she wasn't breathing properly. I tried to wake her and couldn't. I carried her down to the car and brought her here. Aegina was off somewhere, good thing too."

"And what did they do to her, Gerald?" Billie looked fearfully at the bandages wrapped around Paloma's head.

Gerald looked at the bandages now too. "They opened her up and looked inside her brain for a hemorrhage. They found it and did whatever they do. It was big, they said. Then they said we must wait and see, but a doctor told me he thought it was unlikely she'd wake up." He looked at Billie. "He thought she was more or less gone."

"Gerald . . . Gerald, I'm so . . . Oh, it sounds so absurd to say I'm sorry. Does Aegina know all this?"

"Well, I've told her, more or less, but she doesn't really want to hear it."

"No, of course not," said Billie. She looked at Gerald as he glanced up at her. "So what happens now?"

"I think they're waiting for me to tell them when to turn off the machines."

Billie stood and went to the window and looked out at the street, the buildings, the lights, the dark. Thoughts came to her like Russian dolls, each opening and revealing another inside, only the dolls kept getting bigger.

"God, Gerald."

Five

On *his whiny Rieju,* Luc sped up the hill away from the sea, past small villas, slopes of pine, and terraced olive groves. Through the narrow streets of the *polígono,* the bike's echo running the gauntlet between tall stone buildings sounding louder than the engine itself. Beyond town, the road skirted the foot of the dark scrub oak, pine, and prickly pear slope of Monte Turó, before bending southeast toward the coast again.

The entrance to the Duhamel house was an unmarked gap in the pines and led uphill on a rutted dirt track. In the dark, Luc remembered the location and contour of most of the holes and rocks not quite illuminated or altered out of shape in the jarring swing of his weak headlamp. The house had no electricity. Luc had rarely been there during the day, so it always seemed a flickering, glowing place, first appearing from the outside as faint embers in the trees.

Émile Duhamel, François's father, had designed and built the place of unchinked limestone himself, with a few laborers, in 1959. It was his response, he said, to the Villa Arpel of Jacques Tati's film *Mon Oncle.* Inside it was an intended maze of odd-shaped rooms and curving passages lit by paraffin lamps and candles. Its windows were irregular trapezoidal or oval openings without glass, with exterior shutters for light, ventilation, or protection from weather. Gas stove, *paraffine* refrigerator in the kitchen. The bathrooms contained open-plan showers and sinks fed by gravity tanks into which water was pumped from the cistern by hand with a large-volume marine bilge pump. Hot water flowed from the tank painted black on the roof. The toilets were outside in a stone shelter over a lime pit, a small row of fenestrated planks set in reposeful cubicles of stone discreetly walled from view of the house and each other but wide-open to the outdoors and equipped with moldering paperbacks.

Émile was of course an architect. He had lived with François's mother, Sza Sza, a painter, for many years, though he was still married to his wife, Béatrice. His two older children with Béatrice often came down to Mallorca for a week or two in the summer. Most nights the house hosted an ongoing salon, guests free to drop in and eat, talk, read, play guitars, flutes, bouzoukis, or records on battery-operated record players, sleep if they wished in any of several ascetic rooms containing simple pallets, coarse sheets, candles and matches, and books: the *essais* of Montaigne, Saint Augustine, the odd volume of the Alexandria Quartet, or Harold Robbins.

The people who came to the Duhamels' were like the Duhamels themselves: a community of non-Spanish Europeans living interesting, at times distressing personal lives, who owned modestly renovated small fincas and either lived on the island year-round, or spent their summers there year after year, often coming down in the spring during the time of the almond blossoms, and their children, and the friends the children might bring down to spend a few weeks with them. They were self-employed professionals, artists, writers, nonviolent sweet-natured criminals, mysteriously self-supporting or genteelly impoverished, living on small annuities or the eked-out proceeds from the sale of ancestral paintings and furniture or a flat or a house, occasionally sleeping with one another in a manner that disturbed no one. In unspoken ways, they recognized one another, and everything they did made perfect sense to them, though they often arrived on the island as pariahs of the outside world, but were soothed and taken in by their steady, tolerant, and nonjudgmental friends and lovers on Mallorca.

It was past eleven but not too late for Luc to turn up chez Duhamel. Lounging on the pillows in the main room, he found the Duhamels, *père et femme*, puffing at a chillum, with Schooner Trelawny, who was in his sixties and always wore guayaberas to house his Old Holborn tins and matches, and Natalie Veilleux, who at seventeen slipped conveniently between generations and lay on her stomach on a dhurrie on the floor, chin on her hands, feet waving in the air, bare thighs rolling beneath them, gazing inscrutably (stoned) at Luc as he came in.

"Lucas!" said Schooner, who knew this was not Luc's name. "Teddy's *just now* gone off in the motor to look for none other than you. You must have missed each other at the one-way in the *polígono*." Teddy was Schooner's sixteen-year-old son, who spent his summer holidays with his father in Mallorca.

"Oh," said Luc. "Has Aegina been here?"

"She and François are in his room," said Émile.

"Thanks."

Luc wound through a labyrinthine passageway to Francois's room. Though François lived in Paris most of the year too, they hardly ever saw each other there. In Mallorca, François was probably his best friend.

They were lying on the floor, side by side, their heads propped against François's bed, a mattress on the floor. Aegina's eyes were closed. Nina Simone was singing "Mississippi Goddam" on the little blue and white battery-powered record player. Despite the open window, the air was filled with sweet, blue hashish smoke. Luc wondered if they'd been fucking, but they were dressed and the sheets were still neatly drawn up to the pillows, although they could have been rolling around on the floor together. He didn't really know what Aegina and François got up to on their own. The three of them were still natural and giggly together, the way they had been as children, but this summer, when Luc was alone with Aegina—not often, but at the Miravista when everyone else was dancing or off in the loo, or at the beach or in his boat—he had become either speechless or prone to idiot wisecrackery, and twitchingly self-conscious about his occasional spots. Aegina was still only fourteen, though in her bikini she looked older. And there was something very different about her this summer. A wildness and impenetrability he hadn't known behind what he knew so well, like a jungle he'd only just become aware of at the back of a beach he'd known forever. He hadn't kissed Aegina, apart from normal cheek-bussing, but he thought about it all the time now. He didn't want to ask François if he had.

"*Salut, mec,*" said François.

"*Salut,*" said Luc. He sat down on the floor between the window and the bed.

François proffered a thick joint. "*T'en veux?*"

Luc took it, put its soggy end between his lips and inhaled, and nodded toward Aegina. "She been here long?"

"Hours, man. She's completely wrecked."

Aegina's head was pushed forward by the edge of the bed, her neck at an awkward angle. He took a toke and handed the joint back, but François waved it away. He was rolling another.

"I'm thinking of having my ear pierced," said François. "Just one. And then I'll put a gold ring in it. Like a pirate."

"You'll look like a *pédé.*"

"No, straight guys are doing it. It'll look cool."

"*Putain,*" said Luc. "Not me. It'll fucking hurt."

He took another deep hit. He would get wrecked too, then.

Six

Sunday it rained, on and off, unusual for summer. In the late afternoon, the sun came out and dried the darkened patio tiles and the flower beds and bougainvillea of the Rocks, and brought out the guests who had been weather-bound in their rooms, tired of their books, scouring old newspapers for anything left unread, staving off or finally succumbing to obligatory sex with their spouses or the people they were putatively fucking.

Cassian and Dominick had spent the afternoon playing backgammon to the accompaniment of desultory drips from the overhanging tiled roof at the corner table beside the bar. They played on into the twilight as guests, still in the beachwear they'd worn all day despite the weather, drifted out to the bar.

A chubby blond woman, Susie Breedham, heaved herself onto a barstool beside them. "Christ, have you two been at it all day?"

"We have, yes," said Cassian.

"*Darling* Susie," said Dominick, "what have you been up to, sweetheart?"

"Wanking when I got bored out of my fucking mind and couldn't stand it any longer. Otherwise sleeping and reading and drinking. Not in that order."

"I'd have been happy to give you a hand if you'd only asked."

"Sweet of you, Dominick. I didn't want to bother you."

"No bother at all."

"I'll let you know if I can't manage by myself."

"Do."

Richard Squibb appeared beside the backgammon players, in his tiny bikini beneath pink potbelly, hands on hips, puffing on his cigar. "Who's won, who's lost?"

"Need you ask," said Dominick. "He's taken forty pounds off me."

"Well, why the bloody hell do you play with him, then?" asked Richard.

Cassian looked up at Richard through his yellow lenses, one side of his mouth slightly raised in a tight-lipped half smile. "He likes playing the loser." He lowered his eyes to Dominick across the table. "That's his gambit."

"Yes, but he keeps losing," said Richard. "I don't understand."

"Richard, will you take that massive smoldering log out of my ear, please?" said Susie.

"Sorry." Richard walked to the other side of the bar. He saw Lulu coming across the patio from the garage. "Lulu. Have you just been on one of your long drives in the campo?"

"I have, Richard, yes."

She paused as they pecked cheeks.

"Wasn't it a bit gloomy in this weather?"

"Not at all, I love it," said Lulu. "But I'm glad the rain's gone, so we can have our live music."

"Yes, me too," said Richard. "He's good, isn't he, old Jackson?"

"Yes, he is." Smiling beatifically, Lulu swept on. "Darlings," she said in answer to several hails, and disappeared into the house.

She'd caught Jackson Rale's catatonic scotch-and-soda set at the Miravista weeks earlier. Mateo had no objections to Jackson playing somewhere else on his union-obligated contractual single night off, so he'd played at the Rocks for the last three Sunday nights, sitting like a Buddha in the shadows beside the pool, an electrical cord snaking up the steps to his amplifier, a hit among the local British and European residents, as well as Rocks guests. Sunday nights had turned into a money-spinner for Lulu. It wouldn't have worked in the rain.

Lulu passed through her bedroom, and ran a bath. She had driven from the other side of Artà, where she'd had a chat with Bartolomé Llobet in El Claustro—"the cloister"—he liked to call it: the small finca he'd fixed up as a sanctuary for study and contemplation during his family summers in Cala Marsopa. The spare dwelling had a small kitchen, books and writing materials, a fireplace, a large bed, and a telephone into which Llobet would voice soft entreaties to Lulu whenever he could get her on the phone. She knew his schedule well, the afternoons when he might call, and she'd instructed her staff as to when she was at home or not to the Spanish gentleman—her lawyer, she described him—who called to advise her on her affairs with increasing urgency as the summer advanced.

"*Querida*," he would say, his deep, sonorous *madrileño* accent in the earpiece making her think of stones grinding together on the shore under the pull of a retreating wave, and continuing in English, "I am here."

Lulu enjoyed Llobet's company. He was intelligent and amusing, but he was an unintuitive lover. One didn't want to have to give directions, and when she did, Llobet became narrowly focused to the point of tedium, requiring her soon to say, "That's lovely, Barty. You can do something else now." And he would.

No one knew of her friendship with the youngest son of the old Nacionalista pirate Juan Llobet, Cala Marsopa's most notorious citizen. Bartolomé Llobet was merely a rich *madrileño* maritime lawyer who brought his large, immaculate family across the sea to the patriarchal home every summer; a local grandee who presided over the opening of the Festa de Sant Llorenç in August, and was a principal of the Banco Llobet. He and Lulu had never formally met, but the previous spring at Palma airport a tall man in a blazer and tie with slicked-back silvering hair had begged her pardon for his intrusion but surely he knew her from somewhere? Of course, he said, smiling with recognition when they had worked it out: *la dama de la Villa Los Roques* in Cala Marsopa. Driving along the shore road, and in town, he had seen her. He was delighted to finally meet her.

He worked assiduously at giving her pleasure. He took a boyish pride in maneuvering Lulu to her climaxes, which she bestowed rather than achieved. They were soft shudders, from which she quickly recovered. He was simple and undeviating in his own requirements, and dependable as good hotel plumbing.

They rarely saw, and never acknowledged, each other outside El Claustro. No one would ever find her there. It was the sense of complete dislocation that she loved. The fact that their association at no point touched any part of the rest of her life, and that that could not change.

But today Lulu had brought the physical side of their relationship to a close.

"*Dear* Barty, it's *much* better this way. Now we can truly be friends and know each other publicly. I can actually see you more often. Sex gets old and I don't want that to happen with us. It's been perfectly lovely, so let's keep it that way."

They spoke in English. Lulu's acquisition of Spanish, now decades old, had plateaued and calcified once she had mastered basic commands and necessary instructions—*el baño absolutamente necesario ser reparada por seis de la tarde*—and Llobet's English, honed through dealings with the international maritime community, was faultless and capable of the subtlest nuance.

He looked at her, dumbfounded. "But *querida*, I don't understand. We have the perfect, indeed, the most *extraordinarily* ideal situation here. Absolute discretion. Fulfillment of our desire for each other, the most charming intimacy and friendship—unless I completely misunderstand you. You don't want to marry me? You know it's impossible—"

"Good lord, no, Barty. I wouldn't dream of marrying you or anybody. No, no, you see, really, I've come to like you too much. I want us to be real friends."

"But we are real friends," he protested. "We have the most delicious, perfect friendship—"

"Yes, but it's hidden away here. We can't be real friends like this, and that's what I want us to be: *real* friends. I'd *love* to have you and Maria come to the Rocks for dinner."

"Maria? And me? Both of us, for dinner?"

"Yes. Why not, Barty? If she's your wife, she must be a wonderful woman. I'm sure we'd be great friends too, don't you think?"

Llobet stared at her. He stood and walked to the door that led into the little garden, where a fountain was surrounded by small orange trees. Then he turned and looked at her with a tragic expression. "Lulu. My darling. You are saying we will not make love again?"

"Yes, Barty. It's been *very* sweet. But let's move on, no?" She smiled at him with a look of genuine friendship.

I'*d like to get* my leg over that," said Dominick, his eyes following Lulu as she crossed the patio after they'd exchanged *darlings*. "What do you reckon my chances?"

"Nil," said Cassian. He shook the red leather dice cup and rolled eleven.

"Really? Why not?"

Cassian moved his pieces.

"Where's she getting it, then?" Dominick wondered aloud. Lulu was at least a decade older than either of them, but age in her case only meant enhancement. "She must be getting it off with someone. Who?"

"It's your move."

"Well, aren't *you* interested?" asked Dominick. "You've known her forever. What's the game, then?" He was pretty sure Cassian wasn't bent. He was about Dominick's age, mid-thirties, not nearly as good-looking, short red hair brushed back, dressed like a schoolmaster on holiday, apparently entirely unaware of what had been going on in Carnaby Street and on the King's Road. Supposedly Cassian had a girlfriend in London, but he never brought her down.

"No, I'm not interested. There is no game."

"You don't want her?" pressed Dominick.

"Don't be revolting. She's a close friend of my parents'. She's like an aunt to me."

Dominick looked at the house like a reconnoitering burglar. "Well, I've decided"—sotto voce—"I decided this winter, in fact—that this is the summer I'm going to give Lulu a tumble. I'm going for it, I can tell you. I'm going to give her such a thrashing—"

"Oh, shut up and play, you idiot. It's your move."

Seven

They were eating *pulpo, calamares a la plancha, hamburguesas* and plates of *papas fritas* at the Marítimo in the port. Florence and Aymar, Sylvie, François, Teddy, Serge and Alain, Natalie, Aegina, and Luc. The gang. *Les mecs de l'été.* They sat at a table out on the edge of the terrace, away from the lights. Francesca, Rafael Soller's wife, would serve them only Coca-Cola or TriNaranjus, but Aegina had given Natalie money to buy a liter of *vino* Planisi to put in Teddy Trelawney's goatskin bota, and they passed the bag around under the table, filling their water glasses. Billie had given Aegina a thousand pesetas "just to spend as you like, sweetie. Treat yourself to something." Aegina used the money to drink more and stay away from the house. Now that Billie had arrived, she visited the hospital less.

"*Mais c'est dé-gueul-asse,* this shitting *pulpo,*" said François, with a show of averting his head as the dish of little saffron-dusted octopuses Luc had ordered was passed around. He stuffed his mouth with ketchup-smeared *papas.*

"How would you know?" said Aegina. "You haven't even tried it."

"I don't need to. *Ça pue.*"

"I love it," said Aegina.

"You'll stink of it," said François.

"I hope!"

When they finished eating, they descended to the dark quay and climbed the stone steps to the top of the breakwater that sheltered the fishing boats and the few small foreign wooden sailboats that found their way to Cala Marsopa. They walked single file out to the end of the wall and sat beneath the tower that held the port's one blinking white light. At the tower's base, they were in the shadow of its large stones. They were untouched by the light and could only see its intermittent loom above them.

Aegina sat between Luc and François, lying back against the wall, pleasantly high on the wine, her legs spread open, knees moving side to side. She wanted Luc or François to kiss her. To put their hands on her breasts. To maul her. Neither had touched her. She knew they both fancied her and that something was going to happen, but it hadn't yet. François was the more relaxed around her. With his French haircut like Jean-Pierre Léaud, he was the better-looking. Luc was moody this summer. And there seemed to be several versions of him going at once: when he spoke to her, about food, boats, people, plans, his large eyes seemed to belong to someone behind him, looking at her from over his own shoulder.

Natalie sat next to Luc, and Teddy was on the other side of Natalie. They passed Teddy's bag back and forth, drinking the wine. None of them spoke, rendered mute by the engrossing sound of the waves that pulsed over the rocks below and their own thoughts.

Natalie was only a year older than Teddy and Luc and François, but she was already in the other room with the grown-ups. She'd brought her boyfriend Marc down from Paris for two weeks last summer and she and Marc had occupied her room at her parents' house as if they'd been married guests. After Marc had left, she'd gone out with a German business-man who drove a Porsche whom she'd met at the Miravista. So far this summer Natalie was on her own. Marc wasn't coming down; they were no longer an item.

Craning his head around her, pretending to look for the bag, Teddy inhaled her unmasked odor of soap and perspiration, and looked down her shirt. He supposed she spent time with them as she was doing tonight because they'd all known one another for years, as she would with broth-ers and sisters, mates, while she waited for this season's mature, hirsute, chain-smoking, car-driving, financially independent lover to appear.

Aegina's swinging knees were knocking into François's and Luc's. It was annoying Luc. Abruptly he stood up. "I'm going. Are you guys coming to hear Jackson later?"

"Yeah, I'm coming," said Teddy. "What time's he start?"

"Ten." Luc started off along the wall.

"Why are you leaving?" Aegina called after him, sounding petulant.

"I've got stuff to do."

He had nothing to do, but he didn't like wordlessly sandwiching Aegina with François, waiting for something to happen that couldn't happen when they were all together like this, and her slamming her knee into him.

The other half of him kept seeing Arabella Squibb coming through the door into his toolshed, looking—maybe it was the rain earlier in the day—just a little like Dorothy Lamour in *The Hurricane*.

J ust before ten, Jackson Rale set himself up beside the pool. Almost invisibly, with great economy of movement for a big man, he brought a barstool up the steps, ran an extension cord from the bar to his amplifier. He got the girl—Sally—behind the bar to make him a Cuba libre. He set it on top of his amplifier, sat on the stool, and plugged in the Gretsch. Soft muted notes floated out over the patio, the bar, the outdoor dining area, like soap bubbles that popped unnoticeably in the bushes and behind the ears. The tunes so well-known that they sounded as natural and subliminal as the waves breaking gently on the rocks across the road. "Mona Lisa," "Smoke Gets in Your Eyes," "I Cover the Waterfront," "Cuando Caliente el Sol," "Perfidia."

Dinner over, the diners drifted to the bar. They took drinks to the tables that had been moved to the edge of the patio. Jackson turned up the beat: "Come Fly with Me," "I've Got You Under My Skin," "I Get a Kick out of You," "My Funny Valentine." A few couples, those old enough to know how to fling and be flung, began to dance. Then, touching the guitar's volume knob, Jackson let fly some well-mannered rhythm and blues: "I Got a Woman," "Blue Suede Shoes," "Maybellene." More dancers came onto the patio, frugging and shaking and waving their hands. White folks dancing like that, they always reminded Jackson of the night years ago in New Haven, opening with another band, he'd caught Pat Boone convulsing his way through "Tutti Frutti." It was something he'd never forget.

Dominick approached the table where Lulu sat with Tom and Milly. "Lulu," he said, pulsating before her in a floral shirt by Mr Fish; white, tropical-weight hipster bell-bottoms; his awful white Gucci loafers, snapping his fingers and gyrating slightly, "may I have the pleasure?"

"Certainly, Dominick." Lulu rose, smiling directly at him, giving every indication of being elevated by pure charm.

Dominick lifted her hand gallantly in his own, and led her onto the patio as if preparing to join a quadrille. As soon as he let her go, Lulu slid easily into the music. Dominick crouched, flapped his arms, and began to circle her like a bird of paradise targeting a mate. He closed in, shimmying upward to his full height and back down again.

Lulu laughed. "You're so funny, Dominick."

As Jackson's number finished, she said, "Thank you, Dominick. You're very entertaining. I'm going to sit down now. Do join us."

She returned to the patio table. Tom grinned companionably at Dominick. "Have a drink, Dominick!" His smile was always wide, white and confident. Tom never suffered any doubt that an unsightly shred of spinach might be lodged in his teeth for he'd had them all knocked out in a motorcycle accident when he was nineteen, and had been fitted with full sets of increasingly better dentures.

"Thank you," said Dominick, "I will. But no, let me get you all something. What will you have to drink, Lulu?" Lulu of course could drink for free, but guests could indicate a particular attentiveness by purchasing her request.

"How sweet of you, darling. I'd love a sherry. A fino, please."

L *uc came up* the pool steps. He stood near Jackson and watched him play. They made eye contact as he entered the musician's field of vision, Jackson acknowledging him with a slight upward nod. At the end of a number when Jackson took a sip of his Cuba libre, Luc said, "Can you play 'Perfidia'?"

"I did that a little while ago. I'll do it later for sure."

"Thanks, Jackson."

"Sure, man."

As Jackson began playing "Tuxedo Junction," Luc turned and saw Aegina rushing toward him. She didn't stop as he anticipated but pushed him backward into the pool. Jackson kept on playing. Aegina skipped back down the steps and ran between the dancers across the patio.

Luc climbed out of the pool and ran, squishing and dripping over the tiles, after her.

Outside the gate, he looked up and down the shore road where it disappeared against the lights of the port to the left and the pensions on Son Moll beach to the right. Then he saw her at the edge of the rocks right in front of him, her glossy hair and back and legs lit by the houses on the shore, standing against the heaving black sea. He walked across the road, squelching in his sneakers.

"Aegina," he called. The waves sucked noisily below, retreated, and came in again louder as Luc came toward her.

"Aegina—"

His call seemed to propel her into the air.

Luc ran to the ledge above the water. "Jesus Christ, Aegina!" he called to her when he saw her head surface in the confused chop below. "What are you doing?"

She didn't look at him. Her head began moving out to sea.

"Aegina! Come back!"

She wasn't coming back. Very quickly her small, dark head moved away into the jumble of glinting black water.

Luc kicked off his sneakers and jumped.

The water felt unexpectedly warm. He surfaced and couldn't see her for a moment. Then he saw her head silhouetted against the fluorescent glow of the town. He caught up with her quickly.

"Aegina."

She continued swimming seaward. Not fast. Luc paddled beside her.

"What did you do that for?"

She didn't answer.

"Why did you push me into the pool?"

"I wanted to."

"Why?"

She swam on.

"It certainly is a lovely night for a swim," Luc said.

A few minutes later, he said, "You know, I'm not sure I can save you, if we keep going."

"Then go back."

"I'm not going to do that . . ." Luc found it difficult to speak conversationally. He wasn't out of breath, but his heart was pounding from Aegina's actions, and the undoubted attention she'd paid to him, which was gratifying, though he wasn't sure what it meant. "Aegina . . . I can't stop you if you keep going . . . well, I can . . . but then we'll just struggle without going anywhere . . . I'm not strong enough to haul you back to shore . . . if you resist . . . I don't even think I can haul you back now if you don't resist—"

"Fuck off!"

"Yeah, but . . . if I go back . . . and you drown . . . and later I say, 'Well, I was out there, but . . . Aegina told me to leave her alone—'"

"Aie-aie-*aie!*" she shouted aloft to the gods.

He was a few feet away but he could smell her warm winey breath on the water.

Aegina looked around, not at Luc, getting her bearings. She swam around him and headed slowly shoreward.

When they reached the ladder cemented into the rocks, they both held on to it for a few minutes and caught their breath.

"You first," said Luc.

Aegina climbed the ladder and disappeared above him. Luc followed and found her lying on her side on the rocks. He lay down next to her. When he'd caught his breath he began to feel the breeze from the sea on his wet clothes and he felt cold. He sat up.

"Aegina."

She was asleep, but breathing quickly through her open mouth. Her black hair was plastered across her face.

"Aegina," said Luc. He pulled her upright. "We're going inside. Come on, wake up."

She grunted.

Luc knelt and bowed forward as if in prayer until his head touched rock and he pulled her over his shoulder.

He staggered up the side street to the gate beside the garage, and then up the path to his toolshed. He knelt again and laid Aegina down on his bed. Light from the pool and patio below came through the little square openings the size of portholes at the top of the walls. He was desperately thirsty. He stayed in the shadows as he walked down to the house and found a stoppered liter bottle of water in the kitchen refrigerator. He drank three long icy gulps and took the bottle with him.

When he returned, Aegina lay on the bed wrapped in a sheet, two small twisted bits of cloth on the concrete floor.

"Aegina? Are you awake? Do you want some water?"

"Yes." She rose on an elbow and he handed her the bottle. He sat on the edge of the bed while she drank. When she finished she handed the bottle back to him. "Do you want to see my breasts?"

"No, it's okay, thanks."

"Look." Aegina let the sheet drop. They were the size of plums, white where they had been covered from the sun, small dark knobs at the center. "They've just arrived," she said.

"I see."

"Do you like them?"

"Yes, they're nice."

"Do you want to touch them?"

"No, it's okay."

She snatched his free hand, pulled it to her chest, and held it against her. He felt the cold hard little buttons.

"Aren't they nice? They'll get bigger."

"Very nice. They're fine as they are."

"No, they'll be bigger. I know, because I'm like my mother."

Luc had heard about Paloma from Francesca, who came and cleaned at the Rocks every day. Francesca only knew that Paloma was in the hospital at Manacor and that it was very bad. I'm sorry to hear about your mum, he'd said to Aegina a few days ago, and she hadn't wanted to talk about it. But she'd been drunk or getting drunk ever since.

"I'm going to take you home," said Luc.

Aegina leaned back, still clamping his hand to her breast, pulling him forward. "I want you to do it to me."

"Do what?"

"*Jódeme.*" She pulled his hand down across her stomach, and then he pulled it away.

"No," he said.

"Why not? Are you a virgin?" she taunted him.

Luc had been asked this before, by boys and girls in Paris. He responded variously. But he didn't mind telling Aegina the truth. "Yes. Are you?"

"Of course I am! What do you think? I'm fourteen!"

"Yeah, well, so you're kind of young—"

"No I'm not. I'm ready. It's time. I want to lose my virginity. And you're older, you should want to do it. What's the matter? You don't want me?"

"Aegina, it's not that . . . you're very attractive. And I like you. But maybe we should wait."

"For what? Now's perfect. Come on." She threw the sheet off her and raised one knee and glared at him. "You don't want me?"

Luc kept his eyes on hers, but he was aware of her small lithe, still damp body, the precocious dark triangle at the apex of her thighs and belly.

"Maybe we should lead up to it, differently, sort of. Sometime when you're not drunk."

"I'm not drunk. And anyway, so what?"

"I'm going to take you home."

Aegina snatched the sheet back up to her chin and sat up on the bed. "I've got my *moto*."

"You can't drive that now."

"How will you stop me?"

"I'll stop you, don't worry."

"¡*Coño!*" said Aegina, sounding like an authentic fishwife. She looked down at her scraps of wet clothing on the floor. "I'm not getting back into those."

"You can wear these." Luc put a pair of his shorts and a T-shirt on the bed, and left the shed.

A*egina, stop it!*" he hissed at her. She sat behind him as they rode out of town on his motorcycle, one arm around his chest, repeatedly grabbing at his crotch with the other hand. At one point her fingers closed firmly around his erection and he twisted violently. "Stop it! We're going to have an accident!"

"Just drive," she said.

He stopped struggling, and they drove on quietly as her hand closed around him and she gently explored, and neither of them said anything.

Both Gerald and Billie were on the terrace, alerted by the extended agonized whine of the Rieju as it came up the hill.

"Go," said Aegina to Luc as she hopped off.

He turned and coasted quietly away down the hill, his mind and body filled with the touch of her fingers.

"Aegina, where have you been?" asked Gerald. "Are you all right? Where's your moped? Did you have an accident?"

"No, I'm fine, Papa. I just didn't want to drive home," said Aegina. "Night!" She ran up the short steps immediately below them to her own room beside the cistern on the ground floor.

On the terrace, Billie said, "Do you have any idea where she's been?"

"They've probably been out at the Miravista, dancing. That was Luc—Lulu's son. He's actually a nice boy."

"Those weren't her clothes, Gerald."

"Weren't they?"

"Gerald . . . this has got to stop."

Eight

L*ife goes on, however.* Gerald needed to sell oil. Early in the morning, he set off to Artà to pick up fifty bottled liters of his olive oil to deliver to Comestibles Calix, the Hotel Castillo, La Fonda, and several other restaurants in Cala Marsopa.

He had joined the Cooperativa d'Artà in November, which enabled him now to market his oil with the stamp *Illes Balears Qualitat*. The previous autumn had been wet, and his trees had produced more olives than he thought he'd be able to harvest by himself. The *cooperativa* sent two men to help him, and they'd driven the filled tubs of green and purple olives to the press for him. The fees to join the *cooperativa* and pay for the work of the men were more than offset by the larger size of his harvest and the few pesetas he was now able to add to the price of each *litro* bearing the appellation *Qualitat*. The old *abuelo* at the press, the grandfather of the olives they called him, whose gnarled index finger held under streams of new oil and raised to his tongue provided the *cooperativa's* quality control, had advised Gerald to harvest two weeks earlier than usual. The resultant oil was the best he'd ever produced. It smelled of *frutas del bosque*. Gerald had initially been upset, thinking that this was because his olives had been mixed with superior fruit, but the *abuelo* had assured him that it was because the olives had been picked earlier and that only his olives had gone into his oil, and that his oil was very fine. There were more bottles than he could find room for at C'an Cabrer, and half of it, several hundred slightly cloudy green liter bottles, remained stored at the *cooperativa*. He drove to Artà and fetched them as he needed to.

He first drove the fifty minutes to the hospital in Manacor. Paloma appeared unchanged, though with the respirator, her color was good and the bruised-looking shadows around her eyes that had appeared after the brain surgery were fading. In Spanish, Gerald told her that he was off to fetch more bottles from the *cooperativa* and that he would return later in the afternoon.

From the hospital it was half an hour to Artà. He said *bon dia* to the old *abuelo*, who smiled at him with an open mouth missing most of its teeth. He filled the back of his Simca with carefully crated bottles, and drove back to Cala Marsopa.

M*ateo Pujols had rented* a small apartment for Jackson Rale up the hill from the port. The apartment belonged to a friend who had bought it for his mother-in-law. The mother-in-law had died in June and Mateo's friend was happy to rent it out furnished for the season.

It suited Jackson because it was in the back streets near a television repair shop, a cobbler, a grocery store, and a plumbing supply yard. The noises that came from these businesses were few and brief and did not go on for hours like the drunken singing of tourists in the streets and bars in the part of town where the hotels and pensions were located.

Jackson slept late in the mornings. In the small kitchen he kept a supply of staples he'd bought from the nearby grocery store: bread, coffee, milk, sugar for his breakfast; chunks of cheese, ice cream, bottles of water, beer, and J&B Rare. He went to the same café in the plaza every day for lunch. Not too many tourists. He brought his sketchbook and pencils and drew the people and the buildings in the plaza. When he sketched, Jackson's mind became agreeably blank. He had no thoughts— he didn't like to think much. It was like a vacation when he sketched. He was always aware of that afterward, when his thoughts started up again: he'd been away on vacation.

He returned to his room at three. Most days now his new woman would come in the afternoon. He left the door unlocked.

Soon enough, she came in. The curtains were drawn like she liked, and Jackson was already lying on the bed, naked, belly up like a basking dog.

"Exactly the way I like you," she said. She shucked her clothes in seconds and advanced up his legs like a cat.

This one liked to throw her head around and slap her long white hair across his black legs and groin and torso. And through her white hair she'd stare at his black skin and play her spread-out white hands all over him, like she was making some piece of art. She'd crawl up his legs, slapping her hair over him and then she would squat and lower herself onto his dick. She was older, near his age maybe, but small and hard like a cat, and she would sit on him like that and lose her mind for a while. Then when she was ready she'd roll off him and he'd get on top—she'd tell him what she wanted and that was fine by him—and he'd start pile driving like the U.S. Army Corps of Engineers, pushing her up the bed till she got her hands flat on the wall above her head and she pushed back at him. He knew when she was getting there because her voice went strangled and then she'd really rip loud with the moans, like someone in serious trouble, and Jackson would have to put his hand over her mouth to keep the noise down while she stared at him wild-eyed, screaming into his cupped palm and breathing through her nose like a racehorse until the snot ran down his hand. He did that for as long as she wanted, pounding away at her while she had her crazy conniptions. She said no letting loose inside and that was fine with him because when she had enough she pushed him off and got on top again and grabbed hold of him with her hands like some native woman pounding corn mush with a log, sitting on top of him pouring sweat until he popped, and she watched that like she was a child watching a chick hatch out of an egg.

She looked at him all breathless and said, "You have no idea what you do to me, Jackson," and he said, "I think I got a pretty good idea." Then she said, "How was that for you?" And he said, "Maybe you could try harder next time," and she laughed in a beautiful way. She was some beautiful woman. They were like a black-and-white photograph together.

She didn't hang around. She was up and dressed and gone as quick as she'd come in.

B*ecause of its location*, Comestibles Calix did not get the tourist traffic. It carried items for more discerning palates—for the seasonal foreign residents and the local Spaniards of the professional class—who prepared food at home and wanted something better than the usual Spanish and Portuguese muck in tins. At Comestibles Calix, you could find glass jars of foie gras from the Périgord, biscuits from Lefèvre-Utile of Nantes, cheddar cheese from Somerset, putrid-smelling *hapansilakka* from Finland, olive oil from Italy and Greece, and bottles of green local oil. Baskets of lemons, bins of olives and almonds. Calix had purchased Gerald's produce from his earliest days.

He parked the Simca a few doors down. Into his straw basket, Gerald carefully placed twelve bottles. He entered Calix through the dangling bead curtain of the entrance.

"Hola," he said to José and Caterina Calix, who stood behind the counter.

"Hola, *Jerol*," said Caterina, her face shifting into an unstable blend of keenly felt sympathy, sadness, brave cheerfulness, and discomfort. José, a red-haired, now graying Catalan, pushing a haunch of *jamón serrano* through an electric slicer, nodded at Gerald with the grim camaraderie of soldiers in a trench sharing a last cigarette.

"*¿Cómo está Paloma?*" asked Caterina.

Gerald shrugged and looked away. "*Vamos a ver*," was all he could bring himself to say at present. He placed his bottles on the counter. Caterina removed some notes from her till, counted them carefully, adding peseta coins, handed them to Gerald, and looked at him. Her attempt at studied calm now gave way with a betrayal of grief.

"*Dios mío, Jerol.*"

Caterina came around the counter and hugged him. Quickly she recovered herself and returned behind the counter.

"*Sí. Gracias, Caterina. José.*"

Coming out onto the street through the beads, which partially obscured his view of where he was going, Gerald turned in the direction of his Simca and collided with Lulu.

She tottered and his hand caught her upper arm.

"Lulu," he said. And stared at her.

She was covered in a film of perspiration, strands of her hair flying, the rest of it untidily gathered behind her head. She looked as if she'd run all the way from the Rocks. She stared back at him, as if interrupted, surprised, disoriented by encountering him.

His eyes flew to the scar on her chin; it was livid, as if pulsing—

Lulu recovered, twisted, wrenching her arm free. "What are you doing here?" she snapped.

Gerald motioned with his hand. "Calix. I—"

Abruptly, she walked quickly past him, down the slight hill toward the port, the center of town. Gerald watched her until she reached a corner and was gone.

He walked to the Simca in a daze. He got in, and through the windshield looked down the street in the direction she had disappeared.

He had been inches from her. He'd felt heat coming off her as if from an old electric fire. He'd felt the warmth and sweat on her arm. A synapse in Gerald's brain sparked a vision, so that he no longer saw the street ahead, but Lulu, writhing naked, hot, wet, on top of him on *Nereid*'s narrow berth, wild strands of her hair clinging to her streaming face and neck and chest. The cabin stifling hot, their appetite for each other at its peak, still awash in the wonder of what they had found.

Gradually, Gerald's vision cleared. He saw the street, people, motor scooters. He started the Simca's engine.

Nine

Billie was in the kitchen making *soupe catalane*. On one of her earliest visits to her brother at C'an Cabrer, she'd brought down a new copy of Elizabeth David's *A Book of Mediterranean Food*. She'd applied many of the recipes from her own well-thumbed and stained copy at home in Sevenoaks to the game and fruit and vegetables she was able to find locally in Kent, but it was always a delight for her to use the book in its proper setting, Mallorca, surrounded by the pale blue Mediterranean. For her *soupe catalane*, Billie was able to use entirely indigenous ingredients, with the exception of celery, which she had not been able to find in Cala Marsopa. She substituted chopped green peppers instead. Paloma was an efficient, if stolid meal maker, always providing plenty of meat (she liked boar) and fish and vegetables, but was chary with lighter fare of salads, soups, squid, and octopus. These, and simple but interesting hors d'oeuvres, Billie enjoyed sharing the fossicking for and preparing with Aegina, but on this visit, Aegina had eaten little and spent no time in the kitchen with her.

"Is she still not up?" asked Gerald when he came into the kitchen, laden with more bottles of oil.

"No, she's not," said Billie. She chopped onions thoughtfully. Then she stopped and patted her streaming eyes with pieces of bread, and turned to Gerald as he came out of the larder. "Gerald, do sit down. I must talk seriously with you."

"Yes, all right," said Gerald, with relief. She was the older sibling, and generally what she said had the pronouncement of an oracle. He sat and poured himself a glass of red wine from the open bottle on the table, and took a bite from a piece of bread.

Billie looked at him levelly.

A *egina appeared* to have been asleep for many years, as if in a fairy tale, cobwebbed and dusted with sleep pollen, thick and cottony and protective.

On the table in her room lay piles of the golden yarn she used to make her Roman foot thongs: a woven strip of gold an inch or so wide that fastened around the ankle, ran across the top of the foot to a loop that fit around the second toe, worn without other footwear. They had become the fashion vogue at the Rocks for the last two years for the ladies who liked to slip noiselessly across the patio and dance in otherwise bare feet. They were sold at the bar and had provided Aegina with some decent pocket money. Her thongs, she'd told Gerald, had actually inspired a Roman toga evening at the Rocks. She hadn't made any since her mother had become ill.

Gerald sat on the bed beside her. He stretched out a hand to the dark hair across her face and gently moved it aside. My beautiful, beautiful little girl. He missed all the children she had once been—the eighteen-month-old, the three-year-old, the five-year-old, the smallness of her then, the whole weight of her against his shoulder when she was asleep— and he could only bear it because she grew into something more precious and extraordinary, more a necessary part of him, with the passage of time. Her face in repose now, mouth open, still looked like a very young child's, as if he had sent her off to sleep the night before with *The Tale of Pigling Bland*. Now he was going to wake her into a harsh world, and wrench her forever out of the happiest part of her childhood.

She opened her eyes and found Gerald's. "Is it about Mama? What's happened?"

"Nothing," said Gerald. "Nothing's happened. But I have to talk to you about Mama."

Aegina hadn't moved, but she was staring at her father, quite awake. "I know what you're going to say, Papa."

He began dissemblingly. "My dear, dear Aegina—"

"She's already dead and we've got to unplug her. I know that."

He looked at her, lying in bed, for some crack in her absolute composure.

"Well . . . I think that's what the doctors have been wanting to tell us."

"They have told us, Papa. Dr. Jiménez said she had no more *función cerebral* and that it wasn't going to come back and that the machine was breathing for her and we had to prepare ourselves to let her go. That's what he said. We have to prepare ourselves to let her go."

"Yes," said Gerald, astonished. It was he who wasn't prepared. Aegina, he understood now, had been preparing, every night. "I think I remember something like that."

"Well, don't you think we should, Papa? Stop the machine and let her go? I don't want to see her like that anymore. She *is* gone."

Aegina reached over and took Gerald's callused hand in hers.

"You've got a lot of your mother in you," he said.

*T*hey *drove to Manacor*, the three of them, in the afternoon. Gerald saw everything along the way as if for the first time. The olive groves, the old limestone walls. He thought about Aegina. He wanted to tell Paloma how amazing she was, and how beautiful Mallorca looked. He wanted to tell her how grateful he was. He wasn't sure she knew that. You didn't go around saying how awfully grateful you were.

What she had done for him.

He kept looking at Aegina in the rearview mirror—had to tilt his head a bit to one side and tried not to do it overtly. She was looking out the window, inscrutable behind her sunglasses that were as large as a frogman's mask. She appeared more composed than he was feeling.

"All right?" said Billie softly.

He saw that she was looking at him. "Yes," he said.

Dr. Jiménez was not at the hospital. The younger man, Dr. Muñoz, was on duty.

"Oh, dear," said Gerald, thinking out loud. "We should have spoken with Dr. Jiménez before coming to a decision."

But Dr. Muñoz was able to help them. They could wait in Paloma's room, he said, until the nurse fetched the priest on duty.

Aegina sat on the bed beside her mother and picked up Paloma's right hand. Gerald sat on the other side of the bed. He looked at his daughter but still she seemed calm and determined. He picked up Paloma's left hand. It was very warm. Billie sat on the bed beside Aegina.

"*Hola, querida,*" Gerald said conversationally to Paloma, as he always did, as if she could hear him. "We love you."

The priest appeared, with Dr. Muñoz and a nurse behind him.

"*Buenos días,*" said the priest. He had very pale skin against which a dense black five-o'clock shadow stood out like charcoal. Small flakes of dandruff dotted the shoulders of his black cassock. Gerald could smell garlic and *sobrasada* on his breath. He had been summoned from lunch.

"Would you like to say anything?" said the priest.

"You mean us?" Gerald looked at Aegina, who shook her head. "No," he said.

The priest made the sign of the cross and began to speak softly. "*Da, quaesumus, Domine, ut in hora mortis nostrae Sacramentis refecti et culpis omnibus expiati, in sinum misericordiae tuae laeti suscipi mereamur . . .*"

When he was finished, the priest kissed the scarlet stole around his neck, then removed it and stepped forward and placed it for a moment on Paloma's cheek close to her intubated mouth.

"Can I do anything else for you?"

"No, thank you, Father," said Gerald.

The priest nodded gently, mumbled a little more Latin, and left the room. Back to his lunch.

"Ready?" asked Dr. Muñoz.

"*Sí,*" said Gerald.

Dr. Muñoz nodded at the nurse, made a quick sign of the cross over his chest, and turned off the ventilator. The sudden quiet filled the room, like the silence of a refrigerator unremarked until it's unplugged. Dr. Muñoz neatly removed the ventilator tube and apparatus from Paloma's face, while the nurse deftly wiped around her mouth with a white cloth. Dr. Muñoz removed the IV drip from Paloma's hand. He and the nurse left the room.

They stared at Paloma. Gerald looked to see if her chest would rise. It did not. Aegina leaned forward and kissed her mother on the cheek. They could hear only their own fretful breathing.

"She looks beautiful," said Billie. "And peaceful."

As she spoke, Paloma's lips parted as if she were about to say something. Her mouth opened—

"Mama!" cried Aegina.

Paloma's mouth fell open until her jaw resumed the position it had known for more than a week around the ventilator tube. Her lips began to turn blue. The color in her cheeks drained away and her skin became sallow. Then a gray, suety white.

Aegina stood and screamed. She screamed again. She ran out of the room.

Billie stood up. "I'll go after her." But she couldn't take her eyes off the swift change overtaking Paloma's body. "My God, it's quick." She touched Gerald's shoulder. "Shall I leave you?"

"Yes, I'll be along in a bit," said Gerald, glancing up at Billie with a small effort at a smile.

But he didn't stay long. He was looking at a corpse. He'd seen plenty of those.

Gerald stood and left the room.

Ten

I'm not the best father, you know," said Gerald gloomily.

"Of course you are, Gerald," said Billie.

They were sitting at the kitchen table. It was three in the afternoon. Aegina had not appeared since coming in late the night before, though this time she'd come home on her moped.

"You are the very *best* father I have ever seen. Certainly better than our old pater."

"He was all right."

"He wasn't interested in us, Gerald. You were too young to see it. He was nice enough, but he really wasn't interested. I'm sorry, but it was sad, seeing the way he ignored you. You were a *boy*, you needed a father. He hardly ever read to you or did anything with you. The only thing that he ever got excited about with you was packing you off to school each term."

"I thought he was good to me, in his way. He was decent, kind—"

"A librarian can be kind and decent. I'm sorry."

"He wasn't taught, you know, to show his feelings."

"Nor were you. But look how you are with Aegina. And you're wonderfully affectionate with each other. Look how you both kiss and hug each other. And you laugh together. Who taught you that, then? Not Dorothy!" Dorothy had been their father's second wife.

"It's just the way we are. It's natural."

"Exactly. You're a natural father. A wonderful father."

Billie got up to put on water for tea. When she'd done that she turned toward him. She crossed her arms and stood implacably by the stove. "However," she said, "have you thought of returning to England?"

Gerald was surprised at this. "No," he said after a moment. "What would I do there?"

"I don't know. You could write some more. People liked your book. You could teach."

"I'm sure it's not as easy as that. You say that, but I think one would have to have been there, doing that all this time. I wouldn't know where to begin. Anyway, I'd have no money."

"You could sell this place."

Gerald looked bewildered. "Well, not for very much. It's not exactly a smart villa. But it does provide me with a living. I really don't see what I'd do in England."

"Aegina's English, Gerald."

"Yes. She's Spanish too."

"Right. But what is she *going* to be?"

"Well—"

"To put it bluntly: is she going to grow up and get a job cleaning rooms at a local hotel?"

"She's going to school."

"Is it a good school?"

"It's all right. She likes it."

Billie turned away and busied herself with the tea.

"I know what you're saying," said Gerald. "What are you suggesting?"

Billie didn't answer. She poured the water into the teapot, brought it to the table with mugs and a pot of milk and the sugar bowl, and sat down. Billie poured milk into the mugs and finally tea. She pushed a mug toward her brother. "You mustn't waste her, Gerald."

Gerald took the mug and looked at it.

Billie continued, gently. "If you're not going to move, she should come back to England with me. There are some very good schools in and around Sevenoaks, and in Kent. They're not all expensive. She's too intelligent to stay here, Gerald. Not that there's anything—"

"No, I know. I've been trying to think of what would be best for her now."

"It's not the education. I'm sure it's perfectly good here—well, I don't know. But it's a question of what Aegina will see of the world, what she will imagine for herself. She can see the view from Mallorca, or the view from England."

"Right." Gerald put sugar in his tea and stirred. "It might be difficult."

"I don't know," said Billie. "Hard on you both, yes."

"And money."

"Yes, all right, perhaps it will be difficult. What's the alternative?" Gerald sipped his tea, trying to see it.

"We'll manage, Gerald. You and I, and Aegina."

"Hard on you, don't you think?"

"No," said Billie. She looked up from her tea. "I'd like it."

I*t was still twilight* as Luc gunned the noisy Rieju up the long drive to C'an Cabrer. As usual, they heard him coming. Gerald was on the terrace when he came to a stop below. He turned off the engine.

"Hello, Gerald."

"Good evening, Luc. I'm afraid Aegina's not here. She's in town having a *hamburguesa* somewhere. With Josefina. Do you know her?"

"Oh, yes." But not well. Josefina was one of Aegina's local friends. A school friend. A *mallorquina*. Luc had met her, but Aegina's island contemporaries didn't generally mix with his group of seasonal locals, as he and François and Teddy Trelawney and the others thought of themselves, because they certainly knew they weren't tourists. Josefina didn't speak English or French, for one thing. She never came to the Rocks; she inhabited another Mallorca. Though he'd spent long periods here all his life, and he knew many of the people who had lived on Mallorca all their lives, Luc wasn't one of them. But Aegina was, through her mother. It was a part of her he didn't know at all.

"You'll know where to find them, then," said Gerald helpfully.

"Yeah, maybe. Thank you. I'm very sorry to hear about Paloma."

"Thank you, Luc."

Luc turned his motorcycle to go, was about to jump on the kick-starter, when Gerald spoke again.

"And how are you doing, Luc?"

"Oh, all right, thank you."

"You're in Paris most of the year, is that right? You go to school there?"

"Yes."

"And you like it, going to school there?"

"Yeah. I guess."

"You'd rather be there for school than here?"

"Oh . . ." as if it had never occurred to him. "Yes. Absolutely."

"Well, you have a good evening," said Gerald.

"Thank you. You too."

Luc rose and stamped on the kick-starter and the bike whined. With a brief, polite look up at Gerald, who was watching him as if he were a strange new set of clothes, Luc leaned to the right and the bike rolled downhill.

Down the long bumpy road to town—across which, years ago, he and François had stretched combined mouthfuls of bubble gum in a long drooping pink trip wire that was run into by the first vehicle to come by, a Guardia Civil on a Vespa, who had screamed at them and chased them into the fields through the twilight, and never found them despite their hysterical and plainly audible giggling.

He cruised slowly through the plaza, past the sidewalk cafés and garish *hamburgueserías* and *loncherías* and *churros* dives where the locals rather than the tourists ate. He turned his bike up the small streets that ran uphill away from the sea, with the little hole-in-the-wall *bodegas* where they would put out a small table and some chairs and serve bowls of *sopa mallorquina*; the indigenous, more mysterious town of which his Cala Marsopa was only a subspecies. *La Majorque profonde*, as his father had once put it, that Luc didn't really, after all these years, know at all. As much as this place was home to him, he would always be an outsider here, as he was in Paris where he had lived, off and on, since he was five, or six, or seven years old—he was never exactly sure when he had started to spend more time in Paris than in Mallorca.

Aegina could disappear in plain view here and he would never find her.

He tooled down to the port, scoped out the diners at the Marítimo, and tore along the quay, dodging squat old fishermen and their wives, until he reached the end of the breakwater beneath the port's blinking beacon. No one out here, not of his group anyway. He looked back at the town, bright, and increasingly unfamiliar as years went by and the town grew and more people whom he didn't know filled the streets in the evenings.

H ey, Jackson."
        Jackson nodded at him. "Hey."

Luc was scanning the dance floor, the tables, at the Miravista.

"Jackson, have you seen, um—"

"Your girlfriend who threw you in the pool?"

"Well, yeah."

"Nope. She ain't been in."

"Okay, thanks."

Someone waving from a table. A crowd from the Rocks, including his mother.

"Lukey, darling!" said Arabella as he reached the table. Arabella and Richard, Milly and Tom, Susie Breedham, Dominick, and his mother. It wasn't rare to see his mother out on the town with friends, but it wasn't usual either. It was because of Milly and Tom.

"Here, Luc," said Susie. She moved her chair, making space between her and Dominick. Luc pulled up a chair.

Jackson began a muted but cheerful instrumental version of "It

Happened in Monterey," and after a moment, Tom began to sing along with the music.

"How very romantic you are, Tom," said Arabella.

"It's a song about a philanderer," said Milly.

Dominick stood up and held a hand out to Lulu. "Come on, then, old flower. Shall we trip the light fantastic once more?"

Lulu laughed immoderately. Luc knew that laugh. His mother had drunk a little—she wasn't drunk by any means, something Luc had never seen—but she was enjoying herself. "Dominick, you're such a fool," she said. But she rose. Dominick led her onto the dance floor and began dipping and weaving like a cobra, waving his arms, fixing Lulu with a grin like Svengali on dope.

His mother only ever appeared to relax—*really*—when Milly and Tom were sitting on either side of her. Milly was like an older sister to her. She had always been there, all Luc's life, away in England mostly, but missed and waited for, corresponded with weekly by his mother, coming down and staying several times a year. Sometimes Tom and Milly came for Christmas. Ahead of their visits, Tom always shipped boxes of food and drink from Fortnum's. Luc knew somehow that his mother never charged them. He knew they'd helped her buy the place. She behaved as if the house were theirs. For a long time, Luc had thought they were part of his family.

Tonight, his mother's mood extended so far as to allow her to enjoy Dominick's oily attentions. He hadn't been aware that his mother had even noticed Dominick before now, although he'd been coming down to the Rocks for years. But now he was amusing her, and her humor was encouraging him. Couldn't be anything there, surely, he thought. Not Dominick. Such a buffoon. Not his mother's type, though that wasn't always easy to spot. She did like writers, but intelligent men, thinkers, dryly humorous—like Luc's father—not bad thriller writers who wore pastel shirts and trousers and white loafers and were so blatantly on the make. She couldn't be that hard up.

Luc stood up. "Well, I'll see you all later—"

"Lukey, *would* you be a sweetheart and take me back to the Rocks?" Susie suddenly implored. "I'm really not feeling well."

"I've just got my bike, Susie—"

"That's fine, darling." Susie stood up a little uncertainly. "You don't mind, do you? It's not far."

"No, not at all, if you're really okay on the bike."

"Fine, really. You're such a star." Susie blew kisses around the table. She took Luc's arm. "Where are we, sweetie?"

A *re you feeling sick?"* he asked Susie once they were outside.
    "No, darling, just a little woozy. You are a *star.*"

"Just hold on to me," he instructed her as they climbed onto his motorcycle.

It was only a short bumpy ride along the unpaved shore road beside the rocks. Susie's arms circled him tightly, her hands gripping his stomach and chest. He felt the warm deadweight of her against his back, as if she'd fallen asleep. He remembered driving Aegina home a week or so ago and the way she had touched him.

When he stopped beside the Rocks' garage, Susie did appear to be asleep.

"We're here, Susie."

"Are we, darling?" She didn't move but still held him tightly.

"Yes. And actually, I've got to get going."

Slowly she released him. Then she fell off the bike into the road. Luc pulled the bike onto its stand and helped her up.

"Are you all right?"

"Fine, sweetie." She leaned against him, wobbling. "Can you be a star and take me up to my room, Lukey darling?"

Her room was one of four on the second floor, reached by the outside stairs at the back of the villa. They had to go up slowly as Susie negotiated each step. "Perfectly all right, darling. Sweet of you to insist, though."

Susie held on to him tightly until they got into her room. Luc sat her on the bed and she fell sideways and he turned on the bedside light. "Oh, turn it off, sweetie." He did and her hand seized his arm and pulled him down onto the bed. "Come lie down with me, sweetheart." Politely, he lay down beside her.

Then he got up. "I have to go find someone, Susie."

"Oh, do stay, Lukey. Come and have a cuddle."

"Bye." He was out the door.

Running down the steps.

A egina sat with her back to the pillow and legs stretched out on Luc's bed in the dark little toolshed. She had Teddy's bota and had been drinking the wine in it while she waited for Luc. She didn't want to go home. She didn't even want to drink any more wine now, but she kept sipping from the bag because he didn't come. She'd been sliding lower and lower onto the bed. She would stay here and he would eventually come.

She heard people arrive, talking and saying good night, laughing, and soon she no longer heard them. Minutes later she heard steps on the path outside. The door opened slowly. A woman's silhouette.

"Lukey, darling, you're not asleep?"

Aegina sat up, suddenly tense. "He's not here," she said.

"Oh," said the woman in the door. "Well, I just wanted to have a word with him about the water-skiing tomorrow. I'll leave you alone."

Aegina stood, dropping the bota, and moved toward the door like a cat disturbed in a closed space. The woman stepped back as Aegina sidled past her.

By the pool lights that filled the evergreen branches and palm fronds, they recognized each other. "It's Aegina, isn't it? It's all right, darling, it's Arabella. You remember, last year I bought an armful of your wonderful little foot thingies to bring back to friends in London. I was hoping to buy some more this year. Have you stopped making them, sweetie?"

"I haven't had time," said Aegina, moving away. She remembered

Arabella and recognized her as the sort of terrifying Amazonian woman she admired and wanted to be when she grew up.

"Don't go, sweetie. I was just looking to check about the water-skiing. I'm sure Lukey will be here in a moment. He was with us at the Miravista."

But Aegina kept going, following the shadows around the house. She left Arabella behind.

A large figure coming from the bar loomed in front of her, blocking her exit.

"A-gee-nah—"

She stopped.

Dominick had a bottle in one hand. His shirt was half open, his chest shiny with sweat. His long hair partly stuck to his forehead and flying away from his head. "How lovely to see you. And unexpected too. How are you?"

"I'm fine," she said, and tried to pass.

"What's the matter? You all right?"

"Nothing." She was small and entirely closed up, her eyes ranging in all directions around him. What a fantastic little minx she was in those incredibly tiny shorts and T-shirt, like one of those gamine French film actresses scaled down to three-fifths size.

She staggered slightly—she was drunk.

"Hang on. Don't be in such a hurry. Look," he held up the bottle, half full. "Champers. Good stuff. You can't say no. Come and have a drink."

He slid his hand around her upper arm. She didn't immediately withdraw—a telling sign. "Drinkies?" He pulled gently. After a momentary hesitation, she let him pull her. He led her to the stairs.

He didn't have any glasses in his room. They drank from the bottle. Several long swigs apiece. It took no time at all once he'd kissed her. She said absolutely nothing but compliantly lay down as he pulled her little shirt and shorts off. "My God, look at you," Dominick mooned, in genuine thrall.

He set about her with all his skills, like a taxidermist, turning her over, lifting her, turning her back again—she weighed nothing. She quickly appeared to lose consciousness, apart from the appropriate respiration and occasional muted cries. Finally, finished, exhausted, Dominick lay back, thinking he must rouse her in a minute and get her out.

When he woke in the morning she was gone. He played it over in his mind. Body out of a fairy tale, or one of the little fairy dancers in a ballet. One of the most fantastic fucks of his life. No entanglement—blessed creature had slipped away like a doe.

His eye caught the sheet and he saw the dried brown stains. He sat up and noticed his hands. He pulled away the sheet and looked between his legs. Fucking Armageddon. He got out of bed and padded across the tiled floor to the tiny sink in the corner of the room. He turned on the tap and looked up into the little majolica framed mirror on the wall.

There was something in his face, framed by his wild hair, of the mad, caught-in-the-act look of *Saturn Devouring His Son* in the Goya painting he'd once seen in the Prado and never forgotten. An impression not softened by the apparent evidence that this Saturn had consumed his boy with lashings of Worcestershire sauce and wiped the gore and condiment across his face with a dripping hand.

Dominick turned on the tap and splashed water over his face.

Never mind the mess. Fucking fantastic. Would she be back for more? Teach her a few things next time.

Eleven

A *gloomy drive* to the airport. To break the unbearable silence, Gerald ventured what he hoped was a constructive comment about letter writing. Billie must get some Basildon Bond. It makes a difference, he said, what you think and write when you're writing on good paper.

"We'll get Basildon Bond," Billie said.

Aegina said nothing.

He dropped them near the door to the departures hall and rumbled off to park the Simca.

Inside, Gerald ordered a *café con leche* for Billie, a TriNaranjus for Aegina, and a *café* for himself. They sipped glumly. Gerald smoked ferociously, surrounding himself with a dense blue cloud. He could think of nothing comforting to say. It'll only be a few months—for people of his generation, used to the war, with uncertain outcomes of much longer separations, such partings were trivial. Aegina, in fact, appeared preternaturally composed: no weeping or lamentations. Thank God. Like this, they could simply sip their drinks while waiting for the flight to be called and look out in agreed-upon contemplation at the strangely abiding *Don Quixote* landscape of crumbling stone walls, tawny fields, and sail-powered windmills that still surrounded Palma's airport.

Billie went off to the loo.

Gerald peered at his daughter through the smoke. She was too composed, he realized. He'd been unwilling to open floodgates of emotion, but now he put his arm around Aegina. "Aegina. Are you all right?"

"Yes."

"It'll only be a few months, and you'll come down for Christmas. And we'll—" Of course, it will be Christmas without her mother. What an idiot he was.

"Yes. I'll be all right. Don't worry, Papa. I'm fine."

She was amazing. Got her strength from her mother.

"Well, what are you thinking?" he asked.

"I'm thinking that my childhood is over. It just ended."

"No, no, not at all. You are still only fourteen—I mean, you're just a girl, Aegina. Don't worry, you're not being packed off to England to grow up, you know. You're just going to school. You'll make new friends. Really, you're still a young girl, you've got lots of time—"

"I'm sure it will be great, Papa. But my childhood is over."

I*t was that ruddy* great darkie guitar player, Dominick realized, chomping away on an *ensaïmada* with quite amusing delicacy in the airport café.

"You're off as well, then, Jackson?" said Dominick.

Jackson gazed at him. "Yes."

"Back to America?"

"No, I'm going to Gibraltar. Got a job playing with a band on an ocean liner for the winter. Going to the Caribbean."

"Fantastic. Lucky old you. I wish I were in your shoes." Indeed, what a swath old Jackson would cut through a shipload of widows cruising for a spot of excitement. "So will we see you back here next summer?"

"I don't know. Depends what comes up."

"All right, well, have fun aboard your ship of music lovers."

Dominick walked on toward his gate with the other people heading for the London flight. He saw two familiar faces: the father, the woman who wasn't his wife—and the girl.

"Hallo," said Dominick cheerily. "Are you off back home too? We must be on the same flight." It *was* Aegina. She looked like a child in her little shirt and skirt and cheap plastic sandals. Terribly sweet. "Well,

Aegina, it was such fun seeing you this summer." He grinned at her. "We must get together next year."

Aegina stepped quickly forward and kicked him in the balls.

Dominick was completely surprised, but he could say nothing because her blow had been devastatingly accurate. He only grunted and crumpled forward, dropping the newspaper he'd bought at the airport shop.

Aegina kicked again, but Dominick's bent posture offered only his shins to her foot. She threw out her arms and launched herself at his chest, pushing him so that he fell sprawling on the hard marble airport floor.

"Aegina?" said Billie.

Gerald stepped forward and wrapped his arms around his daughter. She was a trembling, throbbing coil. He pulled her away, folding her tightly into his chest, and watched the man on the floor kicking his legs like a fallen horse, scrambling to get away.

1956

The Waves

The mother and daughter arrived at the beach first.

"¡Mira las olas, mamá!" yelled the four-year-old girl.

"Sí, son grandes. ¿Qué dijo tu padre?"

"Que tenemos que ser cuidadosos."

"Bueno. Claro," said Paloma.

They crossed the sand to their usual spot. "¿Dónde están?" cried the little girl.

"Ya vienen."

There had been a storm somewhere to the north, said her father, who knew all about the sea, and today the waves at the beach would be large and strong. He was right; they were rolling in as booming funnels and breaking on top of one another close to the beach like something being delivered too fast. As soon as they dropped their towels on the sand, the girl dragged her mother to the water's edge. The foamy water popped and crackled around them. The girl waded deeper, letting go of her mother's hand, and a wave rushed at her. She screamed as it caught her and she fell. Her mother didn't move. The wave surged out and the girl lay in the wet sand, laughing.

"¡Mira, mamá! ¡Ahí están!" she shouted. She stood up and began waving at the woman approaching with the little boy. "¡Por aquí!"

The other woman and the little boy, who was almost six, joined them in the shallows. The two women stood together while the children played around them.

"*Bueno*," said Preciosa. "*Voy a sentarme. Luc, te quedas cerca de la playa y te cuidas de Aegina. ¿Entiendes?*"

On the beach, not far from the water, the women sat on their towels.

"Aie, a madhouse," said Preciosa.

"What now?"

"Oy! Everything, all the time. Take Luc to the beach, she says, while telling me to clean up the breakfasts, clean the rooms, do the laundry."

"She never takes Luc to the beach herself?"

"That one? Never. She never goes to the beach, she doesn't spend any time with him, poor thing."

"And the father? When does he arrive?"

"I don't think he's coming this summer. He's staying in Paris. He can't take her, and I don't blame him—*¡Cuidado!*" Preciosa yelled at the children.

The waves, tumbling closely one atop another, insistently, left no respite after each surge. As the women watched, a retreating wave met a breaker larger than the others. A heap of water rose over the children and swept them off their feet, pulling them into the next wall, which broke and swallowed them in a chaotic vortex of heaping foam.

Both women stood and walked into the water. They grabbed at shiny brown feet, hands, arms, legs indistinguishable from each other, and hauled the spluttering children into shallower water.

"*¡Cuidado con las olas!*" said Preciosa. "Look out for the waves or you'll be carried off to Minorca before we can get you."

"Don't go out any farther," said Paloma.

The women walked back up to their towels. When they had sat down again, Preciosa said: "I saw Gerald down here again the other day."

Paloma stared hard at her. "Did he come in?"

"No. Just walking on the road around Los Roques."

Paloma shook her head. "He's still hooked by that witch."

"But he loves you, surely?" said Preciosa. "Not her. Not that one?"

"It's a sickness," said Paloma.

She looked out at the children.

They were taunting the most vicious of the approaching waves.

"*¡Éste!*" yelled Luc.

"*¡No, la próxima!*" screamed Aegina, screeching like a bird.

Another wave engulfed them. The water carried them under with unimagined force. It twisted and rolled them together so that neither child could tell whether the arms and legs and hands and feet thumping into their faces and bodies were their own or the other's. They were one tumbling creature.

And then the water was gone, and they were left sprawled together on the sand in a moment of unnatural quiet, shrieking and laughing. Shrieking and laughing. Before the next wave broke.

1951

The Way to Ithaca

One

After three years on the island, Gerald no longer walked along the shore in front of Villa Los Roques. During the first year, he'd stopped at the house and knocked on the door on several occasions, but it had never been opened to him. Then he'd been shot by an air rifle while passing the house on the shore road, the .177 lead pellet (he'd picked it up after seeing it fall to the road beside him and put it in his pocket to keep as a memento of Lulu's shifting feelings for him) stinging his thigh and later raising a small bruise. He now used calle Rotges, bordering the high wall at the back of the property, and occasionally he heard voices on the other side of the wall—Milly's he could always make out—but never Lulu's. Other voices, men and women; sometimes a boy's, Milly's son Cassian, he supposed. A little way on, a dirt path led down to the dirt road along the sea, well out of sight of the house. That would take him to the beach at Son Moll and then up to the main road close to his long rutted drive.

Today he saw the man and the little boy again. He'd seen them before along the road here. He couldn't be sure but he thought it was Lulu's husband and son. They ate sometimes at the Marítimo, in the evenings when Gerald was never in town—Rafael had told him. Lulu and her American husband and the baby boy and their friends from the house.

They were coming toward him from the beach; the American man walking, hugging the little boy to his chest. As they drew close, the man nodded at Gerald with the polite acknowledgment of people who know each other only by infrequent sighting. Nothing deep or knowing in that look: he doesn't know who I am, Gerald realized. With his straw hat and threadbare shirt and trousers, Gerald wouldn't be taken for a holiday-maker. A yachtsman, perhaps, or a laborer.

The child was fast asleep on his father's shoulder. Gerald looked closely at its face for signs of Lulu, but it was simply a very small boy's sleeping face—Gerald couldn't tell how old children were by looking at them, but this one seemed convincingly less than two, which would be right. Just a pure sleeping-boy face, unaware of anything in the world.

Gerald nodded back as they passed and walked on.

Two

"**B**ernard! *Good man,*" said Tom when Bernie came in through the gate carrying the straw shoulder bag. Tom appeared to have just woken up. He sat splayed in a deck chair wearing Milly's threadbare yellow dressing gown with traces of a pattern of sprouted tufts. He was blinking in the sunlight, taking in his surroundings—the tiled patio, the open doors to the house, the glimpse of the blue sea beyond the white wall—as if a hood had just been removed from his head.

As usual, Bernie had been the first awake and he'd walked into town from Villa Los Roques along the unpaved shore road to the *panadería*.

"Morning, Tom," he said.

Bernie went on into the house. Lulu and Milly, both dressed, were sitting at the kitchen table, the teapot between them. Milly, half a generation older than Lulu, wearing her usual sensible summer wear: a short-sleeved Aertex shirt, loose skirt to the knees, plimsolls: a schoolgirl's outfit sized for a six-footer. Lulu, a schoolgirl in size against her, wore floral shorts and a sleeveless cotton shirt that displayed the lithe arms and legs that Bernie so admired. They were saying something about "guests" but stopped talking the moment he appeared. Lulu stood up. "I've just put your coffeepot on," she said, going to the stove.

"Thanks," he said. Bernie again was aware of the sense he'd had for a few days: that Lulu and Milly were conspiring about something. He set the straw bag on the table and took out its contents: several round loaves and a mounded paper parcel with its two ends twisted together.

"Ooh, *lovely,*" said Milly, reaching for the parcel, opening it, and pulling out a soft, round, spiral-shaped flaky pastry. "I must have my *ensaïmada* immediately, while they're still hot. Thank you, Bernard. You're a love."

"Yes, you are," said Lulu, as if confirming this after some consideration.

"You're welcome," said Bernie.

Nobody called him Bernie, his preferred name, here. After two years of marriage, Lulu still wouldn't call him Bernie. "I can't, darling," she'd said early on. "I just can't say it. You might as well be called Siegfried. I couldn't manage it." He'd thought that charming at first. She evidently couldn't manage Bernard either. She called him darling, and referred to him by name only when mentioning him to third parties. *Ber*-nard, or *Buh*nud, the way it came out. This, then, was what Milly and Tom and Lulu's friends called him. Bernie was accustomed to the American emphasis on the second syllable, with its prominent American *r*—Ber-*nard*—which people had called him all his life, at school, college, the army, until they got to know him as Bernie. Even in Paris, where he now lived, the French—*Bair-narrrhh*—was more familiar-sounding, and certainly more charming, than *Buh*nud. Good morning, Buhnud. Ah, there you are, Buhnud. They seemed to be talking about someone else.

"Luc asleep?" asked Bernie.

"Yes, darling," said Lulu. She poured coffee from the Moka pot into a cup and handed it to him.

"Did you see Schooner out on the terrace?" asked Milly.

"No."

"Good," said Milly. "He needs his sleep. Well, if you go join Tom, Lulu and I'll bring you your breakfast."

Obediently, Bernie went out to the terrace. He sat in the shade and wished he had a newspaper.

"Poor old Schooner, eh?" said Tom, squinting at him.

"He seemed very glad to be here."

"I should think so, after his epic peregrination around the Mediterranean. And the other business. Poor old fellow," he said feelingly.

Schooner Trelawney had left England under a cloud four days earlier, intent on joining Tom and Milly and licking his wounds among loyal friends. He knew, of course, that for years they'd been going down to the same villa called the Rocks beside the sea—they'd often invited him. He'd gone directly to Monaco by train but it looked nothing like T & M's holiday snapshots. He'd been unable to find them anywhere. A man had suggested the Eden Roc Hotel, so, despite not being in Monaco at all, he'd gone there. The houses along the French coast here looked more like it, but no sign of Tom and Milly, nor any villa of that name. After several days in a wretched pension in Nice, Schooner was reluctantly persuaded by cables sent to and from England to make his way to Barcelona, where he got on the ferry—to *Mallorca* (he'd never heard of the place) not Monaco—and then endured a frightening bus ride across the island, his heart sinking the whole time with the mounting conviction that he was now closer to Africa than to his friends, to a *tiny* little village by the sea that couldn't *possibly* be the place they'd been banging on about for years, and then, at last, long after dark, he was directed to a house on a dirt road beside the sucking sea where he stumbled in and quite miraculously found Tom and Milly, et al. Schooner had collapsed, weeping, managed to get out a few shreds of his awful news over soup and whiskey, before Milly and Lulu packed him off to bed.

"Well, you can't shit where you eat," said Milly quietly as they ate breakfast on the patio.

"I know," said Tom, "but jolly bad luck, all the same. And what about poor Teddy? What's going to happen to him now? He's just a little boy. It's going to be tough on him if Vivian decides to take it further. Do you think she will?"

"It's not bad luck—it's very naughty, and bloody wanton, if you ask me," said Milly. "But yes, there is Teddy, so I don't think she'll shop him to the police."

"Let's hope not," said Tom. "But under threat of that, she can call the shots, can't she. Shut him right out if she's a mind to."

"What happened?" asked Bernie. He had been typing a piece in his room much of the evening and had caught a sense of the thing—an infidelity of some sort—the night before, but now he was lost. "He was having an affair, right?"

"Not exactly," said Milly. "Vivian, Schooner's wife, caught him in his study at home with one of his pupils he was tutoring, in flagrante delicto. It was a boy, of course, which perfectly suited Vivian, because she's kicked him out and threatened to go to the police. Now she'll try to keep him away from their son, Teddy. In England, he can be prosecuted for (a) buggery, and (b) doing it with a child. So he's out." Milly began pouring the tea.

"Poor old chap," said Tom. He turned and looked at Bernie appealingly.

"Sounds tough," agreed Bernie. Without the gauze of love and sympathy through which the others saw Schooner, Bernie understood only that Schooner was a pedophile on the run, harbored by his wife's friends in a house containing his sleeping infant son.

He looked at Lulu. She was quiet. Her thoughts seemed elsewhere. She looked up at him and smiled. "I'll get you some more coffee, darling," she said, then rose and disappeared into the house.

Cassian joined them on the terrace. So obviously Milly's son in every way, with his thatch of her red hair, wearing Aertex shirt, shorts, sandals—a schoolboy's holiday outfit—he looked younger than fifteen. He sat down and spread marmalade thickly across a piece of grilled bread while Milly poured him a cup of tea.

"You missed all the excitement last night," said Tom. "Schooner's here."

"I know, Mummy told me," said Cassian. His broad pale freckled face showed no emotion.

"Did you?" Tom said, looking at his wife.

"Yes," said Milly.

"You told him what, exactly?" asked Tom.

"That he'd been buggering a little boy and been chucked out," said Cassian.

"Really?" said Tom. "You told him that—"

"Of course I didn't, darling."

"I *know*, Daddy," said Cassian, witheringly. "Everyone knows."

"Well, it's an unhappy situation," said Tom.

"I'm sure he'll live," said Cassian, raising his teacup.

"Darling boy," said Tom, with gentle censure, "what a heartless thing to say. I don't think you quite understand what's happened. There's a little boy, Schooner's son, Teddy, to consider."

"There was another little boy, as well, wasn't there?" said Cassian.

Milly broke in. "What are you doing today, darling?"

"Go bathing as usual, I expect," said Cassian without enthusiasm. He took a bite of toast, and even with his mouth closed the sound of the crust being crushed between his teeth was extraordinarily loud.

"I'm going to look in on Luc," said Bernie, rising and leaving the table.

Luc was sleeping in a tiny room beside his parents' bedroom. Its window looked out at the sea. Bernie had made paper airplanes and colored them with artist's pastels he'd found in the house and taped them to the white walls. Luc, at fifteen months old, was sleeping in a small normal bed with no protection around it, but he'd always been good about not falling out of bed. He lay awake, sprawled on his back, his eyes and whole attention on Bernie the moment he came in the door, as if he'd been waiting for him. A beautiful smile spread across Luc's face as he saw his father. "Papa!"

"Good morning, my little boy," said Bernie. He scooped Luc up and hugged and kissed him and then held him so they could see each other's faces. "How are you?"

"Papa, beach?" said Luc.

"Papa has to go into the town to mail a letter," said Bernie. "But this afternoon I'll come back and we'll go to the beach."

"Go beach!" shouted Luc.

Cassian was outside the door of Luc's room. "Bernard, I hear you're driving into Palma this morning."

"Yes."

"Can I come with you?"

"Yes, but I won't be staying long."

"Long enough for a coffee?"

"Sure. I usually stop for coffee anyway."

"Are you leaving soon?"

"I was planning on going as soon as I'm dressed."

"I'll meet you by the car," said Cassian.

B ernie ran up the wide steps into the cool, cavernous, marbled interior of the Correos building on carrer de la Constitució and mailed off his neatly typed pages to the *Herald Tribune* office in Paris. Days earlier, after attending the coronation of King Baudouin, he'd flown straight from Brussels to Palma rather than returning to Paris and writing up the story there. Others were reporting on the abdication of King Léopold III and the succession of his son; Bernie's piece was a more thoughtful assessment of the quaintness versus the value of any monarchy in postwar Europe. It wasn't urgent and he'd wanted to resume his vacation with Lulu and Luc as soon as possible, so he wrote it in the not entirely peaceful holiday atmosphere of Villa Los Roques.

Cassian had followed him into the building to make a phone call and was waiting outside. He was wearing stylish sunglasses, in rakish counterpoint to his shirt, shorts, sandals with socks.

Bernie drove the little SEAT to the Bar Formentor, where, he'd told Cassian when the boy asked him, they would stop for coffee. Bernie liked the place for its view at the head of a tree-lined plaza, for its retention of the feel of an older world, and for the people-watching. Errol Flynn, who came to the Bar Formentor daily for coffee and nonserious shoreside drinking when his yacht *Zaca* was in port (currently it wasn't), was said to have put the place on the map, but Porfirio Rubirosa had come to Mallorca with his third wife, Doris Duke, in the late forties to attend parties thrown by Juan Llobet and was photographed quaffing beer at the Formentor. Other British, French, American travelers—people who

came off yachts or wrote books or made films—had migrated to the Bar
Formentor with the same sort of flocking and homing devices that send
birds on the North American flyway to Central Park: somehow they
simply knew.

Bernie had first come to Mallorca and the Bar Formentor in 1949
with French film director Julien Duvivier and the actors George Sanders and Herbert Marshall during the shooting of Duvivier's *Black Jack*, a
film about an expatriate American smuggler who cruised from port to
port around the Mediterranean aboard his capacious mahogany motor
yacht and got into ceaseless trouble. *Life* magazine, under the impression
that another *Casablanca* was in the works, had borrowed Bernie from the
Trib and dispatched him to Palma for a story on the film to coincide with
its release the following year. Bernie and a *Life* photographer spent time
with the director and his stars on locations around the island, one of
which had been the waters off Cala Marsopa. They met an amusing
group of English people at a house party in a villa above the rocks near
the harbor. Bernie went back to Cala Marsopa after he'd finished his
assignment. Lulu was one of the most beautiful women he'd ever met.
She and her friends Tom and Milly Ollorenshaw were funny in an acer-
bic British way he liked. Bernie made them laugh too, in some American
way that they seemed to like. He invited Lulu to visit him in Paris. She'd
only passed through the city once. It couldn't have been more romantic:
she loved the food, she loved his apartment on rue Jacob; they walked,
drank, ate everywhere. She loved the fact that Bernie traveled, met poli-
ticians, movie people, most of all that he lived in Paris. "A writer living in
Paris, it's ridiculously romantic, you know," Lulu told him. It was as if
he'd given her an elixir. They were married at the American embassy. In
the beginning, she accompanied him on his assignments, enjoying the
trains to Rome, Prague, Bucharest, but then she grew tired of traveling.
Bernie had stories to cover all over Europe every week. She didn't like his
being away. She felt unsafe when he was away, she said. Bernie told her
she couldn't be safer in Paris; she was probably safer in Paris than anywhere. She felt unsafe *alone*, she told him. Bernie didn't know what to say

to that: traveling for his stories, researching his books, it was what he did—it was what she'd said she liked about him.

He'd never seen *Black Jack*, or even heard of its release. *Life* hadn't published his story.

R*eady to go?*" he asked Cassian. He'd finished his *café con leche*, and read a three-day-old London *Daily Express*, the only English newspaper he'd been able to find at the newsstand near the bar. Cassian, not a spirited conversationalist, had taken half an hour to empty his bottle of Coca-Cola with increasingly small sips while looking around the plaza with a mounting anxiousness that was palpable despite his sunglasses and habitual inscrutability.

"Do you mind if we wait another few minutes?" Cassian said flatly. "I'm expecting a friend. He's late. So he should be here soon."

"Sure," said Bernie, masking the gratification of his curiosity with a flick of his wrists to snap the paper open again. He had the opportunity to read in depth the stories he'd glanced over too briefly: a man who had amassed a horde of stolen empty milk bottles belonging to the Putney Dairy in southwest London was helping police with their inquiries; the BBC Television Service transmission from Alexandra Palace had suffered an inexplicable thirteen-minute blackout during the Saturday evening broadcast of the football pools results—

Cassian rose abruptly, skidding his chair back, to greet a tall man who approached their table. The man motioned with a quick hand held at his waist for Cassian to sit back down, and he sat down himself beside him at their table. He was in his thirties, dark—more Arab- or Turkish-, Bernie thought, than Spanish-looking—dressed like a waiter: white open-necked shirt, black pants and shoes. He was immediately uneasy at the sight of Bernie, his eyes flickering questioningly between him and Cassian.

"It's all right, he's a friend of my parents.'"

"You should tell me," the man said with an accent Bernie thought was eastern European, or Levantine. "When I see him, almost I don't come. It's okay, the rest? You will see your friend?"

"Oh, yes, that's all in hand," said Cassian suavely.

The man was carrying a straw bag of the sort people carried to market. He pulled from it a small parcel wrapped in brown paper tied tightly with string and passed it to Cassian beneath the table. He shot another glance at Bernie, and looked again at Cassian uncertainly, his eyes flickering over the boy's shirt and shorts. "Okay," he said. He stood and walked across the plaza.

"I liked your friend very much," said Bernie.

"Actually, he's more of an acquaintance. I've only met him a few times. He's a friend of a friend."

"Ready to go?" Bernie put some peseta notes under his saucer.

"Yes," said Cassian. He stood, holding the brown parcel to his chest.

In the car, Cassian said, "Can we just swing by the Club Náutico on our way?"

"Sure," said Bernie. "Got a friend there?"

"Yes, actually, a friend from London."

"So, what's in the package? Drugs?"

"Good God, no. Just money."

Bernie swung the car into the entrance to the Real Club Náutico and parked near the head of the main quay.

"I won't be a minute," said Cassian, opening the door. He walked down a quay at which a number of foreign motor yachts were moored: British blue and red ensigns, French Tricolors, Dutch, Swedish, Norwegian flags fluttering lightly at their sterns.

Bernie had to smile. For the role of Mike Alexander, the nefarious smuggler and lead character in *Black Jack*, George Sanders had been kitted out by wardrobe with the white, black-visored captain's hat bearing the insignia of an anchor, traditionally worn by actors when their character stepped aboard a vessel of any sort, a striped French fisherman's jersey with a red kerchief tied at the neck, voluminous white trousers held up by a wide belt that carried a sheath knife, and sneakers; a costume that, together with the naturally louche and dissolute cast of George Sanders's features, was no less indicative of his character's business than if he'd worn a sandwich board with the word *smuggler* painted on it. Whereas Cassian appeared for all the world what he was: a schoolboy in shorts, with a slight side-to-side wavering of his still-growing lope as he made his way down the quay. He turned right where the dock reached a T, and Bernie lost sight of him.

He returned, empty-handed, eight minutes later.

"What sort of money, if you don't mind my asking?" asked Bernie as he drove out of Palma.

"Czechoslovak korunas—the old ones, pre-1939," said Cassian.

"Who wants them?"

"I've no idea. People took them out before the war and now people want them back to get the new currency. At the moment they can be exchanged for the new korunas at par, I think. Otherwise, they're useless."

"So, when you're on holiday, you're a currency smuggler?"

"Not always. I'm just helping out some friends. I mean, everybody does it, don't they? Mummy and Daddy do it every time they leave England. You can't have a decent holiday on fifty pounds, can you? Fifty pounds is all you're allowed to take out of England, you know."

"Yes, I know. So what do you all do, stuff it in your pants when you get onto the cross-Channel ferry?"

"Crikey, no. Yachts mostly. At least, everyone I know uses yachts. That's what Mummy and Daddy do. How do you think they're getting the money into Spain for Lulu to buy the house?"

"What?"

"The money for the villa. You can't do a bank draft for that sort of money."

Some minutes later, Bernie said, "No, of course not."

Cassian was looking out the window. He swung his head back to Bernie. "Sorry?" he said.

Three

Early in the year, an editor at John Murray, Ltd—publisher of Byron, Darwin, Livingstone, Conan Doyle, Jane Austen, and Herman Melville, and still publishing sturdy, literate travel narratives—had sent Gerald a letter, forwarded to him by Griffiths at *Yachting Monthly*:

22 *February 1951*

Dear Mr. Rutledge,

For the past several years, I've read your articles in Yachting Monthly, Cornhill, The Listener, *about Odysseus's route home from the Trojan War with the greatest of pleasure. It has occurred to me, now in agreement with others in the house, that these pieces could be advantageously collected into a small but exceptional book.*

I am a keen coastal yachtsman myself, and consequently have read the run of our contemporary sailing literature. Most of it is abysmal: turgid accounts of anchoring replete with gauges of chain and details of muddy bottoms. Your pieces stand distinctly apart. The mix of gentle erudition with travelogue and your sailorly insights into the geography of The Odyssey *would make, we believe, a unique narrative. Such a book would prove attractive to a general reader whose interests go beyond the classical or nautical, yet draw back at the stolidly academic. Indeed, we see in your seamanlike deduction and navigation of the possible route of* The Odyssey *the makings of a small classic of travel literature.*

This may have occurred to you too—perhaps you already have plans with another publisher? But if not, we are prepared to offer you an advance of £750 against royalties, with every expectation that this advance will be earned back in a short time and see us all with a modest profit. If this interests you, please let me know your thoughts by return, with, if possible, a detailed list of your Odyssey *articles— are there any that remain unpublished?—and to what extent they cover the entire route from Troy to Ithaca.*

I look forward to hearing from you at your earliest opportunity.

By the way, where are you? If you are in or near London, I should be very happy to discuss all this with you over a drink at the RTYC.

Yours sincerely,
Eric Pocock

During respites in action—lying in his bunk in the bilgy bowels of, first, the aircraft carrier HMS *Furious,* and then the destroyer HMS *Avon Vale*—Gerald had read a Cambridge University translation of Heinrich Schliemann's account of the discovery of Troy. On August 14, 1868, after picking his way on horseback across a rubble-strewn plateau in northwest Turkey, Schliemann found traces of a circular wall at a place called Hisarlik. "The site fully agrees with the description given by Homer. . . . As soon as one sets foot on the Trojan plain, the view of the beautiful hill of Hisarlik grips one with astonishment." Later that day, Schliemann climbed to the roof of a house at the northern edge of the plain:

With the *Iliad* in hand, I sat on the roof and looked around me. I imagined seeing below me the fleet, camp, and assemblies of the Greeks; Troy and its fortress on the plateau of Hisarlik; troops marching to and fro and battling each other . . . For two hours the main events of the *Iliad* passed before my eyes until darkness and violent hunger forced me to leave the roof. I had become fully convinced that it was here that ancient Troy had stood.

Schliemann dug and unearthed an ancient city that had been sacked by war.

Immediately after being demobbed in Alexandria at the end of the war, Gerald had traveled to Istanbul. He reached Hisarlik and the gouged mounds of Troy by ferry, charabanc, and foot. Afterward, *Odyssey* in hand, he visited the surrounding coasts in a number of craft, large and small. What he saw, he concluded, was what Odysseus (whether a real man or not seemed moot) had seen. Since here was Troy, and to the southwest at a known coordinate lay Ithaca, and between them the mysteries of that ten-year voyage home, Gerald determined then to return in his own small yacht and find his way, navigating by Homer's cloaked directions, from Troy to Ithaca. He'd done exactly that, purchasing and sailing the nimble *Nereid* from Sussex, all the way to the Aegean in 1946–1947, and west back around Italy's boot into the Tyrrhenian Sea in 1948 to explore Corsica and Sardinia as possible sites for the home of the Laestrygonians, and the cave of the Cyclops, Polyphemus. The Strait of Messina, he had always known, must be the location of Scylla and Charybdis, and he had been sure he would find the cave somewhere on the west coast of Sicily. His undoing, like Odysseus's, had been straying too far to the west and becoming enmeshed with a nymph on an island.

With what he had already published, Gerald had most of his propounded route of *The Odyssey* written, with photographs, including the *Nereid* lying to her anchor in the same spots where he believed Homer had placed his hero. Only the most eastern early locations of *The Odyssey*, Troy itself and Ismarus, he had not sailed to himself—the cruise abandoned after the aborted honeymoon voyage with Lulu—but these were known, unequivocal, and he had already visited them in one vessel or another.

He and Pocock corresponded. He sent him all his articles, including several that had not yet been published; he sent his photos and his own rough maps. Pocock sent him a contract to sign, and just a few weeks later, at the dusty Correos in Cala Marsopa, Gerald opened a brown envelope containing a check for £750. A life-altering sum. More money than he'd ever seen, or perhaps would ever see again. What to do with it?

He could buy another boat and, at last, sail back to the Aegean. It was where he had aimed himself and his fascination with Ancient Greece since he'd been a schoolboy in shorts. He had sailed, in one boat or another, to most places he believed were contenders for locations in *The Odyssey*, but he had always believed he could spend a lifetime exploring the waters of Greece and Turkey, or, as he thought of the place in classical terms, Asia Minor, the supposed birthplace of Homer. Mallorca had proved a catastrophic interruption to this grand plan. Something like a terrible automobile crash.

The morning after he received Pocock's letter, Gerald took his habitual morning walk through the olive groves along the ridge above C'an Cabrer, to gaze down the hill, over the town, out to sea.

I could buy a boat, he thought.

Then he turned and looked at the olive trees.

Four

They were sitting under the shaded arbor on the patio overlooking the rocks and the sea, ready for a late lunch, when Bernie and Cassian returned from Palma.

Rested and safe at last among friends, Schooner Trelawney was back in top form. Over lunch, he related the difficulties he'd experienced trying to locate his friends in Monaco.

"Well, you'd said the place was small and that you knew absolutely everybody, so when I stepped out of the train station and beheld the entire, sparkling Fabergé principality spread out beneath me, I was impressed." Schooner looked at Tom. "I must say, m'dear, *you* rose instantly in my estimation. I thought, Golly, Tom *is* doing well. And if, indeed, you knew everybody, then it was a simple deduction that I should start inquiring after you at the palace."

Tom and Milly were weaving in their chairs and hooting. Cassian giggled, more at seeing his parents reduced to helplessness than for Schooner's story.

"You can imagine my disappointment—after such a journey—when nobody at the palace had heard of you. Well, that was the guards, and what would they know? They couldn't care less. Deaf to any logic or appeal. They wouldn't even let me in to ask the prince or somebody who might have been expected to know you. *The Ollorenshaws!* I began shouting it past the guards up at the windows—for all I knew, you were *inside*, at some do." Schooner looked around the table, his eyebrows raised, happy.

Lulu looked sideways at Bernie. Luc sat at his chair between them, impervious to the hysterics and noise of the adults, and Bernie seemed wholly intent on watching his son gather spoonfuls of his lunch of rice and mashed sardines.

A *fter she'd put Luc down* for his nap, Lulu found Bernie in a chair beneath the pines behind the house. She sat down nearby.

"You were positively funereal at lunch. I'm sure you're repelled by Schooner, but you might make an effort not to be so boorishly disapproving among my friends."

"I wasn't disapproving. I simply wasn't amused."

"No, of course not. Your sense of humor doesn't extend beyond Laurel and Hardy. What's going on with you, then?"

"When were you going to tell me that you're buying this place with Tom's money?"

"Actually, it's Milly's money."

"Oh, Milly's money. I was misinformed. I got what little I know from Cassian, who was able to give me the broad details about the financial transfer. Bright kid. So when were you going to tell me?"

"Not until I bloody well had to," she said. She pulled from her shorts a pack of cigarettes and the gold Ronson lighter Bernie had given her, and busily lit a cigarette, blowing a spout of smoke upward toward the overarching pine boughs.

"I might have helped you," Bernie said, "if you'd asked. But you spend your summers here anyway, so why do you want to buy the place?" In the nearly three years he'd known her, even after they were married, Lulu spent all summer in Cala Marsopa with Tom and Milly, who had rented Villa Los Roques every summer since the war. Lulu had come down with them from England, initially to cook, later as an inseparable part of their summer group, which included rotating rooms of friends. After she'd married Bernie and moved into his apartment in Paris, she and Luc would leave the city early in June and not return until after *la rentrée* in early September. Bernie made trips down to see them when he could.

"Because I'm going to make it into a business. I'm going to have people come and stay and eat here for their holidays and pay me money for it. It was Milly's idea. They want to do other things, they want to travel more, but they still want this place to come to."

"Oh," said Bernie. The ramifications spread outward slowly, the way following a moving object will raise the head to broader, unsuspected views. "That'll take a lot of work."

"Yes, it will. It means a big change. I'm going to stay here. I'm not coming back to Paris."

"But you know I can't live here," said Bernie. "I have to be based in Paris—that's my work."

"Of course I know it. You love France and the French. Well, I'm sorry, I hate it there."

"I thought you were feeling better about it. You've seemed happier the last few months."

"That's because I've been planning this for months," said Lulu.

"Let me have one of your cigarettes," said Bernie. After he'd lit a cigarette, he said, "And you want Luc to grow up here? To go to school here?"

"Of course not. I don't want him growing up to be some Spanish oick any more than you do."

"So what are you suggesting?"

"Well, obviously he has to stay here with me until school becomes important—I mean beyond counting and reading and all that, when he's eight or nine or ten, whenever it is they start learning things properly—then he should go to school in Paris and stay with you during term time. He'll come down here in the holidays."

Bernie didn't know what to say. Or, rather, he quelled and swallowed all the thoughtful objections, savage rebuttals, angry recriminations, legal threats, and reasonable entreaties that boiled in his mind and mouth.

He understood that he didn't know Lulu at all. The longer he'd known her, the more of a mystery she had become to him. Over the past year, he'd come to realize that he had almost entirely invented the person he'd fallen in love with. He realized too that she had no idea who he was. They were complete strangers to each other, and they'd been growing more mystified and estranged. Since Luc's birth, the enigma that each was to the other had enlarged into a yawning space between them. Now he was stunned, perhaps, but not surprised.

He smoked. Beyond the abundant, cosseting, superior health and educational services vouchsafed all mothers and children in France, Paris had always seemed to him the unsurpassable ideal garden in which to plant and grow a child. A few days after his birth, Bernie had taken Luc into the Jardin du Luxembourg. Thereafter they wandered regularly into the Lux—a short walk from Bernie's apartment—following their ears and eyes, discovering together more than Bernie had known existed there: the model Breton fishing smacks sailing across the octagonal basin before the palace, the *théâtre des marionnettes*, the gently galloping horses of the carousel. Together, they watched the chess players, and the even more serious boules players, and gazed without shyness at the serene, spectral stone and bronze people frozen mid-*pensée* while the seasons and the centuries drifted over them.

There was the wider Paris he had planned to explore with Luc: the *bouquinistes*, the coal-roasted *châtaignes*, the bric-a-brac of *les puces*, the jungle-rich parade of humankind and the wonder of who all these people were and where they came from, these artists and musicians, filmmakers, writers, academics, White Russian émigrés, Roma gypsies, the Walter Benjamins, the Ben Franklins, the serious wanderers of the Earth, all of whom ineluctably pass through Paris at one time or another. No roiling mobs, or stunting urban canyonscapes, but a world passing by on a human, absorbable scale, like a puttering Mobylette; the entire human story, touchable, instructive, charming, reeking agreeably, inexhaustible but not exhausting—all this he had planned to show his son, Luc.

In his mind now, Bernie saw the life he had fully imagined for Luc in Paris go *pfftt*.

"You think he'll be happy here?"

"Of course he'll be happy," said Lulu. "The weather's pleasant. It's quiet and peaceful. He's already familiar with Preciosa. She'll look after him. There are other children about, not just Spaniards."

"You don't think he'll miss me?"

"I'm sure he'll miss you, though children need their mothers more than their fathers. You're off half the time anyway. You're welcome to come and stay at a hotel and see him on a reasonable basis."

"You'd like me to be reasonable?"

"Yes. Why not? That's what's best for Luc, isn't it? We must put his needs first. Besides, I'm going to be reasonable with you. I won't take any money from you. You need to support Luc, but I've got my own money and I'll make what I need. You needn't worry about me."

"I can see that. You've thought of everything."

"Oh, believe me, Bernard"—how brutal it sounded, to hear her use his name, for once—"I have."

Five

S eñor Gerald!" exclaimed Lestrado Puig, rising to his feet as Gerald came into his office along the street from the *mercado* in Cala Marsopa. "This is a pleasure. Sit, please."

They sat on either side of the lawyer's desk. Early in their acquaintance, Puig had abandoned efforts to speak Gerald's surname, the unpronounceable "Rutledge" with its thicket of confusing consonants, and since they had become friendly, there had been no need—though he could now spell Gerald's surname to a nicety, for Puig represented the owners of C'an Cabrer, the small farmhouse in the hills above Cala Marsopa where Gerald had lived for the previous three years. Once a month Gerald walked into town and paid his rent to Señor Lestrado Puig, who then sent it on to the owners in Palma.

"I have had some good fortune," said Gerald. He explained, as best he could in his now serviceable Spanish, the nature of his earlier voyaging, his published articles, the letter from the publisher in London.

"This is splendid news," said Puig. "You should make an investment."

"I thought so too," said Gerald.

"Do you have an idea?"

"Yes."

Six

For his first night as master of C'an Cabrer, Gerald slept again on the thin mattress in the small room where he had slept for the last three years. In the middle of the night he woke and walked around the other, still-empty, rooms of the house. He wondered how long he would live here. Perhaps he'd buy another boat someday and sail to Greece. Perhaps the book would sell. But here he would stay and live, for now . . . somehow.

The night air coming through the open window of the larger room was warm and smelled of citrus and the trees and vegetation around the house. He stood before the window for a moment and then climbed out onto the solid surface of the cistern at the side of the house and looked down the hill, to the sea. The partial moon had risen late and hung over its scattered reflection on the Mediterranean in the southeast—it hung over the Aegean. Suddenly, now that he could, he no longer had the urge to be sailing away. Was it gone, that long-held desire, or would it come back? For three shore-bound years, during which he had felt marooned, he had wanted to be on a boat again, sailing southeast across the Mediterranean. Yet when he'd seriously considered buying another boat and leaving . . .

He walked to the edge of the cistern top. Put a rail here and he'd have a terrace that overlooked the sea. Knock out the lower part of that window and he'd have a door to his terrace. Sit here and look at the sea and the dirt road between Son Moll and the port, and the villas along the road fronting the rocky shore.

A t the bottom of his hill, Gerald found two letters in his dusty mailbox. One was from his sister, Billie, in Sevenoaks. "So you are a Man of Property! Well done! Swallowed the anchor? I must come down for the *vendemmia*! What larks we'll have!"

The other letter was from Pocock at John Murray. A fear gripped Gerald: what if they'd changed their mind and wanted the money back? Well, it was too bloody late!

Dear Gerald,

Everything going well with the book here; on course for publication early in the autumn; I'll be sending you proofs in September.

The only spot of dissent amongst the savants is with the title. Some feel, and I have to count myself among them, that The Route of Odysseus *is rather too prosaic. It's quite accurate, as far as it goes, but limiting and not exciting. The book is only a little removed from being a gripping travel narrative, and the right title could position it very favorably for reviewers at the Sunday papers, not to mention readers. We've been batting this about a bit. I'm sure you'll appreciate that the word Odysseus doesn't lend itself easily to the possessive:* Odysseus's Voyage, Odysseus's Journey, *etc., as some have suggested here. Odysseus is, in fact, a bit of a mouthful. Odyssey is preferable to Odysseus and also looks better on the page, although, again, this says scholarly rather than fun. Other suggestions have been:* Homer's Voyage, Homer's Ill Winds, *etc., etc. The best of a poor lot, and really not right.*

Can you put your thinking cap on and suggest something less literal; a little more, dare I say it, poetic, Homeric? We are doing same.

Otherwise, all bodes well for a good autumn launch and run up to Christmas.

Sincerely,
Eric Pocock

But "route" was the whole point, thought Gerald, a little tetchily. *Where Odysseus Sailed*—worse. He could think of nothing. Blow the savants; let them come up with it, then.

He *was in the lemon grove* when he heard the sound of Lupe the donkey: the usual one-note honking for which there was no anthropomorphizing a meaning beyond generalized asinine complaint. Lupe brayed often and Gerald was always pleased when Gonzalo, who lived down the hill and across the road and had worked the farm for the owners, took her away. Gonzalo had used Lupe to carry straw panniers filled with olives, almonds, and lemons down the hill. He was surprised to hear Lupe again, for he had let Gonzalo go, intending from now on to do all the work at C'an Cabrer himself and try to live off the proceeds of the produce he would harvest and take to market—he would somehow have to be the beast of burden. Gonzalo had been told of the sale of the farm by someone, Puig perhaps, or the owners, and he had been visibly upset when Gerald told him he would do all the work himself and no longer required his services.

Then he heard the girl's voice. He walked through the trees and found Gonzalo's daughter, the third member of the Gonzalo labor force that had worked the farm. She was standing beside the house with the donkey, which was now quiescent and staring at the wall.

She smiled when she saw Gerald. It was hard to tell her age; Gonzalo didn't look older than thirty-five. His daughter's looks and womanly fig-ure had initially strongly reminded Gerald of the Italian film star Anna Magnani, whom he had seen in a film screened by a faltering projector in a bar in Argostoli, Greece, shortly after the end of the war. The actress had screamed a great deal during the film, and the Greeks in the bar, all men, had shouted back *Anna Magnani! Anna Magnani!* after each of her outbursts, which was how Gerald knew and remembered her name. However, Gonzalo's daughter didn't have the Italian's piercing eyes or volcanic behavior or her appearance of innate intelligence—she seemed more a lobotomized version of the actress—but her heavy-lidded eyes and openmouthed smile that habitually found Gerald had persistently made him aware of her interest in him. Gonzalo usually spoke to her in peremptory or rough tones, and Gerald had twice seen him cuffing his daughter on her arms, back, the side of her head. The first time he saw this they were some distance away through the trees and it took Gerald a minute to be sure of what he had seen. The second time they were closer, and he had called out, "Please do not touch the girl like that, it's not correct," in his awkward Spanish.

"*¿Qué?*" Gonzalo answered, and Gerald repeated what he had said. Gonzalo shrugged and moved away, mumbling. Gerald was pleased to let the man and his daughter go when he returned to C'an Cabrer as owner. So he was surprised and discomfited by her appearance. He looked around but didn't see Gonzalo.

"*Hola,*" the girl said now, swaying slightly in her thin cotton dress beside Lupe's flicking tail.

"*Hola,*" answered Gerald.

"Good, then, here's your animal."

"Pardon me?"

"Lupe. She is yours."

"No, she belongs to your father. She is of Gonzalo."

"No, she is of C'an Cabrer. She is of you now."

"No, I'm sure not. I don't want her. Please take her back to your father."

"He told me to bring her here to you. She is yours now, truly. And she is hungry. You must feed her."

"I don't know what she eats, I can't keep her."

"She eats anything. It's not important."

"No, please, take her to your father. I will talk to him later."

"No," said the girl.

"Yes," insisted Gerald.

"No." She laughed and looked suddenly animated.

"Please take her back to your house."

"No. And anyway you need her, for the work. I can work too if you want. I will come every day and help you."

"No, thank you. I'm going to do all the work myself."

"Ahhh." She smiled, swaying.

"Good day," said Gerald. He turned and climbed up the hill out of sight.

The donkey's braying began again. When he came down to the house, the girl was gone. Lupe was nibbling a bush.

In the afternoon Gerald walked into town and spoke with Lestrado Puig, who confirmed that he owned all the equipment that came with the property, including the donkey. Gerald asked where he could sell the donkey. Puig told him he would find out and let him know.

H*e woke again* in the night and lay beneath the sheet and looked toward the open window. Not a breath of wind in the trees—his trees now—not a good night to be at sea.

Names and lines from *The Odyssey* floated through his brain. *Laistry-gonians . . . and Cyclops, angry Poseidon—don't be afraid of them . . . Hope the voyage is a long one . . .*

That wasn't from *The Odyssey*, but from Cavafy's "Ithaka."

Gerald half rose off his mattress with the urge to look through his books, but remained propped up on an elbow . . . He didn't have the poem with him. He lay back down. He could write to Pocock and tell him to look it up. He didn't remember it all:

As you set out for Ithaka
hope the voyage is a long one,
full of adventure, full of discovery.
Laistrygonians and Cyclops . . .

Hope the voyage is a long one . . .

How did it go . . . ?

. . . Keep Ithaka always in your mind.
Arriving there is what you are destined for.
But do not hurry the journey at all.
Better if it lasts for years,
so you are old by the time you reach the island,
wealthy with all you have gained on the way,
not expecting Ithaka to make you rich.

Ithaka gave you the marvelous journey.
Without her you would not have set out. . . .

Something in there, perhaps? *Ithaca in Mind?* By Gerald Rutledge. Was that the sort of thing they wanted, Pocock and the savants at John Murray? Poetic and Homeric enough for you?

He lay on his mattress and looked at the opaque blue-gray trapezoid of night framed by the bare walls. Around it, the walls and ceiling of the dark room seemed to move, closing in, drifting outward, pulsing erratically with tricks of perspective and the dim light.

Ithaca the Marvelous Journey. By Gerald Rutledge. Except it was hardly that, was it? Mostly a wretched, storm-tossed misery, full of wrong turns and monsters. And some very nasty females.

Seven

A *motor noise* from the distant road, the sort of thing he never noticed beneath the cicadas, but did now because it grew louder and began to whine with effort, until Gerald finally realized it was coming up the hill. A visitor.

He came around the side of the house and saw a young woman pulling a Vespa backward onto its stand.

"*Buenos días*," she said. She was wearing a crisp white shirt, a blue skirt, proper shoes. Her black hair was pulled tightly back into a braid at the back of her head.

"*Buenos días*," said Gerald.

"How do you do. I am the daughter of Lestrado Puig," she said.

"Oh. I am Gerald Rutledge. Pleased to meet you."

"Yes, I know. We have sold the donkey. Someone will come and take it. Here is a check for the sale." She handed him an envelope.

"Thank you."

"*De nada.* Now I take you to meet Calix who will buy everything, all the produce."

"Pardon me?"

"Comestibles Calix. Here in Cala Marsopa. They will buy everything that is produced on the farm: olives, almonds, lemons, carobs. At a good price. It is there that Gonzalo sold before."

She turned to her Vespa and with a firm, practiced motion stamped on the kick-starter with her small black shoes and the engine started easily. She pushed the scooter forward off its stand and sat on the front saddle seat, one leg stretching from her tightened skirt with that foot on the ground. She looked at Gerald. "Get on."

"I go with you?"

"Yes."

"Where are we going?"

"To meet Calix."

Gerald was hesitant. She was small and he didn't see how they would remain upright if he got on the seat behind her.

"It's all right," she said. "I carry my father everywhere. He is bigger than you."

Gerald approached. He raised a leg over the seat and slowly lowered himself. She brought her hand back and pointed at the handle immediately behind her tightly skirted rump between Gerald's legs. "Hold here. Take off your hat." Gerald removed his straw hat and she half turned and pushed it for him under his arm.

The scooter slid forward, turned, and plunged down the hill, bumping on the rutted track. Gerald remained stiffly upright, afraid even to lean his head to one side or the other in case he threw her off balance. She paused briefly at the road, looking quickly right and left, and Gerald felt the warmth coming off the back of her neck against his face, and he smelled perfume, and then the scooter leapt forward and they flew down the road. The speed seemed terrific but now there was no sense of precariousness. He watched her hands efficiently working the throttle and clutch. They were unconscionably close: she appeared to be sitting in his lap, they were spooning in a seated position. He tried to keep his legs away from her thighs. The back of her shirt flapped against his arms, errant strands of her hair flicked across his face.

She sped through town. Gerald tried to anticipate her turns to maintain balance as she and the scooter leaned in and out of the turns, but he was unable to prevent his legs, one or the other on each turn, rubbing up against her thighs.

She slowed abruptly on a side street and came to a stop. "You can get off," she said.

Gerald released the handle, swung a leg off, and stood trembling with the memory of the motor in him as she shut off the machine and briskly pulled the scooter onto its stand.

"Come, please," she said.

They walked through a curtain of beads into the dark cool interior containing shelves of food, baskets of fresh produce.

"¡Hola, Paloma!" said a broad woman wearing an apron, smiling at them both as they came in.

When they were finished at Calix, she offered to ride him back up the hill to C'an Cabrer. Gerald thanked her and told her he had some business in town and would walk home. She shook his hand—very firmly—started the Vespa, and shot away like a hummingbird.

Unusual girl, he thought, the daughter of Puig.

Eight

After their siesta, Bernie and Luc walked slowly along the dirt road beside the rocks until they came to the little beach called Son Moll. Lulu didn't like the beach, so she never came with them or took Luc to the beach, even if Bernie was working. He spread out a blanket. They ran in and out of the lapping waves, and built sand castles at the water's edge.

"Papa! We go see pirates?"

"Yes, Luc, *mon brave*! Let's go see if the pirates are here today."

Crouching, wading on his knees, Bernie carried Luc into the natural cave inside the large rock formation that breached like a whale from the shallows at the western edge of the beach. He had to hold Luc up close to his face to pass through a cleft where there was just room enough for their heads above the water between the two Brobdingnagian clamshell rocks almost closed against each other that made the great whale. They reached an inner grotto, where, Bernie told Luc, the pirates used to hide, and could even reappear at any time. Inside the cool space, lit by shards of sunlight from the imperfect joints of the clamshells, the water made chocky, echoing sounds.

"Arrrgghh, me hearties!" Bernie called out. "Avast, Blind Pew!"

"Bline Pooh!" cried Luc.

"Billy Bones! Black Dog! Long John Silver! Show yourselves, ye swabs!"

"Fifteen men!"

"Ah-ha-harrgh! Fifteen men on a dead man's chest, yo-ho-ho, and a bottle of rum!" they sang together.

After a while, Bernie said, "Right, then, young 'Orkins. I don't see no pirates today, matey. We best be off."

"'Orkins!"

Clutching Luc to his chest and face, Bernie waded out again through the water that glowed pale blue from the light beneath the rocks. He felt the smooth wet skin of his son against him, beneath his hands, and the life inside this most perfect bundle, and the trust his son felt that no matter how dangerous the cave looked and what might appear there, Bernie would keep him safe.

Luc fell asleep in his arms as he walked back along the road to the Rocks.

Coming toward him, he saw the man he'd noticed several times on this road, walking between the beach and the town. Not a Spaniard, obviously: sandy-haired, northern European–looking, but not a tourist. Thin to the point of emaciation, tanned, threadbare clothes, a decrepit straw hat; he looked like a manual laborer of some sort.

Bernie nodded to him, and the man nodded back as he passed.

1948
August

A Sailor's Seasons

R afael Soller was on the quay as Nereid approached at less than a walking pace. His shirtsleeves were rolled up, his thick arms covered with black hair held away from his body, eager to push off, to catch, to help as needed.

"Bon dia, Gerald."

"Bon dia, Rafael."

The boat drifted alongside, squeezing gently against the hemp fenders hanging down the side of the hull. Gerald stepped onto the quay holding the bow and stern lines.

"Give me one," said Rafael. Gerald handed him the bowline and Rafael wrapped it many times around a small bollard and threw in two knots for good measure. Gerald tied the stern line to an iron ring set in the concrete. They shook hands.

"So, Gerald—" Rafael was suddenly unsure of what to say next. He looked at the Englishman awkwardly. "How are you?"

"I'm all right," Gerald answered. He looked up at Rafael. "Have you seen my wife?"

"Yes." Rafael's eyes flicked over the boat, away from Gerald. "She returned a week ago. I have seen her, but I have not spoken to her."

"Is she still here?"

Rafael looked up at Gerald and lifted his chin in the direction of the house above the rocks across the harbor. "Maybe at the house. I don't know."

Gerald too looked across the harbor for a moment, his eyes squinting as if to focus better. He looked back at Rafael. "Rafael, there was an accident. I'm going to sail to Palma to have some work done on the boat. May I leave some things here with you, in the bar? Some bags, some books? To have them off the boat while the work is being done? I will take them when I come back."

"But yes, of course. When do you go?"

"Today. Very soon."

Rafael was surprised. "You are leaving again today?"

"Yes."

"Then, give me something to carry," said Rafael.

"No, thank you. I have to pack up. I'll bring them to the bar later. Thank you."

G*erald walked around* the port and then along the sandy road beside the shore above the rocks. Past white villas with tiled roofs and shutters closed either for the season or against the midday light.

He opened the iron gate in the wall in front of the large house with sage-green shutters. The house spread around a courtyard and a fountain visible through an inner gate. He pulled the bell knob beside the green front door.

After a minute, the boy opened the door. "Oh, it's you," he said. Despite the unruly carrot-colored thatch of hair and the smooth, freckled face of a twelve-year-old, he gazed at Gerald with the freighted appraisal of someone cognizant of the entire range of human failing. A tall, large-boned woman in her late thirties appeared beside him. She glared at Gerald.

"Cassian, leave us," she said firmly.

With a retreating glance, the boy disappeared.

"Oh, *Gerald!*" said Milly Ollorenshaw. She stepped just beyond the doorway, pulling the door half-closed behind her.

"Hullo, Milly. Is she here?"

"She saw you come in on the boat and she left. She doesn't want to see you."

"How is she?"

"As I told you on the phone—she's alive, thank God!"

"I must talk to her, Milly—"

"I don't know what you could possibly say. How *could* you have *abandoned* her like that? After what happened? And what do you think Tom and I thought when you telephoned from Sardinia asking if we'd heard from Lulu? We were frantic! I don't know what to say to you, Gerald. It was *unspeakable* of you."

He'd phoned once, from Cagliari. He'd been told by both Tom and Milly that Lulu had arrived back in Mallorca but did not want to speak with him. "Milly, I understand that Lulu couldn't know where I went and what I did, and so you don't either. I did it for her. I had to get them away. And I did. It took a bit of time, I know. But when I went back, she wasn't there."

"*Did you think she'd be sitting there, knitting you a cardigan?*" Milly shouted at him. She was furious. "She was *naked*, Gerald! She had to beg for clothing! We had to send her money! I don't know *what* you did, Gerald, and more to the point, nor did Lulu. She only knew that you'd gone and left her there!"

"I know. I came back as soon as I could. I can explain—"

"*Gerald!*" She took a deep breath and looked at him with not entirely unfriendly distress, sadly. "Whatever you have to say doesn't alter what happened to Lulu. It doesn't alter the fact that you left. Do you understand that? No explanation will change that."

Gerald was silent, pale.

More gently, Milly said: "Once someone loses trust, that's it, Gerald. It's gone. It's broken. You can't repair it with explanations. You can't wheedle trust back from someone. She will never forget that you left. Whatever your reasons . . . well, they don't matter, don't you see? It doesn't alter anything. I'm sorry, Gerald. Do you remember what I told you? Lulu needed someone whom she could *trust*. That was *all* she needed—but she needed that."

Gerald looked down at Milly's enormous feet in dirty plimsolls. He looked up at her. "When will she be back?"

"She's gone off in the car with Tom. She doesn't want to see you. You should go."

He drew something out of the pocket of his trousers and held his hand out. "Will you please give her this."

It was a roll of film.

"What is she supposed to do with that?"

"Please ask her to have it developed."

"Why?"

"It will show her what I did. I know it doesn't change what happened to her, but it will show her why I left—I got them away, you see, otherwise I don't know what would have happened—and . . . well, it'll show what I did."

Hesitantly, Milly reached out and took the roll.

"Do have her develop the film. Please."

"I'll give it to her, that's all I can do," said Milly. "Now I must ask you to leave, Gerald. I'm sorry. We've all been enormously upset, as perhaps you can imagine."

Unhappily—generous by nature and unused to being dismissive—Milly turned away and closed the door.

Gerald went out through the gate and walked quickly away toward the harbor.

H e *unloaded* four bulging sail bags, and a small bag of Lulu's clothes, from the small yacht and carried them to the Bar Marítimo across the field of black fishing nets that had been spread out to dry in front of the fishermen's storage caves. They were heavy with books. He and Rafael heaped them against the stone wall in the narrow back room beside demijohns of wine and crates of beer. He returned to the boat and came back with a wooden tool chest, his typewriter, and the varnished dovetailed box holding his sextant.

"You won't need the tools in Palma?" asked Rafael.

"I'll have most of the work done by the yard's carpenters. I expect they'll have their own tools."

"Yes, of course."

Rafael stood on the quay as Gerald hauled aloft the stained brown mainsail, held to the mast by wooden hoops. The canvas flapped idly in the light wind.

"I'll take the line now, thank you, Rafael."

Rafael untied the line he had knotted earlier, unwound it from the bollard, coiled it quickly, and threw it to Gerald, who dropped the coil on the deck. The yacht drifted slowly off the quay. The two men were still close enough to talk quietly.

"So, you will come back, when, in a week or so?" asked Rafael.

"Yes. It depends on the work. But I'll see you soon. Thank you for your help, Rafael."

"It's nothing. Go with God, Gerald."

The yacht made a slow U-turn, and Rafael now saw on the other side of the hull a gash of blue paint, streaks of dirt, and a depression where two planks were cracked halfway between the deck and the water sliding by.

"Now I see it," Rafael called, walking down the quay to stay abreast of the boat. He pointed toward the broken planks. "The work that needs to be done. What happened?"

Gerald leaned out and looked down at the damage, as if noticing it for the first time. He shrugged. "An accident. A fishing boat."

Nereid was gathering speed. Her course wove through the moored fishing boats past the end of the breakwater. She was sliding past the houses above the rocks. Gerald stood on deck at the stern and looked up at the house with the green shutters.

G erald *walked* into the Marítimo three days later.
        "Gerald!" said Rafael. He looked out at the port; he hadn't seen the boat come in. "So soon? You come from Palma?"

"Yes. I came on the bus." Gerald seemed subdued. He sat down at a small table.

"On the bus?" said Rafael as he poured Gerald a Cognac. "And the yacht? They are doing the work, in Palma?"

"I lost the yacht," said Gerald.

"What?"

"She sank."

"She *sank*? The *Nereid*?"

"Yes."

Rafael stared at Gerald. "Your boat—she is gone?"

"Yes." Gerald raised the glass to his mouth and drank the burning liquor.

Rafael was filled with disquiet. He had been aboard *Nereid* many times; he had drunk wine and Cognac with Gerald in the little cabin, seen his charts and his sextant and heard Gerald's ideas about the navigation of the ancient Greeks. The Englishman was a sailor of a type Rafael had never met; he knew more about the sea and navigation than his father's oldest friends, who knew only the waters around Mallorca. Gerald was English, a race famous for its sailors; he had sailed from England, itself a feat, and he had sailed the little *Nereid* without an engine all over the Mediterranean with one hand on the tiller and a book in the other, and it was the last thing Rafael could imagine that Gerald could ever lose his yacht, even in a storm—but there had been no storms.

"Where did this happen?"

"Off Cabrera. In deep water."

Rafael poured himself a Cognac. He knew the loss of the boat was a disaster for his friend, and like the death of a loved one. He was hesitant to press Gerald for the details.

"How, Gerald?" he said finally.

Gerald's eyes squinted and he looked out over the port. "The damage was worse than I'd thought. She came down hard on a wave and started a plank below the waterline. I only had time to put the dinghy in the water and get in before she sank. I managed to get to the shore, but the dinghy got quite badly smashed on the rocks and that sank too."

"My God," said Rafael. He stared furtively at Gerald as you stare at a man whose wife has drowned. What would he do without his boat and all his books . . . "But what incredible luck that you unloaded your books and the other things."

"Yes," said Gerald.

"Then . . . what will you do, Gerald? Where will you go? You can stay here, in the back, for a few days, of course, but then . . . ?"

"Thank you, Rafael." Gerald drained his glass and rose. "I'll find something."

When Gerald reached the door, Rafael said, "Where are you going now?"

"I'm going for a walk." Gerald smiled at Rafael, as if to reassure him.

Gerald would not see himself reduced to Rafael's kind offer to put up among the crates and demijohns in the back of the Marítimo. It wasn't going to be like that.

In one of his sail bags, he'd packed the rubber canvas groundsheet that had been part of his naval kit on shore maneuvers. With this and a few other essentials, he made camp under the small pines above the shore at Cala Espasa, to the north of Cala Marsopa. He made small fires of pine and scrub oak that snapped inordinately but burned sufficiently to heat tins of beans, and he slept tolerably well wrapped in his groundsheet. He was on maneuvers again.

When he woke in the mornings, he read beneath the pines from the small Cambridge editions of Marcus Aurelius (always immediately useful) and scraps of Hesiod. Not a compulsive adventurer—Hesiod's only sea voyage was from the city of Aulis, on the Strait of Euripus, to the island of Euboea, a crossing of just under two hundred feet. Yet Gerald admired the Greek poet's seamanlike instincts about when came "the timely season for men to voyage" and when they should remain in port.

What, he wondered, would Hesiod make of this season?

1948
August—A Week Earlier

Cyclopes

G erald *could never* have imagined such ... *flights* of lovemaking. Édith, the French widow in Alexandria during the war, had been appreciative, instructive, and very kind to him. Six-foot-two-inch Felicity at Oxford, keen and sweaty, solid as a pony, great pale shanks revealed in the fumbling of damp tweed beside the gas fire, had been like weekend rides at a gymkhana.

Beside these, Lulu was a kinetic wild child. She made love to him with a feral hunger. She showed him everything: first, what he wanted, then what she wanted. Their lovemaking became an obsessive preoccupation, anticipated, ritualized, deliberated over. A fascination. A drowning in sensation that was new to him.

The mesmerizing animal sight of her as she sat astride him now in the moonlit cabin, panting like a runner, slim muscled arms raised with hands gripping, pushing, at the cabin beams overhead, sweat streaming from her face and neck, soaking her hair, rilling down her small breasts and torso, pooling between her thighs at the junction of their sucking groins. Her hips drove forward and backward with the insistent motion of piston arms. Gerald watched her—an almost fiendish sight in the bars of moonlight coming through the portholes—amazed as always that such a thing could take place anywhere near, let alone on top of, him. It happened almost every night: at some point they came out of sleep together, shedding sleep for this feverish embrace.

Then he lost all thought, as a locus of sensation seized the base of his spine and he stiffened, broke with her rhythm, and Lulu quickly slipped off him, moved down and lowered her face and hands over him as if in prayer and deftly midwived his shuddering contractions. He felt the vibration of her vocal cords driving back into him as she hummed a long note and then he heard her take a breath, and she said, "You taste of the sea."

An inchoate emotion flooded through Gerald and he began to weep. It only lasted a few seconds, no more than an involuntary spasm in the chest as he squeezed his eyes shut against the tears. It happened often when they were finished—fortunately Lulu never seemed to notice, for he wouldn't have been able to explain the sudden loss of his composure. Except to say that she made him happy.

She got off the narrow settee and stood upright (almost, at five-three, beneath the cabin roof) and rubbed the slick wetness across her face and body like lotion. "Come on." She disappeared up the companionway steps and Gerald heard a splash. He followed her up, with admiration, but always a kernel of anxiety at her readiness to leap off the boat in the dark. It was something he had never done before knowing Lulu.

On deck he saw her wriggling in the water beside the boat like a small porpoise. He looked around, uneasy at her exposed nakedness, but the little bay four miles south of Trapani was deserted. They had ghosted in at dusk, eaten a simple meal, and fallen asleep, both tired after the slow crossing in light air and hot sun from their last anchorage on the small island of Favignana.

"Come on, darling!" Lulu called from the sea. "Come in! It's unbelievably warm, like a bath!"

It would be, long into the night after the heat of a Sicilian summer's day. Gerald looked around: now bathed in moonlight, there was no sign of a dwelling of any kind on this rocky stretch of the coast. "I'm coming, my darling."

He rigged the small rope boarding ladder to the cleat at the stern and hung it over the side—he was always careful about the ladder and it had proved worthwhile. Then, naked himself, he dove in.

He swam toward Lulu but she vanished beneath the surface. He couldn't see beneath the mercury-seeming liquid surrounding him. In the salty water, he ran his hands over the human film that still clung to his skin, instinctively touching his genitals, faintly surprised to find things there as they had always been. Lulu's head quietly broke the surface thirty feet away like a water bird's. It began to move toward the shore.

"Lulu, darling, do come back," called Gerald. "It's the middle of the night."

"No! We're going into the beach—come on!"

Gerald felt uncomfortable going far from the yacht without a stitch on him—and in the dead of night—but they were quite alone. Before they'd gone to bed, he'd hung the paraffin anchor light in *Nereid's* rigging, the lone sign of Man anywhere around them. The coast here in the pale moonlight appeared unchanged since Homer's time—that is, it bore the ancient, worn-to-nub appearance of countless Mediterranean shores: torturously indented limestone crowned with a scrub of stunted, goat-nibbled vegetation; whereas, of course, in Homer's time, twenty-eight or so centuries earlier, the shores had been densely forested—younger-looking lands, barely peopled, with so much history yet to play out. Gerald had sailed these waters in HMS *Furious* six years earlier during the obliterating tumult of war—history was always war—but now the land and sea appeared quiet and peaceful.

He struck out after his wife.

They had sailed from Cala Marsopa a week earlier, crossing the emptiest stretch of the western Mediterranean in light winds; a gentle and pleasurable introduction to travel under sail for Gerald's new wife. By now, August, the season was half over. He'd once hoped to be finished with Sicily and be across the Ionian Sea, exploring the Ionian islands—Ithaca itself—but he'd never expected to spend two months in Mallorca. He had long discounted Spain or the Balearics as a location for any part of *The Odyssey.* There was little in Homer to account for a passage so far west in the big, black, slow ships of Odysseus and his men—unless one considered the wild card of the "floating" island of Aeolia, whose "cliffs rise sheer from the sea," a six-day, six-night row—westward? southward?—from the land of the Laestrygonians. Homer himself was no seaman, Lawrence had decided during the four years he'd worked on his translation, but the poet had listened to navigators and stitched their stories together, situating lands and peoples in relation to one another in the seascape of his mind's eye. So, for a firsthand view, a definitive rejection of the western Mediterranean for the geography of *The Odyssey*, Gerald had sailed southwestward to the Spanish islands, a two-day reach from the Strait of Bonifacio.

Tom and Milly Ollorenshaw had espied his red ensign in the port and brought him up to the villa for dinner with their cook-houseguest. They asked him where he was headed in his little boat and he told them about his effort to decode and explore the geography of *The Odyssey*. What a clever idea, they all said.

"But I recognize this," Lulu, Tom and Milly's friend, said, with genuine amazement, when she ducked her head and came down the companionway steps the first time and saw the interior of *Nereid*'s tiny cabin: the tongue-and-groove pine trimmed in teak, the small gunmetal stove with its aluminum kettle, the shelves of books, the cushioned settee berths, the paraffin lamps, the beams, the portholes. "It's Mrs. Tiggy-Winkle's cottage! I want to live here!" She turned to him, their heads close enough under the hatch for him to feel her breath in his face while she said seriously, "You have to take me with you, now."

"All right," Gerald said easily.

But from that moment on, he imagined it.

He took them all sailing. It was amazing to Gerald how clumsy Tom and Milly were, unable to find the natural locations on deck or in the cockpit where one could sit comfortably while the yacht heeled or pitched gently, how often they got in the way of the tiller, sheets, or the swinging boom, grabbed the wrong things, almost fell overboard. "Well, that was exciting!" said Milly when she stepped carefully onto the stone quay afterward, "And I'm *jolly* glad it's over!"

Lulu, on the other hand, asked him to take her out again. She was like a cat aboard the boat, small and quick and balanced. Right away she got the hang of pulling the sheets when Gerald tacked. Under way, she liked to sit on the bowsprit over the creaming bow wave. At other times, Gerald would find her below, sitting on a settee, looking around the cabin. She lay down experimentally on the settee berths and looked up at him. "I love this little boat."

She asked him to show her how to work the Primus stove, and she quickly learned to preheat the burner with alcohol, pump the tank, and ignite the pressurized paraffin as it vaporized in the burner. She made them tea. "*So exciting,*" she said.

"But why don't you have an engine?" she asked him. Gerald explained that in a boat as small as *Nereid*, there was little room for fuel tanks, so that an engine could not be run for long, only a few hours, which would hardly help much on a long passage. Engines were useful for getting a yacht in and out of harbors, but again, such a small boat sailed almost as well as a dinghy and he could maneuver it handily in the lightest of airs. Without an engine, he had more room, no noise, no engine breakdowns, no smell of oily fumes.

"So you can just go," she said, marveling, "by untying your ropes and pushing off. Anywhere that's touched by water, can't you?"

"Yes, that's the idea."

"You could sail from here—from Cala Marsopa—to the Caribbean, then?"

"Yes."

"What would you do for food? And water?"

"Well, you stop here and there. Like here. The world's not a desert."

"And you're going from here to Greece?"

"Yes."

One afternoon they sailed to Cala Gat, the small cove with a tiny beach smaller than a tennis court below the lighthouse on the very eastern tip of Mallorca. Gerald anchored and Lulu made them lunch: bread, sardines, cheese, wine, olives, peaches. Then she took off her clothes and dove overboard. "Come in!" she insisted. Gerald put on his swimming trunks, hung the rope boarding ladder, and joined her in the water. They swam and then they climbed back aboard up the rope ladder. She went up first; Gerald's eyes involuntarily followed her lean hindquarters swaying above him until he forced himself to look away. He was amazed and touched by her unself-consciousness, by her trust. "Come and lie down," she said as she stretched herself out in the sun on deck.

As he lay beside her, he had a view of the beading seawater drying on her stomach, and much else.

Then she sat up and looked at him, pushing her hair out of her face. "God, Gerald, look at how you live. This is glorious."

"It's not for everyone."

"More fool they. Then everybody would live like this."

She grinned.

"What?" he said.

She kissed him. Then she took his hand and led him below and made love to him. Even that first time, it was beyond anything Gerald could have imagined.

Later she said, "Can we spend the night here? Do we have to go back to the port?"

"Tom and Milly will be worried about you."

She laughed softly at him. "No they won't, darling."

She made them dinner: bully beef and asparagus from Gerald's tins, bread, wine, cheese, the rest of the peaches. Gerald watched her, surprised by her ease and enjoyment of what she was doing.

As they ate, she asked him to show her where he was going.

He cleared the tiny saloon table, put their plates on the settees beside them, and spread out beneath the light of the paraffin lamp his creased small-scale chart of the Mediterranean. Look, here's Troy, he said. What, the real Troy? she asked. Yes, right here below Istanbul; it was discovered by a German about seventy years ago. And here's Ithaca, the home of Odysseus; about six hundred sea miles between them. Two weeks' easy sail, depending on conditions, but it took Odysseus ten years of unintended detours. A lot of famous trouble. This island, here, Jerba in Tunisia, I think, is the Land of the Lotus-eaters—"

"Shall we be Lotus-eaters?" she said, pulling him toward her.

The next afternoon, when they sailed back to Cala Marsopa, Lulu asked Gerald if they could anchor off Villa los Roques. She wanted to swim from the boat to the rocks on the shore and climb up them to the villa. The sea was almost calm, there was little swell. Of course, said Gerald.

"Come on," said Lulu, when he'd let go the anchor, and she dove overboard.

Gerald lowered the ladder before following her.

When he reached the rocks, Lulu was already climbing.

"Careful," he said.

Lulu turned to look down at him, paddling below, and smiled. "Darling, I do this every day." Perhaps she didn't turn away and look down every day, or for whatever reason, she slipped. Her arm shot out for a handhold but she missed it. Gerald watched her fall: she arched forward and he clearly saw her chin strike a projecting nub of sharp limestone. Her head snapped back as she came away from the rock face and fell backward into the water beside him.

When he pulled her up, she was facedown. He rolled her over, got an arm under her head, and lifted her face clear of the water. Her eyes were closed, but she was breathing easily. Blood streamed from a gash on her chin, swirling in the water around her face like red ink. Otherwise, she looked peaceful: asleep; as if she might open her eyes at any moment. Kicking to support them, Gerald used his other hand to smooth away the hair from Lulu's face. He could see that it was already shot through with premature gray. He had never seen anything more beautiful.

But she was quite unconscious. He looked up: no way to climb up that lot with her. He adjusted his arm, wrapping it around her and keeping her head on his chest, and struck out with the other arm toward the boat.

When she awoke, Lulu looked up and saw Gerald's face.

"What happened?"

"You fell. You've cut your chin—no, don't touch—" He stopped her hand and wrapped it in his own. "I've got a bandage on it. It's all right, though you might need a stitch or two. It threw your head back quite sharply. How do you feel?"

"Bit of a headache. I can feel the chin, now that you mention it." She looked beyond him, her eyes ranging over the interior of the little boat, then back to Gerald's face. "How on earth did you get me aboard?"

"Put you over my shoulder. I had the ladder down. Wasn't difficult. No getting you up those rocks, though. We'll go ashore in the dinghy when you feel up to it."

Her eyes looking at him grew large and still. "You saved me."

"Yes. Well, I wasn't going to go off and leave you." He grinned at her.

Lulu lifted her arm and placed a cool hand against Gerald's cheek. She moved her thumb across his mouth, looking at her hand, her thumb, his face. "Gerald," she said, "take me with you."

"Where?"

"Wherever you're going. To Greece."

He imagined it again. "I'm not sure how long I'll be. I mean, I won't return soon."

"Marry me. Then we won't be in a rush."

He stared at her, all thought falling away except the phrase: *Why not?*

"I'll make you happy, Gerald. I'll make you as happy as I feel right now."

He knew he should think for a moment, but what was there to think about? What if all the years ahead could go on as the last two days had been?

"Gerald," she said, very quietly, as if she were about to point out a hummingbird nearby and didn't want to scare it away, "I love you."

"I love you too."

"Then it's simple. Take me with you."

"All right," he said.

She pulled his face down. "Watch out for your—" he said as she kissed him.

Tom and Milly thought it a splendid idea. Well, why *not?* they said. Milly shrieked and hugged them both. Tom, in loco parentis, had a friendly chat with Gerald. He reported to Lulu and Milly that Gerald had little or no money, but he was intelligent, well educated, his idea about *The Odyssey* was really quite smart—but never mind all that: Lulu, you're never going to marry some duffer in a bank. I'm sure it'll be all right.

While Lulu's chin was being stitched in the doctor's office, Milly told Gerald that although Lulu probably wouldn't mention it, not right away, she'd had a beastly time of it growing up: neglectful parents, who at one point had actually lost her while traveling in Belgium, then died; a succession of indifferent relatives; boarding school in Scotland—well, it had all been jolly unpleasant for her until Milly and Tom had discovered her as a ward of friends in London and taken her on, initially as a cook. . . . Anyway, all she really needed was absolute trust and safety. If he gave her that, they'd have no problems.

Go on, the both of you, Tom and Milly said, sail off in your little ark and please come back and stay with us next summer.

It all happened very quickly. Lulu and Milly made a simple, summery white wedding dress. Gerald had a blazer, his old school tie, and presentable flannel trousers folded away on his boat. Tom made the arrangements and drove them into Palma where Gerald and Lulu were married at the British consulate. Tom stood them a wedding dinner of suckling pig at La Fonda in Cala Marsopa.

For a wedding present, Gerald gave Lulu one of several copies of *The Odyssey* he carried aboard the yacht. "This is quite an interesting translation." He opened it. "You see, it says it's by T. E. Shaw—the pen name of T. E. Lawrence, of Arabia. He knows his way around a good story. He's got some interesting things to say about Homer in his Introduction. I don't have anything else to give you, but I can promise you an odyssey."

"Oh, darling! That's all I want." Lulu hugged and kissed him fiercely. "We *will* have an odyssey, won't we!"

And they sailed away.

S*he was a strong swimmer;* unable to catch her up, he followed her all the way in to the shore. They could see rocks beneath them against the pale sand in the moonlight. Lulu walked out of the water and lay flat on the sand, faceup, legs and arms spread.

"Come and lie beside me," she said. "Nobody's here to see you now," she said.

Gerald was not yet a blithe naturist. He'd learned to enjoy swimming naked in the sea with Lulu, but not where anybody might see them. She was completely indifferent to such a concern, and he'd had to caution her when she wanted to leap overboard in anchorages where other craft were anchored or might appear.

He sat down beside her. He heard a bell somewhere above them— sheep or goats.

"Is that your cave up there, then?" she asked.

"That black hole we saw coming in? I think so. We'll see."

"So this is where the Cyclops lived?"

"Perhaps—if he lived."

"Tell me again," she said, "it's to do with some fog, right?"

Gerald's heart swelled every time she asked him questions about his investigation of *The Odyssey*; how she wanted to understand what he was doing. No one else had. "That's right." He told her how Odysseus and his men had sailed from the land of the Lotus-eaters and landed in the morning at an island in fog, where they'd found a spring coming down to the port. There wasn't much fog in the Mediterranean, especially in the south, but it could occur here off the west coast of Sicily. The island of Favignana—"where we were yesterday, you remember the spring"—was where Gerald believed Odysseus encountered fog and then sailed on a short distance, exactly as they had in *Nereid*, to the mainland of Sicily, where both Odysseus and now Gerald and Lulu had found a cave.

"How do you know it happened?" Lulu asked.

"Well, no one knows for sure. But I think it's like any faith. You could say the same about the Bible. You believe in it, or not, depending on whether you have faith, regardless of reason or lack of absolute proof, because it makes—"

"Look," said Lulu, rising on her elbow, "another boat's come in."

Gerald turned his head from Lulu and the shore. The navigation lights were dim, but against the moon-splashed water he could make out a sagging, neglected-looking fishing boat, forty feet or so long, coming around the headland to the north, moving sluggishly into the slight scalloped bay off the beach.

"Guardia Costiera," Gerald said, quietly, as if to himself.

"What's that, darling?"

"Italian coast guard."

"It looks like a decrepit fishing boat."

"It probably was. Beggars can't be choosers. But even in this light you can see by their ensign. The little flag on the stern."

The boat was still moving slowly forward and the loud rattle of chain running through a hawsepipe came across the water.

"They're not the best seamen either." Gerald could never have brought himself to let go chain while a boat was moving forward and have it scrape down the side of the hull, a most slovenly bit of mismanagement. It bespoke slovenliness in other things, an entire attitude to life. "I think we should get back to the yacht."

"Oh, do let's lie here, darling. They're not going to see us."

"They'll see the boat and the anchor light. They can be officious little men. They'll be very bored, and we're a foreign yacht. Almost certainly they'll come alongside to see our papers."

"Not tonight, surely?"

"They may. And if we're not aboard, they may board the yacht. Come on."

Gerald stood, crouching, as if to remain unseen, for in the pale light he thought they might be visible on the beach from the Guardia vessel. He moved quickly into the water. "Lulu, darling, do come now. We must get back to the boat."

They were not far off the beach when Gerald saw the rubber tender coming away from the Guardia boat, making toward *Nereid*. Several figures ineptly deploying short oars like paddles; voices across the water. The rubber boat had no directional stability and crabbed along, half spinning with each of the paddlers' efforts counteracting the others. But slowly it drew closer to the yacht. It would be awkward without clothing; their nakedness would be visible. "Quick as you can, darling," he said.

The voices in the rubber boat quietened, then grew more animated, and Gerald realized that they'd been spotted. The boat's zigzag course altered, grew jerkier as it moved faster, and he saw they would be intercepted before they reached *Nereid*.

"*Buonasera*," called Gerald, with the cheerfulness of an English holidaymaker.

"*Buonasera*," came the reply, with a measured vacancy.

The men in the boat—there were three of them, Gerald now saw—continued talking in a more subdued tone. He could understand nothing. He spoke a modicum of Italian, what he needed to obtain food, drink, supplies in Italy, but they were speaking Neapolitan, the dialect he'd heard in southern Tyrrhenian ports. As they drew to within a few feet of them, the men ceased paddling and drifted. Their eyes were shadowed but he could tell they were looking at the swimmers. The rubber boat was some sort of ex-military life raft, oblong, with no discernible bow or stern; the air chambers sagged under the weight of the three occupants, indicating a leak in the rubberized canvas or at a valve.

"*Inglese?*"

"*Sì*," said Gerald. He and Lulu continued swimming toward *Nereid*.

More talk in the boat, a real conversation now. Gerald could now make out the paddlers: not officious little men, but youths in filthy, ill-fitting uniforms. Not seamen or sons of fishermen but city boys ignorant of boats and the water beyond basic training—perhaps one of them knew something about engines. Gerald had seen them in every poor Italian port he had visited since the war, singly and in groups, unemployed, staring incomprehensibly at his small boat, and at him as he moved about and came and went. In these ports he had paid a small fee to the designated unofficial watchman who, somehow, kept such boys from pilfering anything stowed on a boat's deck or looting its contents below. These three were the lucky ones: employed and given uniforms and authority and let loose in a leaking tub with a vague mandate of enforcing maritime—

The jabbing oar caught Lulu's shoulder. "Ow!" she said, with unconcealed annoyance. A young man in the rubber boat giggled and the others commented in tones as if critiquing a bocce toss. All three began using their oars to pull Lulu closer to their boat, as if she were a tortoise. Gerald shouted something and pushed an oar away. An oar hit the back of his head with force, making a crunching noise that he heard in the middle of his brain. Another oar hit his face with a blinding, stunning smack.

He was rolling underwater. For a moment he couldn't determine which way was up, but he understood everything very matter-of-factly.

He surfaced to an empty view of water and coast, heard noise, turned in the water, and saw Lulu, clearly naked in the moonlight, wriggling, emitting hoarse grunts, fighting as she was pulled aboard the rubber dinghy by the three men as if she were a large struggling fish. The men were laughing, one of them barking excitedly like a man baiting a dog. They were thirty feet away. Once they had her flopping in the bottom of the boat, they sat on her and began paddling back toward the Guardia Costiera vessel. Gerald heard noises from Lulu, he saw the men struggling, and heard slapping sounds, then angry shouts from Lulu.

He swam as fast as he could after the rubber boat. It moved jerkily, rocked by tremors, but the men were now paddling with urgency, heading toward the Guardia boat. Then he heard a splash—Lulu had managed to jump overboard. He could make her out, swimming strongly, pulling ahead of the dinghy. A minute later he saw her climbing out of the water just before the dinghy reached the beach. Her white form in the dark moving up the steep rocky bank, and the three men jumping out of the dinghy in the shallows, climbing after her.

Now Gerald turned toward the beach—the sooner the better, for he would be faster on his feet than swimming. He came ashore some distance from the rubber boat, lurched in the shallows, lost his footing on a rock and fell. He rose gasping from the sand. He could hear them somewhere above.

They were in the cave.

Gerald scrambled up the rocks. He made out a path through the vegetation above the beach and ran along it until it widened below a rising escarpment of limestone arching over a dark hole—the cave—in the rock face ahead. The path led into the cave. Out of it came the sound of men, and noises from Lulu. She was moaning, or grunting: short hoarse harrowing exhalations.

Gerald sprinted toward the black hole in the rocks. He was unaware of anything, only that he must get to Lulu, and a sense of murderous power—

He didn't see the sheep and ran headlong into the huddled group. He fell hard across the shaggy backs onto the dirt among them. As he scrambled up, the sheep bolted, leaping over him, stampeding into the cave. Gerald ran after them.

"*Ma che cazzo?*" The city boys, spooked, interrupted, alarmed by the inrushing animal shapes, swore in fear. "*Cazzo! Merda!*" The sheep collided with the Italians, leapt and bleated, terrified. *Baaa! Baa! Baaaaaaaa!* Gerald ran into an upright figure and drove his fist at head height into some bony extremity and heard a yelp of pain. He saw a shape, taller then himself, and rushed at it, hands forward, pushing a man who cried with fear as he fell under the legs of the whinnying sheep, now a writhing, leaping mass of shapes in the cave.

"Lulu!" Gerald called. "*Lulu, run!*"

And he saw her, he thought—outlined against the light at the far side of the cave, a slight figure among the bounding woolly shapes bunching and leaping toward the light, bleating and crying, escaping onto the path beyond—then he didn't see her.

The Italians were getting to their feet, yelling angrily, and coming forward from the walls of the cave. Gerald turned and ran out of the cave—away from the bolting sheep, to draw the men toward him—along the path the way he had come in.

It was darker: cloud had obscured the moon. He almost shouted for Lulu, to see if she had come this way and not out the other side of the cave, but he caught himself. Behind him, shouting, the Italians emerged from the cave mouth. If he found Lulu here, they would catch both of them. Gerald turned and scrambled down the rocky slope to the beach. Would they see that he was alone? He called urgently, as if hurrying Lulu on with him, *"Come on, darling!"*

As Odysseus escaped the Cyclops's cave by riding beneath a ram, then drove his sheep down to the shore, so Gerald ran beside the waves in the dark. He heard the Italians on the path behind him, calling to one another. He couldn't see them, but he distinctly heard three voices shouting angrily, and he could tell they were moving fast. She was not with them, then.

He ran through the waves making splashing noises, varying his stride, trying to sound like four feet. *"Come on, darling!"* he yelled. *"Swim, darling! Make for the yacht!"* Then he dove in and swam as fast as he could, urging Lulu on, talking for both of them.

He heard them on the beach launching the rubber boat, splashing in the shallows. They wouldn't be able to see that Lulu was not with him. *"Come on, darling! Almost there!"*

Gerald swam in sustained panic, a tremendous amount of splashing. When he reached the boat, he climbed the rope ladder. *"Get below, darling! I'll get us under way!"* he shouted. No time to lower the anchor light—good, they would see him moving away, and hopefully come after him. He hauled the mainsail and gaff aloft—they would see that too, the shape against the sky. No time to haul the anchor in, either: on the foredeck, he let the chain go, clattering noisily to let them know exactly what was happening, until it had all run out of the chain locker and he untied the knot that held the last link of the bitter end to the bitts below and it slipped overboard. He raised the jib and held it out to catch the faint breeze, the evening wind coming off the land, until the bow fell away and the long bowsprit pointed out to sea. Back in the cockpit he tightened sheets as the yacht gathered way. It had been no more than four minutes since he'd crawled aboard.

From the cockpit he looked astern: he could only make out the darker shape of the rubber boat against the satin dark water as it beetled toward the Guardia Costiera vessel. *Nereid* was moving well, her lines and spars creaking quietly, the water burbling along the hull into the wake. He'd be several miles offshore before they caught up with him—ample time for Lulu to get far away from the cave and go to ground—

Had she got away? He thought over what he had seen and heard: the slight figure running out of the cave with the sheep. The three men—he was sure—coming out of the cave behind him, shouting. They could not have come after him so fast dragging an unwilling Lulu—he'd have heard her too—or even an unconscious Lulu. Or was she lying bleeding on the floor of the cave? Lulled by the familiar sounds of the yacht under way, safe for the moment, he tried to clear his mind of fear and think clearly. He had seen her. She had got away, he was sure of it now, running out of the cave on the far side with the sheep. She had got away, that was all that mattered.

Gerald began to sob, a dry reflexive heaving that stopped the moment he looked back and saw the shape of the Guardia boat moving away from the shore.

Was he moving too fast? He didn't want to lose them before he'd drawn them away—they weren't sailors, but street thugs in a slow tub. He looked up and saw the anchor light swaying in the shrouds, the sails against the night sky. They could see that. They would follow him . . .

Then, of course, he wouldn't be able to lose them. They'd catch him, and probably kill him, unless he could reach some sort of safety first. But the wind was off the land, blowing off the cooling shore beside the warmer sea, and it would blow like that until after dawn. He couldn't make Trapani, which lay to windward. He would have to lure them out to sea. How far would they come, the lumpen city boys, before they grew afraid and turned back toward land?

Could he get them far enough?

A n *hour later—two?*—dawn filtered slowly through a humid haze, and Gerald found he'd lost them. Had they turned around? He hove to. He threw the lead and found hard bottom at six fathoms.

Long minutes later, the haze was burning off and he saw the pale shape of the Guardia boat less than a mile away on the beam. They saw him too: the vessel's shape narrowed as it turned toward him. Gerald let the sails draw and the yacht moved ahead, steering itself, while he threw the lead line again and again. The soundings gave him a picture of the bottom contour in his head, shoaling irregularly but growing shallower as he advanced: six fathoms ... four and a bit ... five ... three ... seven ... three—all of a sudden he saw the bottom: lighter, browner patches against the darker blue. He looked to the north and saw that the Guardia Costiera vessel was gaining on him—the wind that had blown lightly but steadily all night was dropping, his speed slowing, while their engine chugged on.

Three fathoms ... four ... three ... three—a very light patch ahead, the sun picking out the weedy rock beneath the surface.

The distance between the two boats was closing fast. Gerald could see a man in the bow, peering intently toward him. Three hundred yards ... two hundred ... Another man joined the first on the bow—with a man at the helm, all three were aboard.

He heard them calling. The words undecipherable but the threat, the intent in the voice, clear. The boat was coming on at its full speed, barely five knots, but *Nereid* had slowed to no more than two. Gerald barely had maneuverability. Now the Guardia vessel angled away from him, then curved back until it was heading toward him once more, but on his beam: it was lining up to ram him amidships—to sink him. Its commercial build and displacement left no doubt about the result of such a collision.

Gerald hardened the sheets and headed closer to windward, giving them more of a target but at the same time gaining a knot of speed, a little more maneuverability for the only move that could save him.

The Guardia boat was ten yards off, aiming straight for the midpoint in dainty *Nereid*'s hull, when Gerald pushed the tiller down. The light, swift little boat's bow veered off sharply, suddenly, leaving him end on to the slowly charging boat. They would still collide, but it would be more of a glancing blow, he hoped. The Guardia's curling bow wave pushed *Nereid* off just before the two hulls met. . . .

It was a solid sideswipe that Gerald felt all through his body—he heard a crack of the thin frames in *Nereid*'s hull beneath him.

"Pezzo di merda succhiacazzi!" shouted from immediately above him. Other shouts. One of the men—they were close enough to touch hands—locking his eyes on Gerald's, swung at him with a length of chain. Gerald stepped nimbly back and the chain wrapped around *Nereid*'s shrouds, shaking the whole rig, and was torn from the Italian's hand as the Guardia boat swept on. The other man on deck was pointing at Gerald, jabbing his finger in his direction, staring at him like a madman. He shouted an incomprehensible insult. The boat turned away and arced across the water in a long, lazy, confident loop that would bring it back on a course toward *Nereid*—

Abruptly, the two men on deck were thrown to their knees and fell sprawling as the Guardia vessel bucked once, rose, slewed sideways, came to a shuddering stop. Its own stern wave overtook it, lifting the boat and settling it down again, rocking slightly, but otherwise immobile on the surface of the clear undisturbed sea around it. . . .

S even years earlier, in July 1941, Gerald had been aboard HMS *Furious* as it approached the Strait of Sicily on Operation Substance, a supply convoy from Gibraltar to Malta. Reports had been received of U-boat sightings off the Gulf of Tunis. The convoy hove to for thirty hours in the vicinity of Skerki Bank, whose shallow reefs were thought to bar the approach of submarines.

During the heat of the day, in no breeze at all, the ships wallowed in the slight swell, engines idling, generators thrumming, their steel plating turning to hot plates, burning men's hands and feet. In the afternoon, the men were permitted to swim. They were lowered overside in boats, and taken a safe distance away from the ship and its idling propellers. The Mediterranean was warm and clear and blue. They could see the reefs of the bank beneath them as they swam.

"Oy!" shouted one of the swimmers. They looked: one of the sailors was standing upright in the water, hand on hip, one leg crooked in front of the other, the pose of a model on a runway. No land in sight, the horizon all round vanishing between sea and sky, while he stood in calf-deep water. He looked around his feet theatrically. "Seen any fucking U-boats, tosh?"

They swam toward him and clustered around the barely submerged top of the reef, jockeying for standing room, pushing one another off, waving and shouting at the ship. Someone said, "You fink them bloody navigators 'ave any bloody idea 'ow fucking shallow it is?"

Gerald was sure they didn't. He'd seen the charts, and it showed no soundings indicating such a hazard, although parts of the contour of Skerki Bank were drawn with a dotted line indicating that chart data was incomplete. The ship was fortunate not to have run aground and been holed.

Other swimmers found shallows close enough beneath the surface to stand on. The effect, on a sea that was empty in every direction except for the idling convoy ships, was dreamlike, unreal.

The all-clear came just before midnight and the convoy steamed off into the strait toward Malta.

That day, Gerald marked the spot, as near as he could, on the chart he carried with him in his kit, with his copy of *The Odyssey*, all through the war. Later, in an Admiralty pilot of the Tyrrhenian Sea, he read:

"... in places, depths of less than six feet have been reported on Skerki Bank ... the cause of the total loss in October 1804 of H.M.S. Athenian, sixty-four guns ... Skerki Bank sits at the crossroad of three thousand years of east-west Mediterranean maritime commerce ... countless vessels through the ages have also perished on these banks. ..."

K eeping an eye on the color of the water ahead and beneath him, Gerald trimmed *Nereid*'s sheets and ghosted slowly toward the grounded Guardia Costiera vessel—not too close, they might have firearms aboard. The men were running up and down the deck at the rail like worried dogs, staring down into the water around their boat. Two of them were shouting at the third, the helmsman who had been steering. All three disappeared into the wheelhouse; the engine whined at an unnatural pitch; dense blue-black smoke rose from the exhaust stack behind the wheelhouse. Gerald could see froth at the stern. The vessel lurched, shuddered—would they get off?—but it did not break free. When the engine noise subsided, another shudder went through the boat—the bottom was grinding to pulp on the rocks—and it slid slowly backward, the stern settling deeper into the water until the rear deck was awash, the bow pointing unnaturally upward. The men on board, yelling frantically, converged on the rubber boat, which lay half deflated on the foredeck. One of them began pumping air into its collapsed chamber with a foot pump.

As Gerald sailed slowly round the Guardia vessel, about a hundred feet off, the men threw their rubber boat over the rail and jumped down into it. They began paddling toward *Nereid*. They glared at Gerald as they came closer.

He stepped down his companionway. When he reappeared on deck a moment later, the rubber boat was fifty feet away. He let them come on. At twenty-five feet he raised the large brass and wood Webley Very pistol and fired. The whooshing flare drove straight into the boat, the rocket propellant packed to carry it three hundred feet into the air continuing to throw flame around the bottom of the boat while the sulfur flare ignited, burning a large hole in the air chamber. The Italians leapt screaming into the water. At least two of them had been burned by propellant or sulfur. They abandoned the drooping remains of the rubber boat and swam back to the wrecked mother ship.

Gerald continued to sail slowly around the Guardia vessel as its three crewmen hauled themselves aboard by the swamped stern. As water filled it, and its frames and structure cracked and gave way with progressive breakage, the boat was perceptibly sliding off the reef. The men climbed to the foredeck, now the highest point above the water. They called to Gerald, pleading, demanding (he presumed, he didn't understand them) his assistance. Slowly he sailed closer, pushing the conspicuous brass Very pistol into his belt, looking at the water—didn't want to run aground himself and have the Italians board him.

When he was about forty feet away, he raised the Agfa Solinette and took several exposures.

Then he steered off. He went below to stow the camera, and when he returned to the deck, he steered east, eased sheets, and the yacht picked up speed. In a very short time, he could no longer hear the men's screams. In half an hour he could see nothing astern but the lightly ruffled surface of the sea.

L ulu! Lulu!?"
   It was just past noon. In daylight, the cave was littered with rubbish, old tins, the remains of fires, the droppings of sheep. Otherwise quite empty.

"Lulu? *Lulu!*" he called.

He ran along the path up and down the shore north and south of the cave, yelling her name frantically. He climbed the rocky slopes above the cave, looking for hiding places among ledges and in the vegetation.

"Lulooooo . . . !"

He trotted along the beach below the cave and explored the rocks at either end of the cove. He grew panicked and irresolute.

She was alive, obviously, and she had gone. Gone where—naked? Some dwelling along the coast . . . Trapani?

Gradually, another concern crowded into his brain. Although it had been night, there had been a moon. He knew that if anyone had seen *Nereid* at anchor off the beach at the same time as the Guardia vessel, they might remember. If anyone saw him anchored here now, they might remember. He couldn't go ashore and ask questions, talk with the police. If the Italians had been rescued, they might appear at any moment. At some point, Italian maritime authorities might alert ports around the Mediterranean to report any sighting of a small white-hulled sailing yacht flying the British red ensign. That might ultimately be connected with the death or disappearance of three Italian coastguardsmen.

He must leave.

Naked, hurt or not, Lulu had gone. Somehow, he knew, she would return to Tom and Milly in Mallorca.

He sailed again before dark. He steered northwest for Mallorca. He would stop in Sardinia and find a phone.

2005

Old Photos

One

Y ou're too late, I'm afraid," said the woman outside the service hall.

People leaving the Crematorio de Cala Marsopa recognized people just arriving. For convenience, Pompas Fúnebres González, the town's only undertakers, had scheduled the Davenport and Rutledge services back-to-back.

"Who are you?" the woman asked, her crepey, jellied wattle shaking as she inclined her head forward to hear better.

"Aegina Rutledge," said Aegina.

"Oh, yes! So it was your *father*? Wait—I'm not sure I understand. Then you and Lukey are half brother and sister?"

"No, different parents, all round."

"But your parents were married to each other at one point, surely? I mean—no, hang on—I remember you. You're Lukey's little friend, the sweet little Spanishy girl. Good *lord*, that was yonks! I bought pairs and pairs of those little slipper thingies you made—that was you, yes? I gave them to everybody. You probably don't remember me. Arabella Squibb. Are you still making them?"

"No," said Aegina.

"Well, you've missed the service at any rate—but it's so nice of you to come."

"Excuse me," said a man, sixtyish, glancing briefly at Aegina. "The car's over here, Mummy." He steered the older woman away.

"A-*geee*-nah!" A once tall, emaciated man, in his seventies but looking twenty years older, in blazer and black jeans with lank shards of white hair came, hip and knee sensitive, down the steps outside the service hall, moving stiffly toward her. "I know, *Picture of Dorian Gray*. But it's been well earned, I can tell you. Perhaps you don't remember—"

"I remember you, Dominick."

He grinned. "And I remember you." He was suddenly close enough for her to smell the miasmal breath that poured over the mushroom-hued National Health dentures. "You . . ." he said, drawing it out, "look—"

"Go away before I throw you down the steps," said Aegina.

Dominick looked at her blankly. Another man appeared behind him.

"Dominick, stop pestering nice people," said the man. "My condolences to you, Aegina."

It had been a number of years, but Aegina recognized the gingery hue of skin beneath the flaking scabs and blotches. "Thank you, Cassian," she said.

Coming out of the hall, Luc spotted Fergus and Charlie standing together, nodding and saying hello to people they knew. Charlie about thirty now, he guessed, with his mother's Spanish hair, his father's height. He was pleased to see that Fergus was bloated and balding, the little piggy features of his massive pudding face arranged in an expression of insincere commiseration that didn't hide his piercing fascination with the crowd coming out of the crematorium. He was asking Charlie about the identity of this person and that, and Charlie nodded or gave him a name.

Luc looked elsewhere. A reflexive triangulation drew his attention to Dominick, leaning oilily toward Aegina, babbling as Cassian pulled him away.

She saw him as he came toward her, and her expression softened.

"How are you?" he said.

Aegina made a gesture, part shrug, half a head shake. "All right." She looked at him closely. "How are you?"

"Okay . . . I don't know. Strange. I miss her, in fact."

"Of course you do."

Luc made himself look away at the small crowd. He noticed the number of local Spaniards arriving for the Rutledge service. "I don't know half of yours. Gerald was really more part of the local community, I guess, wasn't he?"

"Yes," said Aegina.

He looked back at her, into her face as if it were a map telling him where to go now, because he didn't know when he'd see her again.

The Gerald crowd was growing around them. Aegina was greeting people. Her extended Puig family, the indigenous island side of her that he had observed but never known. Penny and François and the now utterly grown-up Bianca. Luc realized he had to rejoin his mother's group.

Then he remembered. "I have something for you."

"Oh, yes?" She was distracted by the other people.

"It's from your father."

Aegina looked at him, then a short, stout woman embraced her passionately.

"I'll call you," Luc said, moving away.

Aegina nodded at him over the woman's shoulder.

L*uc could hear* the same braying of old from the bar, outside the window—all his life (he'd mostly been here during the summers) the ambient sound of his mother's home. He was lying fully clothed on the bed, in the room at the far end of the barracks. Half of the rooms were occupied by those who had flown down for the funeral—

Oh, please. He could hear someone coming slowly up the tiled stairs. Along the hall . . . the inexorable knock at the door. Fuck offfffff!

A woman's head appeared around the door, sweetly peekabooey. "Luc, are you all right, sweetheart?" Sarah Bavister, his unwilling long-ago shipmate aboard the ill-fated luncheon cruise of the *Dolphin*. "Can I come in?"

"Sure."

Sarah's Pouter pigeon *poitrine* had swelled with the year, until she now had the shape of a jug on a short-stemmed base. She sat down beside him.

"How are you doing, sweetie?" She was drunk.

"I'm all right, thanks. Tired. How are you?"

"Why don't you stay in the house, sweetie? In your mum's room? Or in the study? No one's in the study. Wouldn't you be more comfortable there? We could see more of you, instead of making this epic trek to the far end of the barracks—or is that the plan, sweetheart?"

"No, not really. I'm just more used to it here."

"You're *sure*?"

"Yes. This is sort of my room, really."

"I understand, darling."

Sarah looked at him, wading through years of gooey memories. "Darling, darling, Lukey." She picked up his hand and held it hard against her bosom, kneading his wrist painfully. "You will come and have dinner with us, though, won't you? I don't know what it is but it smells good. And you've got to eat, pet."

"No, I know. Sure. I'll be right down. Everyone else okay?"

"Oh, yes. You know this lot. But it is the *saddest* possible day for all of us. And we do want you to be with us, darling."

"That's very sweet of you, Sarah. I'll be right down."

"Good."

She leaned forward, her chest pressing down forcibly on his, smothering him in a rancid admixture of booze, body odor, and Chanel No. 5, almost spraining his wrist. She kissed his cheek wetly. "Soon, then?"

"Yes. I'll be right down. Thanks, Sarah."

She rose and went to the door and looked back at him. "We all love you so, so much, darling Lukey, sweetheart darling. We're not going to leave you alone."

"Love you too. Thank you."

He would never move into the house. His mother's room was empty now, but someone would want it. Come summer, there would be a feeding frenzy for *Lulu's Room* on the booking site. This *far* end room in the barracks, his room, was geographically closest to the only place where he had ever felt at home at the Rocks: the long-dismantled tool-shed against the back wall of the property. The only room that had been exclusively his, unbookable for guests, undesired by anyone else; his boy-hood home at the Rocks, the haven for his hormone-addled intrigues, the dank refuge of a thousand lonely wanks.

And the place where, long regretted, one night he could have done something more with Aegina than play the noble grown-up and take her home.

His mother was gone. Strange now: the house, the Rocks, without her. People wandering around as if looking for her. Something essential missing.

Was this grief, this weird non-Lulu atmosphere?

He didn't doubt that she had loved him, in her efficient, streamlined way, and he had, of course, loved her, in a mute, nondeclarative, resentful way. He didn't remember his mother ever saying, "I love you, darling." Nor his saying anything along those lines to her. They hadn't been like that with each other. They'd sort of simply taken the notion of each other for granted: someone crucial—if annoying or disappointing—but always there. Somebody who, however poorly she had expressed it, had loved him. Now there was nobody—except Sarah, and everybody down at the bar, his ersatz family, shuffling through the house, talking about his mother as if she'd been theirs.

None of them would have come and found him floating out at sea.

Two

It was warm, but still only spring, yet the Marítimo was almost full. Older people mostly—that was, Luc's age, and beyond. The usual British, German, northern European retirees. The terrace was pleasant in the sun. Fishing boats and wintering yachts filled the enlarged marina, but there was little noise. The town was busy, though not the carnival of flesh and summer. Conversation on the terrace was muted and polite.

Luc stood as Aegina came out to his table. She was wearing jeans, a short cotton blazer over a T-shirt, espadrilles.

"You look very well," he said. "Great, actually." He knew her age, fifty-three, to the day, but she'd been lucky—or very disciplined—both, probably. Slimmer than she'd been when he'd last seen her . . . ten years ago? The hair still dark—not a single gray strand? Must color it, but well. The Latin skin wrinkle-free except for some warm weathering around the eyes. She still looked the way he always thought of her, no jarring adjustment. Luc knew he looked, at his best, like every other man in his mid-fifties: beginning to sag noticeably under the jaw, the spare tire no matter what one did, his father's thinning hair—though his father had died before it got too bad.

"Thank you." She looked at him closely. "How are you doing?"

"All right. Feels a bit strange. How about you?"

"Yes: strange. I can't quite take it in. I suppose it will take time. I'm—" She was going to say: *I'm glad I have Charlie.* Instead she said: "Is it difficult for you with people at the Rocks now? Or is it a help? You know them all."

"I don't know what life down here is like without them. They've always been here. They'll all be gone in a few days. Then maybe I'll know."

"I'm sure they all love you."

"That's what they say."

"Well, it's true, Luc. Why wouldn't it be? You're part of someone they love. And they love you too, of course they do."

A waitress appeared. She was in her twenties, bristling with piercings. She asked them for their order in English with a characteristically sibilant Dutch accent.

"How did you know we spoke English?" Luc asked her.

"Her," the waitress thrust her spiked lower lip at Aegina, "you can't tell, but you, it's easy."

They ordered salads and *agua con gas*. Luc watched the waitress walk away and turned to look beyond her, into the bar inside. "I don't know anybody in this place anymore."

"Will you keep the Rocks?" Aegina asked.

"Yeah. For now, anyway. Sally's running the place. It makes its costs. Actually, it's doing well. There are people who come through the website now. What about you? Will you sell?"

"C'an Cabrer? Oh, no. It's home to me, more than anywhere. And it's Charlie's too. He loves it, and he still loves coming here. So, no, we'll keep it. Not that you can sell a property in Spain now anyway."

"No, right."

"Luc, Charlie and I both watched *Ryan*," she said. "We absolutely loved it."

"Thank you."

"Was he really a spy, your father?"

"I'm not sure. He could have been. He used to vaguely mention doing what he called his State Department work. But I really don't know. I made all that stuff up."

"I was very moved by it. I saw you, of course, and your father."

Luc's greatest success had come only in the last two years, with the

French television miniseries, broadcast in Britain and many European markets, about an American journalist, Ryan, living in Paris during the Cold War. Under the cover of reporting European events for an unnamed American newspaper based in Paris, Ryan was a minor CIA operative through the decades after World War II. The series' popularity and critical acclaim stemmed from the mix of Ryan's cloak-and-dagger work with the more quotidian drama of raising a child in Paris as a single father. There was something of the tenderness of François Truffaut, several critics had noted, in the relationship between Ryan and his growing, sometimes fractious son. Luc's French agent was now "talking" with HBO, AMC, and other television companies about producing an American version of the series. It would be like drug money, his agent said, the sale to the Americans, with an executive producer credit, but Luc was worried that the Americans would also ruin it. A not entirely unpleasant dilemma.

"You know, I never thought much about my father—I didn't see him—while he was there. I've been thinking about him a lot. When I look back now, he seems a shadowy character."

"I'm sure you miss him."

"I'd like to see him again. Talk to him. See who he really was."

"And have you got someone in Paris?"

"Just Sophie."

"Who?"

"Sophie—my made-up girlfriend, years ago, when we went to Morocco. You had somebody too—"

"Dennis! Yes! But do you really have someone? I hope you do."

"You do, huh?" The likelihood of meeting anyone who wouldn't make him feel even lonelier seemed increasingly remote. Life was a dwindling process now, not a building proposition. He couldn't imagine being with someone new, opening up, feeling appreciated and understood, without having to explain his dubious non sequiturs and increasingly arcane or redundant frame of reference. "Not really. But I have friends. You know. A sort of life. You? Are you seeing anyone?"

"I have been."

"Ah." Why did that feel more desolating than the death of his mother? "That's nice."

"It has been."

"Not an unqualified statement."

"No. One changes. Or things change."

"Who was it? Or is it?"

"Was—nobody. Someone I thought I understood, but in fact, didn't."

"That I understand."

Their salads arrived.

"*Gracias*," said Luc automatically.

"Yeah, no problem," said their waitress.

"You wanted to give me something?" said Aegina.

"Yes." He pushed a small manila envelope in front of him across the table. "I found an old shoe box in my mother's closet. It contained the certificate of marriage between her and your father, and a divorce document, for same. Also an undeveloped roll of black-and-white film, old one-twenty stock. The bloke at the *fotografería* in town still does film processing."

Aegina drew a handful of photographs from the envelope. They were glossy and new. "Oh, my God," she said softly.

Luc shifted his chair so that he could look at them with her. "Obviously taken by your father. I guess she took the one of him."

"My God, Luc. Look how beautiful your mother was—look at her hair: it's almost black."

"Is that his boat?"

"Yes," she said.

"Not Mallorca, is it? Looks more like Italy or somewhere."

Aegina looked at him. "It's the honeymoon voyage."

"So it would seem."

Her father had always kept his old Agfa Solinette aboard the boat. He had carefully photographed anchorages, ports, views of small coves from the hills rising above them, harbor approaches from the sea, stretches of coastline all over the Mediterranean. These photographs, adeptly composed and exposed, always in contrast black-and-white, some dating back more than sixty years, had illustrated his articles and his one book. Visible in many of those old photographs, resting peacefully at anchor against a backdrop of an ancient Greek or Italian fishing village, lay a small, pretty, white-hulled sailboat, his beloved *Nereid*—on which, Aegina knew, her father and Lulu had sailed from Mallorca on the day after their wedding in July 1948. A short time later they had separated, and *Nereid* had sunk. There had never been any further, or more specific, details. When she had asked her father, several times, why he had no photographs from that summer, he told her they'd all been lost when the boat sank that September. Yet he'd managed to save the camera, and the important books, and everything else of any value that had been aboard the yacht.

"Can I get copies of these?" she asked.

"These are yours," said Luc. "I made an extra set for you."

She went through them slowly. "It's so strange—to think of them together."

"On a little boat too. She hated boats."

Aegina looked at him. "What *happened* to them? He would never tell me."

"She wouldn't tell me either," said Luc. "They fell out—that's the way she put it: 'We fell out,' she said. And that's all she ever said."

Aegina handed him three photographs. "What are these?"

"I was wondering if you might know. If he ever said anything about that. It looks like a shipwreck."

Three photos of men waving, in obvious distress, from the bow of a wrecked, apparently sinking fishing boat.

"No," she said. "He never mentioned anything like that."

"I suppose they saved whoever it was." He gave the three photographs back to her.

She pulled a photograph from her handbag and handed it to him.

"Oh, jeez," Luc said.

He stared at the faded color shot of himself and Aegina—so *young*—leaning against a ship's rail, both smiling awkwardly into the camera.

"I've never seen this," he said. "Where is this?"

"It has to be on the ferry. Minka must have taken it. I don't remember her giving it to me. I found it a few days ago."

"I would guess on the way to Morocco," he said, unable to look at her, "rather than on the way back." It sounded flippant, he immediately regretted it.

She took it from him and put all the photographs in her bag. She looked up at Luc. "Did you know that your mother seduced Charlie?"

Luc stared at her, trying to read her face. It betrayed nothing. "When?"

"On her birthday. When he was fifteen. It might be called rape now. Certainly child abuse."

"No, I didn't know that. I'm sorry to hear it."

"Are you surprised?"

"No." Not at all. "I won't be absurd and apologize for her. But . . . I'm sorry to know that." Then, he couldn't help it, "Thanks so much for telling me."

"I'm sorry. I really didn't mean to." Aegina stabbed a fork into her salad. But she put it down and looked across the table at Luc. "Do you know how I found out?"

"No." Luc wanted to get up and dive headfirst over the iron railing to the concrete quay below, but he sat still and modulated his voice into a pleasant tone. "Why don't you tell me."

"Charlie never actually told me—he wouldn't tell me who it was, only what happened—but I put it together. She gave him the Moroccan shirt—the original, the one I brought from London. I saw it in his room after the party—he kept it for years. He thought he was in love with her. And of course, she didn't want to see him again, like that."

Luc remembered Charlie wearing the shirt the night of the birthday party.

"Fuck," said Aegina. "I'm sorry, Luc." She reached across the table and pulled his hand out of his lap and wrapped hers around it. "I don't know why I told you—except I think I've been wanting to for years . . . I'm not sure why. And it's the Rocks . . . it wasn't easy for me there either. I'm sorry."

She let go his hand, put the photographs in the envelope and the envelope in her bag. She pulled out a twenty-euro bill and laid it on the table.

"I'll get it," said Luc.

"No, it's all right. Let me. Thank you for the photos. I'm so sorry . . ." Aegina stood up abruptly. "I'm sorry," she said again. "Bye."

"Bye."

She walked away.

Luc turned his head and watched her until his eyes filled and he could see nothing but an unfocused wash of light and color.

He looked back in the direction of the boats spread below until the port came back into focus. He looked down the long quay ending in the small port light that blinked at night. He looked out toward the sea, which today sparkled with a harsh relentlessness.

The chair grated on the tile and Aegina sat down beside him. She'd pulled it around the table until she was right beside him. She put both hands on his arm and he turned to look at her. He saw that her eyes were wet.

"Come up to the house for dinner."

"No, thanks. You've got Charlie and Fergus there. Family time."

"They're both going back to London tomorrow. I'm staying on for a bit. Come up tomorrow."

He blinked again. He felt her hands tighten on his arm. "Come up, Luc." She was looking into him in a way he remembered from long ago . . . the toolshed one night.

"What time?"

"Seven."

Aegina leaned forward and kissed him on the cheek. She drew back and her thumb moved gently across his cheek where it was wet. Her eyes wandered all over his face and finally came back to his eyes. "You'll come, right?"

"Yes. I'll come."

"Seven."

"Yes."

"Good," she said.

She stood again and walked across the terrace. He watched her as she got into her rented Renault Clio, and followed the car until he lost it down on calle Llobet.

He looked back out across the port, this time to the rocks and the dirt road along the harbor.

He felt suddenly strange. Off-kilter, weak . . . dizzy? Was he going to have a stroke . . . *now?*

After a moment he realized what it was.

He was filled with joy.

2005

Together Again

G*erald came* to the surface gasping, wheezing, unable to get his breath. The water felt icy, making it even harder to breathe. He kicked instinctually—sharp pain shot through his legs again. His knees were on fire, but the cold water began to numb them. His hands flailed, attempting to paddle—he touched flesh.

He twisted his head and saw Lulu facedown in the water close by. He pulled at her, managed with tremendous effort to turn her faceup, but submerging himself again. He kicked, screaming in pain, though this came out as a few bubbles. His chest spasmed trying to inhale, and he knew he would only suck in water. He kicked and somehow surfaced. He could only blow bubbles in the water around his mouth. One hand found Lulu again, the other feebly paddled; he went under again. Surfaced . . .

So he brought them both to the rock face, where he could move no more, but hung onto a button of limestone while holding Lulu's head, her face anyway, out of the water, against his chest. He looked up but saw only the rock rising to the sky. "Help . . . *Ayuda*," he exhaled aloud, several times.

Gerald looked down at Lulu. She was breathing. Strands of pure white hair were plastered untidily across her tan face—she looked disturbingly half drowned. He would have smoothed the hair away if he'd had a third hand. Then a small wave washed over her head. With a great effort Gerald lifted and held her more tightly against him. Her face emerged from the water with her hair perfectly drawn back from the hairline, as if she herself had tilted her head back underwater and rose face upward through the surface. Now she appeared groomed, and lightly asleep, as if she would open her eyes at any moment and look directly up at him from the cradle of his arm against his chest.

Now, at last, he could tell her.

As he opened his mouth to suck in breath to speak, another wave, a larger wave, washed over them, broke against the rock and pulled them away from the shore. Gerald lost his grip on Lulu. She floated away from him.

"Wait . . ." he bubbled into the water. His hand found some piece of her clothing. He pulled at her. But he was underwater. She hadn't heard it yet. He was going to say:

I did come back, you know. With the sheep into the cave. You got out the same way Odysseus did . . . out of the very same cave . . . Then I lured them away—you never saw the film I gave Milly, did you? That would have shown you. I got them away from you and I took care of them—

Did she hear? Where was she?

Suddenly he knew that she'd fallen from the rocks. She'd cut her chin. He'd got his arm around her. He held her head up out of the water and looked into her face. She was only asleep. Her hair was shot through with gray; it would be white before long. It was the most beautiful thing he'd ever seen. She was all right now. He'd saved her.

Gerald cradled her head against his chest and struck out strongly for *Nereid.*

ACKNOWLEDGMENTS

I could not have written this book without the love, nonjudgmental support, and belief in me and my work that I've received from my brother, David. I can't imagine what or where I'd be without him. At best, living in a highway culvert, screaming at passing cars for interrupting my exquisite daydreams. I'm also inexpressibly grateful for the love and support I've received from Liz Sharp, Cynthia Hartshorn, Matthew deGarmo. Ports through all storms.

Many people gave this book generous editorial help. At Antioch University in Los Angeles, Steve Heller was my first, last, and most sanguine mentor. Also at Antioch, Dan Bellm, Gayle Brandeis, Jenny Factor, Seth Fischer, Christine Hale, Tara Ison, Jim Krusoe, Alistair McCartney, Bernadette Murphy, Susan Taylor Chekak, and Howie Davidson and Audrey Mandelbaum. I want to thank Antioch friends Mary Guterson, Vanessa Franking, Wendy Dutwin, Wendy Fontaine, Eric Howald, Ashley Perez, Rachael Warecki, Marcia Meier, Arturo Sande, Daniel José Older, Elizabeth Earley, Susan Nunn, Christina Lynch, Christine Buckley, Lee Stoops, Andromeda Romano-Lax, who are all somehow part of this book.

Joan Juliet Buck, Tony Cohan, Damien Enright, Kim Dana Kupperman, David Nichols, Peter Selgin, and Liz Sharp all read the book in various drafts and offered constructive help, and hope. Kim Dana Kupperman also gave an early draft its first copyedit, and got me a job.

I'm grateful to Michael White, of the MFA program at Fairfield

University, Connecticut, and Mark Spencer and Diane Payne of same at the University of Arkansas at Monticello.

I'm grateful to my writing students, all of them, everywhere. It always seems they are allowing me to work out my own stuff on their time.

In Los Angeles, and elsewhere, Annie Nichols for so much over many years.

Many people, in many places, were kind to me in ways that directly and indirectly helped me during the writing of this book, and afterward: Jon Billman, Dick Bloom, Selma Bornstein, Olivia Brown, Susan Burks, Jo-Ann Chorney, Peter Collier and Jeanne Davis, Bridget Conway, Tom Corwin and Marlene Saritzky, Larry Cronin and Marla Reckart, Ruth Ann Duncan-Thomas, Lindy Elkins-Tanton, Leonora Epstein, Meg Files, Josephine Franzheim, Roberta Franzheim, Rick Gilmore and Donald Craig of Rick's A/C & Radiator, Waco, Texas, Doug Grant and Kathryn van Dyke, Kate Griffin (especially!), Amy Hagemeier, Kim Hayashi, Sheyene Heller, Kelly Horan, Martha Kennedy at AJ's, Tucson, Arizona, Elaine Lembo, Herb McCormick, Flo and Georgie Neve, Stephanie Pearmain, Richard Podolsky, Karena Rice, Jenny Rider, Bennett Scheuer, Aurelie Sheehan, Sue Slutes, Isabelle Stone, Jut Wynn.

I'm extremely grateful to Jennifer Haigh, whose novels inspired me as I wrote this one. And to Richard Russo, whom I often observed scribbling in composition books at several cafés in Camden, Maine. He made it appear quotidian and possible. And both have been generous to me since I've completed this book.

Kate Griffin and Georgie Neve found me my extraordinary agent, Patrick Walsh, who (while on holiday in Africa) scribbled also: hundreds of suggestions throughout a bulky manuscript that considerably improved the novel before he promptly sold it. Thanks also to Clare Conville, Carrie Plitt, Alexandra McNicholl, Jake Smith-Bosanquet, Henna Silvennoinen, David Llewelyn, Dorcas Rogers, and all at Conville & Walsh. Also in London, David and Anita Burdett, Isabel Costello, John and Sarah Standing, and, not least, Gillian Stern.

You can never sufficiently thank your editors for their leap of faith, and all the people in a publishing house who prepare and send a book out into the world. My visionary editor Sarah McGrath and her team at Riverhead Books would be any writer's dream assembly of book hatchers: assistants Danya Kukafka and Sarah Stein; publicity savants Jynne Dilling Martin, Claire McGinnis, Margaret Delaney, and Alexandra Primiani; art director Helen Yentus; marketing team Lydia Hirt, Kate Stark, Mary Stone; copy chief Linda Rosenberg and copy editor Martha Schwartz; managing editor Lisa D'Agostino; and Geoff Kloske, the publisher supporting all of this good work. In London, I want to thank editor Susan Watt, Jon Watt, and copy editor Lizzie Dipple, of Heron Books/ Quercus Books.

The Rocks is entirely a work of fiction, its characters not based on the living or the dead. But while writing it I remembered with great affection Nora, Luis, and Claudine Cumberlege. Also a number of men and women I knew only slightly in Mallorca when I was young, people who would not have noticed or remembered the boy who watched and long afterward reimagined them.